P9-DEL-802

INTO NO MAN'S LAND
© 2016 Richard C. Bachus

All rights reserved. No part of this publication may be repro-
duced or used in any form or by any means, graphic, electronic
or mechanical, including photocopying, recording, taping, or
information and retrieval systems without written permission of
the publisher.

Hellgate Press
PO Box 3531
Ashland, OR 97520
email: sales@hellgatepress.com

Editor: Harley B. Patrick
Book design: Michael Campbell
Cover design: L. Redding
Portrait courtesy of the author
Background photo:U.S. Army Signal Corps

Library of Congress Cataloging-in-Publication Data
available upon request

Printed and bound in the United States of America
First Edition 10 9 8 7 6 5 4 3 2 1

INTO
NO MAN'S
LAND

See! We teachers really can write.

RICHARD C.
BACHUS

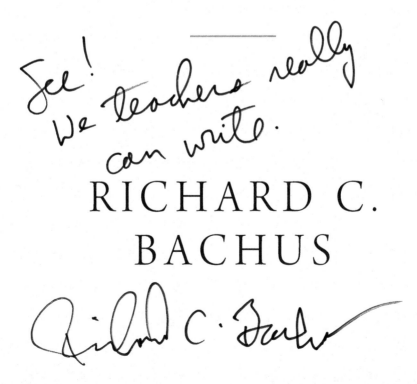

For Carol, my delight

CONTENTS

AUTHOR'S NOTE

Anyone who has spent much time in the military or in a military family usually organizes their memory by place — the string of posts, homeports, and countries that a soldier, sailor, or marine gets sent to. In this same spirit, this novel is organized into 13 Parts, with each part named for a geographical location — a location as specific as a house to as broad as an entire country. These part names are not meant to serve as datelines for the opening (or even primary) location of the action in each chapter. Neither are they always the most significant places within the terrain of each group of chapters. Rather, they are more like mileposts on the journey that the main characters are undertaking. I hope you enjoy the trip.

PROLOGUE

DAWN WAS A LETHAL TIME OF DAY. *The soldiers on both sides of No Man's Land expected raids every morning. But the gas attacks, bursts of machine gun fire, the artillery barrages, and the sniper bullets had become so routinely random, that the expected hour was as good an opportunity to attack as any other time.*

And so, Capt. Kurt Radtke climbed onto the fire step of an observation post a few hundred yards out into No Man's Land. It was still about an hour before dawn, but Kurt liked to scan the wires and shell holes before his eyes adjusted to the first faint morning light. The night position for Petty Post 4 (the official designation for the seven-foot-deep hole that Kurt and a platoon of American doughboys were standing in) lay out in front of E Company's main firing trench. From there, Kurt could not only see all the way to the opposing German trenches, but he could look back to his own lines to make sure that none of his boys' heads were sticking up above the parapet.

Even after twelve days of living in the trenches of Alsace-Lorraine, Kurt still hadn't gotten used to the stink of the front lines. The morning air was completely still, and Kurt could pick out individual smells all around him. Neither side had been able to reach the remains of the two German scouts that Kurt's men had killed with a volley of rifle grenades two nights ago. There was the stench of the Petty Post latrine to his left, mixed with the sharp odor of lime dust that was used to keep the flies at bay. And there was a particularly sour smell coming from under his own uniform, which he had worn continuously for almost a month now.

Kurt did not actually think much about these foul smells. In the past couple weeks, however, he had spent so many of his waking hours in darkness that he had become attuned to each sound and smell of the mile-long sector of the trenches that he was responsible for. He could navigate E Company's trenches at night using his nose and ears almost as easily as he could using his eyes during the day.

As the light gathered in the east, Kurt strained to see through the antenna-like trench binoculars that allowed him to look over the parapet without getting his head shot off. Kurt only had a few more minutes to look around before the "morning hate" began. This daily routine of grenade explosions, "blind" machine gun strafing, and rifle fire not only helped relieve the tension of the long night, but it was intended to ensure that no enemy raiders lay in wait for a dawn attack. Kurt's troops knew to keep their fire away from their own platoons that were occupying the petty posts and preparing to move deeper into No Man's Land, but the men in the petty posts kept hunkered down during the morning hate, just in case.

Satisfied that E Company's lines were secure, Kurt turned to his left flank, where Company M was holding the line. Petty Post 5 was four hundred yards to the north of Petty Post 4, and Kurt could see that Capt. Gansser's men were preparing to move up to the advanced observation post. A short burst of machine gun fire erupted in the distance, and the morning hate began on the far side of No Man's Land as the Germans cleared the ground in front of their main firing trench.

Kurt's men opened up in a split second, as he climbed down off the fire step to avoid getting hit by friendly fire. Kurt stepped under the steel-roofed canopy of the post dugout to check with Lt. Simons who had also been scanning No Man's Land for signs of trouble.

The roar of the firing drowned out Lt. Simon's voice for a few moments. And then, the morning hate trailed off into occasional dislike and random irritation. Capt. Radtke looked out from under the dugout canopy and noticed that the clusters of remaining leaves on the two trees that still clung to life beside the trench quaked as if moved by a sudden wind. There was nothing natural about the force that moved the air, however. Flying dirt, shrapnel, and bullets ripped through the trees, and a few more fresh, green oak leaves fluttered down from the branches and into the mud at Capt. Radtke's feet.

Kurt waited a few more minutes to make sure all was quiet. When the leaves in the trees above the petty post hung quietly again in still air, he climbed back up to the fire step for a last look around.

For all the devastation of No Man's Land, Kurt was still surprised by the amount of life that managed to hang on in the half-mile-wide strip between the opposing armies. Not only were there still clumps of trees both in front of and behind the lines, but the few patches of undisturbed ground between the shell holes were covered with a mixture of yellow-flowered weeds and young stalks of wheat. Kurt realized that the wheat must have reseeded itself four times since the war began. No man or woman had sowed these deadly fields since 1914 — only the wind and the wild birds had cultivated what was left of these wheat fields. Indeed, all of No Man's Land had been fertile farmland before the cannons' shells and soldiers' spades tore it up.

Kurt thought about the acres of stump land around his wife's hometown back in Northern Michigan. Some of it was already starting to grow back into forest, and some of it had been cleared for hay fields and pasture. Now that the logging boom was over, some of that land could be had for just a few dollars an acre. Kurt planned to buy some of that land for Sarah when the war was over. It was worth a lot more to Sarah and to him than it was to the lumber companies, which were already closing down the mills and moving on to new forests. Kurt's mind drifted, and he thought how strange it was that the value of a particular piece of land could rise and fall because of decisions made hundreds of miles away. Kurt imagined what it would be like if the human sweat and blood that soaked into an acre of earth played a part in its worth. How much would those stump fields in Northern Michigan cost if the lives and toil of the Ottawa Indians, the immigrant loggers, and the homesteaders were factored in? Who would be able to afford it? And what would one have to do to earn that land? If that system were used here in Europe, Kurt thought, what would this ground in Alsatian Germany cost after so much blood had been shed to buy it and hold it? Many wars had been fought over this same land. But in this war to end all wars, a group of Americans far away from their home turf were charged with the duty of keeping this ground from an enemy intent on reclaiming it. Capt. Radtke shook off a wave of weariness, and knew he would protect this fractured field as if it was the land he would someday buy for Sarah.

The smoke from the morning hate cleared almost straight up into the air. This was a good sign, Kurt thought to himself, because the Germans usually only used gas when the wind was at their backs. The only sign of movement came from an odd breeze that was rustling the grass that grew along the edges of the Petty Post 5 trenches. Kurt marveled at how quickly the wheat and weeds had grown since the last time he had examined Capt. Gansser's sector.

Suddenly, Kurt realized that he wasn't looking at odd winds and fast-growing grass. In an instant, he saw that Petty Post 5 was about to be ambushed by a German raiding party heavily camouflaged in grass. Kurt leapt off the fire step, grabbed a signal rocket from the dugout to call for artillery to fire around the edges of Petty Post 5, and sent a runner to alert his own men and to warn Capt. Gansser of the ambush.

"Sgt. Miller, get your crew back up on that machine gun and start strafing the grass along the edge of Petty Post 5," Kurt said. "It's crawling with Bosche!"

Before Sgt. Miller could take two steps, a single pistol shot rang out from Petty Post 5. As Miller reached the machine gun and Kurt got back up on the fire step with his trench binoculars, the grass along Petty Post 5 rose up as though the ground was exploding into the air. Kurt saw dozens of German troops getting to their feet, firing down into Petty Post 5, and tossing potato-masher grenades down on top of the Americans in the trench.

The platoon manning Petty Post 4 began to mount the fire step to shoot at the Germans who were 400 yards away, but a firehose stream of lead from a pair of German machine guns drove them back down into the trench. One private who was standing next to Kurt was knocked right off the fire step when a machine gun bullet glanced off his helmet. The German machine gun fire was so intense and precise that the men near Kurt couldn't even get their rifles over the parapet. Kurt gathered a Lieutenant and some sergeants together.

"Those guys are getting clobbered over there, Captain," Sgt. Swartz said. "And those damn gunners got us pinned down pretty good. Any bright ideas?"

"Remember that old road farther out into No Man's Land that runs parallel to our main trench?" Capt. Radtke said, as the German grenades thudded from the bottom of the Petty Post 5. "There's still enough of a ditch on this side of that old road that we can get a squad over to Petty Post 5. We'll be able to crawl right up to the raiding party's flank and drive them off without exposing ourselves to the main German line. Lt. Simon's squad provides covering fire from here. The rest of you meet me up where that old road crosses our trench with half of the men from your platoon."

Kurt grabbed a box of rifle grenades to pass out to the squad, and headed up the trench to the spot near the old road. Kurt didn't actually decide to lead the squad, but he soon found himself scrambling out of the petty post trench and crawling on all fours towards the beleaguered men of Company M. He had been out here once before, and recognized the large shell crater where they found the dead French soldier on Kurt's first full day on the line. As he drew closer, Kurt saw one big, grass-covered German fall face first into the trench, and another one throw his hands into the air and fall backwards into a shell hole. There were still some Yanks putting up a fight in Petty Post 5.

Kurt and his squad only made it about a hundred yards away from Petty Post 4, however, when he heard the shriek of incoming artillery shells. Even as Kurt called out to warn his men to find cover, a wave of fire and earth rose up in front of him. The last thing Capt. Radtke remembered from that instant was the ground that he had sworn to protect falling out of the sky and burying him.

~ PART 1 ~
# THE SHACK

———

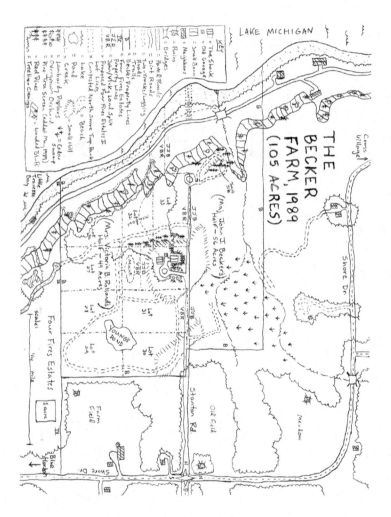

LAKE MICHIGAN

THE BECKER FARM, 1989 (105 ACRES)

KEY

- [⊞] = The Shack
- [□] = Old Garage
- [▦] = Small Barn
- = Neighbors
- = Ruins
- = Bridges
- = Paved Roads
- = Dirt Roads
- = Two Tracks/Logging Roads
- = Becker Property Lines
- = Four Fires Estates Property Lines
- = John/Viking Land Split
- = Proposed Four Fires Estates II Lot Lines
- = Contested North Shore Top Bank
- = Lake
- = Creek
- = Pond
- = Lombardy Poplars
- = Overgrown Orchard
- = Pine Tree Screen (added Nov. 1989)
- = Red Pines
- = Tree Line/Clearings
- = Beach
- = Small Hill
- = Cedar Swamp
- = 1 acre
- = Wooded Bluff

Cross Village ↑

Shore Dr

(Mr) John J. Becker's Half - 56 Acres

(Mrs. Victoria B. Rhoads) Half - 49 Acres

378 VBR

378 VBR

Lot 33

Lot 32

378 VBR

Lot 31

Shack

378 VBR

Lot 37

Lot 31

378 VBR

Lot 30

YOUNG'S POND

Lot 30

Stanton Rd

Old Field

Meadow

Four Fires Estates

Scale: ¼ mile

1 acre

Farm Field

Blue Herons ←

Shore Dr.

Little Traverse Bay N ↑

Chapter 1

AUNT VICKY'S LEGACY to her only remaining heirs is on its way. The United Van Lines shipping bill lists a cedar chest stuffed with four oval oriental rugs, a rocking chair, an antique desk, a dresser, and five cardboard boxes containing "personal effects."

The cab of my old red pickup is warm and dry, despite the snowstorm raging outside. As I sit in my truck waiting for the moving van, I'm thinking I should be grateful to get anything at all from Aunt Vicky. We weren't exactly close. Still, I can't help feeling that the old lady stiffed me.

The family property that lies just a half-mile down the road behind me is said to be worth about $750,000. My grandfather — Col. Joseph L. Becker — set it up so Dad and Vicky (Dad's sister) weren't allowed to sell the property during their lifetimes. As a result, the property has remained virtually unchanged for more than thirty years. Seven years of legal battles have somehow freed Dad and Vicky from some of the restrictions of the Colonel's will. Before they both passed on, they split the property and were preparing to sell all of Vicky's half and some of Dad's half once the remaining challenges to a clear title were eliminated.

The sheets of snow swirling just beyond the windshield have a hypnotic effect. My eyes don't know whether to focus on the flakes in front of me, the gust-strewn cloud of snow out in the middle of the intersection, or the ghostly tree trunks beyond that. Time also seems out of focus. I can pick a point and see its detail, but the past, present, and future all seem to be before me at once.

Today is April 14, 1989 — exactly two years since Dad passed on. He would have only been 60 last month. Aunt Vicky, Dad's senior by eighteen years, outlived him, passing on this January, at 77. My sister, Sally, and I are doing all right under the circumstances, but the circumstances aren't getting any easier as a result of the three bequests from the previous generations of Beckers. Realtors, developers, and lawyers are circling overhead, but all we have inherited so far are legal problems.

Waiting around for bequeathals isn't exactly what I planned to be doing in my mid-20s. Just a few months ago, I was in the heart of *The Christian Science Monitor's* busy Boston newsroom and on my way up. I was writing articles at a steady rate on top of my junior editing responsibilities. I was sitting in on staff meetings with Henry Kissinger and Jessie Jackson. And I was next in line for the investigative reporting seminar. I was looking forward to the future. This Northern Michigan farm and a need for someone to look after family affairs, however, has me looking back to the past. Things are starting to come to a head here, and somebody has to take care of business. With Sally down in Grand Rapids trying to steer through the rough waters of a troubled marriage and my mom starting a new career down in Florida, that somebody became me — the youngest, the prodigal son.

The death of Maj. John J. Becker, my father, couldn't have come at a worse time. He spent the last eleven years of his life working overseas, while the rest of his family lived stateside. He always supported us financially — even after the divorce — and we kept in touch every month or so. There were even visits every few years — both here and overseas. Dad's extended hiatus, however, was about to come to an end. Just before he died, he was making arrangements to come home with his new fiancé, and Sally and I were starting to get reacquainted with him.

Aunt Vicky is another story. Her death—and the way she has treated her kin—has only increased the distance she kept from her brother's family while she was still living. I keep telling myself that Vicky had every right in the world to will the proceeds of her pending property sale to the people closest to her, but I feel that something is not quite right. Her father entrusted half of a special family place to Vicky, and now that it has become a sizable real estate fortune, Vicky is posthumously cashing it in for a final farewell to her best friends and favorite charities. The sale of Vicky's share of the land isn't final yet, but it feels like Vicky's half of the property has already gone to her estate in Tucson, been whittled down to next to nothing, and come back as old furniture and a few boxes of miscellaneous stuff. Not what the Colonel had in mind for his grandchildren, I imagine.

It's not that I've got anything against those folks in Tucson, but I visited Vicky's neighborhood a couple of summers ago and it didn't look like any of her friends were down to their last six hundred bucks, like I am. All I can do is try to focus on Dad's half of the property, which will be divided between Sally and me and Mom. We can only hope there will be something left of the farm by the time the inheritance-tax collectors, the state bureaucrats, and the lawyers get done with Dad's estate.

Outside my pickup, the Lake Michigan winds are kicking up the snow into a mid-April ground blizzard. I peer through the swirls of white and gray and try to see the moving van that is probably still crawling up Shore Drive. I told the lady truck driver I would wait for her at this rural intersection with my headlights on.

The crossroads of Shore Drive and Stanton Road aren't much of a landmark — even to most of the locals. If there were a map to my world, however, this is where the four-pointed compass rose would be drawn. No matter where I am, I can usually get my bearings from my fix on this small point on the Earth. To the West, down the gravel section of Stanton Road lies the old farmhouse, which my family calls "The Shack." Since January, I've been calling it home. Just beyond the farmhouse, Stanton Road ends at the edge of a 100-foot-high wooded bluff that slopes down to Lower Beach Trail, then the beach, and into Lake Michigan. To the North, Shore Drive heads straight for a mile before curving toward the bluff and following its winding, wooded edge north to Cross Village and Wilderness State Park at the northwestern tip of Michigan's Lower Peninsula. To the East, Stanton Road is paved and as straight as a midwestern fence line. The eastern terminus of Stanton Road is only a few miles from here at the base of the high ridge that forms the western highlands of Pleasantview Valley. To the South, lies the small resort town of Blue Harbor, and four or five hours drive beyond that are the flat farmlands and busy cities of Southern Michigan.

We call the 105 acres and the small, rustic house that the Colonel bought in the early '20s a farm, but my people haven't been farmers since the turn of the century. Ottawa Indians and white settlers were the last to farm this land. When the snow melts, you can still see dozens of moss-covered rock piles at the edges of the meadows and even in the middle of the second-growth woods. The rocks attest to a back- and heart-breaking effort to grow crops here. Like most of the homesteads in Northern Michigan, the fields have long been abandoned for warmer places or easier ways to make a living. Winter can last for six months up here.

This property was meant to be a place where an old soldier and his wife could spend the last summers of their lives. It should have been a simple arrangement for the property to pass from one generation to the next, and from that generation to Sally and me. It should have been, but there hasn't been anything simple about the passing down of this property for more than three decades. It would be easy to just sign some papers, get what money we can, and walk away, but I, for one, have decided to stick around.

The rounded fingers of snowdrifts are already spilling into the middle of Stanton Road along the open field, so I'm feeling better about telling the truck driver to meet me here instead of trying to get a semi down the half-mile dirt road. When I talked to the driver yesterday by phone, we agreed to shuttle Aunt Vicky's things from the moving van to the farm house in my pickup.

I flick the high beams when I see the moving van crest the hill, and the driver downshifts through her gears as she carefully descends the gentle slope to the intersection. She turns her rig right and comes to a stop on the paved section of Stanton Road. That's east on my internal compass.

I climb out of my warm pickup, cross the road, and walk up to her idling Peterbilt tractor as she hops down from the cab while putting on a navy-blue, Michelin-Man-style down coat.

"You're brave," I said as I reach my hand out to greet her. "I'm glad you made it all right."

"You must be Nick Becker," she said, shaking my hand with a boa constrictor grip. "Good gracious, haven't you folks ever heard of spring up here?"

"We hear about it now and then. It must be nice."

Her nametag says Linda. She is probably in her mid-fifties, small and wiry, with a dark gray ponytail sticking out of the hole in the back of her United Van Lines baseball cap. She has a western drawl, and I ask her where she's from. She says she lives southeast of Tucson, near the Mexican border in a town called Fairbank.

"Is that anywhere near Fort Huachuca?" I ask.

"Sure is. Fairbank's about 15 mile north of the fort as the buzzard flies. How do you know about a hole-in-the-wall place like that, anyway? Were you in the service, son?"

"No, not me. My father and grandfather were, though. My dad was a major in the Army. One of his few pieces of advice to me was to stay the hell out of the Army. I'm a freelance writer."

"Well, that sounds like an interesting job, but it still don't explain how you got to Fort Huachuca," she said.

"My dad's buried in the cemetery there. He died two years ago. My aunt — the same lady who left me the stuff you just hauled from Tucson — said my dad once mentioned that he wanted to be buried there. And she just died in January."

"I'm sorry to hear about your losses. I kind of wondered if that was the case when I saw that the shipment was coming from an estate," Linda says, as she climbed back up into her rig. "We get loads like that every once in a while, and no matter how much nice stuff there is, it isn't usually that much of a comfort to the family getting it."

We decide to back the moving van across the intersection onto the gravel side of Stanton Road. There is a clear stretch near the intersection where gravel still sticks through the hard-packed ice and snow. The traction looks good and the snow-drifts don't start until farther down the road where the woods give way to an old field. I watch for traffic appearing out of the swirling snow as Linda backs across the intersection.

With the moving van safely parked, Linda hops out again and opens the side door in the middle of the trailer. She turns to me with a puzzled grin. "So let me get this straight. Did your people come from Arizona, then?"

"No. We actually came from right here and other parts of Michigan. It was just my aunt who ended up down there when her husband — another Army guy — retired. I guess Fort Huachuca was the closest Army base to Tucson. My aunt's husband is buried there, too. That's how my father came to visit the Fort in the first place," I said.

"I've been to every state in the Lower 48 myself, but you military folks sure do get around."

Linda told me about her family's little ranch in Fairbank along the San Pedro River as we transferred Aunt Vicky's stuff into my pickup. I could probably get everything in one load, if I applied full Becker packing power to the task, but the rocker is bulky and I have to bring Linda back to her truck anyway. If Linda is a professional packer, I am at least semi-pro. In my two-dozen years, I have moved more than a dozen times. Even after my father left my mother, sister, and me to civilian life when I was twelve, we continued to keep moving every two or three years, like we were trying to keep in practice or something.

With our combined experience, Linda and I have the pickup packed within minutes. Only the occasional "turn it clockwise," or "let's set it on this end" interrupts our conversation.

Linda's great grandfather was one of the first white settlers in Cochise County, she tells me. At one time her family owned about twelve square miles of some of the best high desert grassland in the state. Her grandfather had about 240 head of cattle before the Depression hit. Now, she lives on a 200-acre ranch with her brother and his family, who own a gas station/convenience store on State Highway 90.

"I don't remember too much of the scenery down there, Linda, but I do remember the mountains rising up to the south of Fort Huachuca and the long valley stretching down from the highway to the fort. I'll have to get down there again and get a better look next time. Speaking of scenery, you probably didn't get to see much of Lake Michigan in this storm. Are you heading out of town right after you're done with this load?"

"No. I got a room at some fancy hotel between here and town — the Gazebo Garden, or something like that. I passed it on the way over."

"Well, I hope you get some sense of where you are before you have to take off tomorrow. It's pretty incredible around here, too," I tell her.

I feel a twinge of regret when I think that this traveler from the Southwest might leave here in the morning darkness without ever getting a good look around.

"Is this all part of your farm?" Linda asks, as we head down the road towards the farmhouse with the first load.

"No, this field belongs to some neighbors. Our property starts up ahead at the tree line. There's 105 acres. About 75 acres are up here on top of the bluff, and another 30 acres are down on the beach. We've got about 1,000 feet of beachfront down there. You wouldn't believe how nice it gets down there in the summer. The beach is sandy and, depending on the wind and waves, the lake bottom usually is, too. The sand is so clean it squeaks when you walk on it. And the water is clear down to 30 feet after a few calm days. This is probably the last big piece of undeveloped property left on the shoreline between Blue Harbor and Cross Village."

I realize I'm starting to ramble, and ease off a bit. I haven't had too many visitors since I moved Up North, and this trucker doesn't need to hear my whole life story just for dropping a few things off.

The snowstorm is petering out. Although the wind is still kicking up snow devils, the cloud cover is breaking up overhead. Patches of blue appear and disappear from the graywhite commotion above.

I show the lady trucker the old fence line that marks the start of the property as we head into the woods. The mixed hardwood and pine forest is a quiet shelter from the gusty wind. The road through the woods climbs, then drops, then climbs again like a roller coaster as we near the farmhouse drive. To the north, the woods slope down into the dark cedar swamp that surrounds Cummings Creek. The creek lies about a quarter of a mile north of Stanton Road. On the south side of the road, the land rises higher to the flat apex where the farmhouse has stood for close to a century.

The farmhouse is barely visible from the road because of the dense second growth that has filled in what used to be an orchard between the road and house. Pines and spindly tall maples have grown up through the old apple trees. Some of the apple trees are long dead, but most have high, awkward branches shooting up into the new canopy. The apple trunks and main branches near the ground are black with decay. Amid the tall, straight, nearly uniform new pines, the old orchard trees look like iron sculptures left in an unlikely place. Only the gleaming-white new blanket of snow on both the pines and the apple trees seems to tie the scene together. Vertical streaks of snow plastered on the tree trunks show the direction of today's wind.

A beam of sunlight breaks through as we reach the end of the apple-pine tunnel. Fine specks of snow — stirred by the wind — catch the light and twinkle like shiny confetti floating down from the sky. The pickup bounces into the clearing that holds the old garage, the farmhouse, and the small barn, which sit on a football-field-size hill that is the highest spot on the property.

The driveway ends in a circle behind and to the right of the house. Lombardy poplars rise out of the middle of the driveway circle. The poplars once formed a straight windbreak with a large alcove around the barn to keep the north winds at bay. I can still make out the original line of poplars as I pull into the circle, but new generations of poplars have undone most of the planter's order. The old trees, which were probably grown by an Ottawa farmer, sent runners through the topsoil. There are clusters of Lombardies all over the clearing — wherever the ground is not mowed or driven on.

On the west edge of the circular drive, a spur of the driveway leads straight ahead to the old garage, and then to the right, where the barn sits facing the house. I drive clockwise around the circle and pull up to what used to be the kitchen back stoop.

Even with a fresh layer of snow covering the frozen mud and the cinder block foundation, the back of the farmhouse still looks like a WW I foxhole. The clapboard siding is torn off and only a layer of old tar paper, the planks of wooden sheathing, the framing, and some turn-of-the-century wallboard separate indoors from outdoors. Except for the kitchen, The Shack isn't insulated. Between the edge of the driveway and the kitchen door, there is a five-foot deep hole with a concrete footing and block foundation. The new foundation outlines an addition that will bring the east wall of the house out another six feet.

The original farmhouse is a simple affair. The main part of the house is a two-story rectangle with a fieldstone fireplace running up through the middle. There's a shed roof covering the kitchen and small dining area on the back side of the house, and a covered front porch on the west side of the main rectangle.

"Doing a little remodeling, eh?" Linda says.

"We were. My dad and I and a carpenter friend of ours started to fix this place up about two and a half years year ago, but everything has been in limbo since my dad died. I hope to get the project going again this summer."

Linda and I take the cedar chest into the house first, and the planks over the hole sag from the weight of two people and Aunt Vicky's heaviest heirloom. Once inside, the warmth and wood-smoke surround us.

The kitchen is still intact. There are four windows in this part of the house, but it has always been fairly dark in here. The brightest things in the kitchen are the big propane-gas refrigerator and the wood cook stove with its white enamel sides. It was about five below zero when I got up this morning, so I had the cook stove going, as well as the big stove in the living room to take the chill off. My dad and I gutted the living room, so there is a heavy wool blanket tacked across the doorway to keep the living room drafts out of the insulated kitchen.

As I struggle to pull back the blanket with my foot, Linda can't help but notice the big galvanized washtub sitting in front of the cook stove. Next to the washtub is a tray table with soap, shampoo, conditioner, a razor, and a small metal camping mirror. Traces of wet footprints trail across the wood floor to the kitchen table, where my bathrobe and sweater hang off the back of a chair. The kitchen table is strewn with newspapers, a pile of notepads, books, and a little 512k Macintosh computer. A printer sits precariously on one of the kitchen chairs with continuous-feed computer paper hanging over the back of the chair. The kitchen is doing quadruple duty as a cooking area, dining room, washroom and office.

Linda is polite enough to only say, "Cozy" as we pass into the living room. We set the chest down. Linda stretches out a kink in her back and takes a look around. With the walls gutted, the skeleton of the farmhouse framing is exposed. The old dark 2X4s are actually two inches by four inches, unlike the skinny stuff you get from the building center these days. The room is bare, except for a pair of fifty-five-gallon drums that have been converted into what Dan the carpenter calls a double-barreled stove. He installed it himself a decade ago when my dad let him live out here for a few years. Dan had lots of friends and for most of the '70s and into the '80s; The Shack was kind of a commune.

The double-barrel stove is just one of the artifacts left over from that era. Wood goes into a door cut into the end of the bottom barrel, which sits horizontally on steel legs. The top barrel — attached to the bottom barrel by another set of steel legs and a short section of stove pipe — is for trapping the heat and dispersing it into the house before the hot air is drawn up an unfinished chimney of cinder blocks. There are little steel tabs sticking out of the cinder-block joints. Dan never quite got around to putting the brick facade around the cinder blocks. He did, however, get Dad to install a phone line and electricity a few years ago, which have come in handy for someone who makes his living making calls and using a computer.

Linda sees the steep, narrow staircase leading upstairs to the two small bedrooms, and takes in the bare living room. Her grin seems to say she's been through renovations like this before. Then, her jaw drops.

"Holy Cow," she says, as she gets her first look at Lake Michigan through the windows. The Alberta clipper that blew the snowstorm down from the Arctic has, just as quickly as it came, blown the clouds and snow out of the area. It may still be snowing a few miles away, but here at the Becker farm, the sun has burst across the land and lake.

"Want a better look?" I ask Linda, as I open the door to the front porch. She follows without speaking.

The front porch, which is filled with wood for the stoves and fresh snow drifts, looks out over the flat yard of the farmhouse hilltop. The yard drops off sharply to an open meadow about two hundred yards wide. The sunlight makes it almost painful to look at the bright snow-covered meadow. The snow on the field is riddled with drifts that show the patterns of the spirited jig the cold wind has been dancing to since last night. The trees that grow on the side of the bluff have started to fill in the clearing my grandfather cut for his lake view, but there is still plenty of lake left to see.

Today, Lake Michigan is alive. To the left, the edge of the ice sheet covering Little Traverse Bay is being ground and splintered by loose chunks of ice. White-capped waves are hurling the chunks against the edge of the sheet, making more chunks. Even at this distance (it's about a half mile to the water) I can see the waves swelling under the floating pieces of ice like a white bed sheet unfurled across a bed. The waves seem to slow down as they pass underneath the frozen flotsam near the edge. Even over the clamor of the wind, I can hear the ice groaning and cracking. The radiant white of the ice sheet to the left is being challenged by the cold, dark blue and foaming white of the open water to the right. Stray ice floes dot the open water. They may have broken free from the heavy ice anchored to the beach up shore, or they may have come from the ice pack around Beaver Island northwest of here. Massive waves are sweeping in from the northwest almost perpendicular to the shoreline below us. The waves are loud enough to compete with the wind for attention. The cobalt-blue sky is now free of clouds. Lately, I've noticed that the colder it gets, the richer the blue in the sky becomes.

We can see for miles in the clear air, which has been scoured by the winter wind. About six miles south across the mouth of Little Traverse Bay, is Charlevoix County, I tell Linda. And those islands way out there to the west are the Fox Islands. Beaver Island is just out of sight to the right.

"I never imagined it would be so big," Linda said. "I always thought is was just a big lake, and that you could see across it. That's like the North Sea out there."

Chapter 2

THE MOVING VAN has moved on, and I have finished my dinner. The water that comes out of the hand pump at the kitchen sink is icy cold. I use a small gas stove to cook, but the old wood cook stove can heat up water and keep me warm at the same time. I filled the tank on the side of the cook stove when I sat down to eat the chicken fajitas I made, and the water is boiling by the time I'm ready to wash dishes.

There are only a few electrical outlets in place and even fewer electric lamps, so after washing up, I light every kerosene lamp in the house. I want to get a good look at the furniture and boxes sitting in the middle of the living room.

I know nothing about antiques, but the rocking chair, desk, dresser, and cedar chest look like they may be quality stuff. From what little I know about Aunt Vicky and my grandparents, I assume that the chest and rugs come from my grandparents' tour of the Orient in the 1930s. My mother told me that Joe and Anna Becker traveled to Japan and China after Joe's tour of duty in the Philippines was over.

My mother — Janice Whittier Becker of Ft. Lauderdale, Florida — is one of only three living links to Joe and Anna's lives that I know of. The other two are Patty Kensington, an old friend of my father's who lives here in town, and Lu Ann Wilson, Aunt Vicky's best friend in Tucson and the executrix of her estate. The only other link I have is what lies before me in the middle of the living room and this old house.

Joe and Anna Becker had been dead seven and eight years, respectively, before I was born. Growing up, I knew them only as old photographs hanging in the hallway and the reason my father brought us Up North to the family property. I didn't even know Anna's name for sure, until a few months ago. She was simply, "my grandmother." Joe — or "The Colonel" as he is usually referred to — was only a small leather box with the initials JLB on top. My dad used to keep the box with his fly-tying stuff in the spare bedroom. The box was filled with medals, bars, shoulder patches, and epaulettes from Joe's half-century of military service. And, of course, there were the swords. They were only ceremonial with dull edges and fancy etchings on the steel, but I imagined you could run somebody through with them, if the need arose. Beyond a vague sense of reverence for my grandparents, a feeling of connection to this place, and some pride in my family's eighty-year military history, I really don't know these people.

As a kid, I even had a recurring dream in which my sleeping brain confused my grandfather with Colonel Sanders. Now that I am twenty-four, my dreams are still pretty weird, but my knowledge of who my grandparents were has progressed beyond any confusion with the Kentucky Fried Chicken king.

I don't believe in ghosts, but lately the dead have been coming into focus all around me. It started with Dad. A few months after he died from a series of massive strokes, I started to learn more about him then I ever had during his lifetime. There were the family secrets that Mom and Sally shared with me. Like the huge fight they had shielded me from in high school. After retiring from the Army in 1979, Dad had spent a couple months living with us in St. Louis before flying off to Turkey for his first civil service job. One day when I came home from school, I had been told that Dad had gotten a lead on a job that he had to accept sooner than he expected, and went to Washington to prepare for the job. He returned a couple of weeks later to give his final goodbyes and pick up his stuff.

The real story, my sister told me after the funeral, was that Dad had walked into the garage of our suburban townhouse to find Sally cheerfully washing Mom's silver VW Rabbit near the open garage door. Sally, who was getting ready for a big date, had gotten a bit of water inside of the garage and sprayed some of Dad's things in her teenage enthusiasm. Dad, who was better at taking care of his things than his family, erupted into a temper tantrum at the sight. He called Sally a "stupid bitch," for "flooding" the garage. When Sally jumped right back in his face with equal vigor, he slapped her down to the hard, wet concrete. Before either of them could do any further damage, Mom, a five-foot tall Christian Scientist — more prone to prayer than violence — walked in and lashed out at Dad with all the fury of a Missouri twister. With two justifiably shrieking Valkyries on his tail, Dad fled town and, later, the country.

Even then, I was aware of the effect Dad's outbursts had on our family, but I wasn't on the receiving end of them as often as Sally and Mom were. More than half the time, Dad could be a lot of fun. He had dozens of nonsense names for his children, took us camping, went to church with us, held our hands, wiped our noses, wrapped us in bear hugs when he took naps on the sofa, and bought us lots of toys for Christmas. There were plenty of good times, but they became more and more fragile as time went by.

The other way I got to know Dad better was through his things. The remnants of his life were shipped from his bachelor quarters at the Burtonwood Army Depot in England straight to Mom's new house in Florida. Inside, I discovered we had more in common than we knew about. There was all of the gear of an outdoorsman. Cross-country skis, downhill skis, fishing rods, waders, a tent, sleeping bags, and every other piece of equipment you might need outside.

And there were the photos from all over the world: Vietnam, Germany, England, Italy, Switzerland, France, Japan, and Tunisia. The pictures reminded me of the life of travel and adventure that I had sampled when Dad was still with the family and when I spent a year abroad for college. I wasn't interested in a military career, but my newspaper-career plans offered the promise of travel as an overseas correspondent.

The crate from Burtonwood also contained reams of legal papers on our property. Dad had spent the past seven years of his life trying to get clear title to this land. Even though he spent most of his time elsewhere, the papers showed that the land I am trying to claim as my home was constantly on Dad's mind and in his heart.

The leftovers from the lives of two generations of Beckers have been flung to the far corners of the world. With Dad's passing, and now Aunt Vicky's death, these fragments have regrouped and returned to the place they came from. And I am the only witness who cares whether these pieces pass into obscurity or not.

Chapter 3

I SPENT ENOUGH time riffling through the boxes before dinner to determine that they do not contain jewels or 50-year-old American Telephone & Telegraph stock certificates. There is nothing here that would instantly help me get over the fact that some guy named Larry, the Humane Society of Tucson, and other unknown Arizonians will soon be getting the money from half of our family's property.

Aunt Vicky was never close to Mom, Sally, and me. Aunt Vicky was in college by the time my Dad was born, so they didn't really grow up together. And once Dad went to Germany on his own, what little connection we had to her was reduced to Christmas cards, annual exchanges of presents, and a couple phone calls a year. Visits were rare.

Aunt Vicky never had any children of her own, and Sally and I were her closest living relatives. We didn't necessarily expect anything from her estate, but I had held out a glimmer of hope that Aunt Vicky might leave some of the property to her family.

Sally did not share my optimism. Since Dad's funeral, Vicky had practically disowned her niece over a sunburn. The day before the funeral, my sister and I had spent the afternoon lounging around Aunt Vicky's backyard pool in the April Arizona sun. The cool air deceived us unwary Midwesterners into staying out a little too long. I went in after an hour or so, but Sally — ever the sun worshipper — didn't.

The next morning she awoke with a serious case of sun poisoning. Sally could barely get out of bed, but she managed to drag herself to the funeral by wearing nothing but a light sundress and espadrilles, she told me later. There was a tent set up over the coffin at the Ft. Huachuca cemetery, and Sally survived the full military honors without complaint. The air was cold under the shade of the tent, and I can only begin to imagine the mixed sensations of cold and burning that Sally must have endured along with her mixed feelings of loss and release over our father's death.

After the visit, Aunt Vicky accused Sally of intentionally staying out in the sun too long. Familiar with at least one version of the father-daughter fights, Aunt Vicky presumed that Sally made herself sick to get out of going to Dad's funeral. Vicky would never forgive Sally for the alleged offense. What little Aunt Vicky did leave to her heirs, was only left to me. I'll have to see if Sally is interested in any of the old furniture the next time she comes up.

Whatever glimmer of hope I had of re-establishing relations with Aunt Vicky ended a year after Dad's funeral. While spending a few weeks traveling with some college buddies Out West after graduation, I took a side trip to pay my respects. It was my first real effort to get to know more about the Becker family history. I left my buddies in Bend, Oregon, for a few days and caught a Greyhound to Tucson. She was not in good health, so I stayed at a cheap motel near the highway. When I called from the motel, the first thing she told me was that she had tried phoning me to tell me not to come. When she allowed me one hour to visit, I unwittingly showed up an hour late. Apparently, Arizona doesn't feel the need for daylight saving time, I discovered. She showed me a few of the pictures that now lie before me in these five cardboard boxes. Then, after about 45 minutes, she sent me packing. It was the last time I saw her.

These odd family memories wash over me as I bend back the cardboard box flaps to peer into someone else's memories.

The first box contains the antique chandelier that Aunt Vicky's friend Lu Ann told me about. Lu Ann said Vicky had told her the chandelier once hung here at the house. It's Victorian, with a rose-colored glass bowl and an indecipherable nest of copper pieces and clear-glass beads that are meant to hang from underneath the bowl. It looks like it was originally an oil lamp, but was converted to electric.

It occurs to me that the chandelier is like some magic boomerang that was thrown from this house, traveled the spinning course of Aunt Vicky's adult life, made a 180-degree turn in Tucson, and has returned to the spot it was thrown from. I spend a couple of minutes trying to figure out how all the pieces go together, before my curiosity compels me to move on to the other boxes.

I'm drawn to a tattered, green photo album with black pages. Inside are photos and postcards from when my grandparents were stationed in the Philippines in the 1930s. There are dozens of pictures of Philippino natives, some with white, hand-written captions. There are Moro and Igorot natives, and some unnamed beach-dwelling group with men who have wild, flowing hair. They look like the guys who were hired to play the exotic, oriental pirates in the Swiss Family Robinson movie.

A man named Mamma stares at the camera with a smug grin on his face and 14 beautiful, young wives at his side. The crisp black-and-white postcard shows Mamma clad in skin-tight pants that almost look like lycra tights, except for the buttons running up the outside of Mamma's calves.

I do a double take when I flip past a picture of a group of male and female natives lined up with sarongs around their waists and stern expressions on their faces. After closer examination, the ball on the grass in front of them turns out to be a severed human head. The clubs, spears, and knives that were probably used to obtain the head are displayed in neat X patterns on the grass surrounding the trophy.

At first, I dismiss these pictures as mere souvenirs picked up by my grandparents to show their friends back home. It's possible that there were still headhunters in the Philippines in the 1930s, but I don't think the gruesome custom was something my grandparents witnessed, firsthand.

My assumption is overturned a few pages later. I come across a series of grisly photographs showing the decapitated body of a man splayed out in the mud with a rope around his ankles. The photos are too out-of-focus to be the work of a professional postcard photographer. I pull the picture out of the four mounting corners glued to the album page. On the back, in my grandfather's dramatic cursive are the words: "Caluxto Guzman, Negrito — Escaped prisoner of 42nd Co. killed by Pudo, Alabo and Sugilap."

I scan the remaining pictures a bit more carefully. Scattered among the postcards and pictures of Philippino life are photos of Joe in his white tropical suit and black tie, which match his prematurely white hair so well. In one such picture, Joe is on the deck of a boat with a Philippino gentleman, similarly dressed. Above the picture is a business card that reads: "J. Hashim Alzeney, Official Sec'y to H. H. Sultan H. M. J. Kiram." Next to the card is an autographed postcard of the sultan himself, "Captain Becker, Best Wishes from Muhammad Jamalul Kiram, Sultan of Sulu."

I had always been told that Joe and Anna did not live ordinary lives, and now I see how extraordinary their lives were.

In another box, there are several yard-wide, panoramic photos rolled up into tubes. Most are formal portraits of the Army regiments Joe served in, the troops lined up by company and platoon wearing those classic Smoky-the-Bear campaign hats that were part of the uniform of the day. I can pick out Joe easily in the crowd. He was 6-feet-tall and apparently had a knack for always ending up in the middle of group photos.

But this next panoramic group portrait comes as a complete surprise to me. The caption reads, "Dedication Zero Monument — Old Spanish Trail — San Antonio, Texas — 3-25-24." White-whiskered cowboys mounted on their horses and armed with six shooters at their sides and rifles in leather scabbards are surrounded by hundreds of San Antonio residents. On the right side of the picture is a line of mule-drawn covered wagons and stagecoaches filled with more Old West veterans. There are a couple of younger men in Army uniforms, but Joe is nowhere to be seen in this picture and I haven't the slightest idea what the Beckers had to do with the Old Spanish Trail. I can only guess that my grandparents must have been stationed in Texas at some point in Joe's career.

Even with the double-barreled stove blazing, it is too cold in the living room to spend much time in there. The stove does wonders for making the bedrooms upstairs warm and cozy, but I can practically feel the cold being sucked up through the floorboards by the draw of the hot stove. I grab an interesting armful of papers from another box and retreat into the insulated kitchen.

There are envelopes filled with more photographs. One envelope has a sandwich-size stack of black-and-white postcards in French that I assume Joe brought back from WW I. It doesn't appear that he ever mailed them, but some of the postcards bear Joe's notes on the significance of these places. There is even a set of postcards from Champlitte, a small French city where I once spent the night in a youth hostel during my junior year abroad.

A manila folder labeled "Estate and Will of Joseph Becker" slides off the stack of papers and spills over the French post-cards spread across the kitchen table. As I start tucking these legal documents back into their folder for future perusal, I come across the Colonel's Last Will and Testament.

These three yellowing pages set in motion a legal battle over this property that has spanned three decades and affected two generations. Our family's lawyer showed me the will for the first time last year, and I don't entirely understand how it has caused so much trouble. What I do know is that a single para-graph — a mere 127 words — made the difference between a normal transfer of property from one generation to the next, and the mess my aunt and father and, now, my sister and I have had to deal with. I read the words again trying to understand what my grandfather had in mind.

> *I give and bequeath all my real property to my issue, in equal shares. Share and share alike, except such property as I may own in Emmet County, Michigan. Such property as I may own at the time of my death in Emmet County, Michigan, I give and bequeath as life tenants to my issue, with right of survivorship, and with the remainder to my grandchildren, if any, by right of representation. In the event that my issue leave no surviving issue, then I give and devise my said realty in Emmet County, Michigan, to the State of Michigan, to be maintained and managed by the State Department of Conservation as a nature preserve and memorial to my wife, ANNA JOHNSON BECKER, whose name it shall bear.*

It's clear that this place meant a lot to Joe and he didn't want it sold off as soon as he died. It's also clear that if there wasn't any family to take over the place, Joe wanted the property to become something special that would serve as a testament to

Anna. Cyril J. Cushman, our family's lawyer, helped Vicky and Dad get around the life tenancy restrictions that barred them from selling the property during their lifetimes. And now it is only the State of Michigan keeping the grandchildren (i.e., Sally and I) from getting Dad's half of the property. The state says it still has a claim to at least some of the land because of Joe's will. And we still have to resolve the lawsuit against North Shore Township, which claims an acre of our property as a public park. I don't fully understand these problems, but I intend to get to the bottom of them when Cushman gets back from his annual winter migration to Florida in a couple weeks.

I talked with him by phone the other day and he said the township lawsuit is scheduled for a hearing next month. The title issue goes before the Probate Court in a couple of months. Cushman seems like a good guy and a capable attorney. He knew both my father and aunt fairly well, and I was able to joke with him about the "vast fortune" that was coming from Aunt Vicky's estate. He told me not to spend it all in one place. Things are quiet on the legal front right now, but I've got a lot of questions for Cushman.

In the meantime, if there are any answers to the question about Joe's plans for his family's future, I suspect that I'm more likely to find them in these boxes than I am to find them in court.

Chapter 4

AMIDST THE PAPERS is a tight bundle of letters — there must be six or seven dozen such bundles in the boxes. I untie a musty smelling string and finger through the letters, most of which are neatly folded in their original envelopes. This bundle of letters is from Anna — my grandmother. They're written to her mother — my great-grandmother Dianna Johnson. I pick one with a return address of Mrs. Joseph Becker, Capt. 45th Inf., Fort Wm. McKinley, Rizal, Philippine Islands

> *Wednesday — May 13, 1931*
> *Aboard the U.S.S. Grant*
>
> *Dear Mother —*
>
> *We got the letter from you in New York — and I wrote to you from there.*
>
> *Vicky came at 12:30 on Saturday and we spent the afternoon shopping. On Sunday, we had Uncle Emil and Jane and Russell and their son for dinner and supper — and all evening. In the morning (Sunday) we went to Central Park with the baby. He enjoyed it, and after dinner — Jane and Russell drove Vicky and me out to see Major and Mrs. Montgomery at Fort Schuyler. They were at Ft. Ontario until Dec. 15 and lived where the Poore's live now.*
>
> *We had good luck shopping at Wanamakers and got several dresses a piece. I found a lovely brownish dress — a small figured print for $8.75 and it goes well with my*

coat and I bought Vicky a lovely gray coat — it is beautiful — for only $16.50. Won't take time to tell you all about the clothes, now. You will never guess who we ran into while shopping — Harvey Higginbotham and his wife. Right out of the blue, he came up to Vicky and me and greeted me with a loud hello. He was polite enough, but his wife seemed to have no idea who I was. She was lovely, but looked to be half his age!

When I told Joe about the chance encounter later that day, he, at first, pretended not to remember Harvey, then said, "Oh, I remember that scoundrel well enough."

We had a lovely trip to Panama — very smooth sailing, but hot as we neared the Tropics. The second night out, we had a reception on board for the Congressional party who are making this trip. They are Rep. and Mrs. Hooper of Michigan and Rep. and Mrs. Saytor of Colorado — also Rep. Hill of Washington State & Mrs. Hyde, wife of the Secretary of Agriculture.

Imagine me beside the Colonel in Command of the boat — the only Army lady in the receiving line with all those notables. It certainly was an honor. We danced afterward and it was a lovely evening.

It is dinnertime and Joe and Vicky have Towser in the children's dining room. He won't eat, but seems to be O.K. On the train to New York, he said he couldn't wait for you to come visit and play "Goodness Sakes."

We have a lovely stateroom on the promenade deck and I am sitting by the open door looking out on the low mountains along the Central American coast. The sea is calm, but there is always a roll — and hence my peculiar writing. We got into Colon Harbor Sunday about 10 PM, but did not dock until 6 in the morning. We spent the day looking

*around and Joe bought a white Palm Beach suit and hat.
We saw the old places where Joe lived 22 years ago.*

*Vicky was invited to France Field on Monday night,
and on Tuesday, the Army fliers — whom she visited
there — came thru the Canal with us in their planes. They
flew overhead and circled and dived and did tail spins
until we were all through the Canal. Then they formed in
line and flew home. My, but they gave a wonderful exhibition of flying skill. There were six planes.*

*I enjoyed going thru the Canal. It took from 6 AM until
noon. We did not stop at the Pacific side, so we did not
see our quarters of four years ago at Ft. Clayton. Instead,
we sailed right on out into the Pacific. We are in sight of
land all the time now, and will be all the way to Frisco. A
woman aboard is getting off at Corinto, Nicaragua, in the
morning and I will mail this by her.*

*We are all so delighted that the ship is not going to make
direct crossing from Frisco to Manila, as was reported, but
instead we will stop at Honolulu and Guam.*

*There is a hop in the Social Hall tonight and Vicky is
going. She is dolling up now in her new white chiffon dress.
It touches the floor all around and makes her look slim
and slinky.*

*Later: It is now 7:30 and our meals are at 7 — 12 — and
6. We are at the first sitting in the dining salon. The
second sitting is 3/4 of an hour later. The food is
good — always — a four course dinner and three course
lunch. My, I wish you were along. You would love the
meals and lounging on deck in a long deck chair like a
chaise lounge. Nothing to do but eat and bathe. The bath
steward calls us when the bath water is drawn and we
parade in for a salt water bath — with a bucket of fresh
water to rinse in. The ocean water leaves one feeling sticky.*

All afternoon, we have been watching some huge black fish — at least 25 feet long. They have followed the ship and leap out of the water every few seconds. We have seen sharks and whales.

On board the other evening, I was talking to a Lt. Col. Ohmstead, when Mrs. Hooper passed by. I said she was reared in Michigan, not far from my old house. He asked me where I lived (Mrs. H. was from Cheboygan). I said Blue Harbor and he said he had an Aunt there years ago — Mrs. A. A. Cox. I told him I used to sit with Lynne Cox in school, then we had a great visit. A. A. and Lynne are dead, but Mrs. Cox lives in California and he will see her there.

I hear thunder and see chain lightning. I hope the storm clears the air. It is very hot, but not as hot as Monday in Colon. It seemed so good to be back there again, but I wondered how I stood the heat for two years. I probably just got used to it.

We have moving pictures nearly every night on the after well deck, and other amusements in the Social Hall. We had church on Sunday — a good sermon and singing. We have five chaplains aboard. One is retired and is going to Manila with us and then on to Borneo to look up plants for the British Research — something or other.

There is so much talking outside that I can't write as good a letter as I'd like to, and can't remember all I'd like to tell you.

Oh yes — one thing is that the girl Vicky rooms with is a girl whom she went to school with in San Antonio. Another girl came aboard in Colon who graduated with her at Balboa in Panama. The San Antonio girl is a chaplain's daughter. Vicky was feeling a bit blue about having to leave college under the circumstances, but seeing her old chums has restored her spirits.

I can hear the party music. The hop is about to begin, and the wind is blowing the curtains and the rain is on.

Lots of love to you, keep well,
Anna

I can almost hear the party music and smell the tropical rain on the breeze as I set Anna's letter down and rise to stoke the kitchen stove with another log. Anna keeps me up reading until 2 AM.

~ PART 2 ~
BRIDGETOWN, BARBADOS

Chapter 5

I'VE SPENT THE past two weeks sifting through the lives of the last two generations of Beckers. The letters, documents and photographs are in chronological order now — divided into five eras defined by Joe's career. I've named these periods: "Early Years: 1800s to 1909," "Salesman to Soldier: 1909 to 1919," "Texas to Peru: 1919 to 1927," "Upstate and Far East: 1927 to 1934," and "Back to Michigan: 1934 to 1957." Within each era, I've separated the papers and photographs by individual family member, so that I can read or examine all of Anna's letters and pictures between 1909 and 1919, for example, as they unfolded in her life.

I just finished going through the first two decades of Joe's life. The skeleton is all there, and I find myself fleshing out the bones with the colors, emotions, and candor that lie between the lines and behind the images. The acidity and dust from the old papers turn my eyes red, and I decide to spend the rest of this bright Sunday afternoon getting some fresh air out on the property. The past week has brought wave after wave of warmer air from the southwest, breaking winter's back. The daffodils have speared through the remaining snow banks along the front porch and it will be May tomorrow.

Wet snow still lingers in the shaded woods, but the meadow out in front of the farmhouse has shed its white overcoat for a brown undershirt. There's even a touch of green starting to show. The path that leads from the farmhouse, across the meadow, and down the bluff, however, still shows two fading ribbons of white where my cross-country skis packed the snow down over the winter.

After the last hard freeze and before the new spring grass takes hold, comes mud season. The circular driveway out back is a soggy mess. A pair of red Gortex gaiters over my Sorel boots keeps mud from splattering my jeans. The sun on my face, as I step off the front porch and head for the meadow, makes the day feel warmer than the 50 degrees registering on the thermometer.

As I reach the lip of the low hill the farm sits on, dancing tails of pink that dot the meadow stop me in my tracks. Like neon signs in the middle of a desert, the surveyor's stakes — topped with plastic ribbons — jar my brain out of the dusty past and into the messy present.

Although I knew the stakes were out here and even noticed their tops sticking out of the snow earlier this winter, the sudden thaw has freed the pink ribbons to wave in the breeze. Homer Robertson's development plan for half of the property has left the drawing board and been driven into the soil of the Becker farm.

From the yard, I can see that the stakes outline three large building sites in the meadow — at least there won't be wall-to-wall condominiums here. The pink-fringed outline of a gravel road runs along the base of my little hill, north to Stanton Road and south to Four Fires Estates. Homer's deal with Aunt Vicky seven years ago allows him to begin preliminary development, even before her estate is settled. Homer may simply be abiding by the terms of the agreement, but it feels like a dark tentacle has reached up from the neighboring development to my front porch.

Homer introduced himself a couple of years ago as "an old family friend." His older sister was one of Vicky's playmates when Vicky was a little girl living in Blue Harbor. Homer's father owned the farm that bordered ours. And when Homer's old man finally died in the '70s, Homer turned that 300-acre family farm into Four Fires Estates, an upscale, gated, resort development. Retired General Motors executives from downstate snatched up the bluff-top and beachfront vacation homes within a few years. The development provides 24-hour security, three tennis courts, nature trails, beach access, and stunning views of the bay. The GM execs and their families think they have died and gone to heaven, but it is only money and not good deeds that have allowed them through the pearly white security gate. Homer's construction company holds the exclusive right to build the 3,000- to 8,000-square-foot homes in the development. In the past decade, Homer has transformed himself from rusty-pickup nail banger to millionaire developer.

In 1982, Homer came up with a plan to help Aunt Vicky out of "the terrible mess" caused by Joe's will. Vicky was in her seventies and having health and financial problems when Homer contacted her in Arizona. Vicky talked my father into letting her sell a purchase option to Homer for $75,000 on her half of the property. Although she couldn't sell her half of the property while she was alive, the deal guaranteed that Vicky's estate would sell her property to Homer after she died.

My father was never thrilled with the plan, but he acquiesced. After all, it was Vicky's property to do with as she liked, Dad told me during the summer we gutted The Shack, with plans for a brighter future. Dad would have liked to see the property stay in the family, but the property taxes were already more than he could afford, and I don't think he wanted to saddle his kids with that burden. Dad wanted to hold on to about half of his share of the land. He was keeping The Shack for old-times sake and for Sally and I to use if we wanted to, but he had his sights set on building a new log home among the red pines in the northwest corner of the property. He would not begrudge his sister what little money she could get for the place. And, as it turned out, the money paid for medical care that probably kept Aunt Vicky alive a few more years than she would have lived without it.

To facilitate the deal, Vicky and Dad agreed to stake out their individual halves of the property. They had the land surveyed and appraised to make the split as fair as possible, and put the agreement in writing. Dad got the fifty acres on the north side of Stanton Road, plus five acres on the south side of the road. The five-acre tract encompasses The Shack, barn, garage, and the little hill they sit on. Vicky took the remaining 50 acres on the south side of Stanton Road. The Shack and outbuildings were appraised at only about $25,000, but Vicky had more beach frontage, which made each half of the property worth about $375,000.

The deal was a bit risky for Homer because of the state's claim on the land, but Homer is confident our family will end up with most of the property. Vicky's agreement allowed him to make improvements to the property before the sale is final. Homer figures that if the state has any luck in court, it will take a smaller chunk of more-expensive beachfront property over the bluff-top property that he is waiting for. Homer said possession is nine-tenths of the law, and he believes that pounding a few stakes in the ground gives him more of a stake in the property than the state will ever have.

An old Realtor friend of my dad's said Homer is making the pre-sale improvements so that he can line up buyers ahead of time. Homer's millions are tied up in other projects — some of which aren't proving to be too successful — and he will have to borrow from the bank to buy Vicky's property. If Homer lines up buyers first, the bank will probably overlook some of the shaky projects he has sunk the bank's money into over the past few years.

For $75,000, plus preliminary development costs, Homer has the inside track on getting one-half of one of the most valuable pieces of property on the shore — at a bargain price. Homer stands to make enough money to cover his bad investments and still walk away with another million.

It may have been a good deal for Homer and Vicky. With the outline of the scheme driven into the dirt before my eyes, however, it is clear that The Shack will soon be surrounded on three sides by estaters and their huge houses.

Homer told me to feel free to stroll through Four Fires, use its nature trails, tennis courts, and beach park whenever I want to. Homer used to hunt deer, squirrels, and mushrooms on our land, and his offer seemed natural enough at the time. But the new Four Fires Estates owners have been less accommodating. Three summers ago, a white-haired lady wearing tennis shorts over her bathing suit ran up to me while I was lying on the beach near the Four Fires property line. She marched passed the development's "No Trespassing, Private Property" sign — which was aimed in my general direction — to tell me that I was on private property. I was a bit startled, at first. But when I told her that she was right and that my family owned the private property she was standing on, she turned back without a word of apology.

Being around people with money is nothing new to me. Having attended private schools from 6th grade through college, I never experienced any overt class discrimination. Adolescent cliques were the worst signs of snobbery, and they were always open to ridicule by the less popular. I probably have more in common with these estaters than with locals like Dan the carpenter, but the new summer people have fortified their exclusivity with gates, fences, "no trespassing signs," and inflated real estate prices.

Later that same summer, I walked the half a mile to the northernmost paved road in the development. It was the closest access to pavement from The Shack. I was tired of having to throw my bike in the pickup and drive the sandy dirt road to get to the pavement on Shore Drive.

As I peddled past the long driveways with polished brass streetlights, I told myself that the development was, at least, a classy piece of work. Homer could have cut down every tree and built a more generic subdivision. Most of the homes are far enough from the development's road that I could only see cedar-shake roofs through the trees. Each house sits on a lot of ten or more acres and the road is at least a hundred yards from the bluff line. Each lot includes the entire bluff, all the way down to Lower Beach Trail. Homer kept most of the woods and fields intact with plenty of open space for deer, wild turkeys, and other critters.

Most of the estate owners only spend three months a year up here, anyway, so I don't mind that these people are trying to enjoy some of the same things I enjoy about Northern Michigan. It's just that they seem to want it all to themselves. Almost every time I've passed through Four Fires and encountered the people who have homes there, I get suspicious looks. I wave and smile, but I can almost feel them saying, "Who is that person and what is he doing here?" It has gotten so that I feel like a thief anytime I cross the property line, despite Homer's open invitation. This winter, I have stayed on my side of the property line, but even here within sight of my house I am beginning to feel the same sense of uneasiness.

As I cross the staked-out future road, the land beneath my feet still belongs to my family. But I can feel it slipping away. I put the pink ribbons behind me and reach the woods that grow on the side of the bluff. I feel safe from the eyes of unseen estaters. The path under my feet is the same trail that I have taken to the beach since I was a kid. The Indians who lived here before my grandfather bought the property, wore it into the side of the bluff. There used to be four or five houses at the end of Stanton Road. The Shack is the only house that has survived the years, but piles of old boards and field stone foundations still mark the spots were the Indians lived. I wonder if a similar rubble pile will someday be all that my family has to show for its time on this land.

In a couple of minutes, I reach the bottom of the bluff and Lower Beach Trail. It's cooler down here by the water, and I can hear the last of the ice chunks scraping against each other near the water's edge. The beach is free of snow, and the shelf of ice that stretched from the beach and out into the lake is now shattered into a million melting pieces, gathered up in a thin line along the beach. The pieces are bobbing up and down in the calm water, waiting to become one again with Lake Michigan.

I head up the shore to check on Cummings Creek. Wind, ice, and shifting sand change the creek bed from year to year. A formation of Canada geese cruises by, just over my head. I hear the swish of their wings coming up behind me before I see them. Their leader honks only after the last goose in the group passes by.

Further up the shore, I come across a three-foot-long lake trout that has washed up on the beach. There is no dead-fish stench coming off this lunker. On closer inspection, I see its gills still pumping. The lakers come close into shore to spawn in the spring, but I don't know if they are supposed to die after they spawn, like the salmon do.

I grab the big trout firmly in front of its tail with my left hand and cup its soft underbelly in my right hand. Stepping to the very edge of the water, I move the laker's body gently back and forth to force water through its gills the way my dad taught me. Just before the bite of the cold water makes me pull my hands away, the fish thrashes and darts into the shallows. It settles near the pebbly bottom, its gills moving and its fins oscillating to maintain stability. Suddenly, it flicks its tail and disappears under the line of bobbing ice.

Rinsing the fish slime from my hands with lake water and sand, I rise to my feet. Beyond the band of melting ice, Lake Michigan stretches out before me with all the promise of a schoolboy's first day of summer vacation. Behind me lie lawsuits, developers, an unfinished and unfinanced remodeling project, and an uncertain future. Before me lies a wide-open expanse of bright blue possibilities.

My grandfather probably felt the same way as he stood on the Wisconsin shore eighty-eight years ago at the start of a journey that would eventually bring him to this side of Lake Michigan — though, by a route that would take him far from a direct path. To the southwest, I can only see as far as the Medusa Cement plant near Charlevoix. If I could see great distances along the curve of the Earth and across time, I could see Joe looking exactly this way from the Milwaukee Municipal Pier.

Joseph L. Becker would travel half a world away to get to the Michigan side of the lake, but in the summer of 1901 all he wanted to do was get out of Wisconsin.

Chapter 6

BACK HOME IN Ft. Atkinson, they called him "Josie," but from now on he wanted to be called "Joe."

In the summer of 1901, Joe was 15 and old enough to fend for himself. At least that's what he had told his Aunt Annika before setting off for Milwaukee. Uncle Horst was away on business that week, and Joe would be long gone by the time old Uncle Horse-Face got back. Back at the farm, there were stalls to be mucked out, stumps to pull, tack to be oiled, and a field full of hay ready for harvesting, but Joe wasn't going to waste another drop of sweat — or blood, for that matter — on that old drunken bastard, Joe told himself as he walked down West Michigan Street towards the waterfront.

Ever since the expense money from Joe's father stopped coming in last January, Horst had heaped more work and more whippings on Joe. Joe wasn't going to take it anymore, even if it did mean losing the $1,000 that Horst was holding in trust until Joe came of age.

There were no big ships on the pier yet, so Joe wandered up the shore until he found a park where he could get to the water and out from under the noonday sun. Setting down his rucksack under a weeping willow near the beach, Joe unlaced his hobnailed boots and tossed his straw hat aside. He wanted to strip down to nothing and dive right into Lake Michigan, but there were ladies with parasols and men with bowler hats strolling along the paths near the beach. There were some children playing in the water up the shore a bit, but they wore fancy swimming outfits. The best Joe could do was to pull off his sweaty wool socks and pull up the legs of his overalls above his knees.

The coolness of the water seemed to reach from the pads of his sore feet, all the way up to his brain. It had taken Joe two full days and the better part of this morning to walk the 52 miles from Uncle Horst's farm to Milwaukee. Joe had savored every mile, stopping to fish a couple of times, sleeping against the first haystacks of the summer, and making the most of every offer of hospitality along the way. He still had the two smoked whitefish that Mrs. Olafson had wrapped in butcher paper and given him this morning.

Joe waded out to knee depth, bent over, cupped his hands and splashed Lake Michigan on his face and over his head. Cool streams of water washed away the hot droplets of sweat and the powdery layer of dust left by plodding horse hooves and the spinning wheels of wagons. Joe was even covered with the dust kicked up by a horseless carriage — the first he had ever seen — that had passed him on his journey.

Still standing in the lake, refreshment pouring down his back, Joe checked the horizon again. Looking to the northeast, Joe's sharp eyes picked out a tall plume of smoke and steam among the ore barges and fishing boats plying the waters near the city.

Joe kept an eye on the white dot at the base of the distant smokestack cloud as he returned to his rucksack. He dug out the smoked fish and some bread, had a quick lunch, and put his socks and boots on as the ship steamed closer. He could make out the starboard paddle wheel now, churning the blue water into white spray. The golden eagle emblem on the side of the wheelhouse clinched it. As Joe lifted his rucksack and hiked back down to the city pier he was certain that the paddle frigate coming into the harbor was the ship he was waiting for — the U.S.S. *Michigan*.

———

The journey that Joe was about to make was the start of a life that would lead him towards becoming the father and grandfather that I am coming to know. It was a journey quite different from the one mapped out by the lives of his father and family. What I know of Joe's first fifteen years of life I know from his own hand, written in his late teens. A high school English teacher assigned Joe the task of writing his autobiography, and it has survived from one generation to the next.

AUTO-BIOGRAPHY
OF J.L. BECKER

My father was a German, and came from a province near the Oder River when but a child, with the rest of his father's family. There were seven children, of which he was the youngest.

My grandfather had a small plot of land adjoining the estate of Von Bismarck. My Uncle William, older than my father and now deceased, used to tend the sheep and would look over the wall and watch Bismarck and his friends riding to the hounds for hunting. Grandfather Carl decided he was not raising his sons to fight Bismarck's wars, and so, in 1856, he took his family to Hamburg and got passage on a sailing ship for the U.S.A. Arriving in America, my grandfather and his family came west and settled near what was then the village of Watertown, Wisc.

My mother's family was also German, but they were from a province near Berlin and spoke an entirely different dialect than my father's family.

My father at an early age chose the trade of blacksmith and in the year of 1884, he met and married my mother who was then Elizabeth Burchhardt, and lived near Ashippun, about 15 miles N.E. of Watertown.

Buying a home in London, Wisc., Dane Co., he set up a business as a smith, running his own shop and became very successful at what he had chosen for his life's work.

Upon the 10th day of February 1886, I made my appearance in this great and glorious world. For one short year my baby eyes saw my mother, then she died of that painful disease known as spinal-meningitis. At her funeral, I was taken away, my Aunt Mrs. B. Hartwell of Oconomowoc having persuaded my father to let her take care of me. In her home, I lived happily as a child usually does when it's surroundings are agreeable.

One of my earliest memories comes from an incident that occurred when I was three. I remember it quite plainly. I was sitting at a sand pile at play and near me feeding, was my aunt's large black dog Prince. In wagging his tail back and forth, he happened to strike me in the face. Insulted, I proceeded to punish him, which I did by giving his tail a very vicious tug. The dog turned on me with a snarl and bit a hole through my right cheek. I yelled with pain and my kind aunt, running from the house and seeing what had happened picked me up, took me in the house and dressed my very painful wound. The dog died an ignominious death at the hands of the hired man, later that day.

When I was five years old, my father married again and I was taken to live with him and my step-mother in Deerfield, whence my father had removed to. I was certainly dissatisfied with this change for I had grown to love my home with my Aunt Louise and continually longed for it.

At seven years of age, I entered school and having a rather mischievous nature, I suffered chastisement upon several occasions from my teacher who I will always remember as being a most estimable young woman.

The population of this little town was mostly Norwegians and my playmates were not over scrupulous about carrying away my playthings. Near our house was a long hill, which when covered with snow made one of the longest and best sliding places I ever knew. The boys used skies and toboggans and were experts in descending the hill and doing long jumps over slight elevations, while flying along at lightening speed. I used to envy those boys exceedingly, but now, excuse me, I don't mind having kept my neck in one piece.

My father decided to change his place of business again and moved to Ft. Atkinson. We had moved into our new home and I was out in the garden one afternoon watching my father break the soil preparatory to planting. A neighbor boy came along and sat down on the fence nearby and watched also, I picked up a piece of dirt and threw it at his bare toes, he returned the compliment good naturedly and before we parted we were sworn friends. Those next few years were a period of joy for me, for I went swimming in the old Rock River every day, tramped in the woods, played circus, imagined myself to be a wild westerner and did wonderful feats of strength and endurance.

Carlton, for this was my chum's name, and I managed to find apple orchards and melon patches within a radius of a few miles of home and we did do ourselves justice, too. Whenever a circus came to town, we were the first boys to get under the sidewalls of the big top and find a good seat to enjoy the performance.

Between the summers, I was a schoolboy again, and it was irksome work, for I wanted to be fishing. I could see the green fields and the shady knolls in the woods. My listless manner in school brought many reprimands.

When I was 13, tragedy struck our home again. My step-mother took sick of typhoid fever and pneumonia. She became ill on Oct. 1, 1899 and died a week later. Shortly thereafter, my father moved again, this time to Oconomowoc to take over the blacksmith shop of his deceased brother — Mr. Bertram Hartwell. My dear Aunt Louise had also died, and since she and Uncle Burt were without children, they left the business to my father.

As for me and my stepbrothers and stepsisters, we were left in Fort Atkinson with my mother's brother's family. It was only sup-posed to be a temporary arrangement until my father could build the Oconomowoc business back up and sell it, returning to Ft. Atkinson. Our stay with Uncle Horst and Aunt Annika, however, lasted for two years.

Joe didn't tell his teacher and classmates much about those two years, but the dark hole in this part of his autobiography would later be filled in with probate court documents and let-ters to and from attorneys. It was much more than wanderlust that drove Joe to the Milwaukee Municipal Pier.

Joe wanted to the be the first one to greet the crew of the U.S.S. *Michigan*, but a small crowd had already gathered on the pier as the *Michigan* lowered her sails and maneuvered into place. Piloting this double sidewheel steamer alongside the pier was no easy task. She could use both sail and steam out on the lake, but steam power worked best in port. Joe and the crowd stood quietly watching as the *Michigan's* portside paddlewheel turned a few times to angle the bow towards the dock. Joe could hear officers barking out orders that were repeated up and down the deck.

The *Michigan* was rigged as a barkentine — three masts with three square sails per mast. Her entire hull was painted bright white. The ship had approached the city with her three foremast sails and two graceful jib sheets unfurled, but it was the ship's hissing, chugging steam engines that did most of the work. Just to the rear of amidships were the round wheelhouses that enclosed the port and starboard paddlewheels. The gold-painted leaf clusters and curling fiddlehead at the bow of the ship were the finest, most majestic things Joe had ever seen in his short life. The emblem on the wheelhouse depicted an eagle perched on a shield of red, white, and blue stars and stripes. The eagle, poised to take flight and strike, filled Joe' belly with butterflies.

Carl, the dirt-flinging chum, had given Joe a copy of "Our Naval Apprentice" the autumn before Joe's journey. It was sort of a "Boy's Life" for young naval apprentices. Joe had waited all winter to reach the age of 15, so that he could enlist and go to sea. And now, his dream of escape was right before him. He could feel the rumble of the old gun ship's engines as sailors casually jumped on the pier to secure heavy ropes to the pier's massive iron cleats. He smelled the oily coal smoke still puffing out of the ship's single stack, located just behind the small wheelhouse. Joe saw the crew work with clock-like precision to bring the 164-foot-long, iron-hulled frigate up to the pier. Joe and Carl had leafed through back issues of "Our Naval Apprentice" so many times that they knew the measurements and history of nearly every Navy ship in the fleet as well as some kids know baseball player stats. In less than five minutes of approaching the pier, the gangplank was lowered, and officers in shining white uniforms stepped ashore to shake hands with men in civilian clothes.

Joe moved in closer to the knot of uniformed men in time to hear one of the officers introduce the commander of the *Michigan* to David Rose, the mayor of Milwaukee. Commander Bill Winter stood a good three inches above anyone else on the pier. His short-cropped, prematurely white-gray hair was just visible below his tight-fitting white cap. The Commander held a dark wooden pipe in his left hand as he shook hands with his right. As a puff of pipe smoke blew past the Commander, Joe noticed the color of the smoke matched the man's hair almost exactly. Joe realized he was unconsciously lifting his left hand to his mouth as the Commander lifted his pipe to his lips.

When I first saw the photographs of the *Michigan* and its crew, I thought Commander Winter *was* Joe. It wasn't until I sorted out the photographs by year that I realized the man with the pipe wasn't my grandfather. When compared side by side, the two men in their '40s look like brothers. But as Joe first stood near his future doppelganger, he wouldn't have recognized him as such. At fifteen, Joe was still about six inches away from his eventual 6' 2" stature, and his rugged good looks were buried beneath teenage gawkiness.

While Joe only mentioned Commander Winter in one of his letters in later life, I can't help but imagine that Joe saw in this man something of what he wanted to become. By Joe's early twenties, he and his pipe were constant companions. When he later took command of his own company, the men nicknamed him "Smokey Joe." But beyond the impressive uniforms, the pipe, and a life of adventure, I think Joe longed for companionship and the kind of respect from others that didn't depend on the circumstances into which he was born. Joe longed to earn the kind of respect he instinctively felt for Commander Winter and some of the other crewmembers he saw. But before Joe could become the man he wanted to be, he had to confront the man he was running from.

––––––

Joe hung around the dock long enough to find out the crew's schedule for the day. There was a small parade down W. Michigan Avenue at 2:00 PM. At 3:30 PM, there was a baseball game between the crewmembers' team and some local boys, calling themselves the Milwaukee Stars. After dinner, the ship was open for public tours and for signing up new recruits. The navy was looking for 5,000 mechanics and young naval apprentices, and Joe was more than happy to become one of them. Joe decided to take the tour before signing the next few years of his life over to Uncle Sam.

––––––

A tattered, yellow newspaper clipping that Joe held onto all his life offers the spiel that Joe must have received as he stepped aboard the U.S.S. *Michigan* for the first time. From the date of the Milwaukee Journal article and the reporter's description of the soft evening breezes, Joe may have even had the same tour guide as the one in the article. Next to the "Home Doctor" column that shows a cure for "La Grippe" and a technique "to prevent smoke from a lamp," the headline reads: "Historic Old Vessel In Milwaukee This Week: Dozens of Young Men Enlist—"

> *The United States gunboat Michigan steamed into port this afternoon and docked at the city pier at 12:35 o'clock. After a formal dress parade, the gangway was soon thrown open to visitors who are ever eager to avail themselves of*

the opportunity of inspecting Uncle Sam's historic old war vessel.

A visit to the old craft, especially when lead by Yeoman Charles Wallace, an able seaman and tour guide, is an experience not to be missed.

She is classed as a fourth rate iron cruiser and she is 163 feet, 9 inches in length, 27 feet broad of beam, with a 9-foot draught of water and a displacement of 685 tons.

The Michigan is the first iron-armored gunboat in the world, and was a great curiosity in her early days.

According to Yeoman Wallace, the Michigan was built in sections at Pittsburgh in 1843, transported overland by canal and wagon, and put together and launched at Erie, Pa., in 1844, amid much pomp and ceremony, as befitted one of the first iron vessels built.

It is stated that people came from far and near to see the "iron pot," as they called it, launched, fully "impressed" with the prevailing idea that the hull of a vessel built wholly of iron must surely sink under her own weight.

"Those critics thought they were right when the Michigan was first launched," Yeoman Wallace said. "As she began to slide down the ways into Lake Erie, she got hung up on the ways and stuck fast. No one could get her moving again down the ramp and the anxious crowd soon went home. When the shipyard workers returned the next morning ready to complete the launch, though, they found the pride of the Navy had launched herself in the middle of the night."

The vessel was originally outfitted for four 32-pound carronades and two 68-pound Paixhans guns, but an agreement with Britain limited the munitions of warships on the Great Lakes to a single 18-pound cannon.

Changes in history and our relations with our Canadian neighbors have lifted tensions and changed the armaments onboard. The Michigan's current battery consists of four 8-pounder Hotchkiss; two 6-pounder Driggs-Schweder; two 1-pounder Hotchkiss, rapid fire guns; and there are two Gatling and one Colt's improved rapid fire guns mounted on carriages. The later are the same class guns used on board battleships and cruisers during the Spanish-American war, and which proved so effective against the attacks of torpedo boats and in picking off the gunners and crews of Spanish vessels.

The Michigan's guns have never been fired in battle and are mostly used to help lakeside port cities celebrate our national holidays. The Michigan's history, however, has not always been so sleepy. She helped quell the Fenian raid when 1,000 men tried to take over Canada near Buffalo in 1866. And earlier, during the war, she acted as guard ship over the confederate prisoners at Johnson's island.

While anchored at Sandusky, Ohio, taking on supplies, the Michigan was the target of a bold plot by the confederates to capture the warship, release prisoners on the island, and terrorize the principal cities of the Great Lakes. Through the bravery of a petty officer left on board as a guard, the plans were thwarted.

For the last forty years, the Michigan's work has been peaceful. Her principal duty, in addition to protecting our lake commerce, is to make her migratory voyages every summer from port to port, enlisting apprentice boys and mechanics between 15 and 35 years of age, for the navy. The pay ranges from $16 to $75 a month. Hundreds of boys and men have been enlisted yearly on the great lakes and sent to the training station at Newport, R.I.

Commander William Winter, who is in charge of the Michigan, has been in the service since his graduation from the naval academy at Annapolis in 1875. As a gentle afternoon breeze drifted over the deck, Yeoman Wallace fielded questions about Commander Winter. Even this enterprising reporter was not allowed to speak directly to the commander who is much too busy to deal with the press.

Commander Winter has cruised through European waters, north and south Atlantic and Pacific oceans, and has touched at ports in nearly every part of the globe.

At the outbreak of the recent Spanish-American War, he was stationed on the Castine, in blockade duty on the coast of Cuba. At the close of the war he was sent to the Philippines aboard the Castine, remaining there until he was ordered to Erie to command this vessel last year.

The rest of the officers and crew of the Michigan were the first naval detachment called from the middle west to the Eastern Seaboard for duty at the outbreak of the Spanish-American war, and they were scattered to the different fighting ships of Admirals Dewey, Sampson and Schley, wherever a good gunner or seaman was needed. They fought through the war with valor and patriotism, and when the war ended, the navy department reassembled them, officers and men, and transferred them back on board the Michigan as a reward for their faithful service.

The current crew consists of 74 jacks, 8 officers and 24 marines. While the guard of marines on board seems unnecessary, naval history proves that it is unsafe for commanding officers of men-of-war to go to sea without them, as they are the only safeguards to quell mutiny abroad and to preserve discipline to the letter. The marines on board the Michigan are a fine set of men, and they look and act as if they would be able to cope with any emergency ashore or afloat.

Life aboard a man-of-war is not a bed of roses. Usually at 4:30 AM in the summer and 5:30 in the winter, the sailor is roused from his pleasant dreams, given twelve minutes to don his blue jacket, lash hammock and stow it in the settings; then comes a cup of coffee, usually followed by a smoke, which consumes one-half hour. The decks are then scrubbed and everything made to look spick and span. Then the "mess gear" order and he prepares to eat. After breakfast another short smoke, and then more cleaning in for inspection, after which follows an hour's drill at the guns.

The afternoon is usually devoted to repairs about the ship, knotting, splicing and sewing, for Jack makes all his own clothes and repairs them. Then come evolutions at sunset, fall in at quarters, followed by fifteen minutes of setting up exercises, after which Jack has two hours for sport. Finally the bugle sounds taps and Jack hies himself to his hammock, only to be disturbed by reveille the following morning.

Joe slipped off to the recruiter's table before the tour was finished. He didn't have to be talked into signing up, so the beefy marine sergeant put Joe right to work filling out the preliminary registration papers. Within a half hour, Joe was stripped to his under shorts and standing before the ship's surgeon for a medical examination. There wasn't much room for privacy onboard and curious tourists stuck their heads into the surgery's portholes while Joe was poked and prodded.

Joe said the five diagonal scars across his back were from slipping down a riverbank and falling into a thorn bush while fishing. The freshly healed burn mark on his shoulder was from accidentally backing into his Uncle's hot poker while helping out in the blacksmith shop. And otherwise, the surgeon told Joe he was in the best shape of all the boys and men he had seen in the past week. Only about one out of ten passed the surgeon's approval, and on most days dozens of nearsighted, flatfooted, and otherwise disabled fellows left the U.S.S. *Michigan* in embarrassment and disappointment.

Returning to the recruiting table, Joe had his first encounter with military red tape — it certainly wouldn't be his last. Lt. Overstreet — a thin, sinewy Marine who looked to be in his fifties — introduced himself as the ship's recruiting officer.

"Young man, the surgeon says you check out fine and your registration form is in order. The recruiting staff is in support of your candidacy to become a naval apprentice." Joe unconsciously straightened his back and stuck out his chest at the Lieutenant's words.

"The sergeant here says your enthusiasm towards the navy and your apparent maturity of character are admirable. However, in reviewing your certificate of consent, the sergeant has discovered a slight problem."

A knot began to form in Joe's throat.

"Your aunt's signature granting you permission to enlist is inadequate under the Bureau of Navigation's regulations governing the granting of consent to minors by absent parents or guardians. Your aunt's letter specifically states that she and your uncle — a Mr. Horst Burchhardt — are your legal guardians. Unless you have some other form of consent, I cannot approve your enlistment without your uncle's signature, as well as your aunt's."

Joe choked back the tears that were welling up from the knot in his throat. He had come too far to turn back now, and he dreaded defeat more than the whipping he would get if he returned to Uncle Horst's farm. He had to think fast.

Without knowing how he would pull it off, Joe faced the old marine. "Sir, I mean, Lieutenant, you mentioned that I could enlist if I obtain some other form of consent. How long will the *Michigan* remain in Milwaukee?"

"The ship is scheduled to remain tied up here for a week. We shove off for Chicago on Monday."

"If I returned before then with the consent certificate signed by my father, would that be adequate?"

"Just as long as you can prove the man whose hand signs the paper is your father and not some drifter you meet on the road, we will happily sign you on," Lt. Overstreet said with a wink. "Other boys who have had trouble with their parent's consent have tried to trick Uncle Sam, but I have to warn you that falsifying a consent certificate would be grounds for an immediate dishonorable discharge."

"I'll be back by the end of the week," Joe said.

The sun, which continued to hang in the sky until well after 9 PM on these long northern summer nights, was beginning to drop behind the dome of the new St. Josaphat Basilica. The evening flow of recruits had ended and since Joe was the last recruit left onboard, Lt. Overstreet told Joe to help himself to a glass of buttermilk and some supper leftovers in the galley before starting off on his new journey.

A handful of sailors in their undress whites and floppy hats lounged around the galley after completing evening chores that kept them on duty during the mess call. Between bites and gulps, an ensign who was maybe five years older than Joe introduced himself and his mates. Joe asked if he would get to see any action when he joined the navy. The ensign turned quiet for a moment and looked at his mates, before answering.

"Well, there's no guarantee that you won't end up mopping floors if you ain't got any brains or shuffling papers if you can read, but just look around this galley, son. That big fella' over there was lucky enough to have pulled a shore detail the night that the Maine was blown up in Havana Harbor. Otherwise, he would have been in his hammock just one bulkhead away from the main explosion. Most of these boys helped send the Spanish fleet to the bottom of Manila Bay a few years ago. And just last summer, that young kid over there was in the Battle of Peking against the Boxers. You hang around the services long enough and you won't be bored."

Before Ensign Burrows and the rest of the sailors finished their plates, a burly seaman briskly entered the galley and walked straight at Joe.

"Are you Josie Becker?" the sailor asked.

"Yes, I'm Joe Becker," Joe said, startled by the reappearance of the name he had so recently shed.

"Commander Winter wants you in his quarters right away. Please come with me, boy."

"What could the commander want with me?"

"I don't know, kid, you better just come along," the sailor said, leading the way with a white billy club.

Joe was led from the galley in the fo'csle across the well-worn wooden deck, past the small pilothouse, and into the officers' wardroom in the aft section of the ship. From there a small wood-paneled hallway led to the stern cabins. Sweat was beading up on Joe's nose as the shore patrolman gently rapped on a teak door. A polished-brass plaque declared this to be the cabin of Commander William A. Winter.

"Come in. Come in," came the voice inside, which Joe recognized from earlier that afternoon.

"Here is the boy you wanted to see, sir," the sailor said as he motioned Joe into the pipe-smoke-filled cabin.

"You must be young Josie," the commander said as he reached out to shake Joe's hand.

"Yes, sir. Joe Becker."

"Please have a seat," Winter said with a scowl as he relit his pipe. "It is not customary for the commander of a man-of-war to deal directly with naval apprentices, let alone young fellows such as yourself who aren't even enlisted yet, but your presence on board this ship presents certain complications that I felt I had better deal with directly."

Joe's nose-sweat began to spread across his entire face.

"As a civilian, you are not yet directly under my authority, but as a naval officer I am responsible for everything that happens on board this vessel," Commander Winter said as he pulled a telegram from a stack of papers on his desk. "I received this cabled message from a Mr. Horst Burchhardt earlier today. I get a great deal of correspondence every week from parents, teachers and sweethearts of potential recruits recommending why the recruits should our shouldn't be enlisted, but I have never received one quite like this."

The much-faded cable now sits on my desk among Joe's earliest papers. Its dangerous urgency still reads through the telegraphic shorthand.

TO: Naval Captain, U.S.S. Michigan, docked at Milwaukee City Pier

FROM: Horst Burchhardt, Ft. Atkinson, Wisc.

Captain –

Josie Becker, 15, left farm to join your navy. STOP. He does not have my permission. STOP. Forbid him from listing up. STOP. Detain him until I can come to get him back. STOP.

Burchhardt

"Perhaps you can explain this," Commander Winter said as he settled behind his desk.

Joe squirmed in his chair and tried to look the commander in the eyes, but he couldn't lift his gaze beyond the cable Winter held in his hand. Uncle Horst had returned early from repairing a sawmill in Madison. He wasn't supposed to be back for a few days yet. The cable meant that Uncle Horst had extracted Joe's plan of escape from poor Aunt Annika.

It didn't take Joe long to realize this was a time for truth. He admitted that he left the farm without his uncle's permission, but he told Commander Winter the reason for his disobedience. Joe showed the commander the scars on his back and the burn mark on his shoulder. Joe told the commander how Horst had tied him to a barn post and thrashed his bare back with the buggy whip when Joe failed to harness the horses fast enough last summer. The two-inch-long burn mark came from a spring day when an inebriated Horst walked into a glowing hot horseshoe that Joe was pulling from the forge. The shoe barely grazed Horst, but Horst's recoil from the hot shoe knocked him right into the water trough. Joe couldn't help but laugh. The water may have cooled Horst's singed shoulder, but Joe's laughter ignited Horst's fury. Horst knocked Joe face-first to the ground, pinned both hands behind his back and branded him for life with the end of a hot poker.

Joe accurately mimicked his German-born uncle's heavy accent as he told the commander the story.

"You see how dat feels? Nicht so funny, ya?" Horst had hollered as Joe's flesh cooked.

Commander Winter had heard enough.

"Son, I would prefer to see you serving your country rather than this uncle of yours, but I must turn this matter over to civilian authorities. I do not have jurisdiction to detain a civilian minor, as your uncle has requested, so here's what I'm going to do. The police station is several blocks from here. And quite frankly, I have a ship to run and do not have the available manpower to look after stray boys. A member of my crew may not be available to contact the police until tomorrow morning. In the meantime, young Master Becker, there is nothing that the crew and I can do to prevent you from leaving the ship right away. You told the Lieutenant that you have a father who could sign the consent form? Correct?"

Joe nodded in the affirmative.

"I recommend you make haste to find your father. If you return with your father's signature, I guarantee that the Navy will have a place for you."

Joe thanked the commander, grabbed his things, and was back on the road as the sun's last rays left the sky.

Chapter 7

I MAY NEVER know for certain what happened to Joe that night. The dozen or so letters and legal papers I hold provide details without context: a dispute over the cost of two harnesses for the team; the $1,000 trust fund from Joe's mother; a scuffle, a blow to the head. A short, biographical account of Joe's life written in 1978 by his half-brother, Art, just barely mentions a conflict between Joe and Uncle Horst. All it says is that "Horst was harder on Joe than on the rest of us younger children. In 1901, Joe ran from the farm to become a naval apprentice."

I've poured over these fragments several times and there is no clear, direct account. The truth lies somewhere behind the preserved words. More than mere imagination is filling the void. The more I study the lives of Joe and his family, the more certain I am of what really happened on the road to Louis Becker's home.

Joe's long shadow — cast by the rising full moon — preceded him down the old Blue Mound Road as he made his way west. To get to his father's house in Oconomowoc, Joe would have to travel about 30 miles along the same road he had taken from Fort Atkinson. Joe knew that Uncle Horst would be thundering toward Milwaukee along this same road the first thing in the morning, so Joe decided to cover the distance during the night. He was anxious to avoid Horst, but figured he could reach the northerly fork to Oconomowoc before Horst would reach the same junction from Ft. Atkinson. Horst would never guess that Joe was on his way to Louis Becker's house. And if they did happen to cross paths, Joe was confident that he could disappear into the woods and fields along the road without Horst noticing.

Fears of prowling bears and ambushing robbers accompanied him along the way. Joe's long walk into the country night, however, was more troubled by the circumstances that drove him from his home. Uncle Horst was Joe's mother's oldest brother. When she died, Joe's mother, Elizabeth Burchhardt Becker, left $1,000 from the sale of her father's farm to her infant son. Elizabeth's will made Horst the legal guardian over Joe's inheritance until he reached the age of 21.

When Joe was left in Horst's care, a dispute erupted between Joe's father, Louis, and Horst over the interest that was being earned by the trust fund. Louis felt the interest belonged to Joe and should be used by Horst to pay for the expenses of raising Joe while Louis was off in Oconomowoc. Horst, who was apparently having money troubles, had other plans for the interest. He argued that, as legal guardian of the trust, he could do whatever he liked with the interest.

Even before Horst started stealing the money outright, he had cooked the books to siphon the money away from Joe's care and into his own farm and blacksmith business. When a raggedy old plow harness finally fell apart with Joe at the reins, for example, Horst charged the $25 new harness to Joe's expense income, claiming Joe ruined perfectly decent tack.

While Louis and Horst fought over the money in probate court, a judge froze the account until the matter was settled. Louis continued to send "upkeep" money to Horst to pay for Joe's expenses, believing he would be repaid by the interest money when the matter was settled in court. Horst, however, lied to Joe saying Louis' lawsuit caused the court to cut off the "upkeep" payments. Joe would have to work harder to earn his keep. By the spring of 1901, according to letters from Louis' attorney written years later, Horst was simply accepting the payments from Louis without letting anyone know the money was coming in. Louis was, apparently, so tied up with his business in Oconomowoc that he was unable to deal with the matter more directly.

How much of this Joe actually knew as he crossed the stone bridge over the Fox River, I can only guess. The dispute over the money wouldn't be settled until Joe turned 21, but he must have had more than enough to wrestle with on his nocturnal journey.

———

As Joe climbed the steep road cutting up the side of the riverbank bluff, the weight of his worrying and walking finally caught up to him. The moon was already falling below the horizon, and it was dark in the Fox River valley. Near the top of the bluff, Joe left the road and headed up into the woods to rest for just an hour or two, he told himself. Climbing to the top of the bank, Joe found a soft bed of pine needles beneath a large white pine to rest his blistered feet. Looking down the bank, Joe could just barely see patches of the road's sandy-lightness through the dark trees. Joe must have felt secure on his high riverbank perch as he dropped into thick sleep.

Joe awoke with the morning sun high in the trees. It must have been past ten o'clock, he realized through a groggy haze. He sat up and leaned against the tree. He looked to his right towards the road and the river to focus his eyesight. He could hear the river rushing by below the high bank. Craning his neck around the white pine, he noticed that the riverbank road reached the summit of the ridge only 20 paces away. Turning to his left, he was startled to realize that the road switchbacked at the top of the bank and lay no more than ten feet from his left arm. The forest's dark shadows had covered the road the night before, but now Joe was sitting in clear view of the sun-dappled dirt road that led home.

His eye followed the road that curved to the west. Then Joe saw something that snapped him into full wakefulness.

No more than a stone's throw away, Joe saw Hansel and Gretel, the two giant black perscheron draft horses from the farm. They were hitched to the hay wagon. There was no one in the wagon, but a shaft of light gleamed off a nearly empty schnapps bottle sitting on the buckboard.

"Uncle Horst," Joe whispered as he rose to his feet to take flight.

Before Joe could grab his knapsack, he felt a hand grasp the back straps of his overalls. Joe tried to run, but Horst had stepped out from behind the pine, turned Joe around, and had him by both hands before Joe could get away.

"Goot to see you, Junge. You were missed back home," Horst said with a crooked grin.

Horst looked no better for his all-night ride. His black felt hat was cockeyed on his head and tilted back so far it was in danger of falling off. His squinty eyes wandered slightly in his head, as if following the alcohol fumes outward and upward with his every breath. His high, rounded eyebrows were stretched upward with the excitement of having caught his prey. His black and gray beard, which normally covered only his chin and the outline of his jaw, was accompanied by salt and pepper stubble all over the lower half of his red face. Horst stood a foot above his nephew. Even when drunk, the strength of his blacksmith hands was unyielding.

"I found the kleine present you left for me back in the barn," Horst said menacingly. "You will pay for that new harness in cash and out of your hide."

Joe struggled with all his energy to be free of Horst's grip, knowing the high price he was about to pay for the last thing he had done at the farm.

Just a few days ago — although it seemed like a lifetime now — Joe had stabbed and slashed the new plow harness with his jackknife. He'd left it half-buried in the manure pile as a parting farewell for Horst to find when he got back to the farm. At the time, Joe had felt triumphant and free. Now, he only felt overpowered and afraid.

While holding Joe with one hand, Horst reached behind the tree and picked up the buggy whip and a course rope.

"Hold still!" Horst barked, as he tried to tie Joe's hands around the tree, while holding on to him.

Joe squirmed and struggled, making it impossible for Horst to tie him up. Horst gave up on the rope and raised the whip to strike Joe. At an arm's length, however, Joe was too close, and the leather end of the whip harmlessly slapped the ground behind Joe. Horst staggered as he tried to hold Joe in striking distance.

"Verdamte!" Horst cursed in frustration. "This will not work. If I cannot whip you, then I will do to you what you did to the harness."

As Horst dropped the whip and reached into his pocket, Joe reached into his overalls for his jackknife. Horst noticed what Joe was doing, and a cruel smile crossed his face.

"Looking for this?" Horst said as he drew Joe's jackknife from his own pocket.

He must have slipped it out of my overalls when I was asleep, Joe realized.

With the jackknife handle in his left hand, Horst drew out the longest blade by grabbing the back edge of it with his teeth. The blade clicked into place. Horst tried to switch the knife into his preferred right hand, while maintaining a grip on Joe, but he could not. Horst awkwardly slashed at Joe's face — with the knife in his left hand — and threw Joe down to the ground with his right with such force that it nearly knocked the wind out of the boy.

Switching the jackknife into his right hand — and pleased with himself for the tricky maneuver — Horst knelt down over Joe to continue his lesson on "discipline and obedience."

Joe touched his cheek with his right hand and felt a trickle of hot blood begin to flow. Then, with his left hand, he felt something hard sticking out of the pine needles and sand next to him. Joe looked straight into Horst's eyes as he pulled a fist-sized rock out from the forest floor.

When Horst leaned close enough to grab Joe again, Joe swung the rock into the side of Horst's head with a round-house blow, knocking the sweat-stained felt hat to the ground.

Horst's head followed the sweeping path of the stone, taking the rest of his body with it. Horst landed hard, face-first to Joe's side, rolling twice before coming to rest near the road.

Joe slowly rose to his feet and walked over to Horst, still clutching the rock. Horst was lying on his right side. His eyes were tightly closed and a small trickle of blood was forming on the right side of his head, but he was still breathing.

Joe kicked the old man in the stomach with all he had left in him. Then he kicked him again, and again.

Joe knelt down beside the crumpled man. How many times had Joe dreamed of a moment like this? How hard had he longed for this bastard to die?

As Joe raised the rock above Horst's head, a pitiful groan rose from Horst's throat. Horst rolled over into the road and vomited.

Joe turned away from the ugly sight and foul stench and staggered back to the pine tree, letting the rock fall from his hand. The raw pain of the last two years spewed out of him as tears, violent sobs, and — after a few seconds of nausea — the contents of his own stomach.

After the worst of the grief and gagging passed, Joe wiped his eyes and mouth on his sleeve, stood up and walked back over to his moaning uncle. He picked up the rock and looked down at the miserable figure.

After a moment's hesitation, Joe heaved the stone down the riverbank with a yell. The stone tore through the leaves and hit the steep bank with a thud. Joe could hear it crashing down the bank as it bounced and rolled through leaves and underbrush. A distant "plop" told Joe the stone made it to the river.

Joe stooped over Horst and pulled his jackknife out of Horst's loosely clenched fist. Then, he looked around and walked over to the wagon. He let the team sniff him, and caressed their dark faces before reaching up into the wagon. Joe grabbed the nearly empty schnapps bottle from the buckboard, walked back to his uncle and put the bottle in Horst's still-cupped hand. Some of the clear liquid sloshed out onto the dirt road.

Next, Joe took a pine branch and swept away his boot tracks in the dirt. He turned his back on his uncle, and headed west again. He kept off the road for a half mile or so, walking through the cool woods, just to be safe.

Chapter 8

FROM WHAT I know of the rest of Joe's life, Joe made it to his father's house. Perhaps Joe's aunt was waiting there for him and told Louis Becker about Horst's drunkenness and violence. Maybe Louis suspected something all along, but only believed it when he saw the marks on Joe's back and shoulder, and a new cut on his cheek. However Louis came to understand his son's plight, the knowledge was enough to make him splint-up his broken spirit, despite the grief that caused him to leave Joe and his other set of children behind. Within a month, Louis sold his Oconomowoc business and returned to Ft. Atkinson, where his children were returned to his care.

Joe's loathing of his uncle is understandable, but I can only start to imagine Joe's mixed feelings about his father. Whether Louis had known it or not, he had left Joe in harm's way for two years. Some sort of reconciliation must have taken place, though. Louis signed the permission letter that got Joe into the navy. From the date mark of a Milwaukee photographer on the back of one old picture of Louis, I'd guess that Louis may even have taken his son back to the U.S.S. *Michigan* himself before the ship sailed for Chicago.

One letter has survived the years. Joe wrote his father about his adventures at sea. To me, the newsy account of Joe's naval apprenticeship reads more like a thank you from Joe to Louis than simply a letter to the folks back home — a thank you for the freedom Louis granted his son.

February 23rd, 1902

Dear Father,

I received your letters this week. I am glad to hear that you and Arthur and the girls are well and I apologize for being remiss in my correspondence with you all. You asked for an account of my daily life as a naval apprentice and more of that "sailor talk," as you called it, so here goes. Despite the first week when we witnessed the flogging of a sailor who struck an officer, the Navy has been fun.

The U.S.S. Hartford has been my home and the home of 300 other naval apprentices since Jan. 20, when we were transferred from the U.S.T.S. Newport. We left the training station at Newport R.I. in the midst of a cold, dreary ice and snowstorm. It was one of the worst gales that hit the Eastern Coast for some years. I won't tell you of my little experiences then, but be satisfied with knowing that I was far from being in love with Old Father Neptune.

After one month without seeing land, we neared Bridgetown, Barbados. Schools of flying fish swam through the air and porpoises played about the ship as we rolled down on the fast approaching island. The old sea-dogs aboard the ship were continuously telling us of the great things to be seen and done ashore in Bridgetown, of the wonderful curious, strange people, customs and modes of dress.

By 3 o'clock we were tossing down the coast of the island in plain view of the green fields of sugar cane and the tall spreading groves of palms.

Closer to port, we saw small fishing sloops passing by on their way to a night's fishing. The wild Barbadians fish at night with lights and the fish they get are flying fish. These people have an unusual means of catching fish and

*perhaps it will be of interest to you. They fasten a light
to the mast and simply sail back and forth through a
school of flying fish. The fish are attracted to the light, get
out of the water, dart towards it, run into the sail, and
consequently fall to the bottom of the boat where they are
gathered up by the industrious and dark-skinned fishermen. It is a fact that these natives will go out to sea and
stay for days without other food or water than a few stalks
of sugar cane to chew on. The fishermen are fat, good
natured, happy, and liars every one of them.*

*About an hour before sunset, all sails were furled, yards
squared and we proceeded at full speed under steam. It
was sunset last week when we steamed in at the entrance
of the roads at full speed. The lookout on the forecastle
reported a buoy on the starboard bow and, of course, the
navigator, Mr. Dombaugh, the commander, gave it a wide
berth and headed in more to port to avoid getting beached
on the bar. There was a cool breeze blowing, and looking
ashore at the waving green palms it seemed as if this was
certainly paradise.*

*Being the first land we had seen for over a month, and
then coming from a cold latitude to one of warmth,
sunshine, green leaves and sweet smelling blossoms and
ripening fruits, was an experience entirely new to me. But
when catching sight of the stars-and-stripes as they floated
over the consulate ashore, it seemed as if after all we were
not the only people from God's country in this far away
and isolated land. The sight caused thoughts of home and
friends to come to me.*

*Our band came up on deck and seated themselves in their
chairs on the quarter deck and played. Mr. Sharpe called
out, "command rudder" and "bring ship to anchor."*

"Aye, aye, sir" was the answer, and then, from Mr.
Sharpe to the boson's mates in the different parts of the
ship — "All hands bring ship to anchor." The wail of their
pipes went up immediately calling all hands to station and
duty. Men took their places at both anchors, ready, sledge
in hand to knock away the triggers which held them in
place.

"Stand by to let go the port anchor, Mr. Hussey," sings
out Mr. Sharpe from the bridge and from that gentleman
comes the answer, "aye, aye, sir."

Mr. Charles Hussey is in charge of my division and a finer
gentlemen I have never met.

Over go the levers of indicator and annunciator to four
bells astern, then three bells, stop. Mr. Hussey counts "one,
two, three" and says "let go."

A mighty swing of the hammers, a rattle of chains, a splash
of water and foam and our ship swings peacefully at
anchor in Bridgetown Roads.

Immediately from all sides of the ship, so it seems, come the
cries of Negro men and women in small boats and dressed
in light summer garments, calling for permission to come
aboard and sell fruits and sweet meats to the men. I hardly
slept that night, I was so excited and wishing for the morn,
for in the morning my watch was to go ashore and the
mail was to be sent out to the ship.

Next morning at two bells, everybody turned out, and
my, you should have seen the way the boys cleaned that
old tub. She was scrubbed from truck to keel, bright work
cleaned and gear laid up ready for inspection at 8 bells.
Then we had breakfast with fresh meat and fruits. Half
starved as we were, we didn't even lay in cargo when we
were supposed to and kept eating.

Then was the mail distributed and I had seven letters, including yours. I read them all over and over until a volley of shots was heard on deck. I ran up to see what was going on, only to see the trained crew extracting the smoking shells and reloading. I looked aloft to see the British flag waving in the breeze. After this manner, we gave the flag of England thirteen guns in salute, and then the flag was hauled down.

From a battery ashore came an answering salute of 8 guns, our commanding officer only rating that many.

The mates then passed the word, "lay aft all the apprentices of the starboard watch and draw your money."

Everything was dropped and, ranging up in single file, we signed the books for $10 a piece, which the clerk handed to us. Oh, how good the new, fresh money felt. My tenner went down in my socks and I hurried to shift into clean clothes.

At ten o'clock, the liberty party was mustered and inspected and, tumbling down into the boats, we were taken in tow by our steam launch and headed for a place called the careenage, which is a channel running up a small inlet for about an eighth of a mile and in which the fishing craft are moored. We came up alongside the dock and went ashore in a hurry. Poor boys, we didn't know which way to turn, we were surrounded by men, women, and children, beggars every one of them. Others had fruits to sell and curios. All wore rags and were dirty, vile-looking creatures. A more degenerated people I know nothing of. I was not ashore one hour before I found out that these people were the least virtuous of any that it has been my experience to fall in with.

*I singled out a bright-looking Negro lad who seemed
a trifle neater and cleaner than his fellows and, giving
him a quarter which I happened to have in my pocket,
told him to show me to some cafe or restaurant. I was
led through a crowded thoroughfare, full of Negro men
and women, donkeys and carts. The buildings on either
side were of sun-dried brick of various colors and usually
one or two stories high. At last we reached a cross street
which was less crowded and in which were trolly tracks,
coming up it from the careenage. The trolly was hauled
by a donkey and...*

The rest of the letter is missing. What was in the rest of
Joe's letter, I can only guess. What he didn't tell his family may
have been more interesting still. Did he find more than a good
cafe at the end of that crowded Bridgetown street? Maybe Joe
was taken to a beautiful, dark island woman for his first close
encounter with the opposite sex. Maybe the "bright-looking
Negro boy" took Joe to a dark alley, where he and his buddies
relieved Joe of his $10 pay. Or did Joe simply have a nice day
of sight-seeing. I would surely like to know. What I do know
is that Joe would fall ill soon after his first voyage to the Caribbean. Navy docs would diagnose his ailment as acute tonsillitis
and send him home on a medical discharge.

Joe moved back in with his father and half-brother and half-
sisters. He went to Ft. Atkinson High School and joined the
football team. After only a couple of years, though, Joe left
home again for Oklahoma, where he worked in the Cherokee
Nation during an oil boom there. Back in full health, however,
Joe was soon drawn back into uniform. Joe is probably one
of a handful of military men in the history of our country to
have served in all three branches of the military — all four if
you include his Army Air Corps recruiting work prior to the

creation of the U.S. Air Force. He even straddled the divide between the National Guard and the Regular Army. He started his career as a naval apprentice and ended it as a full-bird Army colonel. But in 1905, Joe left the Oklahoma oil fields to join the United States Marine Corps. Was it just the taste of adventure that kept Joe from settling down at home, or was there something deeper he was trying to get away from? I have more questions than answers from this period of Joe's life.

Louis would live to the age of ninety-five, his oldest son outliving him by only a decade. Louis is absent from most of the rest of Joe's life, but towards the end there seemed to be a reunion — two white-haired veterans of life staring out at the camera, with arms locked. Joe is in his mid-fifties visiting Louis at the "Old Fellows Home" in Waterton, Wisconsin, when Louis is in his late eighties. And when Joe is retired and in his late fifties — just after World War II — there is old Louis in his nineties visiting Joe here at The Shack. Joe even took his old man for a boat ride in the harbor with some unidentified geezer friends. With Joe apparently perched on the covered wooden bow of a 1930s-vintage motorboat to get all three men in the picture, Louis' eyes look back at the camera from underneath a crisp-brimmed fedora and from over the top of his droopy, gray mustache. The three men — all wearing formal hats, dark coats and ties, and waistcoats — seem more prepared for business than boating. Louis is caught in a jaunty-looking pose, with one hand on the wheel and another on the gunwale. On closer inspection, though, he is probably nervously bracing himself against the rocking caused by his son's camera angling. Behind Louis' grim visage and Joe's Army posture, however, I detect a warming of old hearts and a softening of hard feelings in these reunion photographs. Perhaps some sons and fathers need lifetimes apart to work out the complications of the relatively few years they spend living together.

~ PART 3 ~
ERIE, PENNSYLVANIA

———

Chapter 9

IT'S BEEN A busy week, and I haven't had much time for Joe, Anna, and Vicky, lately. A few of the regular reporters for *The Northern Michigan Gazette* are off on vacation or out sick, so there has been a high demand for stringer copy. I've been doing five or six stories a month for the *Gazette* since January and a weekly roundup of local news for the four northern-most counties of Michigan's Lower Peninsula.

The *Gazette* just started a Sunday paper, which aims to cover more of the region than just the Traverse City area, so I have as much work from them as I can handle right now. Today promises to be a long one, but on top of the seventy-five bucks I'll earn for my efforts, I'm getting a *Gazette*-paid plane ride to Beaver Island.

The conventional wisdom here Up North is that "a view of the bay is worth half the pay." Today's sights should provide a major scenery-stock dividend.

My day started around 6:30 this morning. I got up to "read my lesson" (that's Christian Science lingo for studying the weekly citations from *The Bible* and our textbook), I showered, got dressed, made a couple of phone calls, ate a quick breakfast at Mary Ellen's Place in Blue Harbor, and drove down to Charlevoix in time to catch the 9 AM flight.

Today's story takes me thirty-two miles out over open water to the largest island in Lake Michigan. I've got a great window seat just behind the wing of a Britten-Norman Islander as it races up the runway for takeoff. It's just me, the pilot, and a mother and daughter who are returning home from a few days of downstate shopping. We circle over Round Lake, where marina workers are busy pulling yachts out of storage and launching them for the summer people. As the pilot banks the plane into his north-northwest route, the morning sunlight shoots down the length of Lake Charlevoix and past the little coast guard station at the inlet. The light fills Round Lake and bounces off the Pine River channel that leads into Lake Michigan. Since the flight is just a 15-minute hop, the pilot takes the plane up only a few thousand feet. From that vantage, every white-capped wave crest, every seagull, every sailboat and fishing boat is distinct. Even the Medusa cement plant shines with epic clarity in the morning light. The three-story-high mining excavator that prowls the bottom of the plant's quarry is still in shadow, but its running lights neatly pinpoint its outline. A cement freighter is tied to the plant's silo-lined pier waiting to fill its hold with acres of dry ready mix. With all of the ice and snow gone and only a few traces of green from lawns and patches of wild leeks in the woods, every square inch of land is open for inspection.

As the plane crosses Lake Michigan to the island, it passes over the Coast Guard buoy tender Sundew and the Beaver Islander ferry, which leave half-mile-long Vs in their wake. Above the dark indigo lake, the blue sky stretches over deep water, forested hills, and sandy beaches with a crispness that I have only seen in this part of the world.

I'm not going to Beaver Island for the scenery, though. I've come to look at junkyards. Islanders have been locked in a battle with the mainland county road commission ever since a road crew came out to repave the island's main drag. Instead of rebuilding the road in one season, the crew ripped up the old pavement and turned King's Highway into a gravel road. Islanders began to suspect that the road crew wasn't ever going to come back to finish the job. There were rumors that the road commission planned to turn the main drag into a gravel road all along. The islanders sued, and the case has been stuck in court for about a year.

Today's junk-car story is a spin-off of the King's Highway story that I wrote back in February — "Bad roads make for bad blood on Beaver Island." Even before the pavement got ground up, the island's 25 miles of dirt and gravel roads had been murder on islanders' cars. Huge pot holes, washboards, mud, and dust have reduce even the toughest of vehicles to junk in about half the time it takes to wear down a vehicle on mainland roads. As a result, few islanders are willing to bring new vehicles to the island. Most folks keep a good car at the airport in Charlevoix and drive a beater around the island. This practice, combined with a stubborn unwillingness to pay the high cost of shipping broken-down vehicles to the mainland, has turned parts of this otherwise-pristine island into a junkyard. The St. James Township supervisor estimates that junkers outnumber year-round residents by about 5 to 1.

On my last trip to Beaver Island, I learned that an automobile recycling program run by Detroit's Big Three is planning to bring a car crusher to the island this summer. The cars will be drained of fluids, crushed, and shipped off the island on barges. The recyclers think that cleaning up the island will be a great way to show that junk cars are really resources waiting to be reused.

I plan to join the township supervisor this morning as she gives these Big Three recyclers a tour of the island's junkyards. Admittedly, this is not the most riveting story I've covered, but as far as I know, no other newspaper, radio, or TV reporters are on to the story, so it's an exclusive. In Northern Michigan, this story will probably make tomorrow's front page.

When I step out of the plane onto the island at 9:20 AM, I've only got three hours to bum a ride to the junkyard, interview the natives and local officials, take the pictures, and catch the 12:30 plane back to the mainland.

At the junkyard, the turns of phrase and word images that will make up my story start to form themselves: "Big Three to crush island's dirty little secret;" "backwoods junk piles;" "recyclers give new life to island's auto graveyards." Not exactly Pulitzer material, but it's a living.

For the photo, I even manage to talk the corporate-engineer recyclers into standing on top of a teetering pile of junk cars with the township supervisor in the foreground.

The only hitch comes when I get back to the airport with only five minutes to spare. The township supervisor gave me a ride back to the grass-strip airport and told me not to worry about getting there early. Time and travel are fluid things on Beaver Island, I'm coming to learn. Maybe it's because there is so much water around, but the rules of travel and time that apply to the mainland, don't seem to work here. Catching a plane is more like catching a cab. I'm told that even the fer-ryboat ride can last a half hour longer or shorter depending on the vagaries of waves, wind, weather, and cargo.

For anyone used to the strict rules and regulations of flying larger commercial airlines, the casual nature of island hopping can be surprising.

In front of the little log cabin that serves as the airport termi-nal, a half dozen people unload fresh produce from the plane that just came in. I find the woman who runs the waiting-room cabin, and let her know I'm there. She already knows who I am and is expecting me. The plane will begin boarding in a few minutes, so I decide to make a much-needed pit stop.

I couldn't have been in the bathroom for more than a minute or two, but when I come out, the woman is gone, the lights are turned off, and my plane is revving its engines. I grab my camera bag and run the short distance to the plane. Keeping clear of the spinning turbo prop, I wave and holler for the pilot to let me on board. He's parked only about 20 feet from me, but he can't hear me over the roar of the engines and is too intent on his instruments to see me standing near his wingtip.

Just when I think he is bound to see me, the engines accelerate and the plane starts to creep forward. Instinctively, I run down the side of the runway, being careful to stay clear of the wing and spinning prop. Finally, the plane brakes to a stop. To my surprise, the pilot is neither rattled nor angry with me for running down his runway. He shuts the engines down, hops out of the cockpit and opens the passenger door for me.

"Sorry, I didn't see you," he says.

"I told the lady at the counter I was here, but I had to take a leak," I explain. "When I got out, the whole place was shut down."

"No problem. Lydia always takes her lunch in the house at 12:30 sharp. She must have thought I saw you when you came in. No harm done."

The entire maneuver takes less than a minute and we are in the air before I catch my breath. As I settle back into my seat behind the only other passenger (an obese middle-age man who takes up two seats), I begin to hear a banging coming from outside the plane. The man in the two seats also notices the noise, as it is coming from just outside the door beside him. He turns and gives me a nervous smile. As he turns back around, his hand catches on a loose black seat-belt strap. As he pulls on the strap to see where the buckle end is hiding, we simultaneously realize that the seat belt is caught in the door.

The loud banging is the sound of the heavy metal buckle bashing against the fuselage as we pick up speed.

The large man turns to me again and shakes his head, then leans forward to tap the pilot — who is wearing headphones — on the shoulder.

"Hey, Bob. I think we got another problem here. The seat belt's caught in the door," the passenger informs the pilot.

Bob the pilot looks over his shoulder and assesses the situation.

"Hang on, guys. We've got to turn around," Bob says.

Bob loops the island hopper around in a tight turn, lands with a gentle plop in the middle of the runway, cuts the engines for the second time on this flight, climbs out of the cockpit, opens the door, shoves the seat belt back in the plane, shuts the passenger door, climbs back into the cockpit, and takes off using no more than 50 yards of runway. The whole maneuver takes less than five minutes. With a strong tailwind, we even make it back to Charlevoix two minutes ahead of schedule.

After my eventful flight, it's a 50-minute drive down to the *Gazette*'s newsroom in Traverse City. I usually file my stories from home via modem or — on rare occasions — dictate them over the phone from the scene of a story. This driving to Traverse City and back only occurs when they want the story for the next day's paper and I've got pictures to go with it. There is no courier service that can get the roll of film down to T.C. I don't mind the drive, but it does add about four hours of drive time to my day and 180 miles to my odometer. The *Gazette* pays a whopping 21 cents a mile to reporters and freelancers, alike. At about fifteen bucks in gas per trip, I figure I only have to make about a thousand trips to pay for a new truck after this one wears out.

Past the shoreline strip of motels, pizza joints, and putt-putt golf establishments, downtown Traverse City comes into view. I grab some Mickey D's on the way in to Front Street. Once in the newsroom, I have a brief huddle with the city editor and then plunk myself down at some absent reporter's desk. I get some more interviews by phone; write an 800-word story before my 5 PM deadline; type up some cutlines for the pics that were developed that afternoon, answer the copy editor's questions about the story, pow wow with the Sunday editor about the next few assignments; and spend an hour and eight bucks on dinner at the Union Street Pub with some of the full-time reporters.

It's about 7:30 by the time I start the two-hour drive home, but it's all in a day's work for this young freelancer.

The drive back from Traverse City offers more "views of the bay" — or more concisely, views of the *bays* (Grand Traverse and Little Traverse). With the days getting much longer now, I enjoy fading sunlight for more than half the trip back to Blue Harbor. U.S. 31 takes me along the bottom of the West Bay of Grand Traverse and up the east shore of East Bay until Old Mission Peninsula comes to an end and the two arms become one wide mouth. Almost-blossoming cherry trees, stump-filled Elk Lake, dairy farms, cedar swamps, and hardwood forests just starting to show hesitant buds line the highway. North of the big John Deere dealership in Atwood, I'm treated to sunset over Cat Head Point and the Fox Islands. I have to wait for the drawbridge at Charlevoix, where the streets are filled with a premature wave of summer people. As I make my way through the streets of Petoskey, the lights of Blue Harbor twinkle across Little Traverse Bay. From the bluffs of Blue Harbor (20 minutes later), I marvel at the lights of Petoskey glistening right back at me.

Chapter 10

IT'S ABOUT 9:30 PM by the time my headlights shine on the wooden plank spanning the excavation in back of The Shack. Inside, there are three messages on my answering machine. I used some of the money from the two *Home Forum* articles that I had published in the *Monitor* to buy the answering machine. This marvel of modern technology even lets me get my messages from remote locations by dialing a four-digit code, which I can never seem to remember when I need it. I hit the "play" button to put the franticly blinking light to rest.

Beep.

"Hey guy, The 6 o'clock news didn't even have a clue about the Big Three guys being on the island. Your story's running on page one tomorrow. Great job. Look, I know you put in a long day, but our cop reporter learned that there may be a hearing on that Mathias murder case over in Gaylord tomorrow afternoon around 3:00 PM. That's the one I was telling you about that's dragged on for three years. Anyway, we might need you over there tomorrow. I'll be in the newsroom by 8:00 AM. Give me a call first thing in the morning. Bye."

That's Sean Cooper — the Sunday editor for *The Northern Michigan Gazette*. I guess he heard about the hearing after I left the newsroom. I'll probably only make about $50 if the Mathias story pans out tomorrow, but at least I'm keeping my foot in the door. Cooper says he really wants to open up a bureau in my neck of the woods and — although he can't make any promises — I might be just the right man for the job.

There is better money to be had writing for regional and national magazines. I've sold two stories to *Snow Country Magazine*, and a third one is in the works. They pay about $800 a pop, but there is so much time between when I write a story and when I get paid, that I can't afford to only go after the big money.

One of my old *Monitor* bosses, who successfully freelanced for about twenty years, told me that he would have fifty articles in the works at any given time, just to make $30,000 a year or so.

Prolificacy both intrigues and frightens me. It took six months from conception to publication for the first article I had published in the *Monitor*. Of course, the *Monitor* articles were done on my own time, on top of my assistant editor duties. The articles have come a lot easier since that first one, but I am still a ways off from fifty at a time.

Next message.

Beep.

"Hi Nick, this is Lu Ann Wilson. I'm sorry it's taken me so long to get back to you, but seeing to your Aunt's estate has got me runnin' circles. I got your letter, and I don't know how much help I can be, but give me a call. I'll be home all day."

Next message.

Beep.

"Hello Nicholas. Cy Cushman here. I just wanted to remind you about the Court of Appeals hearing next week. Why don't you meet me at my office around 8:30 and we will go over to the courthouse together. Don't forget — that's May 8th at 8:30. I'll see you then."

At this late hour, there's not much I can do about Cooper and Cushman, but I think it's not too late to call Lu Ann in Arizona.

"Hello."

"Hi Lu Ann, this is Nick Becker."

"Oh, Nick, I'm so glad you called, I've been thinking about your letter all day."

"You have? I hope my little favor wasn't too much trouble," I tell her.

I'd been looking ahead in the Becker family chronicles, and asked Lu Ann if she had any insight into a minor mystery. My reading has only gotten Joe up to 1905 or so, but I've been wondering about Aunt Vicky's life from 1910 to 1922. While sorting everything into the big metal filing cabinet, I noticed that Aunt Vicky was living with her grandmother, Dianna Johnson, for most of the first dozen years of her life. Anna and Joe lived in a house in Ann Arbor, Michigan and Cambridge, Ohio during those years. Joe worked as a traveling salesman for seven years after the Marine Corps and was seldom at home. But there is nothing to explain why Anna didn't raise Vicky herself.

"No trouble," Lu Ann reassures me. "Listen, I asked around a bit, but nobody here remembers why Vicky was raised by her grandmother. She often spoke of Blue Harbor and her dear grandmother, but it was news to me and Vicky's other friends that her grandma raised her. The only thing I can guess is that her parents just needed as much help as they could get. Times were so much harder back then. I'm sorry I can't be of more help."

I thank Lu Ann for her efforts and give her an update on the township park hearing. Lu Ann is the executrix of Aunt Vicky's estate, and I'm trying to keep her informed about the property because nobody in Arizona — not even the Humane Society — gets their share of Aunt Vicky's money until the title is cleared on the land in Michigan.

"I don't think your aunt knew what she was getting me into when she asked me to manage her estate," Lu Ann sighs over the phone. "People are getting real antsy about the money. Just last week, I was taken to task by that lady probate judge for sending Vicky's antiques and those boxes of papers to you. You wouldn't believe how petty some people can be, Nick. I'm only telling you this in case some of the lawyers representing the charities call you about what you got from Vicky. Those lawyers tried to keep you from getting even what little you got from Vicky. They said that the hand-written list Vicky made of the things she wanted to go to specific people was invalid. I told them I sat in her living room and made the list myself while she told me what should go to who. They said it was invalid because she didn't sign it. The charities get the remainder of the estate and they are scrapping to have as much remainder as possible. They even said that old photographs, letters, and documents might be of some value to museums and collectors and such. It didn't sound very humane to me. Can you believe that?"

It's about time somebody besides me or Sally started to get a little bit ticked off at the way everyone seems to be trying to keep us from our own family's possessions. I've liked Lu Ann ever since I first heard her smoker-husky, yet grandmotherly voice on the telephone last January. Getting along with Aunt Vicky's best friend seems so natural and easy, though, that it makes me wonder why it was so hard to get along with Aunt Vicky. Lu Ann is starting to get up a good head of steam, and I'm not about to interrupt.

"Well, at least the signed part of the will did say that personal effects were to go to people she had on the hand-written list. I told that judge that I only dispersed Vicky's personal effects. So, if anyone calls telling you they represent the Humane

Society of Tucson or the Children's Hospital of Arizona, tell them you only got Vicky's "personal effects."

"I'll swear that two plus two is five if it will keep you out of trouble," I tell her. "I can see why Vicky thought you were such a good friend."

"Some friend," Lu Ann deprecates. "She's only been gone five months, and I find myself mad at her for leaving me with such a mess, even as much as I miss her."

Lu Ann's voice wavers across the miles of phone line between Tucson and Blue Harbor.

"Nick, it's just a real shame how things worked out with your family and Vicky. I told her she was wrong not to leave at least some of the property to you and Sally. You two are her only living relations. She could be stubborn as an old mule. But she was my dearest friend — she was so smart and funny. She and your Uncle Rollie used to have us over for barbeque every Thursday night. They would do their George & Gracie routine in front of the outdoor grill they made. I only wish you could have known the Vicky Rolland that I knew."

Chapter 11

IT WAS WARM enough to sleep with the windows open last night, and I awake to a clear Saturday morning that is all mine. The old wire-mesh screens in The Shack's windows did a pretty good job of keeping the blackflies out. One of them must have gotten through somewhere else, though, because I awoke with a crusty pinhead of blood on my forehead where one of them took a bite out of me in my sleep.

There's probably a story with my byline in this morning's paper about that Gaylord murder case I covered yesterday, but not even the *Gazette* delivers out this far from town. Besides, I'm feeling a bit more caught up in ancient Becker history than current events right this moment. I get in a brisk morning walk before the bugs are fully awake. Blackfly season usually only lasts for a few weeks, I'm told. I make it through the woods relatively unmolested and their is plenty of yard work to do outside, but I think I'll stay inside, all the same. I've got plans to spend most of the weekend at my desk with a young Marine Corps private and his bride-to-be.

Pvt. Joe Becker was getting used to surprises. He had been surprised that the Marine Corps trained at the Philadelphia Navy Yard, but he had grown accustom to the surprise inspections, midnight hikes, and mock ambushes his instructors had thrown at him. He also wasn't surprised that his first travel allowance didn't cover the cost of a sleeping berth. Joe's long legs and neck were stiff from trying to catch some winks in the passenger car during the train ride from Broad Street Station to Erie, Pennsylvania. He was looking forward to walking around town and getting some fresh air, even though the sky was cold and gray, and the leaves of the trees were lying on the ground under a blanket of late-November snow.

As the train slowed on its way into Erie, Joe straightened his uniform, which was rumpled from the nine-hour journey. He pinched the cuffs of his light-blue trousers and ran his clenched fingers along the length of his legs to sharpen the creases. Then he carefully buttoned the seven gold buttons of his navy-blue, scarlet-trimmed dress tunic. He had to crane his neck and turn his head to fasten that last high button at the throat. He checked his reflection in the window as he set the modest marine cap on his head. He didn't much care for the dress cap. The bill was always threatening to slip down and cover his eyes. The caps weren't all that different than the ones worn by members of the Salvation Army, he thought.

An attractive young woman, who got on the train in Pittsburgh with her hands tucked into a white ermine muff, even mistook him for a train-station porter when he went for a newspaper on the platform. Joe wasn't too offended, though. He rather enjoyed the opportunity to talk with a beautiful woman his age. She may have considered herself above Joe's station in life, but Joe just thought she was pretty. He even went along with her demand to carry her bags up to the first-class baggage car. Joe liked it when the young woman's chaperone set the girl straight on the difference between a marine and a porter, and the girl was obliged to apologize.

"Lizzy, dear, this young man is one of the brave heroes who liberated the oppressed people of Cuba and the Philippines when you were a child, not a common baggage handler," the older woman told her traveling companion. Joe tried to explain that he, too, was just a youngster during the war with Spain, but the woman would have nothing of it. "You are part of the same great cause," she said.

"Oh, I beg your pardon, sir," the young woman said, before climbing aboard the train. "Please forgive me."

"No harm done," Joe replied, refusing the tip she tried to give him. "It's always an honor to help a lady."

The exchange with the two women had amused Joe, but he still didn't like the cap of a seagoing marine. Joe preferred the Montana-peaked campaign hats and khakis that were part of the field-service dress uniform. The more Joe thought about it, he realized it wasn't just the style of uniform he wanted to change.

Joe's orders reassigning him to some vessel called the U.S.S. *Wolverine* had come as a surprise. Joe had joined the Marine Corps only four months before he was ordered to Erie. Joe had been traveling around the country since he had left the Navy and then graduated from high school back in Wisconsin. He would work for a few weeks or months in one town, earning just enough to get by and put up enough money to get to the next town. He'd had a string of jobs, from meat packer, to hay raker, to busboy, to oil-derrick tender. Before the age of 19, Joe had sailed to the Caribbean, seen the Grand Canyon, and lived with an Indian family on the Cherokee Nation during an oil boom. When he enlisted at the recruiting station in Kansas City, Missouri, on July 5, 1905, he thought the Marine Corps was his best chance for turning a life of travel and adventure into a career. He especially liked the idea that the marines were usually the first ones into the action whenever there was trouble.

The Marines had been the first American troops to land in Cuba at the outset of the war with Spain when Joe was 12. The Marines had helped rescue the besieged Americans from the Boxers in Peking when he was 14. They were still in the Philippines trying to quell the insurgency. They had protected national interests in Honduras last year. And just last week in Cuba, there were rebel uprisings in the Havana and Pinar del Rio provinces against the elected government. Just before Joe left the Philly Navy Yard he had heard talk of U.S. troops having to return to Cuba. What was it that that young Major Butler had said about the Cubans when he addressed the new recruits back in the summer?

"We fought to win the Cubans their independence and now they are fighting amongst themselves because they don't know what to do with independence." That's what Joe remembered the major — the one they called "Old Gimlet Eye" — saying.

Joe's regiment was preparing to enter the fray in the Philippines just before Joe received the detachment order that was now bringing him back to the Great Lakes. He had actually been standing in the quartermaster's line with the other boots to be outfitted with the tropical field-service uniform when he got word of the transfer. It wasn't the first time in Joe's short Marine Corps career that he had been disappointed by the brass' plans for him. When the Sergeant learned that Joe could read and write, somebody upstairs made him a clerk instead of a rifleman. He still went through the same six weeks' indoctrination that his buddies went through and he was issued the same Krag rifle as everyone else, but after training, Joe spent more time behind a desk than he did learning hand-to-hand combat along with the other members of his platoon.

Joe didn't complain to anyone, but filling out paperwork for shavetail recruits in Pennsylvania wasn't quite what he had in mind. He was still young, though, and willing to make the most out of any situation. After a couple years away from home, he might even get a chance to see Pop and his half brother and sisters in Ft. Atkinson. He always liked Lake Michigan and he hadn't seen any of the other Great Lakes before.

As Joe stepped off the train and onto the Erie platform, he thought that even though this place wasn't exotic or dangerous, it was, at least, new to him. Shouldering his bivy sack and winding his way through the old station, Joe had the feeling that something good might come out of this assignment, despite his initial disappointment. He would put his best foot forward and prove himself to his superiors and shipmates alike. There was just no telling what lay ahead.

It was a short walk from the train station to the city wharf. Joe rounded the corner of State Street and got his first look at the Lake Erie port town. The wide street sloped gently down to the water with solid, rectangular townhouses flanking its bustling sidewalks. Most buildings were only three stories high, but the hard brick and stone walls framing the streets made Joe think that the city's residents must be sturdy, straightforward folk. Joe passed a pillared hall on his right that looked like it had been uprooted from Athens, Greece, and plopped in downtown Erie, but it made the city look more respectable than exotic. Further down State Street, Joe could see the tall masts and smokestacks of the docks. And there among the pleasure sloops, ore barges, and timber freighters was the glistening-white hull of an old friend. The three-masted, double sidewheel frigate was none other than the old U.S.S. *Michigan* — the very same ship on which Joe had launched his naval apprenticeship four years ago. Despite the cold wind blowing off the lake, Joe was cheered by the sight of the familiar ship. He picked up his pace as he made his way downhill to the docks.

As Joe pulled his new pipe from his overcoat and tamped the fresh tobacco down, he remembered the kind-hearted Commander Winter who had offered Joe a way out of his troubles in Wisconsin. Joe wondered if Winter was still in command.

As the entire port came into view, Joe also began to wonder about his assignment. The *Michigan* was clearly the only navy ship in sight. Where was this U.S.S. *Wolverine?* Surely the *Michigan's* crew would know the answer.

Crossing the snow-covered park at the foot of the city pier, Joe was stopped in his tracks by a woman's scream. Joe turned towards the cry of distress and ran towards it without hesitation. Not far from the pier, a small crowd of children and a matronly woman in a long, gray wool coat were scrambling around the base of a large elm tree.

"Come down from there, you infernal beast!" the woman shrieked. "I'll have your hide for this."

Joe followed the fixed gazes of the woman and children, who were all straining their necks looking at something high up in the branches of the old tree. Joe heard the bleating of the black, furry creature before he saw it.

"What the devil is that?" Joe said to no one in particular.

"It's a bear!" the children screamed.

As Joe looked again he could make out the tan muzzle and dark round eyes of what appeared to be a black bear clinging to the main trunk of the tree. In its clenched jaw, it held the handle of a basket.

"He's stolen our lunch," the woman pleaded.

Joe dropped his ditty bag and prepared for action, but he was a bit confused by the scene around him. What was a bear doing in the middle of a busy port town? And why weren't these children the least bit scared of a wild animal in their midst? Just then, Joe noticed the long steel chain that hung down from a collar about the bear's neck. The other end of the chain was wrapped around the base of the tree and paddlelocked. One of the boys started to climb up the tree.

"Don't worry, ma'am, I'll get your basket back," the boy said.

"Wait a minute. What's going on here?" Joe asked, as he grabbed the boy by his ankle. "You can't just climb up a tree after a dangerous animal like that."

"He's not dangerous," the boy beamed back. "It's just Rocky. We wrestle with him all the time."

"And who is Rocky?" Joe asked, turning toward the woman.

"Oh, it's all my fault," the woman said. "Rocky's always getting into people's pockets looking for food. I shouldn't have set my basket down for a minute. That rascal has been known to steal candy from a baby. I spent all morning putting that basket together for the D.A.R. luncheon this afternoon."

"So you know this bear?" Joe asked.

"Oh my, yes. Everybody in town knows Rocky by now. He belongs to one of the marines on the government boat," she said.

"Well, now I've seen everything," Joe said, shaking his head and breaking into an easy grin. "If this bear belongs to a marine, then a marine ought to be the one to get your basket back, ma'am. As for you, young fellow, you're a brave lad, but even a pet bear can lose its good humor when someone tries to take food away from it. You had better let me climb up there. "

"Do be careful, sir," the woman said.

The boy shimmied the few feet back to the ground and Joe took off his cap, overcoat and tunic so that they wouldn't get covered in sap or bear drool just before he reported for duty. Joe, who had been considered an expert tree climber back in Ft. Atkinson, lost no time in scaling the elm branches and trunk to the bear's perch. He had seen a bear once while hunting deer back in Wisconsin, but he had never been this close. Rocky watched Joe's every move, but was more intent on figuring out how to hold on to the trunk with his paws and get into the basket at the same time. Joe moved slowly as he approached the bear, speaking gently to sooth the beast.

"Good bear. Nice bear. How are you today, Rocky?"

A low growl rumbled from the throat of the jet-black animal as Joe sat on a branch just below the bear and out of reach. Rocky looked up, wanting to climb higher, but the large branch above him blocked any escape upward.

Closer to the bear, now, Joe could see that it was still just a big cub. Rocky was probably only about 150 pounds. A cool breeze off the lake blew the bear's stench right into Joe's face. It was a mix of wet dog, peanuts, and molasses, with a slight skunky musk. Joe reached for the bottom of the basket and tugged. Rocky unclenched his powerful jaws enough to emit a fearsome, bleating roar. Rocky let go of the tree trunk with one paw just long enough to swat at Joe's retreating hand.

The bear's sharp claws just missed, but Joe got the message loud and clear.

"Okay, bear, I won't try that again." he said calmly. "I know just what you want."

Joe reached into his trousers pocket and pulled out a yellow piece of taffy wrapped in wax paper. The bear's eyes widened at the sound of the crinkly wrapping coming off. The bear even shimmied down the trunk a couple of feet as Joe held out the taffy to give Rocky a good sniff.

The bear was only a couple of feet away now, and Joe knew that he would probably only have one chance to execute his plan.

"Here you go, little fellow," Joe said, easing the taffy towards the bear's mouth.

Rocky went for the taffy, and in the same instant that his jaw opened to gobble the treat, Joe snatched the basket handle out of the startled creature's maw. Rocky hesitated for a moment while he chewed the taffy and swallowed it. That moment of hesitation was just enough for Joe to start making his way back down the tree with the basket. It didn't take Rocky long to realize he had gotten the short end of the stick, however, and before Joe reached the lower branches, he heard the angry bear's chain clanging down the tree after him. Rocky bawled in outrage at the treachery, as he quickly shuffled down towards Joe. Joe bounced down from limb to limb in a near freefall with the bear just above him.

"Look out," Joe hollered, scattering the cluster of children at the base of the tree as he jumped from the last branch ten feet to the ground below him.

Joe somesaulted forward to ease the impact from the fall. He landed on his feet right next to his bag and clothes — had just enough time to snatch up his things — and ran to the outside of the well-worn circle around the tree. Rocky swiped at Joe's legs, shredding his trouser cuff, just before he was yanked up short at the end of his chain.

The children and the woman, who had all retreated to the safety beyond the reach of Rocky's chain, jumped up and down with excitement, clapping and cheering.

"Hooray for the Marine! Hurrah for Rocky!" the children screamed.

"Oh, thank you, dear," the woman said, as Joe turned over the slightly slobbered-on, but intact lunch basket.

"I just hope everything in there is unharmed," Joe said, setting his cap back on his head.

"It's all wrapped tight in butcher paper. I'm sure it's fine," the woman said. "The ladies won't mind a bit when I tell them how their lunch was saved by such a gallant young private. I do hope you will excuse me, but I'm late. I mustn't keep the

Daughters waiting. I'm sure we will be seeing each other again. Thank you so much."

Joe waved goodbye as the woman started off across the park. He roughly touseled the hair of the boy who had said Rocky was harmless and turned towards the ship, only to find a sergeant standing a few feet away and glaring at him, fists on his hips.

"What's going on, here? And what are you doing out of uniform, private? Is monkeying around with a bear any way to report for duty?"

Joe snapped to attention. With his eyes forward, it wasn't hard to get a good look at the muscular man who was now standing only six inches away from Joe's face. The sergeant's cap was pushed back on his finely chiseled head, showing spiky tufts of short, almost-white blond hair. A long, but neatly trimmed handlebar mustache drooped under the sergeant's long nose. The man's face was ruddy from being outside a lot, but he looked to be only a few years older than Joe.

"No, sergeant. I was just on my way to report for duty when I heard that woman…"

"I saw what you were up to, private. In fact most of the crew did, too," the sergeant said, pointing over his shoulder with his thumb to the marines and sailors leaning over the rails of the white ship.

"I'm Sgt. Olafson and you must be the new boot we've been expecting from the Navy Yard," he said. "And that, over there, is my bear you've been frolicking with. Straighten up your kit, you're wanted on board."

Oh wonderful, another damned Norwegian, Joe thought, as he remembered the unfriendly ski jumpers of his youth. This Norwegian is not only my superior, but he owns a ferocious bear and already has it out for me.

"Yes, Sergeant. I'm Private Joseph Becker, and I'm supposed to be reporting for duty aboard the U.S.S. *Wolverine*. I was just coming to ask for directions from the crew of this fine vessel when I stopped to help the woman get her basket back from your bear. I'm familiar with the U.S.S. *Michigan* from years ago, but I was hoping you or your crew could direct me to the *Wolverine*," Joe said, buttoning his tunic back up.

"Well, you're standing right in front of her, Private. The *Wolverine* and the *Michigan* are one and the same. Some big wigs back in Washington stole her true name for some superdrednaught that's under construction. She was re-christened the *Wolverine* just this past summer. Welcome aboard."

The Sergeant's frown turned to a broad Nordic smile, as he shook Joe's hand.

"I'll have you know that you are the only man besides myself who has gotten away with taking food from Rocky since he was a little cub," the Sergeant said. "Rocky loves kids and females, but he usually doesn't like men — especially any man in a uniform. It probably goes back to when my brother found little Rocky in Cascade County, Montana. Some railroad fellows shot Rocky's mother for sport and left the cubs to die. My brother heard about it in town and walked back down the tracks to the den. There were three cubs holed up in a cave. They didn't mind my brother, but when little Rocky saw one of the railroad men in his uniform back in town, Rocky went for him. Rocky did a lot worse to that fellow's trousers than he did to yours — or so my brother told me, when he gave Rocky to me this summer in Menominee. The last man who tried to get between Rocky and his food almost got his hand bit off. Didn't you see the sign?"

Mounted to the side of a small shack that is apparently Rocky's winter quarters is a hand-painted sign that proclaims:

"Rocky the Rocky Mountain Bear. Kids and women O.K. Men beware. No food near the bear unless you want him to eat it."

"I just charged in without looking," Joe said. "I guess I didn't see the sign."

"As any good marine would," the Sergeant said. "Any fellow who can deal with Rocky as well as you just did has earned one of the most important jobs on the *Wolverine*."

"What's that, Sergeant?"

"You get to bring him his morning bowl of coffee. He likes it with lots of milk and sugar. And he gets grumpy if he doesn't get his coffee at 5 o'clock in the morning — sharp. You can also help with his noontime and dinner feedings. He's always sticking his nose in people's pockets looking for peanuts or maple-sugar candies, but I mostly feed him bread and fruit."

"Yes, Sergeant."

"And another thing, Private. You know that woman whose lunch you just rescued? That's Mrs. Morgan, the mayor's wife. By this afternoon, you'll be famous all around town. And by the annual Thanksgiving party next Thursday, you'll know why Erie is called the Mother-in-Law of the Marines. Mrs. Morgan fancies herself a real matchmaker, and she probably already has several potential wives lined up for you."

Joe's white cheeks reddened.

"I was just trying to make myself useful," Joe said, as he mounted the gangplank to the familiar deck of the former U.S.S. *Michigan*.

~ P A R T 4 ~

CHI-NOO-DING, MA-SHI-GAN-ING

———

Chapter 12

UNTIL A MONTH ago, Anna Johnson Becker — my grandmother — was a stranger to me. There are a lot more letters, clippings, documents, and photographs of Joe's early life than there are of Anna's, but I am beginning to piece together parts of her story, as well. There are only a few photographs and clippings from Anna's life before marriage, but there is a letter written many years later that provides rare insight into the heart and mind of her twenty-something self.

While Joe's life has drawn me into the past, it is Anna's life that is grounded to this place I now call home. It is Anna, the daughter of some of the first white settlers in these parts, who gave her husband, her children, her grandchildren, and future generations of Beckers a place in Blue Harbor. It is Anna and her parents, more than Joe, who I have to thank for being here. She is the native daughter who has tied us to this land of blue waves, white ice, summer sand, tall pines, and deep hardwood forests. Joe simply had the good sense to adopt her hometown as his own.

One of the boxes that came from Aunt Vicky's estate contained an heirloom that I did not stumble upon until a couple of weeks ago. It was loosely wrapped in a felt bag at the bottom of the last box I unpacked. It's sitting on the left side of my desk near me as I shuffle through Anna's papers in my improvised living-room office. At first, the initials A.J.M. on the sterling silver brush-and-comb set threw me, but then I learned her full maiden name — Anna Macklin Johnson — and figured out the traditional monogram style where the last-name initial is enlarged and placed in the middle with first- and middle-name initials on each side.

I don't really know what I'm going to do with an antique brush, comb, and mirror. It's not exactly something a young man has much use for. And, frankly, there's something a little bit creepy about the thought of ever giving my dead grandmother's brush set as a gift to my future wife or daughter. There is something just a little too personal about this heirloom to consider putting it into use again.

Yet, it is the intimate nature of these tarnished silver heirlooms that intrigues me. I imagine that Anna kept them on top of a mirrored vanity in her bedroom. Perhaps they were given to her on the occasion of her 1903 high school graduation. I can almost see Anna sitting before her vanity combing her long, light-brown hair on a light, breezy June evening at the start of a summer that would determine the course of the rest of her life.

She was twenty-two years old in 1906 — the year she first met Joe. She was filled with eager expectation for the newly arrived summer, although she had no way of knowing what changes it would bring. As a warmish breeze rustled the white linen curtains of her open bedroom window, Anna drew deeper into thought. Her reflection gazed back at the young woman who would be toastmaster of the Blue Harbor High School Alumni Banquet at the Hotel Topaque later tonight.

Mrs. Lette Shay, the alumni association president, had specifically invited Anna to officiate the banquet because Anna was such "a shining example of the quality of our town's educational system." She had even said as much in the short *Blue Harbor Independent* article, dated June 14, announcing the upcoming event. Anna's cheeks warmed with embarrassment and a touch of pride at the flattering words the paper had used to describe her when announcing her upcoming role in the banquet.

> *Miss Johnson, second daughter of Mr. and Mrs. James Johnson, is one of Blue Harbor's best-known and most popular young ladies, having resided here since birth. A genial and ever-willing helper in social affairs and a musician of excellent ability, Miss Johnson has won by her estimable character the love and respect of a large circle of acquaintances.*

"Oh, it's just a silly little small-town newspaper," Anna said to herself as she brushed a stray wisp of fine, light hair from her face. "I mustn't let such nonsense go to my head."

Anna continued with her grooming, but couldn't help thinking how the eyes of so many of her former schoolmates, their parents, the school board members, the professor, and dozens of other townsfolk would be on her tonight. She was fairly accustomed to being in the spotlight. She played the organ at the Presbyterian Church every Sunday and she frequently gave piano recitals and spoke at the various social functions she helped organize. But still, a butterfly or two stirred in her stomach as she looked at the young woman who would be officiating tonight's festivities. She began to scrutinize the young woman in the mirror with the kind of balance and level-headedness that she considered among her best attributes.

Anna did not think of herself as being beautiful like her classmate Leslie Higginbotham, who had perfect, white teeth and golden hair that was always carefully pinned up under a sun hat or bow. Although Anna was lulling herself into a contemplative trance with the rhythmic sweep of the silver brush down her own long hair, she did not generally approve of the long hours Leslie would spend fussing over hair, clothes, and appearance. Anna once figured to herself that Leslie's poor father probably spent about a month or two a year running the lumber mill just to keep Leslie in the latest dresses. Anna liked fine, simple clothes, and now that she was out of school, she paid for her own wardrobe with the money she earned from playing at church and from giving music lessons.

To her mother, her female friends, and occasionally to her male school chums, Anna was often self-deprecating. On the back of one dark photograph of her posing in front of huge log piles near the Shay railroad, Anna had written: "I look more like a scarecrow in this than anything I can compare myself to."

But privately, Anna thought slightly better of herself. She looked into her own intelligent, sharp brown eyes, traced a finger across her strong chin, admired her clear white complexion, turned her head to note her long slender neck which curved down toward her even whiter bosom, and told herself that she was "a rather handsome woman, really — if it weren't for that crooked nose."

Looking at pictures of Anna from that time, it is difficult to see the imperfection that so troubled her. Earlier that year when Blue Harbor was covered in a mantle of fresh, white snow, she had broken her nose in an accident, and it was never quite the same afterward. Even now, she couldn't help looking at her nose without thinking about the January 3rd accident and that Harvey Higginbotham.

Harvey's father, Horace Higginbotham, was the wealthiest man in town. The Higginbothams had a big house on the bluff with five porches overlooking the town and harbor. From the easternmost front porch, Horace could easily keep an eye on the Higginbotham Lumber Co. operations at the foot of the east hill that led into town. From the western-most porch,

Harvey could keep an eye on Anna's 3rd Street house, which was tucked up against the base of the long, high bluff.

Anna was three years younger than Harvey and — as a schoolmate of Harvey's younger sister, Leslie — she was a frequent visitor to the Higginbotham household. Harvey was studying business back East at Princeton for most of Anna's high school years, but he was home all summer long working for his father, and spent his Christmas breaks in Blue Harbor. Even after he graduated with honors from Princeton and began working on Wall Street, he still managed to spend ample winter and summer holidays back in Blue Harbor.

It was five months and two weeks before Anna met Joe in the summer that Harvey had asked his old friend Anna to accompany him on a winter sleigh ride through the country. Two and half decades after that ride, Anna recounted the story to her mother in a letter she wrote en route to The Philippines.

Friday — May 15, 1931
Aboard the U.S.S. Grant

Dear Mother —

The seas are calm and the hot weather has driven most of the passengers to the shady deck on the other side of the boat. Our cabin is quiet, at last, and I thought I would steal the opportunity to write you again.

Not much has happened on board since I wrote you the other day, but I have been thinking a bit about that surprising run-in with Harvey Higginbotham back in New York. It brought back a lot of memories of those days back home with you and father during the year when I first met Joe. Seeing Harvey, who is now a wealthy Wall Street man, made me realize how different my life could have been.

*A few nights ago, Joe brought up the encounter again and
I told him the full story of how I broke my nose. I still
remember the ordeal right down to the date — January 2,
1906. You were such a strong advocate for Harvey that I
never told you all of what happened that day... .*

The original plan was for Harvey to take Leslie and Anna
out into the country in his father's sleigh, but when Harvey
pulled up to the Johnson residence, he was alone. Leslie had
come down with a case of the sniffles, Harvey said, and had
excused herself. It was not the first time Harvey and Anna had
been alone together, but, much to Anna's surprise and not
much to her disliking, they found themselves on a first date.

Harvey was a young man who lived in two worlds. Anna
couldn't help noticing the juxtaposition of the top- and bot-
tom-halves of Harvey's outfit as he helped her up into the
small wooden sleigh with iron runners. Harvey's top half was
covered by the same thick, wool Mackinaw coat and wool cap
with ear flaps that almost every lumberjack in the county wore
from November through the end of April — newer and neater
than most, but still the same basic winter gear. His bottom half,
however, was equipped with the gray winter riding breeches
and tall leather boots that Harvey had specially ordered from
Germany. Leslie had teased her brother to no end at the extrav-
agant price of the breeches and boots. When Harvey finally
retorted by reminding Leslie of the numerous dresses she
ordered from Paris, Leslie had pouted for days. It just wasn't
the same thing, Leslie had said.

Anna and Harvey traveled in silence through town for the
first few minutes of the sleigh ride. Without Leslie, there was
a peace to the outing that would not have existed if Leslie had
been along.

"I love Leslie like a sister," Anna said. "But it's surprising how much less noise two people make than three."

Harvey laughed.

"Well, she *is* my sister and I don't mind telling you that as much as I enjoy Leslie's wonderful sense of humor, she's never known how to enjoy the quiet," Harvey said.

Beyond the last Indian Town shack on 4th Street, the sleigh glided through the stillness of the dark cedar swamp on the west end of town. A thick blanket of snow from last Thursday's storm still covered the trees and dormant cattail stalks along the winter haul road. The snow muffled all sounds except for the jangle of the horse-harness bells and the gurgle of springs coming out of the side of the bluff and trickling into the partially frozen pools and ditches along the road.

Harvey's tall buckskin quarter horse, Chieftain, pulled the sleigh up Bull Moose Hill west of town. Harvey broke the peaceful quiet.

"The road monkeys have done a good job of keeping the haul road well iced," Harvey said.

"I don't think that any monkeys live in this part of the world, Harvey," Anna said, with a twinkle in her eye.

"You know what I mean, Anna. Father added a second crew this winter to keep the roads sprinkled from here to the Kijikon Lumber Camp up near Good Hart. With the Bull Moose pulling the sledges, we can bring 40,000 board feet of logs into the mill a day. About fifty percent more than we ever could with just horses. It won't be long until the entire operation is mechanized from forest to finished boards."

"By the time you and your father have the whole thing perfected, there won't be a single tree left standing in the entire county," Anna teased.

While the great lumber booms of the 19th Century had already cleared millions of acres of forests from the Atlantic to the Pacific, logging was just reaching its peak in North Michigan after the turn of the century. The headlong rush to the goldfields, forests, and farmlands of the West had bypassed most of Michigan. White settlers, including Anna's Irish-Canadian parents, had only been allowed to buy land from the Indians since the mid 1870s. In the twenty-eight years since James and Dianna Johnson had moved to Little Traverse (as Blue Harbor was then called) from Toronto, the town had changed from Indian village to booming timber and resort town. By the end of the Midwestern logging boom that Anna witnessed, the Michigan timber harvest would equal more than three times the value of all the gold that came out of the California and Alaska gold rushes. And the steam-and-iron technology of Anna's youth had brought about those changes more rapidly than anyone had ever seen before.

The Bull Moose was a steam-powered tractor that muscled raw timber into town in winter on a road of ice that stretched ten miles into the hardwood and hemlock forests northwest of Blue Harbor. The road monkeys were the crews of young boys and old men who drove the sprinkler carts and rollers along the haul road, turning the soft snow into a rock-hard ribbon of ice. The Bull Moose resembled a cross between a locomotive and a snowmobile. A set of thick, cleated tracks drove the Bull Moose forward at about four miles an hour, and a pivoting pair of runners in the front kept the unlikely contraption on course. A fireman fed the boiler from the back of the engine and a driver guided the runners along the icy track from a seat at the front of the boiler. A brakeman kept the whole thing from sliding out of control on the steep downhill sections. The five log sleighs pulled by the engine made for a train that needed no track, except what winter could provide.

It was late Tuesday afternoon, and the Bull Moose had already returned from the lumber camps with a load of passengers back from New Year's visits with brothers, fathers, sons, nephews, uncles, husbands and friends who lived at the camps all winter long.

"There doesn't seem to be too many people out on the road today," Anna said, becoming more conscious of being alone with Harvey.

"It's a little tricky walking or riding on these ice roads," Harvey said. "Chieftain, here, is shod with special spikes that help him keep his footing on the ice. Yesterday, I had him shoed especially for this ride. You have to know what you are doing to drive a sleigh out here."

To Anna's ears, Harvey sounded confident that he knew what he was doing — maybe too confident. Although Harvey only worked in the lumber company head office these days, his father had made sure that all of his three sons knew every aspect of the lumber business. Harvey was only interested in investments now, but he had spent many a school holiday working right alongside the road monkeys, teamsters, lumberjacks, camp cooks, sawyers, axe and saw filers, and chore boys. If he could handle one of the big horse-drawn log sleighs, he could probably handle this light rig.

... The first half-hour or so of the sleigh ride was most agreeable. Harvey could be a dear when he wanted to be. But after a while, I began to get cold and wanted to turn back. Harvey had a "surprise" to show me that he said I would like, and he insisted on going a bit farther. I insisted that if we were to go on any farther that he tell me what this big surprise was all about, so I could judge for myself whether it was worth continuing. It was getting cloudier and the snow was beginning to fall.

Harvey would only say that there was a new lower beach
trail road that went all the way to Cummings Creek,
and if I could just "brace up" for the rest of the journey, it
would all be worth while. I told him it was getting too late
to go all the way to Cummings Creek...

"Anna, it's less than a mile from here to the creek. We will be back in plenty of time," Harvey said. "In fact, if you are concerned about the time, I'll just get us there a little faster."

Harvey slapped the reins on Chieftain's back and hupped him up to a trot and then a canter. Chieftain's ears pricked back as he leaned into his harness at Harvey's urging. The sleigh flew down the ice road.

"What are you doing, Harvey," Anna said, as she grabbed the iron handrail at her left side with one hand and the front lip of the sleigh with the other.

"I know exactly what I'm doing," Harvey said. "Chieftain and I travel this road together every winter."

"Well, I do not, Harvey Higginbotham, and I do not like this breakneck pace you are keeping. Slow down this instant, or I'll jump out and walk home." Anna said, as waves of both irritation and anxiety swept over her.

"Oh, Anna, don't be so dramatic, we will be there in a few minutes," Harvey said, with a tight grin that could barely contain the irritation he now felt at Anna's lack of faith in his sleigh-driving abilities.

Chieftain kept his course, but the light little sleigh began to gently sway across the ice road. The distance between the runners of the sleigh were slightly narrower than the distance between the ruts left by the Bull Moose. At the faster speed, Harvey was unable to keep the sleigh on the flat spot between the Bull Moose ruts. The sleigh began to slide down into one rut, tipping the sleigh slightly sideways on an uncomfortable angle. There, it would ride the rut for a few moments until the next little bump in the rut would cause the sleigh to "jump track," so to speak, sway across the flat spot, and slide down into the other rut with the opposite runner.

... Harvey would not heed my firm requests and kept going. I'm sure that for him skittering across the ice road was all part of the fun, but, as you know, Mother, I do not appreciate traveling quickly on slick roads. I was angry and hurt that he would not slow down. I, at first, did not know what had gotten into him. I can only assume that he had bragged about his abilities so much that he felt he had to show off...

When Anna finally found her voice through her fear, a few minutes later, she said, "Harvey, I mean it, slow down right now. You are frightening me."

At that point, Harvey still could have redeemed himself. He did slow down to a trot, but instead of consoling Anna's fears, he argued with them.

"Anna, we are not in any danger. Why can't you just enjoy the ride, as I am. If you are so concerned about my ability to handle this sleigh, then you ought to just pipe down and let me concentrate on driving it."

And it was at *that* point that Harvey turned away from Anna to see Chieftain swerve off the main ice road to the new spur of the lower beach trail road that Harvey was not expecting so soon. The new Cummings Creek spur dropped off from the main bluff-line haul road at a steep angle. The ice surface of the spur was not smooth, but was roughed-up by the cleats of the Bull Moose and might have provided adequate traction at a more cautious speed. The Bull Moose crew always slowed down to a snail-crawl before descending this bluff traverse, even when the log sledges were empty. But Chieftain, Harvey, Anna and the light sleigh careened over the edge of the bluff at a strong trotter's pace.

Chapter 13

"WHOA! CHIEFTAIN, WHOA!" Harvey cried as he pulled back on the reins and jammed his feet against the kickboard in front of him.

Chieftain's back legs slid out from behind him, and he started sliding down the ice road sitting on his back haunches. The sleigh began to slide sideways and Anna grabbed for the iron handrail. Chieftain struggled to get traction with his spiked shoes, but Harvey kept pulling back on the reins making it difficult for Chieftain to get back up on his hind hooves. Finally, Chieftain threw his head up and back to relieve tension on the reins, which threw Harvey hard back down into his seat. The jolt caused Harvey to loosen his death-grip on the reins and Chieftain was able to regain his rear footing.

The extra traction abruptly stopped Chieftain in his tracks, but the sleigh, which was already starting to jackknife, kept sliding downhill past the horse. The stantions snapped under the heavy sideways load and the sleigh spun all the way around Chieftain, turning the terrified horse around in the process.

If it weren't for the large red pine on the downhill side of the ice road, the entire sleigh, horse and passengers would have slipped off the road and down the steep side of the bluff. The thick tree trunk checked the deadly momentum of the spinning sleigh nearly knocking Anna across the seat and out the other side of the sleigh. She was splayed out across the sleigh bench, but her strong seamstress' grip on the handrail held.

The crash, however, caused poor Chieftain to completely lose what little composure he had left. With Anna still clinging to the handrail, Chieftain darted away from the edge of the slope and tried to climb the steep side of the road. He was still attached to the sleigh by the unbroken stantion and harness, and panicked. Unable to climb the bluff, he turned left again and, with ears back and the whites of his eyes flashing, he dashed down the ice road trying to outrun the spooky thing he was tied to.

Anna raised her head off the sleigh bench enough to see Chieftain racing downhill at a speed faster than she had ever been in her life.

"Harvey! Can't you stop him?" Anna screamed.

Before the little cloud of Anna's frosty breath was blown away by the rushing wind, Anna realized that Harvey was no longer in the sleigh.

"Oh, my God! Harvey!" she cried out.

Hot tears came to her eyes, but quickly turned cold in the swirling winter air. Without letting go of the handrail, she forced herself to sit up in the sleigh. Chieftain had reached the bottom of the hill, but he showed no sign of slowing on the ice road that cut through the mostly flat cedar swamp and woods between the base of the bluff and Lake Michigan. To her dismay, she saw the reins were out of reach, dragging along the road near one of the iron runners

"Whoa! Chieftain! Stop! Please!" Anna screamed.

The ice road was bumpier down here than up on the bluff and Anna was tossed up and down in her seat as the sleigh leaped over the larger bumps. With each serious bump, Anna noticed that the sleigh was spitting off pieces of wood and metal from the back right-side of the sleigh that had crashed into the big red pine.

She yelled again and again for Chieftain to stop, but the sound of panic in her own voice only seemed to frighten him more.

"Get a hold of yourself, Anna," she whispered.

Up ahead, Anna saw a large log across the road only partially covered by snow and ice. She braced herself for the inevitable jump. Chieftain easily cleared the two-foot-high log, but the runners of the sleigh crashed into the log with such force that the chassis of the sleigh was ripped completely off its runners. The entire undercarriage was left behind on the other side of the log as Anna and the sleigh body crashed flat down on the road.

Anna found herself at eye level to and not far from Chieftain's wildly flailing and spiked back hooves. Chieftain's special horseshoes showered Anna in a hail of cold, stinging ice fragments. She contemplated rolling out the side of the now-ground-level sleigh body, but there were too many big trees and stumps along the side of the road to risk jumping.

And it was at that moment that Anna saw the reins sliding along beside the wrecked sleigh. Without the undercarriage beneath her, the reins were within easy reach. Carefully, she lowered herself down from the seat to the road-level floor of what was left of the sleigh. Wedging herself between the front of the sleigh and the front of the seat, Anna reached out for the reins and snatched them into the sleigh. With coaxing words and a firm pull on the reins, Chieftain slowed from a gallop to a trot, and then pulled up to a complete stop just a split second before dragging Anna through the frigid waters of Cummings Creek, which the haul road forded without a bridge. Anna rolled out of the sleigh before Chieftain got any more spooky ideas.

"Oh, Chieftain, look what we've done to the Higginbotham's sleigh," Anna said, shaking her head at the horse and the wooden wreck before her. "I know it wasn't your fault, old fellow, but Harvey will be so upset."

With Harvey's name echoing in the quiet cedar forest, Anna felt a spasm of tears burst from her eyes as she realized that she had no idea where or in what condition Harvey was to be found. Anna began to run back up the haul road frantically calling Harvey's name, slipping, falling, getting back up again, and running, and falling again.

"You stupid girl," Anna said to herself as she sat up from her fifth consecutive fall on the icy road. Tears of anger, more than self pity blurred her vision, as she realized the impractical choice of shoe wear she had made earlier that afternoon with hopes of impressing Harvey. Her high-heeled boots of Italian leather had looked sophisticated as she had descended the stairs of her house back in town, but their smooth leather soles began to look ridiculous to her as she sat in a heap on an ice road in the middle of the woods five miles away from town. She wished she had listened to her mother and worn her solid winter boots instead.

"How am I even going to get back to Harvey, let alone home?" Anna thought as she lifted her gloved hand to wipe the tears from her eyes. As her beige calf-skin glove came down from her eyes, she was simultaneously shocked by three senses at the same time. Her eyes saw a dark stain of blood on her right glove, just as she felt a wave of pain explode from her nose where her fingers had brushed it. As she involuntarily inhaled at the outset of a scream, she also tasted the blood that was trickling down her nose and into the right corner of her mouth.

"My nose is broken!" she said through a grimace, and the tears of anger began to mix with tears of physical pain. "This is horrid!"

The trifecta of shocks, however, did not cause her to faint away or melt into a puddle of tears. Rather, it galvanized her into action.

… the wreck happened just as I told you, but Harvey did not appear down the road to save me as I said before. I was an utter mess after the wreck, but it was actually me who saved poor Harvey. Not vice versa. I was the one who had to rip the hem of my favorite Tartan wool skirt…

Anna's gaze shot from her own worthless shoes to Chieftain's spiked horseshoes. She carefully shuffled along the road toward Chieftain who stood near the creek still snorting clouds of steam from his flared nostrils, trying to catch his breath. Anna's cooing voice allowed her to approach Chieftain, take hold of his mane for support, and slowly unhitch him from the ruined sleigh and now-worthless harness. Without letting go of the long sleigh reins, she gingerly retrieved the warm blanket on the floor of the sleigh, folded it neatly and threw it over Chieftain's back.

Without stirrups or saddle, Anna stopped for just a moment to puzzle over how to mount Chieftain in an ankle-length woolen skirt. She looked around to make sure no one was watching — quickly realizing how unnecessary her modesty was in this circumstance — and hiked her skirt up to about mid-thigh. Even though she had her dark, winter bloomers on underneath the skirt, she instinctively raised her hand to cover the slightly mischievous grin that crept across her face at the sheer audacity of what she was doing. With an indecorous leap and several wild gyrations, Anna managed to get her torso up onto Chieftain, shimmy her right leg over and around the horse's hindquarters, pull herself up his neck to achieve a more dignified bareback seat.

Once mounted, Anna immediately felt herself on firmer footing and more familiar territory. She had always preferred to ride bareback on long summer rides up behind the Lakeview Cemetery. Her father used to let her ride on their old quarter horse Toronto while he spent the afternoons mowing grass and tending graves in his capacity as Cemetery Superintendent.

> *...Harvey had been thrown from the sleigh near the top of Stormy Grade. I had to ruin the skirt in order to help Harvey after the sleigh broke. You know how much I loved that skirt. Do you remember how the dark green stripes matched my charcoal gray overcoat so well?*
>
> *Anyway, I rode that horse for what seemed like an eternity back up the Lower Beach Trail. Of course, it was just a winter haul road back then. At the bottom of the hill, I came upon Harvey sitting on a big old cedar stump next to the road...*

Harvey sat on the stump with his legs crossed, his head bent forward. He was slowly rubbing his bare hands. Anna rode right up to him. He didn't even seem to notice her approach. The snow had been falling in big, dry flakes for some time now, and Harvey's head and shoulders were covered with cone-shaped white heaps. The wave of gratitude that Anna felt upon seeing Harvey in one piece quickly turned to indignation as she realized Harvey must have been sitting there for a long time to amass such a snowy covering.

"Harvey, how long have you been just sitting there?" Anna asked as her face turned red with irritation. "I have been worried to death about you. And I certainly could have used your help. What are you doing?"

Harvey, who had been sitting with his back to Anna and the road, slowly turned towards the sound of a voice.

"I'm looking for Anna," he said without looking up at her. "And my horse and sleigh. Have you seen my horse? It was here just a while ago."

Harvey turned even further around and looked up at Anna. A dark trail of blood covered the left side of his face leading from a three-inch-long gash on his forehead.

"Oh, there's my horse," he said looking straight at Anna. "There's Anna, too."

Anna's face was now white as she looked down at Harvey from Chieftain's back. "Oh, dear Harvey," was all she managed to say for a moment.

Harvey stood up, avalanching the piles of snow off his head and shoulders. He took a step towards Anna, but started to sway. Anna nearly leaped from the horse to help him, but something stronger than her desire to hold him took over. She realized that she was in a much better position to help Harvey from the back of Chieftain than next to Harvey down in the snow. She wasn't even sure if she could manage to clamber back up on the horse if she got off. Instinctively, she knew that the long sleigh reins she held coiled up in her left hand were like a lifeline connecting the young couple to Chieftain. Those reins were their best chance of survival in the cold, darkening hour.

Although a small woman, Anna was built on a wiry strength developed over generations of hard toil. The descendant of Scots-Irish farmers who first came to the New World in the early 1800s, Anna's people had already cleared the woods northeast of Toronto, Ontario, and prospered by turning old-tree forest into new-tilled farmland. Anna's Aunt Elizabeth Macklin Jackson and her Uncle John Jackson had been the first of the Macklin clan to come to Northern Michigan. Arriving in November of 1874, Anna's aunt and uncle spent two years whittling a homestead out of the woods about five miles north of Little Traverse Bay.

The Jacksons were some of the first white farmers in Emmet County. Their neighbors included only about a dozen white farming families. Since their first arrival in town, the Jacksons had come to know the other inhabitants of the village of Little Traverse. In addition to the 300 or so mostly Ottawa and Chippewa Indians, the Jacksons lived among timber buyers, sailors, and fishermen. In the late 1800s, the town still held remnants of Father Jacques Marquette's influence on the land and its native people. More than 200 years after the intrepid priest explored the Great Lakes and Mississippi, there was still a Catholic church and priest in town and a small handful of *coureurs de bois* — French-speaking trappers and traders in buckskins and furs. Men and women with names like St. Leger, Joutel, and Madame Pettier were among the leading citizens of the rough-hewn village.

After getting her own place up and running, Elizabeth invited her younger sister Dianna and her husband, James Johnson, to join them in Northern Michigan as neighbors. In 1878, James and Dianna accepted the offer and left Canada for the tip of Michigan's Lower Peninsula. Although both Jacksons and Johnsons left the hardships of homesteading for the comforts of town before the end of the decade, the print of pioneering was forever etched into their lives.

Whether Anna's mettle was inherited or developed, she put it to use that cold January day as the light began to fade from the sky. Although Anna realized that Harvey was injured and in need of help, she also realized that he was in serviceable enough condition to help her get him up on the horse. Though unsteady, he was, at least, still on his feet.

"Harvey! I need you to take hold of these reins," Anna said in a deliberate voice, tossing the coiled length of leather strap into Harvey's arms. "Pull yourself up onto the road and I'll help by holding onto the reins, too. Just don't pull too hard or you'll pull me right off the horse."

Harvey said nothing, but did exactly as Anna told him to do. Like a schoolmarm giving instructions to her youngest pupil, Anna talked Harvey up out of the ditch beside the road and next to Chieftain.

> ... *The knock on Harvey's head from the crash made him so woozy and limp that I don't know how I managed to help him up on the horse. My fingers and feet were already numb from the cold, and I didn't think we could make it back home in the dark. Then, I remembered visiting Mary Jane Keegonee a few summers back at her grandmother's home about five miles up the shore from town.. You'll remember Mary Jane as the beautiful Indian Princess in the Hiawatha Paegeant for many years before the Great War.*

> *Instead of turning back toward town, I bandaged Harvey's head with the hem of my skirt, turned Chieftain around, and headed back deeper into the forest towards Cummings Creek...*

With Harvey's arms wrapped around her waist and his head pressed heavily against her, Anna kept Chieftain at a slow walk while she scanned each side of the haul road. Even with Harvey barely conscious and the situation still dire, she couldn't help but notice every point of contact between their two bodies with a mixture of alarm and enjoyment. His right cheek bobbed rhythmically up and down on her left shoulder blade with each of Chieftain's steps. His arms, thickened by more than a dozen years of work in the woods, caressed and hugged her ribcage as Harvey's grip about her alternately slipped and tightened. Harvey's hands held his forearms near his elbows because Anna's trim and corseted waist was so small. Beneath her many layers of thick clothing, her flat stomach warmed with the touch of his arms around her. Sometimes his semi-conscious fidgeting caused his arms and hands to slip down into her lap or up to the swell of her breast. She tried to squirm his arms back into a proper position, at first. But then she simply told herself that he wasn't aware of what he was doing and his touches couldn't be helped. She tried to concentrate on the task at hand.

The new snow was already beginning to cover the frantic tracks from her earlier passages down and then up this road, but she was looking for older signs along the way. Although the blood had ceased trickling from her own injury, her whole face ached and she felt lightheaded. While the horse beneath her and Harvey behind her kept most of her body warm, she was startled to realize that she no longer had any feeling in her feet, which hung loosely below Chieftain's belly. She knew they couldn't stay out here much longer. There were several deer paths intersecting the haul road, some of which she followed towards the foot of the steep bluff to her right only to turn back to the road, but she had a clear picture in her head of the marker for the trail she was looking for.

About two-thirds of the way back to Cummings Creek, Anna noticed an odd bulge of snow in the notch of a forked cedar tree. She guided Chieftain off the haul road to the tree and leaned down to brush the snow away. She revealed a smooth, black rock, about the size of a small watermelon which had been jammed into the notch of the split-trunk cedar so many decades ago that its sides were almost entirely enveloped in the tree's bark.

"This is it, Harvey. Hang on tight, now. We're going to climb the bluff here," Anna said mostly to herself. She was encouraged to feel Harvey's grip tighten around her waist and his head nod up and down against her shoulder. "Okay," he moaned.

The foot of the bluff was only about 30 yards back from the road. From there, Anna could clearly see the wide path, which traversed the steep front of the bluff at a more gentle upward angle. The layers of old and new snow were piled almost up to Chieftain's knees, even though Anna could see that other travelers had packed down most of the old snow on the trail. The The deep snow and the steep trail, however, made a lot more work for Chieftain who had to step high and bound through some of the deeper drifts. Alarmed by the horse's abrupt movements, Anna was afraid Harvey might get bucked right off the back of the horse. Keeping one hand on the coil of reins and reaching one arm behind her to hold on to Harvey, Anna urged Chieftain onward.

As they climbed, the trail began to turn left as it followed the contour of an ancient ravine cut into the side of the bluff. The bouncing and the exertion of trying to hold both reins and Harvey stole the breath from Anna's lungs. As she breathed harder and harder, she could feel her eyelids growing heavier. Harvey's arms hung limply about her waist and his head had slid down to the middle of her back, but Anna felt that the top of the bluff was only a bit farther up the trail.

"Get up there, Chieftain. Go on, boy," she whispered into the horse's ear as she kicked and pressed her heels into his sides. With black spots and white bursts beginning to cloud her vision, Anna rode Chieftain to the top of the trail, where he bounded through the corniced snowdrift at the lip of the bluff.

…It was a miracle that I managed to get Harvey up the bluff without losing him or falling off myself. I was saying my prayers all the way up that path. The strain of it all

almost made me black out, but the last thing I remember clearly until the next morning was a ghostly vision of an upside-down buck walking through the woods on a pole. Of course, you have probably already guessed what that odd vision was. It was none other than Leonard and William Keegonee — Mary Jane's brother and uncle bringing a deer back home on a pole between them...

Chapter 14

ANNA'S EYES OPENED the next morning on the bright, new, unpainted hemlock planks of some unfamiliar attic ceiling. Although a faint, cold draft wafted in from a closed, lace-curtained window at her side, Anna was in a warm feather bed piled high with wool blankets and covered by a green-and-cream-colored quilt. A shaft of bright sunlight coming through that same window neutralized the cold draft with a touch of warmth on her face. Filling the air around her was a pleasing aroma that Anna couldn't quite identify. It smelled like a mixture of cornbread and split pea soup, Anna thought. As she drew in a big whiff through her nostrils, she realized that her nose was no longer hurting. Pulling her hand from under the warm covers to touch her nose, she was startled when her fingertips encountered some kind of cool, moist bandage lying across the bridge of her nose.

"Ke-me-no-pe-maw-tis naw?" came a high, croaking voice from the side of the bed. Anna turned to see a reddish-brown face with high cheekbones and dozens of crinkly lines fanning out from the corners of soft, brown eyes and from the corners of a toothless smile. Long, white hair was bundled behind the old woman's head and swept over the billowy shoulder of her clean, white blouse. A bony-fingered hand with dark, wrinkled skin like dried-out leather reached towards Anna's face. Anna's first instinct was to flinch from the hand, but the old Ottawa woman's twinkling eyes and gummy grin washed all fear from Anna's groggy mind. As the old woman moved closer to the bed, Anna noticed that her dark, brown eyes were reflecting the bright, white light from the window. At the same time, Anna sensed that those eyes also reflected a warm light from someplace both familiar and far away. It was as if the old woman knew all about Anna, but Anna knew nothing about her. The old woman caressed Anna's forehead with the back of her hand, which was surprisingly soft and warm.

"Where am I?" Anna asked.

"Chi-noo-ding," the old woman replied, as though Anna could comprehend each syllable she spoke.

"I've never heard of such a place," Anna said. "How far are we from Blue Harbor?"

"Ke-baw-kaw-tay naw?" the old woman asked, apparently changing the subject. She pulled her hand back from Anna's forehead and pulled it up to her lips, as though feeding herself a morsel of food.

"I'm sorry, I don't understand Ottawa," Anna said. Then, deciphering the old woman's hand gesture, she added, "Yes, please, I would love something to eat. I feel like I haven't eaten in days."

Just then, Anna noticed the clomp of boots coming up the steep ladder-like staircase leading to the rest of the house. A head with shiny, crow-black hair rose out of the stairwell to reveal a pair of big, round eyes like black pearls. And below those eyes, came a bright smile that Anna instantly recognized.

"Mary Jane!" Anna cried with delight.

"Anna, I'm so glad to see you're awake. Welcome to our home," said the young Indian woman who emerged from the stairwell carrying a tray with a steaming bowl of something that immediately caught Anna's attention.

"Anna, I hope my Aunty Margaret didn't confuse you with her old, Indian words. She speaks English just fine, but forgets sometimes and talks in the old way."

"Oh, she was very kind. I didn't even know where I was, but she made me feel right at home in an instant," Anna replied. "I could tell that she was taking good care of me."

"I brought you something to eat," Mary Jane said, holding the tray in front of Anna's nose as Anna sat up in the bed. "Aunty Margaret, take the beech leaves off of Anna's nose, so she can eat."

"There was one thing that your aunt said that I was wondering about," Anna said. "I thought I knew every little local name and lots of the old Indian names for places around here, but what was the name you gave this place, Margaret — chi-new-something?"

Aunty Margaret's smile widened as she nodded her head up and down and said, "Yes, Chi-noo-ding, Chi-noo-ding. That's it."

"Ohhh, yes," Mary Jane nodded in accord. "I have not heard that name in a very long time. The old people who lived in the long houses here use that word. It's just the name for this little place along the bluff. It means, uh, Place of Storm Wind."

"That sounds quite impressive. How did it get that name?"

"Whenever big storms come off of Lake Michigan or "Ki-tchi-go-mah Ma-shi-gan-ing," as they say in our language, this is the landfall. For some reason, the storm winds always seem to hit here first," Mary Jane explained.

"You know, I did notice that a lot of the treetops at the edge of the bluff were broken off. I like that — Place of Storm Wind," Anna said, tasting the words in her mouth as she repeated them. "Chi-noo-ding."

Auntie Margaret tugged on Mary Jane's skirt to bring the two younger women back into the present. Mary Jane was still standing over Anna with a tray full of food. "The quay-zayns — I mean — the girl is ready to eat," the old woman said, slipping a wet packet of leaves stuffed with some kind of moss from Anna's face. "It helps keep the swelling down — good medicine," Aunty Margaret said with a wink to Anna as she set the packet in a bowl beside the bed.

"This looks delicious," Anna said as she dipped a spoon into a yellow-white soup with some kind of meal and pieces of pork. "What is this?"

"There isn't really an English name for it," Mary Jane said after thinking for a moment. "It's a hominy type of soup — the eye of the corn kernel cooked in clean lye to remove the husks, washed and cooked and seasoned with fresh pork. We call it Ba-nu-ga-si-can-uk — old family recipe. Do you like it?"

Anna couldn't answer until she swallowed the fourth spoonful that she had wolfishly shoveled into her mouth as soon as the tray was set in front of her. "It's delicious, thank you very much. Is there any more?"

But before Mary Jane could answer, Anna dropped the spoon into the bowl with a clatter and gasped as though a ghost had just passed by the end of the bed. She sat bolt upright in the bed and was starting to extricate herself from the covers when Mary Jane put a hand on her shoulder to hold her in place.

"Where's Harvey?" Anna said, as the full memory of the bareback ride up the bluff with a barely conscious Higginbotham returned to her mind. "Is he all right?"

"Everything's all right, Anna," Mary Jane said with a smile. "He's already back in his big house in town by now. Uncle William and my oldest brother Leonard got a message to your families last night, and Mr. Higginbotham's mill manager — Mr. Newark — came and fetched Harvey home this morning. He'll be just fine."

Anna was relieved to hear that Harvey was safe at home, but as she continued to eat her Ba-nu-ga-si-can-uk, a slight lump started to form in her throat making it difficult to swallow. "But why did he leave without me?" Anna asked.

Mary Jane beamed back at Anna surprisingly oblivious to Anna's anxiety. "Harvey said something about having to get back home for some meeting with his father. But I think he wasn't exactly thrilled to find himself surrounded by a bunch of Indians — especially Uncle William who told off old Mr. Higginbotham last spring when he quit. Harvey said thank you and even paid Leonard and Uncle William $5 each for running into town last night. Mama told him we would be happy to take care of you until you were well enough to go back home."

"Well, I'm glad he even remembered me, after that nasty cut on his head," Anna said, somewhat mollified. "I was quite concerned about him yesterday."

"Oh, I think you were on his mind plenty," Mary Jane said. "It's just that he was embarrassed when he woke up wearing Papa's old night shirt and realized that Mama and Aunty Margaret had put him in it in order to dry out his clothes. Leonard and Uncle William also teased him a bit too much about being saved by a girl."

"Oh, no," Anna said. "Now he's going to think I'm some kind of brute."

Mary Jane could control her mirth no longer and burst into a fit of giggles, which she tried to cover with her hands.

"You are merciless, Mary Jane. What on earth is so funny about that?" Anna said, her flash of indignation fading to a smile with Mary Jane's infectious laughter. Aunty Margaret was laughing, too.

"Anna, ever since the 9th grade, you have had a gift for worrying about bad things that have never happened and probably never will," said Mary Jane.

"Go on and tell her," said Aunty Margaret as she cleared the empty tray from Anna's lap.

"Tell me what?" Anna said.

Mary Jane had to take Anna's hands and sit beside her on the bed to steady her own giddy excitement. "I know exactly how Harvey feels about you," she said.

"How? What did he say?"

"It wasn't what he said, but what we saw," Mary Jane giggled. "Mama made me stay out in the kitchen when they pulled Harvey's thawing-wet clothes off of him. They handed them to me so I could hang them by the cook stove to dry. When I went to hang up his shirt, I dropped his coat on the floor…"

"And what does this have to do with…"

"Something fell out of his coat pocket, Anna. It was an engagement ring."

"No. I can't believe it," Anna said. "I had no idea he was even thinking about marriage."

Anna grabbed Mary Jane around the neck and Mary Jane hugged Anna around the waist as both young women began to laugh and cry at the same time.

> … As you know, the Keegonees took good care of me, but what you don't know is that they discovered the "surprise" that Harvey was planning for me at the end of what was supposed to be a picturesque winter sleigh ride. Just as you expected, Harvey was planning to propose to me that day. I was so embarrassed when I remembered how we were bickering just before the sleigh cracked up. Poor Harvey, no wonder he was acting so funny. There he was trying to set up a romantic proposal, and I fought him all the way. I guess things didn't quite work out the way he planned them, but I suppose it all worked out for the best. If we quarreled that much over the proposal, I can't imagine the

marriage would have gone much better. Well, you know how the rest of the Harvey story ended, but I thought it was about time you knew the whole story.

This trip has really made me appreciate the riches that Joe has brought to my life. We have certainly had our rough spots, and we sure don't have the kind of money that Harvey must now have, but just look at where Joe's career has taken us — California, Texas, Panama, and now we are off to The Philippines. Who ever would have guessed that your small-town daughter who "lived with the Indians" would become such a world traveler living among such notables? We certainly are having a grand time.

Love to You,
Anna

Although Dianna knows what happened to Harvey and Anna after they both returned from Chi-noo-ding, Anna has left me hanging. As I scan through letters and clippings from the 1900s, though, I get bits and pieces of information that fit together into a rough picture puzzle of a near-miss marriage and an aborted relationship. Harvey's "surprise" proposal never survived the wreck of the sleigh and the brief convalescence at the Keegonees' little farmhouse at the top of the wind-battered bluff. Harvey's concussion healed soon enough, but his ego was more deeply bruised.

Given time, Harvey might have come around again, but the opportunity that Harvey and Anna missed the day she broke her nose was never to present itself again. Anna was able to get a ride back to town in Uncle William and Leonard's sleigh. Anna was quickly swept up into the arms of family who — along with the Higginbothams — had spent a frantic evening trying to find out what had become of one of its dear children.

Days later, when Anna was recovered and tired of waiting for Harvey to reappear with the engagement ring or, at least, an explanation for why he hadn't contacted her, Anna discovered that Harvey had ended his vacation pre-maturely and whisked himself back to work in New York. Harvey's sister Leslie had some unsatisfactory message to relay to her friend Anna about "pressing business concerns" back East.

The few additional mentions of Harvey — other than Anna's May 15, 1931 letter written aboard the U.S.S. *Grant* — are cordial, but given no more or less weight than references to the host of other friends and acquaintances who flow in and out of the Johnson-family correspondence. Years later, Mary Jane Keegonee Sagataw — who remained Anna's friend and expert seamstress for decades after Anna left Blue Harbor — mentions meeting Harvey's first wife when she came in for a fitting one summer. According to one letter, Mary Jane is "dead certain that the three-stone diamond engagement ring behind Mrs. Higginbotham's four-stone wedding ring is the exact same ring" that fell out of Harvey's coat pocket onto her kitchen floor.

By 1910, however, the Higginbothams and other timber-baron families like them had cut down just about every tree around Blue Harbor. The Higginbothams sold all of their Michigan holdings, including the five-porch house on the bluff, and moved on to the next big timber boom in Seattle, Washington. It didn't take nearly that long for Anna's affection for Harvey to play out. By the summer of 1906, Anna's nose was completely healed (leaving only a tiny bump), and her heart was ready to move on to new shores of its own. A white ship was already steaming towards her with a young Marine private who would drive any lingering thoughts of Harvey to the back of her mind.

Chapter 15

AFTER A QUIET but exciting weekend pouring over Joe and Anna's papers, Monday morning comes with a jolt. I'm sitting at the plaintiffs' table of the Emmet County Circuit Court waiting for the Michigan Court of Appeals to take the bench. My family's lawyer, Cyril J. Cushman, is busily digging through his briefcase on the table looking for a transcript or something. He's still tan from Florida and his white hair seems even brighter for the darkness of his skin. I notice that Cushman really has to stretch his arms to reach the papers because his prosperous, round belly keeps him from pulling his chair up closer to the table. And yet, he manages to wear his prosperity well in a blue, neatly pressed, two-piece suit with a red, plaid vest. A gold watch fob straddles his scarlet-covered stomach and disappears into a vest pocket where he keeps an antique gold Elgin watch that he regularly pulls out and flips open to consult the hour. He showed it to me once, and it seems to keep excellent time. I notice that there is also an accurate timepiece at the front of the courtroom that also gives the date — May 2, 1989. I suspect that Cushman — who's active mind is always turning — needs something to keep his hands busy, too. I think Cushman's dignified demeanor is also calculated to throw off his opponents. One minute he's a grandfatherly Burl Ives gentleman. The next minute he's coolly cutting some witness to pieces. I'm just glad he's on our side.

Some of the Becker family's legal adversaries are gathered behind the defendant's table for what should be the last round of Becker vs. North Shore Township. This is only one of the legal battles I've recently inherited. This battle is over a sixty-six-foot-wide corridor of our land that North Shore Township says is a public park. Back in the '40s, the township cleared some trees on this beachfront parcel when the Colonel was away and nobody was watching. Despite decades of protest from the Colonel and, later, my father and Vicky, the township kept treating the corridor like a public park. The township says it now owns the former right-of-way by "adverse possession" — by what we laymen would call squatters' rights. We Beckers, however, say it is our land and has been so for more than sixty years.

My family's refusal to just roll over and let the township take property, which has been in the family since 1924, hasn't exactly endeared us to the local populace. To most of the public gathered to watch the hearing, the Beckers are the ones trying to take away one of the few public accesses to the beach. To them, we are not a family simply trying to hold on to what is rightfully ours. To them, we are outsiders. We have the local newspaper to thank, in part, for this skewed perspective on our family's case. The Little Traverse Times has painted the township as the champions of the public good. Yesterday's headline announced the historic first-ever appearance of the Michigan Court of Appeals in Petoskey this way: "State Appeals Court to Meet on Public Beach Park." Only at the end of the story does the reporter mention our family's contention that the beach property is neither public nor a park.

Other news types are here as well. Obviously, I couldn't cover this story for the paper I have been stringing for — The Northern Michigan Gazette. Even I would have a little trouble being very objective. There was quite a bit of discussion among the Gazette editors over whether or not to even cover a story that involves one of their regular freelancers. They decided they could be objective, as long as they mentioned the Nick Becker-*Gazette* connection in the story. The *Gazette* has sent a seasoned reporter up from Traverse City. I met him just a few minutes ago. I'll have to remember the odd sensation of being on the other side of a reporter's notebook the next time I am wielding the pen. I noticed how he didn't seem to be writing anything when I told him the key points of the case, and he scribbled furiously when I thought the interview was over. I hope he doesn't go too far out of his way to show how objective the *Gazette* can be towards one of its freelancers. There is even a fresh-faced TV reporter tucked in the corner of the courtroom with her camera. News has been pretty slow this month, and it doesn't take much to get the Northern Michigan press corps going. They are more interested in the first-ever appearance in this part of the state by the Court of Appeals than in our puny lawsuit, anyway.

At the other table, the township supervisor and constable are whispering quietly to their attorney, with occasional sharp glances towards me. Neither Sally nor my mother was able to fly up for the hearing. With few apparent allies at my side, I am beginning to feel the focus of unfriendly eyes on the back of my head.

I wish Dad, who started this fight five years ago, were here to finish it. Despite the stern looks I'm getting from the next table, I suddenly have to lift my hand to cover my mouth. I feel the muscles in my face rising upward into what must look like a smart-alecky grin.

The last really good laugh that my father and I had was at the expense of some of those guys at the next table, as well as the weasly looking reporter from *The Little Traverse Times* who is seated a few rows behind them. In 1986, I drove up from Leelanau after my camp counselor job ended, and met Dad at

The Shack. He had flown in from England a few weeks before with news of his engagement to Melinda, a fashionable middle-aged British woman who lived near the Burtonwood Army Depot. Dad worked as a civil servant there after retiring from the Army.

Before starting in on the demolition work for the remodeling, Dad and I took the bluff trail down to the beach for a swim. We marched down to the "alleged township park," as we called it. The township had just then won a round in the Becker vs. North Shore Township lawsuit. To our astonishment, township officials — they were a nameless, faceless enemy back then — had set two picnic tables and erected a sign on our land proclaiming the area the "North Shore Township Beach Park."

Dad threw down his beach towel and went after the offending lumber. He tried to tip the picnic tables over, but they were anchored to a new concrete pad with chains. He went after the sign, but the beefy 4X4 legs were stuck fast in concrete footings buried beneath the sandy forest floor.

"Come on, let's go," Dad said after working himself into a red-faced sweat. He was pissed.

To be honest, this wasn't my favorite side of my Dad, but I've got to hand it to him — when he got angry at anything outside our family circle, he could be very effective in protecting who and what was inside the circle.

Even after a summer as a camp counselor, it wasn't easy keeping up with my old man — a track star in high school — as he hoofed it back up the steep bluff.

After we changed into jeans and T-shirts (on Dad's orders) he threw some tools into the used red pickup he had just bought. It was supposed to become his retirement truck — who would of thought it would be mine a couple of years later. It was a bit far to walk down to the beach with heavy tools, so Dad fired up the engine and called for me to get in. We sped down Stanton Road leaving contrails of khaki dust in our wake. Dad burned a little rubber as we took a right on Shore Drive. A mile later, we made another sharp right and bounced down unpaved Lower Beach Trail to get to "the alleged township park."

Dad had been in the Army Corp of Engineers for twenty-three years, and he was as good at tearing things down as he was at putting them up. Dad snipped the chains on the picnic tables with heavy bolt cutters. Then, he pulled his own thick chain out of the pickup bed, wrapped it around the top of the sign posts and to the truck frame. A few yanks with the four-wheel drive engaged and Dad had ripped the sign, the 4X4s, and their footings right out of the sandy soil. We piled everything into the pickup and drove back to The Shack. That night, Dad had a beer and I had a Vernors around the roaring burn pile as we watched the township's feeble attempt at "adverse possession" turn to ash.

The really good laugh came a few days later when Dan the Carpenter stopped by with the latest edition of *The Little Traverse Times*. A headline on the bottom of the front page read: "Vandals Strike Township Park." A black-and-white photo showed the township constable standing over the deep tire ruts in front of where the sign had stood. The photo caption said: "township officials vow to bring perpetrators to justice."

Dad thought that was the funniest thing he had ever seen. He laughed so hard that tears came to his eyes, and Dan and I laughed with him. Of course, we never got caught, and — even if we did — the township couldn't have done anything about it. The township park, after all, is on our land.

That's why I am in this courtroom today.

"All rise," the bailiff orders, " The Michigan Court of Appeals is now in session, the honorable judges Walter Allen, Gilbert Glen, and John Ranick, presiding."

Judge Glen seems to be the moderator, and he tells us to sit down. After some preliminary lawyer stuff, Judge Glen sums up the court's understanding of the case, so far.

"The parcel in question is a strip of land 66 feet wide and about one acre in area. It follows the Stanton Road section line down a steep bluff and to the shore of Lake Michigan. Although Stanton Road ends at the top of the bluff, the township claims the Stanton Road right-of-way does not end there, but extends all the way down to the water's edge.

"Two years ago, in an appeal, this court ruled in favor of the plaintiff since the plaintiff had paid taxes on the land, including the so-called township park. If the parcel in question truly was a public right-of-way, then the plaintiff should not have had to pay taxes on it.

"Earlier this year, the township board appealed to the Michigan Supreme Court. The Supreme Court sought additional testimony in January and found evidence that no taxes had been paid on this particular parcel.

"The Supreme Court has remanded the case to this Court to settle one question and one question only. Did the Becker family pay taxes on this part of the property or not? Counsel will please limit any additional testimony to this key question."

The defense gets the first crack at making its case, and we have to sit through nearly an hour of detail about property descriptions, surveying techniques, and land-assessment procedures.

Finally, Graham Stevens, the township's attorney, gets to the stuff he was supposed to get to an hour ago. Stevens looks like a white version of Sammy Davis, Jr. His large, aviator-style glasses are tinted a bit too dark for indoors, but his dark tan makes it seem like he just stepped off a yacht that has motored up from Miami Beach. A gold bracelet dangles loosely from his wrist as he reaches into his pants pocket to jingle a handful of coins. The musical pitch of the tinkling coins matches the pitch to the main chorus of "The Candy Man," and I am doomed to sit through the rest of the hearing with "he mixes it with love and makes the world taste good" bouncing around the inside of my head.

"The defense calls Mr. Ralph Rakowski to the stand," Stevens announces to the courtroom.

The retired township assessor removes his sweat-stained NAPA Auto Parts baseball cap as he ambles through the swinging gate that separates the litigants from onlookers. In his late-sixties, Rakowski wears a baby-blue golf shirt and blue jeans with cowboy boots and big, shiny belt buckle which, on second glance, is the Detroit Red Wings logo. Before coming into the legal arena, he smiles nervously as he fumbles to stop the swinging gate, which squeaks noticeably. He waves hello to his buddies behind the defense table, before stepping up to the witness stand. I detect a slight odor of Old Spice and stale cigar smoke after he has passed by.

After he's sworn in, Stevens runs him through the preliminaries — name, address, occupation — and proves to everyone that yes, indeed, Rakowski does know something about the facts of the case he has been summoned to testify in.

After 25 minutes of technical questioning about how this retired township assessor came up with an assessment for our land, it all boils down to this guy's word that he mentally discounted the tax bill for the beach property without keeping any record of doing so.

After some softball questions to demonstrate what a swell guy Rakowski is, Stevens sits down and Cy is up to bat.

Cy Cushman slowly stands beside me, pulls out his gold watch, snaps the watch lid open, winds the knob and checks the time against the courtroom clock on the wall above the judges' heads. It's the first time I've seen him in action before the court, and I notice that I'm leaning forward in my chair ever so slightly during the long pause before he says anything to Rakowski.

CUSHMAN: *Good morning, Mr. Rakowski.*

RAKOWSKI: *Uh, good morning.*

CUSHMAN: *When you made your assessment of the Becker beach parcels, sir, did you put anything down on a piece of paper?*

RAKOWSKI: *Notes of my own? Yes.*

CUSHMAN: *All right, and where are those notes?*

RAKOWSKI: *I didn't keep those. Those were all miscellaneous, more or less.*

CUSHMAN: *All right. So any record that you made that the taxpayer might be able to see in order to determine how you made the assessment, is just so many dollars on their tax bill?*

RAKOWSKI: *That is right.*

CUSHMAN: *And can you tell us how much you took off for the park assessment, say, in 1983?*

RAKOWSKI: *No, I can't*

CUSHMAN: *How about 1986, the last year that you were the assessor?*

RAKOWSKI: *No, I can't*

CUSHMAN: *Can you tell us how much you took off for the park at any time you were assessor?*

RAKOWSKI: *No.*

CUSHMAN: *Please correct me if I am wrong, but what you are telling the Court is that you didn't include the value of the 66-foot-wide piece of land in your appraisal of the Becker family's property, but you can't tell us what that single acre was worth?*

RAKOWSKI: *Well, I would like to answer that in my own way if I could. You see the assessments were way low...*

JUDGE GLEN: *Just answer the question, Mr. Rakowski.*

CUSHMAN: *You didn't include the so-called park in the assessment, but you can't tell us how much the so-called park was worth. Is that what you are telling the court, Mr. Rakowski?*

RAKOWSKI: *That's right.*

Cushman pauses for a moment, looks up at me over the top of his reading glasses, and turns to the three judges.

"No further questions, your honors."

Stevens gets a chance to make Rakowski look good, but he doesn't add much. Maybe Rakowski's methods were unorganized, but they weren't uncommon compared with general assessment practices, he assures the court.

Before lunch, Cushman makes his closing argument:

"It seems to me, your honors, that the township's case is before this court because of the memory of one witness. Mr. Rakowski remembers with absolute certainty that he did not include the so-called township beach park property in his assessments. His claim of assessing the beach but placing no value on it amounts to government by secret — nobody knew but Mr. Rakowski.

"It seems incredible to me that he can come before this court and testify that he assessed the various parcels included in the Becker family property without making any calculation, but somehow in his mental process he excluded the 66-foot-wide piece on either side of the section line.

"We are talking about property here, your honors, not roadways. There is no road to the beach running down the bluff from Stanton Road. The road ends at the top of the bluff. A road right-of-way is not the same thing as owning the property outright as this township claims it owns the 66-foot corridor. They claim ownership of it, but year after year they sent us a tax bill, which included the so-called beach park in the property description. The Becker family paid the taxes faithfully year after year. And, yet, this officer of the township now comes in and says he somehow deducted the value in his head. Incredible. I think Mr. Rakowski's testimony is self-serving and his credibility as a witness is certainly in question. It is a good thing for the public to have access to Lake Michigan in North Shore Township, but this is not the way to go about it. The court should reaffirm exactly the finding that it made two years ago, and rule in favor of my clients."

We'll have to wait a few days to hear the Appellate Court's decision, but Cushman tells me he thinks the hearing went well.

~ PART 5 ~

BLUE HARBOR, MICHIGAN

———

Chapter 16

I REALIZE THAT my grandparents' story isn't for everybody. Over lunch yesterday with my editor Sean Cooper and a couple of other Traverse City reporters, I began to explain what I was working on. They listened politely for a few minutes, but I could see some of their eyes start to glaze over. When the food finally came, their attention completely disappeared and we were back to talking about murder weapons, county commissioners, and the ratty toupee worn by a local TV reporter.

That response and the need to check up on an old family friend are why I have decided to knock off work a little early today and go into town to visit Patty Kensington. If there is one person who can appreciate what I've found while digging though Aunt Vicky's old stuff, it is Patty. Patty is a couple years older than my Dad would be now. They were best friends growing up. Dad only spent his summers here, but Patty and Dad always kept in touch — even after they married other people and started families of their own. No family trip to Blue Harbor was complete without a stop at Patty's house on the way out to The Shack. Now that I live here year-round, I have taught myself to drive past Patty's house without automatically stopping. Sometimes I even call before dropping in. She is a busy woman, but we still manage to find time for each other a couple of times a month.

As the locally famous columnist in the weekly *Blue Harbor Resorter* newspaper, Patty knows just about everyone in town. Not only does she know a good deal about my family's story, but she is something of a town historian, as well. Patty Kensington spends her days with one foot anchored in the present and the other firmly grounded in the past. Or, more precisely, I should say she keeps all three *wheels* in both worlds. This week's column is a good example of what I'm talking about.

ONLY IN BLUE HARBOR — NEWS OF FRIENDS & NEIGHBORS, RESIDENTS AND RESORTERS.

By Patty Kensington
Monday May 8, 1989

May 8. Good grief! Where is the time going? I made plans this winter. Plans to fight a major battle against clutter. Clutter that I can blame on no one but me. I used to blame my family for the things that cluttered my nest.

#1 All that stuff laying around was theirs.

#2 Because I was SO busy engineering the household, I simply didn't have time to keep everything in order.

I now know that I only deceived myself. I and I alone am responsible for the clutter! My dog, William, and I are here alone. True, he leaves his toys on the floor; but William isn't responsible for the closets, drawers, bookshelves, and the attic (oh the attic) that are jam-packed full.

Now, if you walked into my house, you wouldn't believe what I've just told you. It looks orderly. It even looks rather sparse. That's because every nook and cranny is full.

I have a pact with my friend Jenny Kishawase. If she should hear of my sudden demise, she will rush right over here and start pitching; but in the meantime, I simply must start putting my house in order.

Now, let's see. I'll start with the dish cupboard. These unmatched glasses and mugs. Why do I keep them? Each mug came from someone or some place special. I can't toss them out. All right, I'll leave them.

On to the closets. I should get rid of that gray coat and matching cloche hat. I just can't. I felt so very smart when I wore them. I felt so with it. Oh well. They don't take up too much room. I'll wait. Then there are those four long wool skirts. (Remember when we all wore them, when we were "at home.") I've kept them thinking that I'd cut them off, or make a braided rug, or a jumper for a granddaughter. Heck, I still might. Hang them back. However, I will give this half-finished ski sweater to Carla Windor. I'll bet she'll finish it for me.

On to the bookshelves. Oh oh! Here are the two Iococca books that belong to Sandy and Bill Jones. I'll have to return them. Phyllis McGinley's poetry. Boy, I haven't read these in a long time. And here's Ginny Fester's book of E.B. White essays. Guess I'll stop. Make a cup of coffee and read a bit. What's this? White's first essay is about, of all things, clutter. He and his wife Katharine are moving to Maine after 20 years in their New York apartment. What to do with all of those things? He writes so well. His language is so precise and clever. That does it. Not only am I lousy at throwing out and straightening, I can't write like E.B. White. I give up.

— P.K.

The rest of Patty's column, which sits beside me on the bench seat of my pickup, is filled with the "News of friends & neighbors, residents and resorters" part. Patty's multiple sclerosis put her in a three-wheeled, electric scooter years ago, but she still manages to get around town in her Subaru and keep tabs on who is marrying whom, whose birthday it is, and who is in town visiting. Sally, my mom, and I even made it into her column last year when we all came up for a week of vacation at The Shack. Patty — who is one of the few people who thinks I look like my dad and accidentally calls me by my dad's name all the time — listed me as "John" in her column. It was a classic Kensington slip. Neither carelessness nor senility are responsible for this recurring confusion, though. She's always quick to correct herself when she introduces me as my father to someone new. It's just Patty's way of seeing both the present me and the past John at the same time. Coming from her, I take it as a compliment.

Patty's house is at the north edge of Blue Harbor. It's a rambling, brown, two-story nestled underneath huge red pines, with a two-pole, split-rail fence separating her yard from Shore Drive. Near the edge of the bluff, Patty's house overlooks a dark cedar forest, the church steeple of Holy Childhood church, and a small bit of the bay.

William's wet nose and wagging tail greet me as I mount the few concrete stairs up to Patty's porch. A white-haired gentleman in khaki pants, faded blue sneakers and a red windbreaker is stepping out of Patty's front door just as I step in. Since moving here, I have come to learn that Patty doesn't need to get out much because the world comes to her doorstep almost every day. Resorters and locals alike check in with Patty for conversation and a good cup of coffee.

"... and don't forget about the Kiwanis pancake breakfast next week," the gentleman says as he backs out of Patty's front door.

He doesn't notice me, at first, and I move to hold the screen door open for him without startling him.

"Oh, hello, young fellow, I didn't see you standing there," the man says to me.

As he maneuvers to open the door for me, he calls back into Patty, "It looks like your next gentleman caller is here to see you, Patty. I best be getting home."

"Who's there, Hal?" Patty calls back from the kitchen.

"It's me, Nick Becker."

"Oh, Nick, come on in."

"Hal, do you know who this is?"

"Can't say I do," he says to her. "Hi, I'm Hal Campbell," he says to me with a handshake.

"Hal, this is Col. Becker's grandson. You remember the Colonel and Anna who used to live out at the end of Stanton Road. Nick here is living out at the old Shack. He's a fine journalist and he has moved to live here year 'round."

"Oh, yes, I remember your grandparents and I knew your father, too. I was sorry to hear about your father passing on so young. It's nice to meet you, though."

Hal seems like a real nice guy and he asks me about myself and my writing. He reads five newspapers a day, including *The Northern Michigan Gazette*, and has read my articles. He doesn't say much about himself, though. I quickly realize that he is a Campbell — as in Potter & Campbell, the huge multi-national soap and detergent corporation. This guy with the ratty tennis shoes who will be flipping flapjacks next week down at the Parish Hall is a billionaire several times over.

As summer approaches, this town becomes filled with summer people, most of whom are wealthy. There are plenty of run-of-the-mill auto company executives here, but Blue Harbor in summer is also home to many of America's most illustrious industrialists, their families, and descendents. The corporations that make such things as Coca-Cola, Bissell carpet cleaners, Packard motor cars, and Wrigley's gum have generated so much wealth that some of these summer people have not had to work for five generations, even though some of them still do.

What's interesting to see, though, is that the super-wealthy like Hal are not the ones driving the newest sports cars and wearing the latest designer clothes. They are usually the ones driving some old, yet immaculately maintained convertible VW Bug or — as in Hal's case — a 1970's Ford station wagon. Unlike some of the Four Fires Estate owners I've seen driving around my neighborhood in Cadillacs and Jaguars, the people with the big money — the old money — like to blend into the local population. Sure they may have several yachts, four other houses around the world, and a huge mansion-like cottage on Blue Harbor Point, but you wouldn't know it to look at them, and I think that's the way they like it.

Before any more black flies can get into Patty's house, Hal shoves off and I shut the screen door behind me. Patty is standing up at her sink (with her scooter behind her) washing used Zip-Lock plastic bags. In a land of Republicans, Patty is a die-hard Democrat and an environmentalist at heart. I saw her reusing her Zip-Locks like this last month, and I have tried to follow her example. She isn't just pinching pennies; she believes it's a tragedy to throw all that plastic away after only one use. I figure that if someone whose hands only move at about half speed can take the trouble to wash plastic bags, then an able-bodied young man like myself had better start reusing and recycling everything he can. My barn is already filled with some pretty good stacks of newspapers, plastic bottles, cans, and glass jars that I need to haul to the recycling center. Like Patty, my nooks and crannies are quickly filling up.

I take my usual seat on the dining room side of Patty's low-slung kitchen island. It's table height, which not only makes it great for guests to eat at, but is the ideal height for Patty to work at from her scooter. It's pretty amazing what she can do despite her limited mobility. Her kitchen leads out to a back deck that she recently had installed. The deck allows her to drive her scooter outside and over to her Subaru, where she can slip herself into the driver's seat. I often worry about how quickly she can react out on the road, but I see her driving around all the time like nobody's business. She's something else.

"You know, Nick, I was just thinking about you the other day."

"You must have been cleaning your closets out again. Did you run across a piece of brown lint that was kind of the color of my hair, and decide to keep it to remember me by?"

Patty turns her head to give me a quizzical sidelong glance. She gives me a fake scowl and then leans her head back and laughs till she has to wipe a half a tear from the corner of her eye with the back of her hand.

"Oh, you've got me down to a tee," she says. "That's the problem with writing a column. You just sit down and write the first thing that pops into your head, but that junk ends up coming back to bite you."

"It isn't junk, Patty, and nobody is biting. I loved your column. I'm exactly the same way; only I don't have much closet space to cram my stuff into before guests stop by. I've got boxes of Aunt Vicky's stuff spread all over my living room."

"Well, how is that going? Have you found any treasures in there yet?"

"Alas, Aunt Vicky must have spent the family fortune, but I am finding some pretty good stories..."

"That reminds me," Patty says as she eases back into her scooter and drives it over to join me at the kitchen counter. "My friend Gladys was showing me some of her old family pictures the other day, and she was telling me about the government boats that used to come into the harbor. It knocked some cobwebs out of some corner of my cluttered old brain.

"I remember sitting out at The Shack with your father one stormy summer afternoon. Your grandmother was making a pie... oh, I can still smell her apple pie... and the Colonel, who was sitting in front of the fireplace smoking his pipe started telling us about how he first came to Blue Harbor on the same old government boat."

"That's right," I blurt out. "That's what I have just been reading about in Aunt Vicky's old letters."

My grandparents' lives have mostly been unfolding to me through dusty old letters and photographs, and it's electrifying to hear a living person actually voice something about the Colonel and Anna out loud. I am so eager to connect the written word and silent photographs in my living room to Patty's warm-blooded recollection, however, that I rattle off everything I have learned about Joe's experiences with the U.S.S. *Michigan/Wolverine* and about Anna's life before meeting Joe.

Twenty minutes later, Patty — who has followed my narrative with heart-felt interjections of "amazing," "that's wonderful," and "incredible" — resumes her story.

"As I was saying, the Colonel told us the whole story of how he first met Anna. He told the entire story while rocking back and forth in that old wicker rocking chair. Do you still have that out there? He hardly even looked at us while he spoke, but kept staring into the fire. Your dad and I were sitting on the sofa trying to dry out from getting caught in the thunderstorm after fishing down in the creek. I don't remember the entire story, but I remember the unusual way your grandparents used to interact with each other. He always referred to her as "Mrs. Becker," unless he was speaking to her directly, then it was "dear" or "Anna" or "honey." And she always called him "The Colonel" when talking to others about him, but always "Joe" to his face.

"The Colonel had the warmest, most tender way of speaking about your grandmother in the story, but whenever he would come to a part in the story that he didn't remember so well or Anna thought was wrong, she would call out a correction from the kitchen. The Colonel found this most aggravating and sometimes they would stop to politely, yet firmly, squabble over some point in the story. Your dad and I started to get pretty uncomfortable during some of the arguments. But by the end of the story, the two younger versions of your grandparents in the story were very much in love, and even the older versions of the couple there in The Shack were smiling into each other's faces and holding hands. I didn't know them very well, but it was the only time I ever saw them show much affection towards each other."

Chapter 17

———

JOE SURVIVED THE winter of 1905-1906 in comfort and grace, living aboard the rechristened U.S.S. *Wolverine*. The *Wolverine* in winter was a sailor's delight. With Lake Erie locked in ice part of the time, the old iron-hulled fighting ship seldom left port. Officers and crew alike eased into a routine of regular hot meals, morning drills, daily cleanings and inspections, and plenty of free time for winter sports and shore leave in downtown Erie. The officers and a few, select members of the crew measured their days by the string of gala parties that local dignitaries threw for their naval guests. In turn, the Navy men threw parties for the local dignitaries.

Despite the efforts of Mrs. Morgan — the mayor's match-making wife — Joe managed to make it through the Christmas and New Year's balls, a handful of debutante dinner parties, the St. Valentine's dance, and the Spring Cotillion without getting engaged or otherwise tied down. Joe's picnic-basket rescue led to several party invitations. His duties as platoon clerk also required him to attend the rest of the season's parties, where his superiors loaned him out to check hats and coats or invitations at the door of some city councilmen's uptown mansion. While the long Pennsylvania winters may have been heaven for most of the old salts and leathernecks aboard the *Wolverine*, Joe was itching to get out of port.

I have only one photograph of Joe's time spent in Erie. A long, elegant dinner table set with silver is in the foreground. Behind the table, an equally elegantly dressed cluster of civilians and naval officers faces the camera with bright smiles and stiff, white collars. Off to the right side stands Joe holding a serving tray topped with champagne glasses. There are several pretty girls standing just in front of him, peering deeply into the camera. Joe's gaze, however, is elsewhere. He's looking off to the right at something that is, perhaps, outside a window. Joe shows only his handsome, maturing profile to the camera, but to me he looks like a man who is more eager to set sail, than to settle down. Little did he know that setting sail in the spring would actually bring him several steps closer to settling down.

Joe and Anna were born and raised only about 200 miles from each other as the crow flies, but it was the sea that brought them together — a vast fresh-water, inland sea of interconnected lakes bordered by more shoreline than either ocean coast of the Lower-48 United States. It's a sea that holds one-fifth of the planet's fresh surface water — the Great Lakes.

When Joe met Anna, the lakes were the highways of the Midwest. It's all turned around now with the ribbons of concrete and asphalt between cities defining what is remote and what is civilized for most people. At the opening of the 20th Century, though, the waterways were still the best way to get around, and Blue Harbor's deep-water basin was a regular port of call on the U.S.S. *Wolverine's* annual Great Lakes cruise.

Although Joe's travels had already taken him far from Wisconsin to the Western Prairies and over the Atlantic Ocean to Barbados, he had never been to the far shore of Lake Michigan — the big, blue water he was raised near. Joe was destined for more exotic shores later, but first he had to get to the Michigan side of his familiar Great Lake friend.

Joe didn't get to see much the first time he ever steamed into Blue Harbor at the start of the season in June 1906 because his duties kept him below deck in a closet that had recently been converted into the communications cabin to house the new wireless telegraphy equipment that the Navy had ordered for most ships in the fleet. Joe and an electrician's mate named Porter sat back-to-back in the cramped, stuffy compartment on two-hour watches two times a day. Porter was in charge of the wireless and adept at sending and reading Morse Code, but Joe had been assigned to record any incoming messages because Porter's ham-fisted penmanship was so bad that none of the officers could read it.

The only problem with this new duty was that the U.S.S. *Wolverine* was the only ship on the Great Lakes with a wireless. There were no other ships to communicate with, and the old, iron-hulled warship was hundreds of miles out of range from any shore station that had one of the new wireless sets. Commander Henry Morrell insisted on maintaining round-the-clock "wireless watches" over the airwaves, however, in case of unforeseen emergencies and to train his men for future duties in which such technologies would become commonplace.

To relieve the monotony of this duty, Joe and Electrician's Mate Porter spent the hours reading, smoking, and playing Tic-Tac-Toe with a big piece of chalk that Joe found on the sidewalk while on leave in Sault St. Marie. They weren't allowed to waste paper on games and the chalk could be wiped off the cabin walls with a quick sweep of an arm before any officer could stick his head into the communications cabin.

By the time Joe's "wireless watch" ended, the *Wolverine* had already weighed anchor a few hundred yards off the city's main pier and most of the crew had been shuttled to shore for a pre-arranged baseball game with a local team comprising resorters and shop owners. While many of the larger towns along the *Wolverine's* annual route welcomed the government boat, the Navy maintained an uneasy relationship with the town fathers of Blue Harbor. The Navy's annual summer visits were too short for the sailors and marines to establish the kind of relationship with the town fathers of Blue Harbor that they enjoyed in Erie, but these visits were long enough that some members of the crew found time to enjoy some of the town daughters.

It was one thing for crewmembers to get to know the waterfront women who frequented the hotel bars and pool halls or the untamed Indian girls who no longer lived under the watchful eyes of Holy Childhood nuns. But it was quite another thing when both the daughter of the town's newspaper editor and the daughter of a prominent Blue Harbor Point resorter bore children nine months after the last visit by the *Wolverine*. The newspaper editor's daughter eloped with her sailor husband and moved to Newport, Rhode Island, but the summer resort girl was not seen again for several summers until she returned with two young children and her husband, a balding middle-aged vice president in her father's corporation. Few spoke openly about such things, but everyone knew why the summer resort girl's oldest son looked nothing like his father, but the younger son did. The mayor and town council had launched a letter-writing campaign to the Navy Department to re-route the government boat to a pier across the bay along Petoskey's growing waterfront. In the meantime, the town leaders as well as the officers of the *Wolverine* tried to keep the young crew fully occupied with an exhausting program of events including parades, band concerts, an Indian exhibition, and fireworks displays. The officers refused to deny shore leave to the crew, so the town leaders did their best to keep the sailors and marines engaged in structured activities where they could be carefully watched.

Other than the usual admonitions for the crew to behave in a manner befitting the uniform while ashore, Joe knew very little about all this as he climbed topside to breath fresh air and to brush the chalk dust from the sleeve of his uniform. The bright, June sunlight hurt Joe's eyes after a few hours below deck in the dim electric light. The wooden planks of the main deck were still wet in spots from a thorough scrubbing down, all lines were neatly coiled and stowed, and the afternoon's laundry was flying high overhead drying on the halyards of the main mast like crepe-paper streamers hung for some patriotic festival of blue and white. But there wasn't a seaman or leatherneck in sight, so Joe pulled out his pipe and walked to the rail for a good look around.

The ship lay at anchor in the middle of the harbor with its bow pointing due west — from what Joe could tell by the angle of the sun. From the port side, just aft of the rounded paddle-wheel housing, Joe looked across the flat water to a line of trees dotted with docks and cottages. This line stretched off to the east and narrowed to a sandy point that dived almost straight down into the deep, dark waters. Through the line of trees, Joe caught glimpses of more water behind the cedars, pines, and cottages. Joe figured this must be the Blue Harbor Point resort that Porter had told him about. A row of five matching sailboats were moored near the shore, along with others of varied size and shape. He could see three little boys lying on their stomachs at the end of a dock, heads peering down into the clear, clear water. Two of the boys held sticks with strings tied to the ends of the sticks. They didn't actually appear to be fishing, and Joe wondered what they were up to. The light breeze and still water carried their voices out to Joe, and he realized from the snatches of excited chatter that they were after crayfish, just as Joe and his chum Carlton used to do with chicken gizzards back in Ft. Atkinson. Joe and Carlton used to tie a gizzard to the end of a weighted string and let the morsel sit on the river bottom until a crayfish crawled up to it and grabbed the gizzard with a claw. The crayfish were so intent on eating that they usually wouldn't let go and could be hauled straight up to shore. While Joe was too far away from Blue Harbor Point to see much more than a reddish-brown dot at the end of the string, he knew exactly what the boys on shore were up to when they pulled something up from the water and onto the dock. Joe laughed out loud as he saw the boys dancing around the dock trying to grab the crayfish and toss it into a bucket without getting their fingers or bare toes pinched by powerful little claws that didn't like to let go once they got hold of something.

This scene seemed a lot different from the Blue Harbor Point that Porter had described. A couple of years ago, Porter had been repeatedly rebuffed by a succession of pretty society girls from the resort who he had tried to get to know by sneaking hooch into a Methodist Ladies' Auxiliary picnic on the beach at Zorn Park. Porter concluded that the girls at the picnic and, hence, "all these God-damned, rich-ass resorters were a bunch of frigid snobs." But from Joe's first look at the three boys who were probably sons of wealth, he didn't see how they were all that different from the people he grew up with.

"What ya' laughing at, Becker," came a brogue-ish voice from behind Joe. Joe turned to find Seaman Murphy strutting towards him. Murphy had drawn deck watch instead of shore leave and was making his rounds up and down the port rails until the rest of the crew returned from the baseball game.

"Just some boys trying to keep their toes from getting pinched off by crayfish."

Murphy squinted towards shore, but shook his head.

"Your eyes must be a damned sight better then mine," Murphy said. "I can make out two or three blurs, but I sure can't see any cursed crawdaddies from here. Listen, your pal Roger told me to tell 'ya to meet him over to Zorn Park after the game. The Methodist Ladies' Auxiliary is throwing some dinner picnic, and Roger gots some skirt he wants you to meet."

"I've never been here before ," Joe said, "how do I find the place?"

"Ach, you can see it from here, lad. Come over to starboard and I'll point it out for ya." Murphy said, grabbing Joe by the arm and leading him across the deck to where the town of Blue Harbor lay stretched out along a couple miles of shoreline on the north side of a horseshoe-shaped harbor that opened into Little Traverse Bay a half mile beyond the *Wolverine's* stern.

Joe's eyes followed the sailor's white-sleeved arm and ruddy finger out across the water to a bustling intersection of gravel and sand streets, dark-canopied carriages, telephone poles, and clusters of meandering summer resorters in wide-brimmed hats and suits.

"That's the corner of Bay and State streets over there. Bay runs along the water, for obvious reasons, and State heads up into the main part of town before it jogs left over there and cuts up the side of the bluff. Do ya see where I'm talking about? Zorn Park is that open, grassy area just up from Bay and State and in front of Holy Childhood."

Joe followed each sweep and jab of Murphy's finger while taking in the rest of the town. The main part of the town was tucked between the harbor and a steep, brushy bluff with a long staircase running straight up to its summit. The downtown was only two or three blocks deep, but a mile or so long. There was a two-story, brick hotel on the northwest corner of the Bay and State intersection, and a sprawling complex of attached white buildings connected to a wooden church with a high steeple farther off to Joe's left, just beyond the park. A railroad station with broad, sweeping eaves sat next to a set of tracks between the shore and the brick hotel. A hodge-podge of storefronts, warehouses, boat liveries, and homes sat all along the rest of the waterfront. Right in front of Joe, a long dock stretched out into the harbor flanked by passenger vessels. On one side of the dock lay a hulking steamship that Joe identified as the *Manitou* from the white letters painted on its black prow. The *Manitou* was easily three times the size of the *Wolverine* and hundreds of passengers were debarking in their finest summer travel clothes. Two smaller, double-decked ferries called the *Thomas Friant* and the *Gracie Barker* were docked on the other side of the pier with smokestacks puffing.

"Thanks for the tour, Murph," Joe said.

"'Murph' now, is it?" the old salt said, giving Joe a crisp rap on the shoulder with his white nightstick as Joe started to walk away. "Is that any way for a young whelp of a jarhead to address his betters, eh? Is that what they teach you lousy leathernecks at the Philly Navy Yard these days? Don't you know how to talk to a gallant man-o'-wars-man who has served aboard Dewey's own flagship in Manila Bay?"

Joe knew that everyone called him Murph, but he wasn't entirely sure whether the veteran sailor was truly offended by such informality or not. Joe was pretty sure that Murph was just pulling his leg, but he turned around and faced him squarely anyways.

"Yes, Seaman Murphy. I do know how to address my betters, Seaman Murphy, and will do so if I happen to come across any," Joe said with a straight face.

"That's more like it, Private Josie Becker, now get your kit together down below and shove off or I'll be takin' your shore leave for ya." Murphy grinned.

———

Joe and Anna didn't fall in love at first sight, but by the second look, Joe, at least, was sold. Anna wasn't the girl that Roger wanted Joe to meet — that girl turned out to be the red-headed, freckled friend of a girl Roger was interested in. Joe dutifully stuck with his friend and the redhead for the picnic dinner, but the redhead and her friend wanted ice cream and sent Joe to fetch some. Joe discovered a handsome, young woman with a white bow in her hair who was dishing out ice cream that had been wheeled over to the park from a place called LaFontain's Ice Cream Parlor, just up the street from the Bay and State Street intersection. The young lady with the bow in her hair was scooping ice cream from several buckets packed in ice on a small handcart. The handcart proclaimed that LaFontain's offered "the finest hand-made ice cream since 1895 and the first soda fountain in Northern Michigan." Even the older women of the Auxiliary who were working at the picnic seemed to defer to this younger woman, and Joe was impressed with her graceful sense of command. Even the two stylish, middle-aged women standing in line in front of Joe and apparently whispering about this same young lady had good things to say about her — something about how well she handled herself as Toastmaster at last weekend's Alumni Banquet.

"Mrs. Shay, you are doing a lovely job with the chicken sandwiches. After they are gone, though, be a dear and help Mrs. Sipple over at the pie table," the young woman in the bow said to a matronly Methodist lady with a tray full of sandwiches in her hand.

"I'd be delighted to, Anna, everything seems to be going swimmingly," the woman said as she disappeared into the crowd.

"Two chocolate ice creams, please," was all that Joe managed to say, at first. But in his head he kept saying the name he had just heard over and over again so that he wouldn't forget it. "Anna, Anna, Anna ..."

Another Methodist lady appeared and peppered Anna with questions about the lemonade and there were several people in line behind him, so Joe procured two bowls for the redhead and her friend and vowed to return later to get some for Roger and himself.

By the time Joe returned, the ice cream crowd had dispersed and Joe and Anna found themselves alone on the edge of the park filled with picnickers.

"Hello, Anna, my name is Joe — Joe Becker."

Anna looked up from the cart to see a tall, young man smiling at her. He stood straight with his hands clasped behind his back. His jaw was strong, but his closely shaven face looked soft to the touch. Although he looked confident under his blue, leather-billed marine cap and eagle-anchor-globe insignia, Anna detected no audacity in his light-brown eyes — only a friendly openness.

"Do I know you?" Anna asked, dipping her chocolate-ice-cream-covered hands into a puddle of icy water at the bottom of the cart.

"Not yet, but I would like the pleasure of making your acquaintance."

Anna wiped her cool, wet hands on the white apron she was wearing and reached one of them out to Joe.

"I'm Anna Johnson. It's a pleasure to meet you, Mr. Joe Becker."

Joe and Anna lingered over the melting ice cream for a short while chatting easily. Anna was interested in hearing about the places Joe had been. But just as Joe was getting to know this competent and striking, young woman, he was pulled aside by Sgt. Olafson. Shore leave was cut short.

Chapter 18

SEVERAL DAYS PASSED by after Joe's first meeting of Anna, which he carefully noted in his pocket notepad with a star next to the date of Monday, June 18, 1906. It was Thursday, June 21st before Joe got the chance to have any free time on shore again, but when he did, he had a strong hankering for ice cream.

From under the canopied awning of LaFontain's Ice Cream Parlor, Joe could see that the place was packed. He had to wait a few minutes for people to come out before he could get in. Each time the glass door opened, the din of clanking plates and the tingle of spoons digging to the bottom of glass parfaits spilled out into the street.

Over the cheerful clatter of chattering resorters and raucous sailors and marines, Joe heard a sweet, smooth voice. It was her voice again — the girl who had been asking him about New York at the picnic that first evening in Blue Harbor.

What was her name again, Joe thought to himself. Ann? Annette? No, it was Anna. That was her name, he remembered, as he found himself walking toward that delightful sound.

Ducking under fast-moving trays that would not otherwise clear his 6-foot, 2-inch stature; dodging a chair shoved from a table by the fitful child of a soap magnate; and weaving through a cluster of sundae-swilling shipmates, Joe made his way towards her without taking his eyes off of her. He could see her face reflected in the mirror behind the soda fountain. What was it about her, Joe wondered. She was pretty, but she wasn't even the prettiest woman in the store. Anna's fair-haired companion was easily attracting more attention from Joe's shipmates and the other men in the room. Anna's nose even seemed a bit crooked, Joe noticed. But Anna's beauty was better suited to Joe than that of many other young women Joe had met. Her green eyes held an intelligence that Joe had not seen in a long time. Her straight line of a mouth and square-ish face were plain, but when she smiled and laughed with her friend, her face radiated a quiet warmth that pulled Joe closer. While many girls had set their eyes on Joe with the idea of settling down, here was a woman that Joe could see was strong enough and competent enough to come with him on the journeys he had in mind for himself.

Joe slowed as he neared the long marble-topped counter. Anna's voice was occupied in a serious discussion with the fair-haired, young woman at her side on the challenges of playing a Schubert piano solo for an upcoming recital. Anna's back was turned to Joe. He leaned against the counter politely waiting for a pause in the girls' conversation, but he couldn't take his eyes off Anna's light brown hair, which was tied into a single loose bun with a big white bow.

Joe had to restrain himself from reaching out to touch her hair. There were so many different colors in her ringlets — sun-streaked highlights, auburn locks, and dark brown wisps, which had freed themselves from the bun and dangled lightly across the back of her white neck.

As he stood there listening and looking, his mind and heart reached out to her in a way he had never experienced before. Although he barely knew her, he yearned to be part of her memories and for her to be part of his. He envied the school-mates who had grown up with her in this town, even her family — though he hadn't yet met them. He wanted to see her as a little girl skating across the smooth harbor while the dock-workers cut ice blocks to store for the summer. He wanted to see her first piano recital at the spring pageant. He wanted for her to feel the first warm Caribbean breeze that he had felt aboard the *Hartford*. And he wanted her to have seen the sun setting over the Cherokee hunting party, just as he had seen it in Oklahoma two years ago.

Before she even knew his name, he wanted to be able to laugh with her about how difficult that Schubert recital had been, and to hold her wrinkled old hand in front of the fireplace while reading a Christmas card from their grandchildren.

Anna's companion, Leslie Higginbotham, noticed the tall marine in his undress blue jacket and cap and khaki pants leaning against the counter. Leslie's eyes alerted Anna to Joe's presence, and Anna turned around to the sun-browned face she had seen before.

"Do I know you, young man?" Anna said with her chin held high to look up into Joe's eyes.

"Surely you remember me from the picnic last Monday," Joe said. "I'm Joe Becker. Remember, we talked about your upcoming trip to New York? I've been carrying around the arts section of the New York Post all day hoping I would run into you again. We get all the major newspapers on board. It's a couple days old, but I thought you would enjoy reading about the concerts."

Anna's sharp eyes softened when she realized Joe had been paying attention to her that day at the park. She had, of course, recognized Joe instantly when she turned to him, but she was still a bit peeved that he had vanished just as she had asked him about his last trip through New York. Anna hadn't recognized the sergeant's stripes on Olafson's shoulders, and she had thought Joe a bit rude for cutting her off in mid-sentence when Olafson had whispered something into Joe's ear.

"I must apologize for my hasty departure the other day," Joe explained. "While at the picnic, Sgt. Olafson noticed a sailor there who was supposed to be on duty aboard the *Wolverine*. We had to round him up and get him back on deck before any officers noticed his absence. I tried to get back as soon as I could, but that jack gave us the slip and we spent an hour chasing him along the docks before we got him on board. By then, shore leave was over and I haven't had leave until just now. For some strange reason, the first thing I wanted to do once I got ashore was to get that scoop of ice cream you never got the chance to give me. What a nice surprise to not only get another chance at that scoop, but to run into you, as well."

Anna's displeasure with the handsome, sandy-haired marine had melted the moment he pulled out the Post. She smiled up at him as she asked Joe to join her and Leslie for an ice cream.

Joe procured a table for the threesome and managed to get in three bites of his Velvet Parfait when a sailor's voice, reaching above the noisy crowd, yelled, "Fire! Everyone get out!"

Joe jumped to his feet and began clearing a path for Anna and Leslie, but two of Joe's marine buddies grabbed him by both arms and hauled him out of LaFontain's before Joe had a chance to help the two young women out of the "burning" building. They didn't stop dragging him until they were across the street and behind an alley.

"What the hell are you doing? There are civilians back there who need help," Joe said as he angrily shook himself free of Roger and Gilbert's tight grip.

As Joe turned to run back to the restaurant, his two buddies bent over laughing. Their odd behavior was enough to stop Joe from racing back.

"What is wrong with you two? What's so damn funny?"

"Wait, Joe, wait," Roger managed to say between guffaws. "There's no fire. It's just — It's just a little *Wolverine* tradition."

"No fire?" Joe said as his shoulders and jaw slumped.

"Every year… " Roger struggled to gain his breath, "… we all pile into that place and spoon down a gut load of ice cream. Then some sailor yells 'fire' and we all run out."

"What's so damn funny about that?"

"Well, did you get any ice cream?" Roger asked with a smirk on his face.

"Yeah, a few bites."

"And did you have to pay for it?"

"Well, no."

"None of us ever do. That's the tradition. We call it the old fire-and-ice gag," Roger said as Joe's anger turned to a broad grin.

"I'll be damned," Joe said. Then he shook his head and smacked Roger on the back of the head.

"Hey, what was that for," Roger complained.

"You idiots may have conned a few free sundaes out of old Mrs. LaFontain, but you may have lost me something far more valuable," Joe said as he turned back down the alley towards the ice cream parlor.

"Where you going, Joe?" Gilbert said.

"To find a girl I've already lost track of twice this week."

"You can't go back there," Gilbert said. "Those waiters and the police officers will be looking to take the tab for all those scoops out of the first uniformed hide they come across. We're going to hop on the dummy train and head to a beach out past the Ramona Park Hotel. You better stay away from downtown till things quiet down."

Joe made an about-face and walked out the other end of the alley, leaving his pals behind.

Chapter 19

"FIRST THINGS, FIRST," Joe said to himself, jingling the coins in his pocket.

Joe heeded his friend's advice up to a point and stopped himself from heading straight back to the ice cream parlor. Instead, he circled around the backside of the block until he re-emerged on the sidewalk at the west end of Main Street — a full block up from the waterfront and a half a block up from the ice cream parlor, which he planned to steer clear of for a while.

Joe kept in the shadow of a tasseled canvas awning that gave shelter to a small storefront that identified itself as Swenson's Souvenir Shop. Through the glass, Joe could see that the small store was crammed with all manner of tourist knick-knacks. There was a short barrel filled with toy wooden tomahawks, several stands with picture postcards of the town and harbor, a model railroad set of the narrow-gauge train that Joe had seen climbing the hill out of town from his ship, and a glass case of polished stones unlike anything Joe had ever seen before. A label in the case identified the fossil-filled rocks as "Petoskey Stones." The tiny round fossils, rich browns and grays, and smooth finish reminded Joe of a freshly caught brown trout right out of the old Rock River back in Wisconsin.

Joe didn't have window-shopping in mind, though, and he took a good look around to get his bearings. The high-steepled, catholic church in a new coat of white paint with light-gray trim was just off Joe's left, and Joe realized — from his vantage point and the postcards in the window — that all of Main Street was lined up to frame the front face of Holy Childhood Church.

Main Street itself stretched out before him like a rifle shot — straight and long. Even from the wood-planked sidewalk, Joe could see straight down the wide, flat, packed-dirt main drag of Blue Harbor, along the clapboard false-fronts of downtown stores, through a tree-lined residential section, and on up to the base of East Hill, where the rutted road angled up the bluff on its way towards more summer resorts and inland farms. Long wooden signs, held in place with wire cables jutted out into the broad street and declared open season on the wallets and purses of both resorters and locals, alike. Two hardware stores on opposite sides of the street battled for attention with opposing signs that had the largest lettering in the entire town. The hardware store on the shaded, south side of the street seemed to have a leg up, though, with four-foot-high letters painted on its second-story facade, in addition to the sign hanging out over the sidewalk. "DRUGS," "DRY GOODS," two stores offering "GROCERIES," and a host of other businesses lined both sides of the street, but there was no sign of Anna.

The streets and sidewalks were neither so busy that Joe could simply disappear into the crowd, nor were they so empty that he risked drawing immediate attention to himself if the LaFontain's waiters or the local policemen were still on the warpath. Joe did not want a bunch of angry townspeople on his tail as he searched for Anna, but he did want to make amends for some of the damage his pals had done to his reputation before he found her once again. This fine, young woman — who clearly must have been friends with the LaFontains considering her earlier picnic duties — probably thought Joe was a complete scoundrel. She probably wouldn't want anything to do with him now, but he figured he could at least try to set the record straight. A straight-on charge back to the ice cream parlor was out of the question, but Joe thought he could regain some of his lost honor with a flanking maneuver. All he needed was the right scout for the mission.

Just then, a young boy, wearing a light wool suit with knee britches stepped out of Swenson's with a toy tomahawk in his hand and a straw hat on his head that was as big as a sombrero. He looked up and down the street, as if searching for his parents or an older sibling. There was something almost girlish about the cherubic face framed by a light-brown, pageboy haircut, but Joe noticed a fierce determination in the little boy's eyes. Not finding who he was looking for, the boy dutifully sat down on the shaded bench in front of the souvenir shop. Joe watched the boy slaughter imaginary white settlers with his newly acquired tomahawk for a moment until the boy looked up and noticed the tall, uniformed stranger.

The boy immediately jumped to attention and saluted. Joe returned the salute and stepped toward the boy.

"At ease, Little Chief," Joe said.

"Are you a real Army man, mister?"

"Actually, son, I'm in the United States Marine Corps. What tribe are you in?"

"I'm not really an Indian, I was just playing. I'm Ernie. I'm going to be seven in one month. What's your name?"

"Private Joseph Becker, at your service."

"Golly, I've never met a marine man before. What does a marine do?"

"Well, it depends on the situation," Joe said, taking a seat on the bench. "Mostly, we're the ones they send in when there is trouble on foreign shores. We're usually the landing forces for the Navy when we have to fight in far-away places like The Philippines, Cuba, Nicaragua, or Panama."

"That sounds great. I want join up and travel around as soon as I'm old enough. Who are you fighting here, though? This isn't very far away. We just came up from Chicago on a big boat, and we just left last night," Ernie said as he climbed back up on the bench next to Joe.

"We aren't fighting anybody at this exact moment," Joe said. "I'm serving aboard that big white government boat out in the harbor. Maybe you saw it when you came in?"

The boy's face scrunched up in disbelief. "That white thing with three masts and big water mills on the side? That's a navy boat? The one with all the underwear and britches hanging from the lines?"

"That's the one."

"Are you joshin' me? My sister Marcy said that was a laundry boat."

Joe slapped his knee and chuckled. "Well, Ernie, I've never heard that one before. Just don't let the captain hear you say that or he'll have you scrubbing the decks with a toothbrush for a week. The *Wolverine* may have been around since before the Civil War, but she's still one of the fastest ships in the Great Lakes."

"I bettcha' I've seen faster. My daddy's a doctor and he told me that Mr. McCormick has a new gasoline-engine yacht that is faster than any boat on Lake Michigan."

"Well, that may be so, but I bet it doesn't have an eighteen-pound cannon."

"Gee, it has a real cannon? Boy, would I like to see that."

"Well, I'll tell you what, Ernie. If you come down to the pier on Saturday, you can get a free tour of the whole ship."

"Saturday? Oh, rats! On Saturday I'll be at our cottage on Bear Lake. My folks are just hanging around town for a couple of hours visiting some friends before we catch the train to

Petoskey. Then we have to take another train to Bear Lake, and then a boat up to our place. Mama doesn't ever want to go anywhere once we get to the cottage."

"That's too bad," Joe said reaching into his pocket for change. "How would you like to go on a little scouting mission for the Marine Corps, instead? I could probably make you an honorary marine for about ten minutes if you took the oath."

"Yeah, I'll do it. Daddy says I'm a born sharpshooter. I already know how to handle a pistol and a rifle. Plus, I have my own 20-gauge shotgun. Daddy only lets me have three cartridges a day, and I almost always come home with three squirrels."

"That might come in handy, but there probably won't be any need for shooting on this mission. For this mission, you have to be discreet — kinda quiet like an Indian in the woods."

"Oh, I can do that. I know lots of Indians. There's an Indian camp about a mile behind our cottage. We go huntin' and fishin' with 'em all the time."

Joe held up his right hand. "Raise your right hand and repeat after me. I, Ernie, swear to uphold the honor of the United States Marine Corps..."

"I, Ernie, swear to uphold... what was the rest of it?"

"... the honor of the United States Marine Corps..."

"... the honor of the United States Marine Corps..."

"... for the next ten minutes or until I complete my assignment."

"... for the next ten minutes or until I complete my assignment."

"Excellent. Now here's your assignment. Do you know where LaFontain's Ice Cream Parlor is — just around the corner?"

"Yep," Ernie said, nodding somberly.

"Take this silver dollar to Mrs. LaFontain and tell her it's to pay the tab of any marines who might have accidentally left without paying. And also, it's to pay for the ice cream of Miss Anna Johnson and her friend. Be sure to ask Mrs. LaFontain if Anna Johnson is still there. If she is, tell Miss Johnson that I send the money with my compliments. Do you think you can remember all of that?"

Joe made Ernie go over the message a couple of times just to make sure. Ernie shoved the dollar in his pocket and started to head for the corner.

"One more thing, Ernie. Tell Mrs. LaFontain to give you a dime out of that for your troubles and head straight back here, but make sure nobody follows you."

"Yes, sir," Ernie said, snapping a salute and disappearing around the corner.

Joe sat in the shade of the awning and closed his eyes for a moment, just listening to the sounds of the bustling resort town. A high blast of a whistle from down by the water signaled that the dummy train was backing into town. Joe could hear the rumble and clank of the passenger cars pulling up to the depot ahead of the locomotive, which was still a couple of blocks away. Blue Harbor was the end of the line, and Joe figured that they must call it the "dummy" train because it always pulls into town backwards. Even if his eyes were open, Joe wouldn't be able to see the train from where he was sitting, but he realized that there mustn't be any siding to turn the train around on, so it must simply back its way around the bay from Petoskey. It only goes forward on the return trip from Blue Harbor back to Petoskey, Joe guessed.

Overhead, seagulls cried back and forth to each other as if negotiating over some crayfish just plucked from the shallows. Horses clomped through the streets pulling creaking wagons, and pedestrians called out to friends they met along the sidewalks. The church bell rang out two o'clock from the

Holy Childhood steeple. Joe smiled as he pictured Roger and Gilbert trying to stay out of sight down at the depot for a half an hour until the train left for Menonaqua Beach and points beyond.

Joe opened his eyes and was surprised to find a young girl standing right in front of him. She wore a white frock with a blue and white-stripped kerchief tied loosely around her neck like a little sailor.

"Excuse me, sir. Have you seen a little boy with a big straw hat?" The young girl — though slightly taller and with shoulder-length brown hair — could have been young Ernie's twin.

"You must be Marcy," Joe said. "I bet your looking for Ernie."

"How did you know?" Marcy said, cocking her head to the side slightly.

"Ernie and I just had a nice chat. I sent him on a quick errand and he should be back in a minute or two."

"That little dickens is gonna get me in big trouble if he doesn't get back here right away. I told Mama I would stay with him, but he's always running off on his own. Mama said that as soon as the bell struck two o'clock we were to head back to those people's house over there. Just 'cuz Mama used to dress us up like twins, Ernie always thinks he's as old as me, but I'm eight and a half years old, and he's still six."

"Well how far away is that house?"

"It's just a few blocks away on Third Street. Mama made me remember the man's name — Mr. James Johnson."

"Johnson? Your folks are visiting the Johnsons?"

"Well, sort of." Marcy shrugged. "Mama's friends — Mr. and Mrs. Ralph Connable — from Petoskey came over to meet us on the steamer. And then, we had to go meet some of their old friends from Toronto — the Johnsons — who live here in Blue Harbor. Daddy said Toronto is in Canada, but that's southeast of here. It's all very confusing to me, but they seem pretty nice for grown-ups."

"Do they have a grown daughter named Anna?"

"I don't know. They have a nice dog named Taffy, though. He's a Welsh terrier," Marcy said, looking over her shoulder anxiously. "Look, mister, I would love to stay and talk, but I've got to find Ernie and get back to the Johnsons or Mama will be very cross with me. Mama said ..."

"Just a minute, Marcy, I've got an idea." This little girl was his best lead on Anna, and he wasn't about to let her skip away. The train didn't leave for another half an hour, anyway. "I wouldn't want you to get in trouble on my account, but why don't you wait here with me for a minute or two until Ernie gets back. And then, you can show me to the Johnson house and I will be happy to explain what kept you. Don't worry, I won't let you miss your train."

Marcy squinted one eye at Joe, as if lining up her sights on him to take full measure of this stranger. She scratched her chin and then put both hands on her hips.

"Mama said not to talk to strangers ... but since you already know Ernie, I guess it would be all right," Marcy said shifting her hips to show that she meant business. "Hey, since you already know my name, all you have to do is tell me your name and you've got a deal."

"Private Joe Becker, glad to make your acquaintance."

"Marcelline Hemingway, delighted to meet you."

Marcy held out her hand and Joe gave it a gentle shake.

The marine and the girl in the sailor dress sat on the bench for a few moments sharing where they were from and how they came to be in this pleasant little town. Marcy liked how Joe didn't talk to her in a baby voice like most adults used when they talked to her. Marcy wanted to be a great artist like her mother when she grew up.

Before Joe could say what he wanted to be when he grew up, Ernie ran around the corner with one hand on his head to keep the big straw hat from blowing off. He was going so fast that he almost ended up in Marcy's lap when he stopped in front of the bench.

"Quick, Private Joe, we better get out of here," Ernie said, puffing between each word. "I paid for the ice cream and got the dime, but Mrs. LaFontain said Anna Johnson had just left. Then, some police officer came in asking about marines and sailors, but I took off running before he got a chance to talk to me. He might be coming around the corner any minute. Oh, hiya Marcy, let's get outta here."

Ernie grabbed Joe by one hand and Marcy by the other, pulling them straight across the street at a trot. There was an alley there between the Parish Hall and a feed store. Before ducking into the alley, Marcy put on the brakes.

"Hold it, Ernie, where are you going?"

"Back to the Johnson's house like Mama said, didn't you hear the church bell strike two o'clock? That was almost ten minutes ago," Ernie said, still tugging on Marcy's unyielding arm. "Third Street is right up ahead at the other end of the alley."

"Oh, I see it," Marcy said, un-digging her heels from the mixture of sand, spilled oats, and strewn hay that filled the alley.

Before Ernie could pull Joe out of sight of Main Street, Joe took one look over his shoulder to make sure nobody was after him and his pint-sized accomplices. Instead of hostile waiters or police officers, however, Joe caught a glimpse of a big, white bow tied up in the light-brown hair he had only recently been studying. Anna and her friend were walking down Main Street in the shade of the hardware store with tall lettering, away from Swenson's Souvenir Shop and Lightfoot's Feed Store.

Joe stopped in his tracks and almost pulled Ernie off his feet without realizing it. Joe felt the tug at his arm and looked down on Ernie and Marcy, who were looking up at him with a matched set of one-eyed-squinting, confused expressions. Joe looked back up Main Street to see Anna's lovely head disappear into a crowd of tweed-capped gentlemen. He knew what he had to do and hoped that doing the right thing would work out for all.

"Come on, Joe, we gotta scram," Ernie said.

"Yeah, Joe, Ernie knows the way. He never gets lost."

"Sorry, kids, I just thought I saw someone I know," Joe said disappearing behind the feed store.

Ernie stopped dragging his new friend and sister behind him, and pulled his tomahawk out of his back pocket to lead them the rest of the way. He made them hide behind a rain barrel for a minute or two before leaving the alley to make a right down Third Street, which ran along the bottom of the long bluff. Ernie stopped to pick off unwary pedestrians with his imaginary rifle and ducked into the bushes a couple of times until an angry mastiff scared the wits out of the boy and startled his companions before it reached the end of its chain and pulled up short about a muzzle-length short of Ernie's knickers.

Joe held the children's hands as they intersected the cross streets on their way down Third Street. First, they crossed State Street, which angled off to the left, traversing the face of the bluff. Then, came Spring Street, which ended at the foot of the bluff. It was quiet along this part of Third Street, which was lined with houses and young elm trees that were only beginning to provide much shade. To their left, the tidy wooden houses at the foot of the bluff faced the downtown and the harbor beyond. The gardens and privies behind these houses backed right up to the steep bluff, which had been clear-cut some years ago, but was beginning to sprout saplings, juniper bushes, and vines.

Where Spring Street ended as a gravelly path at the bottom of the bluff, the wooden staircase that Joe had seen from the ship climbed straight uphill, offering only small landings for the weary who tried to climb it. An elderly gentleman in a bowler and black suit stood about half way up the stairs without moving — except for his shoulders, which rose and fell as he struggled to catch his breath. A rough, wooden sign at the foot of the stairs provided a fitting name and warning for the steps — "Jacob's Ladder: Not for the faint of heart!"

Just then, Ernie and Marcy caught sight of their parents backing down the front steps of a neatly clapboarded light green house two doors down from Jacob's Ladder. The parents and another couple were waving goodbyes to a third couple almost hidden in the shadows of a cool porch, which wrapped around the front and two sides of the house.

A buxom woman with a pleasant, round face spotted Ernie and Marcy and called out to them. "Come along, children, we don't want to be late for the train."

"Coming, Mama," Marcy said, running off before remembering Joe and turning back. "Thank you, Mr. Becker. I'm sure we will be all right. Mama doesn't sound upset."

Ernie, still holding Joe's hand, looked up and thanked him for the dime. "If you ever need me for any other missions, you can always get a hold of me at Windemere Cottage on Bear Lake. Some people call it Walloon Lake. Anyway, we're there all summer. See ya around." And with that, Ernie ran down the sidewalk to join his family and their friends, who were already hurrying across the street and back to the train station. Joe waved to them as they passed by, and Marcy's mother — who was undoubtedly getting a full account of the man in uniform from her daughter — waved back. A tall man in a dark beard, carrying what looked to be a physician's satchel, looked Joe in the eye and tipped his hat. Ernie was excitedly showing his father his new tomahawk. They still had 15 minutes to get to the train, according to Joe's watch.

In the brief moment following the farewells of Joe's young friends, Joe found himself somewhat adrift in the quiet neighborhood. The couple on the shady porch — presumably Anna's parents — had disappeared back into the house. Joe walked toward Anna's porch hoping to catch someone's attention inside, but found only a faint stirring of dishwashing coming out of the house. He turned around and started back the way he came, only to turn around again and return to the house. Surely no harm could come of waiting on the sidewalk for a few moments? There was even a low, concrete embankment separating the Johnson's yard from the new concrete walkway. Joe sat for a while. It was peaceful there.

Joe was lost in thought when a small dog ran right up to him from the yard and barked in his face — not with a fierce growl, but with a welcoming yap. The small terrier was dark-caramel colored with a black saddle-shaped patch on its back. Its bearded face was low to the ground and its cropped stump of a tail was wagging feverishly as it bounced around Joe. In a second, it dashed off and returned with a rag ball, which it dropped at Joe's side near the edge of the concrete embankment.

"You must be Taffy," Joe said, and the dog turned in circles at the mention of his name. Joe tossed the ball across the yard, and the dog whipped out to fetch it like a bolt of lightening. Joe, grateful for the company (especially that of a creature close to Anna), rose to his feet on the sidewalk — being careful not to trespass on the Johnson's yard — and tossed the ball over and over again. In the warm, late-afternoon sunshine, Joe took off his hat and wool blouse, setting them on the concrete wall while he rolled up the white sleeves of his shirt. He ran his thumbs under the navy-blue suspenders and gave them a snap to knock some of the sweat off his damp back. He felt sort of like that little dog did, "I could keep doing this all day long." He lost track of time.

And this is how Anna saw Joe for the third time. Years later, Anna claimed to have no recollection of the first two times she met Joe, despite Joe's numerous retellings of the story. It may have been the third time she met him, but for Anna the sight of the young marine playing fetch with her dog in her own front yard was the first time she really saw the man she would marry.

———

"That's it?" I say, slapping the Formica of Patty's kitchen counter. "What did they say to each other? How did they manage to stay in touch with each other over all those years? What was it that made them fall in love? That's all Joe told you?"

"You know, Nick, isn't it funny the things that people remember when they get older and the things that they forget?" Patty says with her hands folded in her lap, sitting quietly in her scooter. "I'll be lucky if I even remember my own name when I get to be their age."

"That must have been in the late '40s when your grandfather told your dad and me that story... oh, my gosh! I practically *am* their age," Patty says lightly smacking her cheek with her Milton Burle-esque deadpan. "No wonder I can't even remember where I left my tennis shoes."

"That's quite a story, Patty, you must still have something going on upstairs to be able to remember all of that," I come around the counter and give her a hug. "Thanks, that really means a lot to me."

It doesn't take much to get Patty going, and she's reaching for the Kleenex box to wipe away a sudden trickle of tears from her cheek. "Oh, I'm such an old softy," is all she says.

"When you think about it, Patty, it's amazing those two ever did get together. The other day I came across an article about the *Wolverine* in Joe's old papers. It was in something called the *Journal of Erie Studies* from the 1950s. It included the ship's summer cruise itinerary," I tell her slowly, trying to match my paper facts with the living words of her story. "The ship was only in Blue Harbor for a week that year and Joe was shipped overseas sometime in 1907, according to his service record. So, whatever happened between Joe and Anna must have happened within a day or two of the time Joe met the Hemingway kids. That's so wild — you're not just pulling my leg? Joe and Anna's family really knew the Hemingways?"

"Well, they mostly just knew the Hemingway's friends the Connables through some Toronto connection, but I remember your grandfather had one bookshelf in The Shack with all of Hemingway's books on it. He told your dad and me that they were too smutty for us to read, but that Ernest knew what he was talking about when he wrote about two things — war and fishing. Your grandmother said Joe secretly believed he helped Hemingway's career by encouraging the young boy to consider the military. "Well, you never know," was all that he would say.

"You're quite a treasure trove of knowledge, Patty."

"Well, most of it is pretty useless trivia, but I'm glad I could be of help," she says with a smile that warms the whole room. "Oh, that reminds me, there is one other thing. After Gladys showed me her old family photographs that pictured your grandfather's ship, she went down to the *Resorter* office and dug through some of their old back issues. She was doing research on her family, but kept coming across articles about the government boats and took some notes for me in case I wanted to write about them in my column.

"Gladys said that the mayor and city council had been petitioning the Navy Department to stop sending the boats to Blue Harbor for years. One article accused the sailors and marines of "unlawful and irresponsible behavior while on leave." After the *Wolverine's* visit in 1906, it was rumored that several young ladies in town ended up having illegitimate children fathered by some of your grandfather's shipmates. The town leaders didn't want the government boat using their port anymore.

"Jeez, you don't think Joe and Anna ended up together because of something like that do you?" I ask.

"Oh, good heavens, no," Patty says reassuringly. "Your Aunt Vicky wasn't born until well after they were married. After a short visit on Anna's porch after the Hemingways left, the ship's steam whistle blew an emergency signal that called the crew back to the ship. It steamed out of the harbor 20 minutes later, and never returned. The only thing that your grandfather got from Anna that summer they met was a kiss on the cheek goodbye and a promise to write to him no matter where the Marine Corps sent him. Joe had told Anna that he didn't have a girl back home to write to, and he would be honored if she would drop him a letter from time to time. It was those letters that brought Joe back to Michigan whenever he got the chance. Now I remember. That's how Joe ended the story that night at The Shack. Isn't that romantic?"

Patty's eyes have begun to leak again, but I don't think Joe and Anna's long-distance courtship is the only memory that has moved her. I have a pretty good idea that the memory she has just shared reaches as deeply into her own past as it does into mine. Patty is still a good friend of my mother's, but I have long suspected that she was more than just a tomboy pal of my father's. If it was just a crush, I could see it dying out long ago, but there is some vein of love that stretches backward from my current friendship with Patty all the way to the feelings that took root there in The Shack on a stormy night in front of a roaring fire — the air laced with Joe's pipe smoke and warmed by the embers of Joe and Anna's original love.

~ PART 6 ~

MANZANILLO, CUBA

Chapter 20

CY CUSHMAN HAS invited me to join him for lunch at the Park Garden Cafe in Petoskey. The Court of Appeals has reached a decision on the beach lawsuit, and Cushman left a message on my answering machine last night that gives me no clue as to the outcome. Either the Becker family has defeated the township's attempt to swipe an acre from us down on the beach for a park, or the park is here to stay. I guess I'll find out in a few minutes.

Cushman's Petoskey office is only a block from the county courthouse. His second-story corner office overlooks Magnus Park out of one window and the historic Gaslight District out the other. His secretary shows me into his office and Cushman waves me toward a seat in front of his desk while talking on the phone to someone else.

The window to the park is open and a pleasant May breeze is blowing in. Summer is on the way, and I can practically see buds opening into full-blown flowers and leaves. I'm looking out over the park as Cushman finishes up a phone call with what sounds like a realtor friend of his. The green belt that cuts diagonally through the center of Petoskey was a busy railroad yard once. Tall maples, carefully manicured lawns, war memorials and a gazebo have replaced old boxcars and switching gear. A single set of tracks runs down the middle of the park, but only the summer tourist trains use the rails these days.

Cushman is standing up at his desk with the phone handset pressed against his face while his other hand fiddles with the gold watch.

"Sorry about that, Nick," Cushman says as he hangs up. "Are you hungry?"

"I can always eat, but what I'm really hungry for is news. What happened with the appeals court?"

"Let me just grab my jacket and briefcase," Cushman says. "We're going to celebrate. Lunch is on me. I'll tell you about it on our way over to the Park Garden."

It's just a quick walk across the park to the old cafe. It doesn't take Cushman long to tell me that the Appellate Court has ruled in our favor. That fight, at least, is over. No more park on our land, Cushman announces.

"Nick, I started this thing with your dad five years ago. It's the most drawn-out case I've ever handled. We lost, we won, we lost again, and now we've finally won. This thing went all the way up to the Michigan Supreme Court. I know it's been a long and expensive battle for your family, but now that it's over, I think your dad would be happy with the outcome."

"Yeah, I only wish he were here to see it," I tell Cushman as we stroll into the Park Garden Cafe.

As we wait for our table, Cushman pulls a folded up document out of his jacket pocket and hands it to me.

"Your dad would have loved this," Cushman says. "It's a copy of the Court of Appeals opinion. You can have this copy and read the whole thing later, but check out the intro on the first couple of pages and the conclusion."

Chutzpah — a delightful Yiddish expression loosely defined as gall. In this panel's prior opinion in this cause, our beloved colleague, Judge John K. Nathaniel, gave us a classic example of chutzpah, to wit: a defendant who, about to be sentenced for murdering his parents, begs the mercy of the sentencing court because he is an orphan.

This case presents another splendid example of chutzpah. The defendant, North Shore Township, claims title to the land in question by adverse possession, even though it continued to assess and collect taxes from the plaintiffs on the small strip of land that it claims as a public park.

Our review of the record convinces us that the trial court clearly erred in finding that plaintiffs John J. Becker and Victoria K. Rolland were not assessed and did not pay taxes on the subject property.

It is undisputed that the land descriptions contained in the property tax bills sent to and paid by plaintiffs included the property which defendant now claims by adverse possession… We hold that the trial court clearly erred in finding that plaintiffs were not assessed and did not pay taxes on the property in question. Accordingly, we reaffirm this panel's earlier holding that the defendant township failed to establish the element of hostile use necessary to create title by adverse possession.

The finding of the trial court is reversed.

Cushman is right; Dad would have liked what the appellate judges had to say.

When I look up from the legal-size photocopies, Cushman gives me an "I guess we showed 'em" grin.

"That's great news," I tell Cushman, but I sound less than enthused, even to my own ears. Don't get me wrong. I'm relieved to put the township park fight behind us, but this five-year long lawsuit has only cleared up the title issue on just one out of 105 acres. The state's claim on the property is still out there. It's not only holding up the settlement of Dad's estate, but it's been weighing on my mind as the probate hearing nears. I'm not afraid of a good fight, but I'm beginning to wonder if all this legal wrangling *is* a good fight. Maybe there is a better reason *not* to fight. I just don't know.

"Where do we go from here?" I ask Cushman.

"Right now, we eat. We're here to celebrate, Nick. We can talk shop after we get some food in us," Cushman says reassuringly.

The cafe is long and narrow with a dark mahogany bar stretching about half way into the smoky interior. There are potted ferns in the corners and oil lamps on the tables. "Rita," the hostess, is expecting us, or at least Cushman, and has a nice table next to one of the small beveled-glass windows towards the back.

Cushman says hello and shakes hands with half a dozen diners on his way back to our table. I check out the ornate tin ceiling and try to blend into the background.

"Hi, Cy"

"Afternoon, Judge."

"Hey, Bill"

"Hey, Cushman."

Cushman gets a coy wave from the well-preserved blond at the end of the bar, and a grunt from the gray-bearded man in the business suit sitting near our table.

Cushman is well known in town and, apparently, well liked. The good-looking young man in khaki pants and red power tie at Cushman's side — yours truly — gets a nod from the blond, but goes mostly unheeded through the lunchtime crowd.

I am not a complete stranger to the Park Garden Cafe, though. I've come here a couple of times to write my stories and file them over the payphone in the back when County Board or Planning Commission meetings have run dangerously close to the *Gazette*'s 11 PM drop-dead deadline. It's a good place to write and the waitresses have always taken good care of me. I tell this to Cushman when he asks if I've been here before.

"You're not the first writer to spend time in this old joint. Did you know that this place was once frequented by Petoskey's most famous literary resident — Ernest Hemingway?" Cushman asks, unfolding his napkin over his crisply pressed, navy-blue suit pants.

"No, kidding. Just yesterday I learned that my grandparents knew the Hemingways," I tell Cushman, trying to sound casual about it.

"Yeah, I wouldn't be surprised if they really did," Cushman nods. "These days, though, everybody's grandparents or aunts or uncles or mother was good friends with Hemingway, if there's a little money to made in it. There are some merchants in town who didn't even come here until after Hemingway died who will swear he shopped in their stores. But Old Ernie really did spend a winter here after World War I writing his first couple of novels and short stories. They say this place was a pool hall that one of his characters hung out in. It was in *The Torrents of Spring*, if I remember correctly."

"I read some of his Michigan stuff in college, but I've never read *The Torrents of Spring*," I have to admit.

"Well, it isn't much of a book. It was mostly a parody of some other writer's work whose name you probably wouldn't recognize, even if I could remember it," Cushman says.

"See that white-haired gentleman at the table near the big-screen T.V.?" Cushman says, lowering his voice. "He would probably remember the name of that other writer."

Cushman directs my attention to a red-faced fellow in tie and blazer holding court with a table full of business types. He's waving a French fry in the air as he tells a story, the punch line of which sends his table into an outburst of laughter.

"That's Young Ernie," Cushman says.

The longer I watch "young Ernie," the more of Ernest Hemingway's features come into focus — the thick jaw, the side-of-the-mouth grin, the roundness of face. Put a white beard and long-billed fishing cap on this guy, and he would be the spittin' image of Papa.

"What do you mean, Young Ernie?" I ask.

"That guy is Ernie the illustrious Chamber of Commerce director, otherwise known as Hemingway's nephew. The Hemingways kept a cottage down on Walloon Lake and Young Ernie's mother still lives there. Sunny was Old Ernie's sister."

"I'll be damned," I say, trying not to stare at Hemingway's flesh-and-blood. "Maybe you could introduce me some time," I suggest.

"Sure thing, Nick."

With a whitefish sandwich and fries in me, I do start to feel a little less apprehensive about the future. Cushman seems equally satisfied after a bowl of morel mushroom pasta.

"Now, you were wondering about where we should go from here," Cushman says, pulling a legal pad out of his briefcase. "I've been giving this a lot of thought, lately, and you and your sister have a few options."

I pull out my reporter's notebook, signaling I'm ready for business.

"I've always tried to be very candid with my clients about the costs of legal action. It's very important that you understand these costs when you and Sally decide how to proceed. We attorneys usually get paid by the hour. My usual fee, for example, is $125 an hour. Sometimes, however, we work on a contingency fee. That means that the attorney only gets paid when and if he wins a cash settlement or judgment for his client. Usually the attorney gets about one-third of whatever damages are paid out.

"When your family came to me for help in getting clear title to the land, they couldn't afford to pay me by the hour. The nature of the lawsuits they wanted to file against the township and the state, however, did not include monetary damages. All they would win, in the end, was clear title to the property their father left them. So I offered them a special contingency-fee deal. Your mother probably told you about the arrangement."

I'm vaguely familiar with the deal, but I don't mind hearing it straight from the horses' mouth. I tell Cushman to give me the details again.

"The deal was simple. After your family gets clear title to the land, I get paid fifteen percent of the sale price of the property or my straight hourly fee (plus expenses), whichever is greater. For years, I sent your dad and your aunt a running balance of the costs and my time. I don't know if Vicky kept you apprised of the costs after John died, so I've prepared a new balance sheet for you and Sally to consider."

Cushman carefully slides a sheet of paper to me across the table. At the bottom of a list of expenses and descriptions of how he spent his $125-an-hour time, is the $85,250 total.

My lunch feels heavy in my stomach, as my eyes travel back and forth across the bottom of the page. The vast majority of this bill stems from the township-park case. Our lawsuit against the State of Michigan has only taken up a fraction of Cushman's time and effort, so far.

I don't deny the value of his work. From what I've seen and read, this was a precedent-setting case. Cushman's attack against the township, using its own tax bills and property descriptions was brilliant. It's just that the fight to hold on to one acre on the beach looks more and more like a victory won at too high a price. If I'm able to hold on to The Shack and some acreage up on the bluff, would it have really been such a bad thing to have a public park just a short walk from my home?

"All right, tell me about the options."

"There are three options — none of the which are perfect," Cushman cautions. "The important thing is to preserve as much of your father's estate as possible, but, unfortunately, all of the options will leave you and Sally with less than there is now. Your first option is to stick with the course your father and aunt embarked on. I will be happy to continue to represent your family against the State of Michigan. As I've told you before, I don't think the state has a leg to stand on. The terms of your grandfather's will clearly state that the grandchildren are to inherit the property if they survive John and Vicky. I could understand their position when John and Vicky were still alive because there was always the slim chance that you and Sally might pass on before John and Vicky. But now that the former life tenants have died, there should be no question about whom the property goes to. The state's refusal to abandon their claim is senseless, and I have already filed a letter of complaint, urging the Attorney General's office to file a brief or drop the state's claim. The advantage of sticking with this plan is that when we win, you and Sally and your aunt's estate will have clear title to the land.

"There are only a few downsides to this course of action. First, there is the cost of litigation. Even if we win fairly quickly, the work of filing briefs, going to court, more legal research, and taking depositions will add substantially to that bill in your hand there. The main problem with proceeding as before is that my fees are close to or may already be exceeding the 15 percent of the sale price of the land. Most attorney's wouldn't put it this way, but to further pursue litigation against the state will only chip away from what you and Sally will be getting from your father's estate."

I'm not really swift with numbers, but after doing the math on my notebook, I figure that fifteen percent of $750,000 is $112,500.

"All right, I think I understand what you're saying," I tell Cushman. "But I'm having a little trouble following your numbers. How come fifteen percent of $750,000 isn't $112,500?"

"That's because the sale price isn't the full $750,000. That's how much the land is worth, but I only get paid from what your family receives from the sale of the land. Your aunt's estate will only get about $175,000 more from Homer Robertson because of the purchase-option deal Vicky had with him. That's on top of the $75,000 she already received from him. And, of course, you won't be selling your entire half of the property because you want to hold on to the cabin and some acreage. When you subtract Robertson's $125,000 discount and, let's say, another $50,000 for the property you won't sell, that leaves about $575,000. And fifteen percent of that is ..."

Cushman has to pull out his calculator for this one.

"Let's see. Well, that's $86,250," Cushman says. "That means I can work on the case for about one more full day before my fees start eating into your inheritance. And the estate still has to go through probate, which will cost three or four thousand — to say nothing of the estate taxes."

"Geez. We aren't on the clock right now are we?" I ask.

"No. I don't charge my clients for my bookkeeping and this chat is on the house."

"So what are the other downsides to suing the state?"

"The other con is basically the unknown. I think it's just bureaucratic red tape that's keeping the state from responding to our initial lawsuit, but if they have something more concrete, then I honestly have to tell you that I don't have a clue what that would be," Cushman says, opening his empty hands on the table. "If they've got something and this turns into another drawn out case, you and Sally could end up spending a lot of your inheritance from your father on attorney's fees. I do not want to see that happen."

"I've got another question, here," I say, looking down at my notes. "In this fifteen percent deal you made with Dad and Aunt Vicky, did you all ever agree how much of the property was to be sold?"

"No. We never really got to that point. It was clear that Vicky wanted to sell all of her land. She told me that it was too far to drive from Arizona for her to ever get any use out of it and she couldn't afford to fly. Now your dad loved this place and wanted to retire up here. He planned to keep The Shack and some property on the south side of the road and keep a plot for a new log home in the red pines north of Stanton Road We never worked out exactly how much he would sell, but we never expected the township fight to drag on as long as it did. That's a decision that you and Sally will have to make now. You also have to keep in mind that, after your father's estate is probated, you and Sally will have to pay substantial inheritance taxes."

"Are there any other problems with this option?"

"Well, the only other problem I foresee is that if the suit against the state goes to trial, there's just no telling how a jury would respond to our case. The law is clearly on our side, but the attorney general may very well try to paint this as two spoiled kids trying to get Daddy's land and the state fighting for public access to Lake Michigan and a refuge for wildlife. That would be kind of an underhanded way for the state to proceed, but there's no way to know how badly they want this property."

"None of that sounds too great. What are the other options?" I ask.

"Settle with the state. That's one approach we could take. Years ago, your dad and Vicky asked me to negotiate with the state. The attorney general was willing to drop Michigan's claim if we paid them one-quarter of the value of the land. At the time, John and Vicky weren't interested in giving up that much to eliminate the state's interest in the property. But it may be worth it now. You would have to give up some of the money from the property, but you and Sally and Vicky's estate would at least have clear title to what is left. Negotiating with the state would be much quicker and less costly than litigation. You may end up with less than if you fought it out in court and won quickly, but then again, you may end up with more than you would have after a drawn-out lawsuit. You and Sally would, at least, have a little more control over your own destinies this way."

The numbers are starting to swirl around in my head. All I really want is to hold on to The Shack and a decent-size piece of land and have enough money to finish fixing up the old place. Even if Sally and I end up with a lot less than Dad's half of the property, we will still be starting off in the world with a lot more than most people our age. I never really expected to come into any inheritance at this stage in my life, and I'm not afraid of making my own way. On the other hand, it doesn't seem right to see the property whittled down to nothing in the process of passing from one generation to the next.

"So what's the other option?" I ask.

"The final suggestion I have is a variation on the first two," Cushman says, tucking his legal pad and calculator back into his briefcase. "I wouldn't ask you this, if I didn't think it would help you and Sally in the long run. But we could renegotiate the contingency-fee deal I made with your father and aunt. I was thinking you and Sally could use the $75,000 from the trust fund your Aunt Vicky set up for you two to either offer a cash settlement to the state or pay me for the legal expenses that have already accrued."

There comes a time in every reporter's life when he or she learns to shut up when a source starts telling you something that you don't already know because the source thinks you already know it. That instinct kicks in right now. The question "What $75,000 trust fund?" is blaring in my head. I resist the temptation to let it out.

"Go on," I tell Cushman, who is too busy trying not to offend me by asking for money to notice whatever look of surprise might have flashed across my face. He seems to think Sally and I have money we don't have.

"Nick, I haven't been paid for the work I've done for your family for five years. I'm not complaining, but getting the money now instead of six months or a couple of years from now would be of great benefit to me. So much so, that I would be willing to set a cap on my fees at $90,000 if you decide to proceed against the state — $75,000 up front and another $15,000 when we win the case. Now, if you want to use the money as an offer to settle with the state, our contingency-fee deal stays the way it has been. That amount is a lot less than the one-quarter they offered before, but even the state might go for getting cash now instead of more land later. Cash has a way of loosening legal logjams even among bureaucrats."

I'm not sure what he's talking about.

"When you say my aunt's trust fund, do mean the money she got from Homer Robertson?" I ask, seeing if I can shake any more information out of Cushman.

"Well, of course, Nick, what other $75,000 would I mean?" Cushman says, suddenly leaning towards me in his chair. "You know, the money that Vicky got from Robertson as a purchase option on her half of the property that she put in trust for you and Sally."

Silence from my side of the table.

"You know, the "vast fortune" you told me about over the phone when I was in Florida?" What he is saying finally starts to make sense.

"Ohh, that's what you're talking about," I tell my misguided attorney, with a smile. "I didn't think you would take me seriously. I'm sorry, Cy, but all Aunt Vicky left me was a few old antiques and some boxes of letters and photographs that belonged to the Colonel and my grandmother. There sure wasn't any trust fund. I was just being sarcastic when I said I'd received the "vast fortune.""

Cushman hesitates for a second and then breaks into a subdued chuckle.

"Why would you have thought that Aunt Vicky put that money into a trust fund?" I ask.

"I apologize, Nick, I should have checked things out with the lawyer in Tucson, before asking you. It's been so many years, that I'm starting to lose track of all the details. You see, I helped set up that purchase-option deal between Mr. Robertson and Vicky. She had a lawyer who handled things for her in Tucson — Betty Fisher, if I remember correctly. I just turned the check over to her, as per her instructions. Vicky told me she was putting the money in trust and was going to use the interest from the money to help cover her medical bills. I just assumed that's what she did with the money. It was out of my hands after I sent the check."

I would like to know a whole lot more about that purchase-option deal, but, glancing at my watch, I see that it is 1:30 PM — just enough time to get to Gaylord to dig around in the court files before another Mathias murder-case hearing.

"Well, I guess that only leaves two options," Cushman concludes. "Settle or keep suing the state. Thanks for joining me for lunch, Nick. I think we made some good progress here."

"I'll talk to Sally before the weekend and try to give you a decision after next week. This weekend, I'm going out of town with a college buddy of mine and his friend and we'll be out of touch for about a week," I tell our family attorney, as we rise from our seats and shake hands.

Ernest Hemingway's nephew is gone and I've really got to get on the road, so there isn't much point in hanging around here anymore. Cushman stays to settle up with the waitress, as I leave the Park Garden Cafe behind and head up East Lake Street to my pickup.

There is still a third option, but it's not one I discussed with Cushman. After I get done digging up the seedy past of this Mathias guy (who was found beat up and frozen stiff in the back of his pickup three years ago), I plan to do some digging of my own. I don't entirely buy Cushman's explanation. It doesn't surprise me that Vicky may have changed her mind about leaving money to Sally and me. What does surprise me, considering the way things turned out, is that she ever considered leaving us $75,000 in the first place. That's all she would ever get out of the place while she was alive, so why wouldn't she just spend it on herself and her doctors? As soon as I get this story filed, I'll be making a few phone calls.

On the way to my pickup, I almost pass by a beat-up newspaper coin box with today's *Little Traverse Times*. I dig out a quarter and slide out the latest local news. Just below the fold on the front page is a story about Cushman's victory in the Appellate Court against the township. Of course, the *Times'* headline puts a different slant on things: "Township loses beach park in legal dispute."

The story is pretty accurate and just states the facts — including the "chutzpa" quote from the opinion. It occurs to me that — in order to make its noon deadline — the *Times* would have had to have gotten a hold of the court decision before Cushman told me about it over lunch. I suppose Cushman could have tipped the paper off before letting me know what was going on. That wouldn't have done any harm, but it seems curious that he didn't run that by me first. Probably, the *Times* got word yesterday from the Associated Press office in Lansing that covers the Appellate Court regularly.

As I scan through the paper for any news that Sean Cooper might be interested in for *The Northern Michigan Gazette*, I come across the *Times'* editorial, entitled "Fighting for Public Lands."

> *Public access to Lake Michigan and the region's inland lakes and streams is a vanishing resource. Even as recently as the 1970s, both tourists and local residents seemed to have ample access to these public waters. But much of that access was neither official nor legal — as a recent court case between North Shore Township and a property owner shows (see pg. 1 "Township loses… ").*
>
> *Ten to 15 years ago, there was still abundant undeveloped private land along the shores that the public was not discouraged from using. But all of that has changed with growing concerns by property owners over legal liability. There have always been a few property owners who go to extremes to protect their privacy. But now the majority of property owners feel they must protect themselves by erecting "No Trespassing" signs every 20 feet along their boundaries. These concerns are legitimate. Just last year, a jury awarded a trespassing snowmobiler who ran into an unmarked barbwire fence $350,000 for his injuries because the property owner did not post his property.*

The time for taking public access to public waters for granted is over. Between Blue Harbor and Cross Village, there are only a couple of public-access sites. The Little Traverse Times applauds North Shore Township for its effort — although unsuccessful — to secure additional public access on Little Traverse Bay.

State, Local, and Federal government should vigorously defend existing public access to the waterfront and pursue all opportunities to obtain new access.

I set the *Times* down on the Mexican blanket cover that drapes over my pickup's bench seat, and look down East Lake Street into Petoskey's Gaslight District. It's a perfect spring day, but the only butterflies I'm aware of are in my stomach. The *Times* editorial is practically a rallying cry for the State of Michigan to kick my family off our own land. Not exactly the kind of attention Sally and I need if we are to go into negotiations with the state. What is most disturbing about the editorial is that people I don't even know seem to know a lot more about my family's business than I do. I've never thought of myself as paranoid, but I'm starting to wonder just how many people are against me. On the other hand, if the editorial weren't indirectly aimed at the Beckers, I would probably agree with it.

Chapter 21

THE DEAD GUY in Gaylord kept me busy all Thursday afternoon and evening riffling through a ten-inch-high stack of court documents. The documents and the hearing only amounted to a three-inch "News in Brief" item in Friday's *Gazette*, but Sean Cooper wants me to get up to speed on the history of the case so I can hit the ground running when I get back from camping with my old college buddy Pete MacSeeney. All of the *Gazette* reporters are back on Monday from a round of spring vacations; so next week was looking fairly sparse assignment-wise, anyway. One of the perks of freelancing is that I can take time off to hang out with the rare visitor to my new northern lair. Since Pete is the first real visitor I've had in almost five months, I don't feel too bad taking time off. All I have to do is make a quick round of "cop calls" Saturday evening and send in a brief or two before I head out.

Pete is a Cape Cod native who ran the Outing Club when we went to Colby College together. He was something of a pied piper for students like me who wanted to do something other than knock off a keg every weekend. When we weren't squirreled away writing papers or studying in the library, we spent our weekends and breaks exploring the mountains, rivers, lakes, and coasts of Maine with backpacks, snowshoes, hiking boots, bicycles, skis, canoes, or some combination thereof. I don't remember if I ever became an official officer of the Outing Club, but for three years Pete had the keys to the club's equipment room, and we put together a lot of great trips for ourselves, our friends, and anyone who wanted to come along.

While we all had different circles of friends at Colby, that core group of hikers, canoers, bikers, and skiers came to become "The Gang" pictured in our senior yearbook two years ago.

Pete's love of the outdoors has been strong enough to pry him out of his beloved New England and into my neck of the midwestern woods where he is getting his masters in ornithology at the University of Indiana in Bloomington. Bob White (yeah, that's his real name), a fellow ornithologist and Indianapolis native, talked Pete into taking him backpacking for a week on Isle Royale, a national park in the northwest corner of Lake Superior. For Pete this is the first chance he's had to see the part of the Northwoods that I've told him so much about. For me, it's a hell of good way to catch up with a friend I haven't seen for about a year. For Bob, however, this is the culmination of a decade-long quest, Pete tells me. Bob has been hiking and car camping before, but he has never been backpacking in his life. Since junior high, though, he has dreamed about backpacking on Isle Royale, and he has been meticulously planning the trip all winter.

Bob wanted to drive straight through to the Isle Royale ferry at the northwest tip of Minnesota and have me meet them there, but Pete was able to talk his eager new friend into stopping at the house of his hospitable old friend when he showed Bob how long it would take to drive from Bloomington to Grand Portage (think Boston to Chicago without any interstate for the last third of the trip). Both Pete and Bob have a limited window of opportunity for this trip between the end of exams and the beginning of summer jobs, so I can understand Bob's anxiousness. Bob has tickets reserved on the first ferryboat of the season for 7:30 Sunday morning.

Even though it's mid-May, the folks in Grand Portage said there is still ice in the bays and snow on the ground, so we may have to wait a day or two to get to the island. But if the ferry *can* get in and we miss it, then we'll have to wait until Wednesday for the next one, which would only leave time for an overnight, instead of Bob's five-day backpacking extravaganza. There is a closer ferry that leaves from Copper Harbor at the tip of Michigan's Keweenaw Peninsula, but that route doesn't open up for a couple of weeks yet. The weather has been in the mid-sixties this week, but it's supposed to get cold again this weekend. Not only has Bob gained another experienced backpacking partner, but I think a few hours of rest at the Becker farm might help ease Bob and Pete out of their frantic grad-school pace and into the quieter, yet less-predictable rhythms of the Northwoods. The wild remoteness of Isle Royale makes Blue Harbor seem like a sprawling metropolis in comparison, so I can only imagine the abrupt transition the guys will have to make between suburban Indiana and the far corners of Lake Superior. I spent most of Friday cleaning up The Shack and packing my camping gear to get ready for my houseguests, so I am left to my own devices until they get here around 4:00 PM on Saturday.

After sleeping in late Saturday morning to prepare for our all-night drive to Grand Portage (we need to leave here around 10:00 PM tonight), I stir up the coals in the fireplace and slip into the wooden chair that sits in front of the desk I have cobbled together in the living room using an old door and some new two-drawer filing cabinets. My visit with Patty Kensington the other day has stirred up the coals of my imagination, and I rifle through the folders of Joe and Anna's stuff to see if I missed any letters from their nearly three years of long-distance courtship.

Apparently, most of these letters did not survive the Becker's many moves, but I suspect that was by design rather than

through carelessness. After all, Joe and Anna would probably be a bit miffed if they knew their grandson was reading
as much of their private correspondence as I've already seen.
I'm sure they considered their pre-marital love letters to be
nobody's business but their own. But with so much of their
lives carefully preserved in writing and pictures I wonder how
they decided what to keep and what to destroy. Like Patty's
selective memory, the Becker record is just as intriguing for
what was left out as what is left in.

Whatever courtship Joe and Anna managed to have in the
few years after they met in the summer of '06 and before they
married in the summer of '09 remains a mostly private matter.
There are, however, a few traces of romance, or, at least, resolve.

Anna Mia —

*Have you my letters? I am waiting to hear from you.
Please write me another letter like the last. Tell me about
yourself. This is Monday morning. Cool and airy and
beautiful.*

*Lovingly Yours,
Joe*

These words are written on both the front and back of a
picture of Havana Harbor in Cuba. In the foreground, hundreds of empty, wooden folding chairs line a harbor side
street. Beyond that lies a carefully manicured park lawn
planted with a few stately bushes and palm trees. Several
colonial buildings of brick and white trim are off to the right,
and a far-away trolley car with a barely perceptible driver is
in the center of the picture. Way off in the background, partially obscured by the tropical haze, is a line of docked ships.
Joe has drawn an arrow pointing to the harbor and an "x"

marking the spot where the U.S.S. *Maine* was sunk some nine years before Joe was sent to Cuba.

Some of Joe's career wishes were coming true. He was promoted to corporal. He was part of a detachment of marines serving in the Army of Cuban Pacification. Not only was he sent to keep the peace in a troubled and obscure corner of the world, but he was finally issued the khaki field service uniform he had wanted to wear since he was mistaken for a railroad conductor on his way to Erie. In his Montana-peaked campaign hat and canvas leggings, Joe looked every inch the marine corporal ready for action in the tropical heat. The only problem was that there wasn't much action to be found at the Marine Corps garrison in Manzanillo, the busy port town on the southeastern shore of Cuba where Joe was sent.

Since the defeat of the Spanish in Cuba in the summer of 1898, the United States had been both helping and hindering Cuba's first steps towards independence. Officially, we liberated Cuba from its Spanish oppressors and were helping the Cuban people to form a democracy much like our own. But behind the scenes, American business interests were gathering up power for themselves faster than the Cubans could consolidate power for a new government. The new Cuban constitution was nearly an exact copy of the U.S. Constitution, with one important addition. The "Platt Amendment" gave the United States "the right to intervene for the preservation of Cuban independence, the maintenance of a government adequate for the protection of life, property and individual liberty, and for discharging the obligations with respect to Cuba imposed by the Treaty of Paris. ..."

While Joe was finishing up his first Great Lakes cruise aboard the *Wolverine* in August 1906, a questionable Cuban election turned into open rebellion by the losing Liberal party, and the incumbent Moderate party president, Tomas Estrada Palma, asked for U.S. help in mid-September. Readily available detachments of marines were sent ashore to guard the Presidential Palace, the Cuban treasury, and American-owned sugar plantations and railroad property on the north coast as the Cuban government disintegrated and a new provisional government was established.

Joe was probably part of the 1st Marine Regiment that arrived in October under Army command and stayed to round up illicit weapons and for guard duty until 1909. According to a history of The United States Marines that Joe must have picked up later in life, garrison duty was slow, but life outside the marine compound in Manzanillo wasn't. Some Cubans didn't much like having their weapons taken away and a new set of foreigners brought in to replace the Spanish. Without guns, anti-American locals mostly avoided open fighting, but found other ways to let Joe and his comrades know that they weren't entirely welcome. "Morning Reports" like the one cited in Joe's book weren't all that unusual.

About 1:10 A M. Privates Haggard, Reed, and Scott reported in from town, the two latter having jumped camp about 12 midnight. They reported having been assaulted by two civilians with a machete and a club. Private Reed presented a badly bruised nose, and Private Haggard three machete cuts and a bruise apparently from a kick to the ribs. All three men were calm and sober. Private Haggard was bleeding profusely from a long wound in the left ear and we sent him to the sick bay and notified Post Surgeon. Later went to the sick bay and saw Private Haggard's wounds and reported the matter (about 2:30 A M) to police headquarters, the doctor giving the necessary certificate.

What a time Joe must have had. By day, Joe and his fellow marines played baseball with local Cuban teams and learned to speak Spanish. By night, they did their best to keep out of trouble. Hostile natives outside the camp, however, were no match for the garrisoned soldier's worst enemy — drunkenness. Officers, sergeants and even corporals like Joe spent almost as much time trying to keep bored soldiers sober as they did trying to keep restless Cubans pacified. Marines were routinely confined to quarters or sent to the brig to sober up on bread and water for a few days as punishment for drunkenness. While the marines took actual guard duty seriously, there was lots of time to kill in between watches. One private even got so drunk one night that he returned to camp without any clothes and couldn't even find them the next day when he was sent under armed guard to recover them.

While Joe was busy battling the evil influences of liquor and midnight machete assaults on the men in his platoon, Anna was engaged in something of a battle of hearts back home. While Harvey Higginbotham was no longer in the picture, his sister Leslie — Anna's best friend — still was. While things did not work out between Anna and Leslie's brother, Leslie still had plenty of eligible cousins, second cousins, and even an uncle or two. Nearly all of them were rich, and after New Year's Day 1907, Leslie embarked on a long trip back East to become better acquainted with society in general and her wealthy relations in particular. While Leslie was certainly on the lookout for prospects of her own, she swore to find a suitable match for Anna with hopes of getting her into the family one way or another.

Despite Anna's protests that she was content writing to her marine friend in Cuba, Leslie wrote weekly letters back home to Anna in Blue Harbor. While Joe was carefully wooing Anna with words and accounts of his adventures abroad, Leslie's letters sought to seduce Anna with a giddy parade of culture, society, and wealth. Her letters are written in a frantic hand, barely legible in spots. Leslie — a sheltered rich girl from the wilds of Northern Michigan — was having the time of her life, and she wanted her best friend to share it with her.

330 *Clinton St.*
Brooklyn, N.Y.
~ or ~
3 *West* 108th *St.*
New York City c/o
I.R. Bateman

Seeing life, Anna Dear. Well some — I am like an English-man who has been in South Africa for years and then finds his feet on the Strand or in Piccadilly Circus. My engage-ments for Friday are a fair sample of the rush, i.e., lun-cheon at one, tea at four dinner at seven. I have a tea on for tomorrow. Had an adorable petit souper *on Monday night. Such a fine time yesterday in two galleries find old French furnishings and being in a fashionable parade on* 5th *Avenue. Today I am staying in being a wise woman but go out to a lecture tonight — Sat. mat. To see the wickedest play in N.Y. Now Anna, don't tell on me but really I like the* Petit soupers, *just lovely refined people — but clever brilliant — cosmopolitan not as some man wrote recently of some village people "virtuous, amiable and tiresome." A few new wrinkles at the little late suppers and some old familiar ones I thought I had forgotten — tangerines with the skin turned into a cup loaf sugar & brandy put in and each one [illegible] it and — how good it tastes — all the*

*men in evening clothes and allowed to smoke cigarettes.
The last one was in the* artistre *apartment of a rich Cal.
girl who was "finished" here at a girls' school and who
is here for the [illegible] gayeties. Went to such a pretty
tea on 5th Ave. — girls who pound. Wore pink satin you
know those soft maves? — old blue pale green and white
and there was a woman in gray who was a picture and
graceful as a cat. The Cal. girl is the sweetheart of Mrs.
Bateman's brother. He is going to take us both to some of
the gay queer places after the theater — have an invitation to tea in the beautiful Waldorf-Astoria and a card to
be shown thru that wonderful Hotel en Refis. I shall have
so much to tell you. I run about a good deal by myself tho
Mr. R's sister in Brooklyn has a fine Excursion Bronphus
but she has been ill for a long time — has a nurse and Dr.
every day they hope she will be able to go to Atlantic City
for a change soon. I [illegible] the [illegible] between the
two places. Mrs. Bateman's apartment is artistic — her
table service exquisite. We have our [illegible] served in
the tiny drawing room first and go thru all the courses.
Mr. B. in evening clothes in a tuxedo always. Mrs. B. is
going to pour at the tea Miss Colby gives for me tomorrow
she will wear a new shade of rose silk — Euphoric — cut
silk ornaments and ivory lace. Her skirt suit is mulberry
not a bit like the ready-made ones and her furs stunning.
Perhaps you would like my skirt suit tho I got it at a smart
shop — black, quite in style (paid enough) but with frilly
lace, white kids and a big bunch of violets in front. Met
Clay West, a delightful gentleman who is some sort of
second cousin to me. He is a pianist, too — told him all
about you and wants to meet you. He has never married,
but dashing in evening clothes.*

Write,
Leslie

Chapter 22

THE SOUND OF tires crunching the gravel on the circular drive behind The Shack releases me from Leslie's whirlwind New York travels, and I look at my watch to see that Pete and Bob have arrived about a half hour earlier than expected. It's only 3:32 on Saturday afternoon. As I stand to put my papers away, I see Pete's head in its customary gray, wool cap appear so quickly out on my front lawn that I guess he couldn't wait to take in the view of Lake Michigan. He must have sprinted around to the front of the house to appear so quickly.

As I step out on the front porch to greet him, I see that Pete is not only checking out the scenery, but he is relieving himself on the weedy edge of the plateau, just beyond my recently mowed lawn.

"Dude, welcome to God's Country," I call out to Pete from the porch steps. "I see that you have already made yourself at home. Mia Casa. Pee Casa. Su Casa."

"Hey, Nick, it's great to be here. This place is awesome. Sorry about the irrigation, but Bob didn't want to stop for the last hour and I was about to rupture something," Pete says, zipping up his jeans and dramatically wiping his hands on his fleece jacket as he runs up to shake my hand.

I feign disgust at touching his outstretched limb for a second just before I wipe my runny nose on my right palm and slap it into his open hand.

"Aw, gnarly," he says as he pulls me in for a bear hug. In a few seconds, we are transformed back to the same goof balls who tried to out-gross each other over dinner in Dana Dining

Hall back in college. Our gross-out antics were mostly verbal, but I have seen Pete do things with cottage cheese that I wish I could forget, and I am an excellent shot with a day-old doughnut hole. It's good to see Pete, and we are laughing our heads off within the first minutes of our reunion.

"Nick, I was actually trying to be polite. I didn't see your outhouse anywhere, and I didn't want to embarrass your other guests."

"Guests?" I ask as I look up to see whether Pete is kidding or not. "I thought it was just you and Bob."

"Bob has been listening to his weather radio ever since we hit the Michigan border, and he is pretty freaked out," Pete says hurriedly in his serious voice. "I guess there is a big snowstorm about to hit the Upper Great Lakes. Bob wants to leave earlier in case the snow slows us down."

We walk around the side of the house to the circular drive where he's parked.

"Well, okay, I just have to do a last-minute round of phone calls for the newspaper after dinner, and then we can hit the road a few hours earlier, around seven. I have to wait for the end of the cops' day shifts or they just give us the same stuff they had in the morning. Does that sound all right? We can take my four-wheel drive pickup if it would make him feel more comfortable and you guys don't mind piling in the cab."

Winter-weather driving isn't something that either Pete or I take lightly, but between the two of us, we have logged many miles of blizzard-bound Maine roads in beat-up old cars and lived to tell the tale. Pete stops me before we round the back corner of The Shack and gives me a knowing look.

"I'll try to talk to Bob, but I think he wants to leave right after dinner. I feel bad about changing plans at the last minute on you like this, Nick, but he's the one who put this trip together and I feel kind of stuck in the middle. I know we could prob-ably make it even if we left at 10 like you said, but I'm just kind of along for the ride on this one," Pete says laying a hand on my shoulder. "Oh, yeah, and there's one other little change in plans you might like a lot better. Come on around to my truck and meet Bob and the surprise member of this expedition."

Two blue-jeaned bottoms and four Vibram-soled hiking boots are sticking out the back of Pete's little, two-wheel-drive Chevy pickup. The tailgate is down and two people are rum-maging through the gear inside Pete's homemade, plywood topper. The butt on the right must be Bob, but the shapely der-riere to the left is definitely not Bob.

"That's Libby Hampton, a friend of Bob's who's decided to join us at the last minute," Pete tells me as we approach. "Bob's been trying to get her to come along all spring, but she was supposed to be heading out to visit her boyfriend Craig in L.A. This guy Craig cancelled on her at the last minute, so she could come along. You'll like her, Nick, she spends her sum-mers backpacking and rafting out in Colorado, and she's even been to Blue Harbor before. Her boyfriend's family has one of those big cottages out on that little peninsula that sticks out into the bay. And she's cute, too. 'Nudge, nudge, wink, wink, know what I mean — know what I mean?'"

Monty Python aside, I am intrigued. As we come up to the tailgate, I catch the sound of a delightful, laughing voice coming out of the plywood enclosure. Her voice is sweet and friendly with a slight Southern lilt to it. As she finishes telling Bob a story about a kid at summer camp who had to wear an extra pair of long underwear on his head because he forgot his hat, she shimmies out of the pickup bed, still kneeling on the tailgate. She shakes her head at something Bob says from under the plywood cap and her long, blond, ponytail — with one of those white scrunchy things holding it up — dances in a beam of sunlight that has managed to slip through the growing cloud cover. The weather has definitely turned colder since this morning's sun, but I am suddenly quite warm in just a chamois shirt and jeans.

My two guests haven't noticed that Pete and I are standing behind them, and I am content to wait a few seconds, even though I have this strange urge to reach out and touch Libby's ponytail with the tips of my fingers. Her hair is so blond that some strands are almost white. I'm no expert, but I don't think her blond comes out of a bottle.

"Boy, it sure is cold up here, Bob. Oh, there it is," she says and pulls on a cute, red ski hat that comes to a long triangular point that drapes down the back of her puffy, powder-blue down vest.

"Hey, guys, here he is," Pete chimes in.

"Hi, I'm Libby," she says, swinging around and hopping off the tailgate with one hand holding her red cap on and one hand outstretched to greet me. Now a bit unsure what to do, I give my hand one last wipe on my jeans before taking hers. In her wintry clothes and rosy cheeks she cuts a figure that is both rugged and pixie-like at the same time. Her remarkable round, blue eyes look up into mine as she shakes my hand.

"Hi, Libby, I'm Nick — Nick Becker, welcome to Northern Michigan."

"Pete has been telling me a lot about you," she says, smiling up at me and shooting a playful scowl at Pete. "Where did you run off to, Mr. MacSeeney? And how long were you hiding behind us?"

"Just long enough to take in the view from back here," Pete says, elbowing me in the shoulder and wagging his eyebrows at Libby.

"Shut up, dill weed," I tell Pete with a smile. "Libby, I see that it hasn't taken you too long to get a bead on this guy. Don't pay him any attention. Pete gets a little loopy after he drives for very long. His girlfriend thinks he's a real gentleman, though. Doesn't she, Pete?"

He nods. "Dill weed" is our inside word for anyone who acts like a complete idiot. It's an old Michigan summer camp phrase that I exported to my Maine classmates. Pete earns the title regularly, but then again, so do I. Actually, Pete is a scholar and a gentleman, mostly, but he is quick to play a sort of wolf-ish, Popeye-esque comedian around pretty women — a few of which have actually dated him for years at a time. They must see something in my 6-ft., blond-haired, good-natured buddy with his Woody-Woodpecker laugh and infectious bawdiness.

Bob finally extracts himself from the back of Pete's pickup and pulls a red anorak over his head while reaching to shake my hand.

"Hi, Nick."

Face-to-face, Bob doesn't look nearly as uptight as I imagined. With black hair and dark-rimmed glasses, Bob looks like a medium-built, slightly nerdier version of Clark Kent. His handshake and broad shoulders reassure me that he will be a solid member of our backpacking group.

"You must be Bob. Thanks for putting this trip together; we are going to have a blast. Why don't you come inside for a few minutes and let the road dust settle. There's water on the stove for washing up and the outhouse is around the back of the old garage if you need to make a pit stop. I know we need to get going this evening after dinner, but I'd love to show you guys around a bit and let you stretch your legs before we do."

"Sounds great," Bob says, and we cross the plank across the excavation behind the kitchen and head in.

After my guests are freshened up and given a tour of the house complete with tidbits of both its Becker and commune history, all four of us head out the front porch, across the plateau, and down the short, steep slope that leads to the green and blossoming meadow. On the drive up, Libby had noticed huge patches of white flowers dotting the forest floor. Libby is from Newport News, Virginia, she tells me, and has never seen the trillium that pops up every spring in the Northwoods. There is a particularly thick patch of it in the woods at the south end of the meadow, so we trot down the slope and on to Homer Robertson's gravel road. I try to ignore the wooden stakes and pink ribbons that mark Homer's development plans, but Pete asks about them, so I give them a synopsis of the state of the Becker property and the legal mess I am currently trying to make sense of as we walk down the road.

"Wow, what a complicated situation, Nick," Libby says. "So what you are saying is that the land up on the plateau where your farmhouse is belongs to your father's estate, but this land down here in the meadow belongs to your Aunt Vicky's estate?"

"Yeah, that's it," I nod.

"Okay, but how does this Homer guy have the right to come in here and start bulldozing roads and staking out house sites if he doesn't own it? Since your Aunt is dead, why can't you just tell Homer to screw himself," Libby says with her pretty, blond eyebrows bent into a frown.

"I wish I could, but it's not up to me," I shrug. "The probate court in Tucson that's handling Vicky's estate has to settle with all of Vicky's creditors and honor the purchase-option agreement she had with Homer."

"Yeah, screw Homer, Nick," Pete says. "What do ya' say you just close your eyes for a few minutes. Libby, Bob, and I can have all these fuckin' stakes pulled in no time and we can dump them over in that Four Fires Estates place."

Pete already has his hands gripped around a nearby stake, grinning up at me and just itching for the go-ahead to destroy a few thousand dollars worth of surveying work.

"Easy there, killer," I say, holding up my hands to stop him. But it's already too late, Pete has yanked up a stake and is pulling it up and stabbing it back into the ground with maniacal glee.

"Die, developer, die! Let Nick's land be free," Pete screams at the soft, black dirt before carefully slipping the stake right back into it original hole.

"Ladies and gentleman, I give you Pete MacSeeney, founding member of the Monkeywrench Gang." I wave my hand towards Pete, who takes a sweeping bow to the audience.

Bob laughs and Libby rolls her eyes at all of us. She is not easily distracted by our clowning antics. "Seriously, there has got to be something you can still do about this," she says.

"Maybe you could make some deal with this Homer guy," Bob says. "If he is so eager to get his hands on this place that he has spent all this money — what did you say about $75,000?"

"That's how much he spent on the purchase option with Aunt Vicky. With the surveying and road building, he's probably got close to $100,000 into this place. I understand that he is trying to line up potential customers before he actually buys Vicky's land because all of his money is tied up in real estate. He needs serious buyers to sign some kind of intent-to-purchase papers so that he can get the financing to buy the rest of Aunt Vicky's land and develop it fully. I'm no business man, but it looks like Homer has put up a little money now so that he can make a lot more money later."

"Well, if this guy is so desperate to line up buyers, maybe you could get him to see things your way by scaring off the next ones that come by," Bob says. "Maybe you could get a few extra acres out of the guy."

"Believe me, the thought has crossed my mind," I admit. "I've spent several sleepless nights dreaming up eco-terrorist schemes to drive them away — collecting roadkill and scattering carcasses about the panoramic bluff sites to give them the true aroma of the outdoors; blaring Jimmy Hendrix from huge speakers (if I had them) on my front porch whenever somebody comes by for a look; or maybe putting up big searchlights and "Trespassers Will Be Shot" signs around the house...."

"Or maybe you need to set up a pen for pigs someplace upwind of these lots," Pete says. "And junk cars. You need a bunch of junk cars piled up around the perimeter of your dad's property. Cape Cod natives have used these tactics for years to keep those Mass-holes from Boston from taking over the place. Old boats and engine parts strewn about work well, but nothing beats a pack of loose dogs. About ten of them is good."

"Thanks, Pete, I'll take that under advisement," I tell him. "All these ideas are tempting, but I just can't quite figure out a scenario where I don't end up with a citation for disturbing the peace or malicious destruction of property. I *am* the only one living within a quarter mile of here. It wouldn't take them too long to figure out who is causing all the trouble."

"That doesn't sound like you anyway, Nick," Libby says. "Let's go look at the flowers."

"You know, it doesn't bother me so much that this won't be my family's anymore. It stinks, but I can accept that." I stop at the edge of the meadow before continuing into the woods. "This place has probably changed hands many times. Hundreds of years ago, the Ottawa Indians ran off some other tribe to live here. The white settlers, including my ancestors, got the land cheap when the Indians couldn't pay property taxes that they didn't even know they owed. Then, the homesteaders sold off the land they cleared to summer people or locals like my grandparents, and now a new set of rich resorters wants to displace us. What really gets me is that this latest wave of people doesn't seem to have any better notion of sharing what we all have here than their predecessors. You'd think we could learn to deal with each other better after a few hundred years. The main problem is that the new folks end up wiping away almost everything that has come before them — including the very things that attracted them here in the first place. Usually, they don't even know what they are getting rid of."

Although the trillium blossoms and waxy wild-leek leaves carpet the forest floor and new buds have popped from the beech and maple trees around us, a cold wind is cutting across the lake and buffeting the branches at the edge of the bluff. When we stepped out on the porch a few minutes ago, I noticed that the thermometer had dropped to 48-degrees.

"This place used to be sort of an Ottawa Indian neighborhood before my grandparents bought it in the '20s," I tell them. "I was reading some of those old letters I showed you in my living room and my grandmother said they used to call this area 'Chi-noo-ding,' which means 'Place of Storm Wind.' On a day like today, you can sure see what they meant."

As we stroll down the gravel road, Pete locks arms with Libby on one side and Bob on the other. Libby puts her arm through mine and we all continue through the forest. With only a glance at each other, we all start chanting, "Lions, and tigers, and bears, oh my, lions, and tigers, and bears!" Off in the distance, I can make out the line of white and red "No Trespassing Violators Will Be Prosecuted" signs that mark the boundary line of Four Fires Estates. Libby has to give me a slight tug to keep up with the others. It's pretty clear who Dorothy is in this bunch and Pete has all the bluster of the Cowardly Lion, but I'm not sure whether I need more brains or more heart to handle the Wicked Witch and the flying monkeys that lay in wait at the end of Homer's road. It sure helps having a few friends around, though.

PART 7

LAS CASCADES, PANAMA

———

Chapter 23

AFTER MY GUESTS' legs have been sufficiently stretched and their bellies have been filled with spaghetti and garlic bread that I cooked with the old woodstove, I return to my desk to take care of my "night reporter" duties for the *Gazette* so we can get going. Pete is dozing on the sofa in front of a warm fire, and Libby is curled up in a blanket on the floor reading in front of the hearth. Bob seemed pretty fidgety during dinner, and has gone out to Pete's pickup to check the weather radio again. Something both wet and frozen has started falling diagonally out of the sky and is bouncing off the windows on the north side of the house with a sound like rusty sheet metal being sand-blasted.

It's only about 5:15 PM and we still have a couple hours of daylight left, but I start in on my "cop calls" while the water boils for kitchen clean up. With a dozen or so city, county, and state police departments in my area, this meat-and-potatoes job of daily journalism can take anywhere from ten minutes to a couple of hours, depending on how much news they have for us. As Murphy's Law would dictate, this evening's calls yield a treasure-trove of news nuggets. There is a car-deer accident over in Indian River; an investigation of bad checks at the Speedway gas station in Petoskey; a fatal rollover in Bay Shore; a Mackinaw City Police Department prisoner who escaped twice in one day; and (my favorite) the return of the Cheboygan State Police Post's Michigan flag that was pilfered in 1971.

It's 6:05 PM by the time I get done with the calls and I still have five good briefs to write up and send in over my

300-baud phone modem. I decide to get the longest item out of the way first.

>CHEBOYGAN — In 1971, a group of youths went on a crime spree, stealing a number of items in what they called "scavenger hunting." One of the thefts was the state flag taken from the Michigan State Post in Cheboygan…

Out of the corner of my eye, I notice Bob pace in and out of the living room where the rest of us are all huddled together for warmth. Bob pulls Pete and Libby into the kitchen. I'm trying to concentrate, but I can still make out part of the conversation.

"… we should clean up the kitchen before we go, Bob. That's the least we can do for him," Pete says in his serious voice.

>… On Wednesday — 18 years later — a woman walked into the Cheboygan post and returned the stolen flag she found while cleaning her attic…

As my fingers fly across the keyboard, I hear the now-familiar sound of Bob's hiking boots approach my desk in the corner of the living room.

>… Knowing its history, she felt compelled to return the flag, a state police…

"Sorry to bother you, Nick," Bob says after clearing his throat. "The weather is getting pretty bad. It's already sleeting here, and the forecast calls for a big snowstorm tonight — as much as twelve inches in the Upper Peninsula."

"I'm going as fast as I can, Bob, but I turned up a bunch of little junk that I have to write up for the paper before I can get out of here. I can be done and ready to hit the road in an hour, easily."

"Well, that's just it, Nick. We need to leave right now or I don't think we will make it. I did some figuring, and I calculate that if the weather slows us down to 40 mph, we just barely have time to make the ferry. I talked it over with Pete and Libby and we have decided to get going in a few minutes. Maybe you could follow behind in your truck when you get done here and try to catch up with us, but we have come too far to risk missing the boat now. The sooner we get started the better. If we go now, we may still have a chance of beating most of the snow."

Bob has my full attention now. Various rebuttals echo in my head. Even in an hour from now we will still be three hours ahead of our original schedule. I might get done sooner, but, then again, getting a jumpstart on the foot of snow that is about to cover the U.P. and northern Ontario sounds like a pretty smart idea.

"You're probably right, Bob, I don't want you guys to miss the ferry, and you should take it easy driving tonight. I'm pretty sure I'll be able to get there in the time I have, but you guys go ahead with my blessing."

"Thanks, Nick, I knew you would understand."

Bob looks considerably relieved. And he heads back to help finish the dishes only to discover Libby leaning against the doorway with a dish towel over her shoulder, the sleeves of her periwinkle turtleneck rolled up, and her arms crossed over her chest. She has a half a smile for Bob that is enough to stop him in his tracks and make me lose my place in my notes.

"Bob, I don't like the idea of heading off into a snowstorm half as much as you macho boys do, but I don't think it's right to leave Nick to drive all night by himself. It's bad enough having to drive through snow, but if Nick still wants to go and he can finish up his work in time, then I'm going to ride with him to help him stay awake."

From behind, I can see Bob's shoulders droop noticeably.

"But, Libby…" Bob says dejectedly.

"That's very nice of you, Libby," I say, "but I don't want to cause you to miss part of the trip. If we don't make it in time, you could get stuck waiting around in Grand Marais for a couple of days with a guy you barely even know."

"Well, I haven't gotten the complete background check on you yet, Mister Becker, but we are going to catch up with these guys before we even reach Canada. I've seen how slow Pete drives even when the roads are clear."

"I really think you should come with us, Libby," Bob says.

"I'm going to go with Nick, and that's that. Let's leave him alone so he can finish his work and you two boys can hit the road."

"Thank you, Libby. I couldn't ask for a better co-pilot for tonight's journey."

I don't believe in bad luck, but I do believe in good fortune. Pete slips in to apologize for having to eat and run.

"You lucky bastard," he says with a smirk. "I was feeling real bad about leaving without you, but now I think you got the long end of this stick. 'Nudge, nudge, wink, wink.' See ya in Minnesota, buddy."

"With that pile of crap you call a truck, you'll be seeing my taillights before you cross the Batchawana River north of the Soo — even with an hour's head start. You drive carefully and let's keep an eye out for each other. Sorry I slowed you guys down with this stuff."

"Take it easy, Nick. We shall meet again."

Chapter 24

BY THE TIME Libby and I hit the road, the sleet has turned to snow and the farm fields and woods are covered in a slushy, white coating that looks more like drippy cinnamon-roll frosting than powdered-donut sugar. As we cross over the Straits of Mackinac on the five-mile-long Mackinac Bridge, Lake Michigan stretches to the west of us and the waters of Lake Huron stretch out to our right. We pay our toll on the St. Ignace side of the bridge, and the last light of day fades as we put the sky-scraper-high towers of the suspension bridge behind us.

Interstate 75 is mostly just wet, so we make good time across the U.P. Bob and Pete only have about an hour's head start on us, so Libby and I settle into comfortable conversation after the initial rush of hitting the road. Libby is going to the University of Indiana to get her Master's and teaching certificate in biology. Even though she is from Virginia and went to a tiny college in Illinois for her undergraduate degree, she chose Indiana because they offered her a full academic scholarship and they provided a program where she could get her masters and her certificate in just two years. I gently probe the issue of the welshing L.A. boyfriend, but her answer skirts the real issue.

"I'm still not sure what I am going to do this summer," she says, "I've applied to several programs that will give me the field study I need for my master's program, but I haven't heard back from all of them yet. I might end up working at Sequoia National Park in California, or doing some ornithology here in the Midwest. Things are a bit up in the air for me right now."

Any more direct questioning seems like it will only sour her otherwise sweet disposition, so I change the subject slightly.

"So, what was the name of that college in Illinois?" I ask, changing the subject.

"Oh, you probably wouldn't have heard of it," she says. "It sits on a high bluff overlooking the Mississippi River in the middle of nowhere. It's called Principia College."

"Principia? Are you kidding me? Did Pete tell you to say that to pull my leg?"

"No, that's where I went. It's a real place," she says on the verge of annoyance over some potential slight to her alma mater.

In an instant, Libby and I realize that there are more than just random sparks behind our growing mutual admiration. Principia is the only college in the world for Christian Scientists.

"You're a scientist?" she asks.

"Heck, yeah. C.S. has been in my family for five generations on my mother's side. I went to Principia Upper and Middle School in St. Louis," I tell her. "Half of my Mom's relatives work at the college. I've been there dozens of times. This is unbelievable."

"I could tell there was something special about you, Nick. I'm not surprised at all."

"How come Pete never said anything to you or me about this little surprising connection?" I ask. "Ever since we were roommates in college and he asked me about my books with those funny little metal markers, he's known something about my religion."

"Well, he didn't know about mine," Libby says. "Pete's a pretty funny guy to hang around, but in the short time I've known him I've learned to keep personal information on a "need-to-know" basis with him. You should have heard how gross he was when I mentioned that I had three blond sisters. Let's just say he wanted to know more about their hair color than I was willing to tell."

"He's a little rough around the edges, but he's usually respectful of the things that really matter to me. I'm sure he'll be as delighted about our little discovery as I am."

Libby and I slip into the usual, long run-down of mutual C.S. friends and acquaintances that carries us through Sault Ste. Marie and into the Algoma region of Ontario on Lake Superior's eastern shore. Libby's favorite biology professor at Principia is my second cousin and she knew my uncle who teaches there, too. Many of her college classmates were my high school classmates, as well. There aren't a lot of Christian Scientists, but the connections between us are usually broad and deep. As we cross-reference the people we know, we even discover that we attended the same wedding together three years ago in Park City, Utah. My cousin Katherine was one of Libby's best friends at a summer camp in Colorado.

By the time we see the green and white "Batchawana River" sign in the darkness, there is still no sign of Pete and Bob. The surface of Provincial Highway 17 has completely disappeared in fluffy, white snow with only three channels of tire tracks indicating where the road lies. There are only three channels because both north- and south-bound traffic share the wider rut in the middle, while the two skinnier, outer channels mark the treads of passenger-side tires in opposite directions. Both Libby and I cease chattering about our pasts as the growing realization of our present, somewhat-dire circumstances comes into focus. Hopefully, Libby's quiet concentration means that she is actually praying for us because my prayers aren't getting much past "Oh, God, we're almost out of gas, too, and I haven't seen an open gas station since we crossed into Canada."

We drive in attentive silence for a half hour without seeing another vehicle or open gas station. With darkness all around us, my headlights illuminate the floating flakes of snow in a hypnotic way. They come at us in a falling arc as the truck slips through the night, making it difficult to keep my eyes focused on the road ahead of me. Instead, they want to focus on the individual snowflakes flying into the windshield. I'm grateful when a creeping tanker truck appears up ahead of us with its outline of yellow running lights and far-cutting headlamps giving better perspective to the wintry road. The semi is chugging along through the snow at only 35 mph, but I don't mind because it's giving my eyes a welcome reprieve from the flying-snow syndrome, and the tanker's dual tires are pushing the snow out of the two channels of roadway that I'm trying to follow. As long as the trucker stays on the road, we will, too. It's only about 11:30 PM, so I decide to hang back behind the truck for a while, and Libby seems relieved to slow down a bit.

"Despite this lousy weather, we're still doing all right," I tell Libby. "I just saw a mileage sign back there that said Thunder Bay is only about 322 kilometers. That's about, uh…"

"Two hundred miles," Libby says before I even figure out how to figure out the conversion.

"Wow! You're good," I say without taking my eyes off the road. "Grand Portage, Minnesota, is only about another 50 miles after that. So, we still have plenty of time to get there before the ferry leaves, right?"

Out of the corner of my eye, I see Libby doing some math trick with her fingertips for a couple of seconds.

"Yeah, we should be okay," she says. "Even if we creep along like this all night, we can still get there in about seven hours, as long as we can find some gas. You wouldn't happen to have a can full of gas back there, would you?"

The needle on the gas gauge hit the red "E" mark a few miles back, but it still hasn't gone past it yet.

"I wish I thought of that. I've got a full 5-gallon can back at home that I haven't mixed with oil yet. It would be pretty ironic to run out of gas with tens of thousands of gallons only fifty yards ahead of us," I say as I read the big green "BP" letters on the back of the tanker, which is partially covered in dirty snow.

"Well, I guess man's extremity is God's opportunity," Libby says, "I'll get back to work."

Within ten minutes, the tanker blows past a brightly lit sign on the right side of the road. Through the vortices of snow whipped up by the passing truck, we can just barely make out the blue-and-white of a "Chevron" sign.

"There's one, Nick," Libby says, clapping and smiling up at the fluorescent beacon in the night.

My pickup fishtails back and forth a bit as I tap my brakes and plow through the two-foot-high snow bank blocking the entrance to the gas station.

"Whew, that was close. I think I know who to thank for this place appearing in the desert. Thank you, Lord, and thanks for the good work, Libby. Can I get you anything from inside?"

"No, thanks, I need to get out of this truck and move around a bit," Libby says slipping on her cute, red cap and down vest. "I'll meet you inside."

Blood begins to return to my white knuckles as I unscrew the gas cap and lift the nozzle to the pump. I have no idea how much gas costs, and the liter-to-gallon, Canadian-to-US-dollar conversion is way beyond me without Libby's quick fingertips and clever mind.

After pushing every button and lifting every lever on the pump three times, however, nothing comes out. Neither the

English nor the French instructions on the pump provide further enlightenment.

"Crap, or should I say 'meard'!"

A warm light glows through steamed-up windows at the café end of this fine "Gas Food" establishment, so I head on in.

Seated around a big circular table in the corner of the café is a group of about a half-dozen of my Canadian "neighbors to the north." A haze of cigarette smoke fills the café and I walk up to the four men and two women around the table.

"Hi! I was wondering if you could please help me with the pump outside? I may be doing something wrong, but I can't get any gas to come out."

There is a flurry of French words and hand gestures across the table, as several members of the group eye me up and down suspiciously and the rest just ignore me. I didn't know there are French Canadians in this part of Ontario, but it doesn't entirely surprise me.

"There is nothing wrong with you or the pump, monsieur," says a man with a rich, French accent flowing from beneath a bushy, dark handlebar mustache. "We are closed, the pumps have been turned off for the night. We open at 6:30 AM. Perhaps you can stay at the motel in town and come back in the morning. It is a terrible night for driving." The man says something in French to an older man with a grizzled, gray beard who gets up from the table and turns off the big Chevron sign outside from a switch behind the counter.

I try to explain my way into a full tank of gas from these likely descendants of French fur traders. I even explain that our ferry to the island leaves at 7:30 AM and we still have about 300 kilometers to drive, but my story only seems to stir a new round of discussion at the table as a younger man in green coveralls named Phil (according to the nametag over his breast pocket) translates to an old woman sitting across from him. He's talking pretty loudly in French, so I can't tell whether the old woman actually doesn't understand English or is just hard of hearing.

I suddenly become aware of a presence at my side, and I turn to see that Libby has returned from the powder room looking as pretty as she did when she went in — only a bit more intense. The man with the handlebar mustache has gotten up from the table and is walking towards us. I can't tell whether he is about to throw us out into the snow or ask Libby to join him for dinner.

"Let me handle this, Nick," Libby says, turning a smile to Monsieur Mustache.

I can't follow the rest of the conversation because it is all in French. Libby speaks the language effortlessly, and all I can do is watch faces and try to pick out the handful of words I do know, mostly from Pink Panther movies. At first, the mustached man, whom Libby is now calling Antoine, shrugs his shoulders and holds out his hands as he speaks with Libby. After a few more exchanges, he is nodding his head and frowning. The back table is now listening carefully to the negotiations. Antoine twists the end of his mustache and seems to yield, but holds up a finger in Libby's face and then taps it across his open palm saying something about "... avec Americaine, no Canadien."

Libby folds her arms across her chest, and I wonder if she has just started a border dispute. Then, she looks Antoine in the eye and says something that makes the peanut gallery in the back of the café begin to snigger.

"Touché, Antoine, I think she has you," says the younger man in the green coveralls. "I'll go turn on the pumps."

Libby is blushing slightly at her victory, but even Antoine is smiling now and he graciously pats Libby on the shoulder. "Your French is very good, mademoiselle."

"What did you say to the guy?" I ask.

"I'll tell you later. Just go fill 'er up, and let's get out of here while we still have our shirts."

After I fill the tank, Libby insists on settling up with Antoine while I clear the snow and ice off the windshield. I hand her a $20 US, but she won't tell me whether that covers it or not. I have no doubt that she made all of the conversions in her head as soon as I hung the nozzle back on the pump.

In minutes, we are on our way again with more than enough gas to make it to Minnesota.

"Thank you, kindly, Miss Hampton. You are proving to be quite resourceful. Nice job with the parlez-vouing. What did you say to that guy, anyway?"

"Oh, just something in French," she says, toying with me. "It's between me and Antoine."

She leaves me with nothing but my imagination to figure out what just happened as we drive through a little village on the banks of the Michipicoten River. The snow is letting up, and a plow has recently cleared our side of the road. There are only two lighted signs near the highway — one for a Royal Mounted Police station and one that blinks "Vacancy" under the words "Mawatam Motel."

"Last chance to stop for the night. Are you sure you want to keep going, Libby?"

"Oh, I'm sure," she answers. "See that motel back there? Guess who owns it?"

"Well, I don't know too many people in Mawatam, but I would venture to say a guy name Antoine?"

"When I went to the restroom, there was a nice map of the area next to the sink," Libby says. "It showed all the businesses in town and who owned them, as well as a R.M.P. post. I noticed that Antoine Tousant was the proprietor of several of the businesses including the gas station-café and the motel.

"When I asked him about letting us buy some gas from him, I could tell that he was trying to get us to stay at his motel. So, I asked him how far it was to the next public campsite. We were equipped for winter camping, I told him. That eliminated any chance of us spending money on motel rooms, so he considered turning on the pumps for us."

"That was smart. Then what did you say?"

"He hemmed and hawed about the difficulty of converting Canadian prices to US dollars. At first, he wanted to make us pay the Canadian pump price in US dollars, but then I noticed the exchange rate posted behind the counter. That would have been highway robbery. I quickly figured out how many liters to the gallon, and since you told me your tank held about 22 gallons, I was able to tell him exactly how much we would pay in US dollars to fill up the tank. He wasn't so sure about the exchange rate due to the late hour, but then I told him that I noticed there was a police station just down the road, and perhaps they could help us settle the matter if my offer seemed unfair to him. That seemed to bring him around, especially when I offered a five dollar tip to anyone who could turn on the pumps for us."

I can only shake my head and laugh. Since I first laid eyes on the Vibram soles of Libby Hampton's boots, I figured she would make a valuable addition to Bob's little adventure. Now, I'm starting to picture her in future adventures with just the two of us. I hope she can picture me there, too.

About an hour later, up ahead in the distance, we see a set of taillights beneath a familiar plywood pickup cap.

Chapter 25

MY PICKUP TRUCK windows are rolled all the way down, and the Eagles are blasting "Out of Control" from the tape deck. I know all of the words, and I don't think old Glen Frye would mind my harmonizing. It's 5:05 PM, May 19, and I am just a few minutes south of Mackinaw City and less than an hour from getting back home. I just said goodbye to my Isle Royale buddies after an early supper back at Audie's Restaurant. I'm cruising along U.S. 31, but they are heading down I-75 to get back to Indiana where the three of them will go their separate ways for the summer.

Our trip turned out even better than expected. The lake-effect snowstorm let up by the time we reached the north shore of Lake Superior, and we arrived with a few hours to spare before the ferry. There was new ice in the bays around Grand Marais and Isle Royale, but the sturdy aluminum craft was able to break through to the island and drop us off. By the following afternoon, the cold weather broke. We were hiking in shorts and T-shirts by the end of the trip. We saw a half dozen moose grazing on the bottom of the island's inland lakes, but we didn't see any wolves, although we heard them howling one cold blue dusky evening. The next afternoon, while hiking a rocky ridge along the spine of the island, we came upon fresh wolf tracks the size of my fist.

What a difference a week can make. All signs of last weekend's snowstorm have vanished, save for a few melting piles of grayish snow back in a Mackinaw City parking lot. A Northwestern Bank sign back there said that it's 78 degrees. Nearly all of the trees have leafed out, and the forsythia, wild cherry, and apple trees are in full bloom. I'm wearing my dirty hiking shorts and a relatively clean, red T-shirt that still smells like campfire, but I don't care because I'm probably in love. Libby and I shared lots of long talks on the way there and part of the way back, we laughed together and goofed off with Pete and Bob on the trail, and we even kissed goodbye in the restaurant parking lot before the boys returned from the men's room to join us. Libby is still officially attached and didn't do anything that her L.A. boyfriend shouldn't know about, but she shed a tear when we had to go. I have her phone number and address in my back pocket, and she has mine in her shirt pocket. We have both promised to keep in touch.

I get a tinge of melancholy as I drive past tiny Pellston Airport, but the after-glow of a great backpacking trip, good friends, and the pleasure of a pretty and clever young lady's company keep me high all the way home. Not only am I looking forward to a hot soak in the galvanized tub (it's warm enough that I might even put it out on the front porch), but I have a new appreciation for the fact that I really do have a home of my own to go back to. There's a lot of work to be done there — stories to write for Sean Cooper, a house renovation to get back on track, a legal mess to untangle, and the story of an old soldier's family to uncover. Nonetheless, I can't wait to get home.

I pull up to The Shack next to the plank over the kitchen-addition excavation so that I can unload easily. A quick look around the house reveals that all is just as I left it, and there's no sign of any raccoons having moved in while I was gone. Joe and Anna's papers from after their marriage in 1909 are on my desk awaiting closer examination, and my answering machine is blinking five or six messages. I hit the play button. There are a couple of hang-ups, a message from Cushman telling me to call him when I get back, and a couple of unexpected messages from Homer Robertson:

"Beep… Hello, Nicolas, this is Homer Robertson, an old friend of your family's. I heard you might be in town. We are going to be doing some work out on your Aunt's property this week, and I just wanted to touch base with you before we get started. Call me. I'm at 526-9957."

And towards the end of the messages: "Beep… Look, Nicolas, we're going to get started Wednesday morning. Give me a call if you're around, otherwise, I may see you out there."

Sweat breaks out on my forehead as I play back the messages and get Robertson's number down on a scrap of paper. What the hell is he talking about? I turn around slowly in my desk chair to look out the living room windows towards the meadow and the lake view, but all I can see is a dark, green band covering up the horizon. My brain can't take in what my eyes are seeing fast enough. I leap from my desk and run out the door and onto the front porch. What I see there trips me up and I almost tumble down the front porch steps. The flat yard at the top of the plateau is still the same, plus a couple of inches of new grass, but a thick line of newly planted pine trees screens off my entire view of the meadow below the plateau and the lake beyond it. There is about a 10-foot stretch of lake view still remaining on the far left side of the yard, but through it I can see a big orange Kubota tractor parked in the meadow with a huge root-ball attachment resting on the earth. Four more pines with their root balls wrapped in burlap sit in the meadow just waiting to finish the job and shut The Shack off from the lake for good. The planted trees — there must be a couple dozen of them — are no shrubs or saplings, either. Each tree is at least 20-feet tall, with thick, healthy branches full of needles. They have been meticulously planted into the side of the plateau's slope in three checkerboard rows. The highest row, planted a few feet beyond where Pete was just pissing last week, blocks most of the view, but it looks like it won't take too many years for the lower two rows to reach full-screening height, either. I can't believe this, why would Robertson do something like this?

I wander through the trees like a child lost in the woods — only this is no wood. It's some kind of bizarre "insta-forest" that has sprung out of the earth in less than a week, like that green stuff that grows on those Chia-Pets I've seen on TV. The trees are all carefully staked and the root balls buried and covered in fresh cedar chips. I have to walk around and touch the Kubota's four-clawed, root-ball attachment to believe what has happened here. Staggering back into the meadow, though, I get the full picture. From the house sites, The Shack has almost disappeared behind the wall of green. Only the second story and the roof peek out over the top of the highest pines. Although my new neighbors will have fantastic views of Lake Michigan from their bluff-top estates, Homer doesn't want them to have to see the old Becker hovel as they drive their Cadillacs and Ford Explorers to and from their new "cottages."

I try to put this in perspective. This side isn't really my family's land anymore, and I know that Homer is just a businessman with customers to please, but I just don't get it. If I had the wherewithal to buy all this land and build a big summerhouse here, would I be just like them? Did Homer even think about standing on my front porch and checking to see what things looked like from our side of the pine-tree wall? Would it have made any difference if he did? Or did he only admire his handiwork from the meadow and see dollar signs? I can begin to feel the blood pounding in my ears as I march up to The Shack to make a phone call.

I punch Homer's numbers out on my phone and wait for an answer.

"Hello, you've reached the home of Homer and Celia Robertson and the office of Four Fires Development Group. Sorry we missed your call. Please leave a message at the beep. If you would like to send a fax, please press..."

I slam the phone down before I even get to the beep. I sit down to calm myself, but I soon rise and head straight out of the house and into the barn. After mixing up some oil and gas in a small gas can, I fill up my new little Poulan chainsaw. I just bought it a couple of months ago to help keep myself supplied with cordwood. I'm starting to get the hang of the thing, but I'm still learning. I slow down enough to remember my gloves and safety glasses, but I am practically running and almost slip on the cedar chips when I reach my first pine-tree target. Between the soft-needled branches of what look to be white pines, I pump the primer on the saw, flip the choke, and give it a couple of pulls. In my haste, I forget to flip the choke off after the first firing, and I flood the damn engine before my chain even gets a first bite. I pull the chord a few more times with the choke all the way open and only make matters worse. I try to clear the engine with the choke closed, but all I smell is gas, and all I feel is the sweat pouring off my head and into my eyes. On second thought, I decide that anger and chainsaws probably shouldn't mix. I head back to the barn for my light cruising axe. It's little, but it's sharp.

Back at the offending pine tree, I try to find a good position to get at the base of the trunk, but it is awkward trying to stand on a steep incline and the cedar chips are loose and slippery. Hunched over with pine needles in my face, I manage to lop off a couple of lower branches to make way for bigger strokes. As I swing the axe back and start to bring it forward, however,

I lose my footing again and the axe head glances off the trunk and bites into my bare shin before I can fully check my swing.

After an initial howl of pain, I clench my lips closed and hop around the yard with my hand over my shin. After a few seconds, I let my shin go without looking down at it, and gather my tools to take back to the barn. A wave of profanity and curses rises from my throat, but I swallow it back down in silence. There is no one to hear it anyway, and my boiling temper has already been reduced to a simmer. Cutting the trees down probably wasn't the best idea anyway. I would just end up having to pay for them in some way, and it still wouldn't change the fact that the Becker farm is changing right in front of my eyes. I can feel the blood trickling down my leg, but on closer inspection, the cut doesn't look too bad. I head back into the house to clean my wound and try to figure things out.

Chapter 26

The Little Traverse Evening Times, Tuesday, Oct. 19, 1909

Blue Harbor
"The Busy Town"

The Johnson-Becker Wedding a Capital Surprise.

The announcement of the marriage of Miss Anna Johnson to Joseph L. Becker is a surprise to the many friends of the young people who have so cleverly carried out their plan. The marriage has been one for some time anticipated by their acquaintances, especially by the friends of the bride, and it was rumored the event would soon occur, but when announcement was made yesterday that the wedding had occurred Aug. 13 at the Presbyterian parsonage at Petoskey, the young people had successfully carried out a capital surprise. The bride, the daughter of Mr. and Mrs. James Johnson, is one of Blue Harbor's best known and most popular young ladies, having resided here since her childhood, and has won by her estimable character the love and respect of a large circle of acquaintances. A genial and ever willing helper in social affairs and a musician of excellent ability, she will be greatly missed. Mr. Becker of Ft. Atkinson, Wis., who was formerly employed in the Isthmian Canal Commission in Panama, but now a salesman for a southern Michigan hosiery firm, is a young man of sterling worth, and the only unsatisfactory fact known of him here is that he is taking from our midst one of Blue Harbor's helpful young ladies. Mr. and Mrs. Becker will leave Thursday for their new home in Ann Arbor with the hearty good wishes of a community of friends.

Joe and Anna's marriage license provides a few more clues about this union of "estimable character" with "sterling worth." They were not particularly superstitious — they were married on Friday the 13th. They weren't above a little white lie now and then for the sake of propriety — they are both listed as "twenty-three" years of age, even though Anna was twenty-five and almost three years older than Joe. And they were both working when they came together in holy matrimony. Anna is listed as a "Music Teacher." Joe is listed as a "Police Officer" residing in Las Cascadas, Panama.

I can imagine what kind of students Anna must have had at her piano, but my imagination can only take me part of the way into Joe's Panama experience. I have spent the better part of this weekend trying to ignore the "insta-forest" outside my windows and studying up on Panama to get a better picture of Joe's time there. The particulars of Joe's first stint in Panama are few and far between — a dozen color-tinted postcards and a few photographs. The polished black boots; high-collared, white shirt; khaki tunic and riding breeches; and campaign hat of the Zone Police Force don't look that much different than the Marine Corps uniform that Joe wore when he arrived in Panama in 1908. One noticeable difference in the photographs, though, is the appearance of a sandy-colored, sweeping mustache above Officer Becker's mouth and the ubiquitous presence of a dark, wooden pipe hanging below.

Joe may not have kept love letters from his Northern sweetheart, but he was always careful to keep his official paperwork in order. A U.S. Marine Corps discharge certificate shows that Corporal Joseph L. Becker was discharged on Sept. 15, 1908 "by purchase" from Camp Elliott, I.C.Z., Panama with "character given on discharge" rated as "excellent."

My guess is that employment with the Isthmian Canal Commission as a police officer wasn't all that different than the garrison duty Joe had been doing for the past couple of years, but it probably paid considerably more than what the Marine Corps offered. Joe left the Marines to get together a stake that would help him and his bride-to-be get settled into civilian life once they were wed.

A few of Joe's carefully preserved postcards bear little notes to Anna like the one from Havana. In his elegant, leftward-leaning script, Joe narrates some scenes to Anna. On a color postcard titled, "One of the Indian Chiefs at San Blas, Panama," Joe writes, "We have Indians here as well as in Blue Harbor. Oct. 11, 1908." On another postcard titled "Birds Eye View of Pedro Miguel, Canal Zone, Panama," Joe puts a big X and writes "Joe to Anna in Grand Rapids. Does this look inviting? Looking towards Panama Canal in back of dark ridge. Station in middle. Feb. 15, 1909."

I trust that Joe had better romantic sense than to only send the occasional postcard. What is clear is that Joe's exotic travels must have provided a needed antidote to Leslie Higginbotham's escapades amongst East Coast society. What I wonder, though, is whether Anna simply admired Joe's worldly travels from afar, or whether she actually envisioned taking part in them herself? Did Anna expect Joe to put all this behind him when he married her, or did she like that part of him enough to want more of it?

While Joe's personal experiences in Panama remain just out of my grasp, he has left me with a detailed record of life on the Zone around 1908 in the form of two old books that he must have purchased while there, and passed on to Anna to give her a better taste of the times and place. Both books — *Panama Pictures* by Michael Delevante and *On the Canal Zone* by

Thomas Graham Grier — provide pictures and accounts of travels across the Isthmus just prior to and during Joe's first stint there, respectively.

George Eastman's invention of dry, roll film and the development of the box camera led to an explosion of amateur photography around the turn of the century. Armed with easily transportable photography equipment and literary inclinations, men like Delevante and Grier traveled the globe to record their discoveries in words and pictures. They wrote and photographed some of what Joe would have seen and lived.

Although water and shipping would not flow through the Canal until 1914, dirt and rock was flying up and down the Isthmus at record speeds in 1908. In the five years since the Americans had taken over the world's largest engineering project from the French, work on the canal had reached epic proportions along the entire forty-plus-mile cut across the Isthmus. The French had moved 82,000,000 cubic yards of earth before they ran out of money, but it would take another 93,000,000 cu. yds. for America and its army of Jamaican, Barbadian, Martiniquen, St. Lucien, French, Spanish, Chinese, Italian, Cartegenian, American, and assorted laborers, clerks, foremen, engineers, and superintendents to finish the "Big Ditch" — to say nothing of its locks, dams, and other earthworks. Since President Theodore Roosevelt had visited Panama in 1906, the ten-mile-wide Canal Zone had been transformed from a mosquito-infested, backwater jungle outpost into a forty-mile-long chain of steam-powered efficiency and U.S. Army-regulated sanitation.

At least two sets of railroad tracks, mostly running along the bottom of the excavation, crossed the Isthmus. By day, the Panama Railroad hauled five hundred trainloads of dirt out of the big cuts and into low areas that required fill. Each of the seventy or so steam shovels (nearly twice as big as a locomotive) working up and down the canal scooped up as much as five cubic yards of dirt and rock per shovel every eighteen seconds and dumped them into railroad dirt cars waiting along side to take the dirt away. Air drills bore into whatever rock and dirt would not yield to the steam shovels' jaws, and blasts (both large and small) could be heard and felt, especially near the big cuts at Culebra and Bas Obispo. As progress was made, the railroad beds and tracks would be shifted to lower elevations so the ground they had rested on could be dug up, blasted apart, and hauled away.

While travelers through the Panama that Joe knew couldn't help but be impressed with the massive scale of the project, it was the little things that were making the difference between French failure and American success. Yellow fever and malaria, which had helped to bring the first efforts of Ferdinand Marie de Lesseps' canal company to a grinding halt in 1889, had nearly been eradicated by the time Joe arrived in Panama in 1908. Ice for refrigeration; screens to cover up the windows and doors of canal company quarters and offices; sewers and clean water for company towns, military camps, and native villages along the zone — all these little things did as much for the completion of the work as all the iron muscle of all the steam engines in Panama.

Cuban physician Carlos Finlay and American bacteriologist Walter Reed had figured out and proved that the pesky mosquito was largely to blame for the deadly fever, and Col. William C. Gorgas of the U.S. Army Medical Corps was placed in charge of "sanitation" work throughout the Canal Zone. Under Col. Gorgas's orders, the jungle was hacked back to the edge of construction areas and installations along the canal, standing water was drained off as quickly as possible, and the towns and work areas were regularly fumigated to keep the mosquitoes from breeding. Sanitation laws were well publicized and strictly enforced. And that's where Joe came in.

Anyone living in or passing through the Canal Zone could be fined or even jailed for violation of the sanitation laws. A worker couldn't even leave a wheelbarrow standing upright during the rainy season for fear of it collecting water and breeding mosquitoes. I don't know how much of Joe's time was spent on wheelbarrow patrol, but an excerpt from Grier's book gives some idea of what Joe's job must have been like.

The Zone Police force is made up of a fine body of men, well qualified for the work; the majority of them are ex-soldiers, who have seen service in Cuba or the Philippines. The force consists of, approximately, three hundred, and is divided among eight main stations and twenty-nine outposts, or out stations, in addition to the headquarters of the department.

In the year ending June 30, 1907, the total number of arrests were 6,236, of which 925 were for violation of sanitary regulations, 787 for intoxication and 1,176 disorderly conduct. Of the persons arrested 365 were females and 5,871 males. The total number of convictions resulting from these arrests were 5,193.

On my return from the Canal Zone I heard the police department being criticized as being lazy. Everyone has a right to their opinion, and I give the figures above to let those who have not been on the Zone form their opinion. The men wearing the uniform of the Canal Zone police force appear to me to be capable, and they were at all times courteous.

*The work of policing the Canal Zone is made difficult by
the mixed nationalities of the laboring classes and their
ignorance of the laws and conventionalities of civilization.
The department has forty-one different nationalities on its
arrest book. In March 1908, there were 586 arrests, and in
April, 591. There were forty nationalities represented in the
591 arrests and fifty-two offenses. There were 146 prisoners
in the district jails on April 30, and ninety-five convicts in
the Zone penitentiary.*

*The convicts were employed in road building; the value of
their work in April, 1908, was $1,580.*

Grier probably only passed through Las Cascadas on a
round-trip train from the Atlantic to the Pacific and back
again, but he clearly experienced some of the Panamanian
terrain and culture that Joe called home for a couple of years.
Grier shared something else in common with Joe, as well. Both
men were living in a new age of industry and science, and they
shared a modern desire to classify and account for the world
around them in numbers and measurable fact. While Grier
was, at times, obsessive in his compulsion to list, count, and
record all that he saw around him, Joe's careful accounting of
his world bore a particularly military stamp — an imprint that
didn't always make sense in the civilian world.

When my mother got to know her father-in-law in the
1950s, for example, Joe's Navy, Marine Corps, and Army ways
were deeply ingrained. Despite the advent of coffee percola-
tors and electric grinders, Joe brewed his coffee in a pot filled
with fresh grounds every morning. After bringing it up to exact
temperature and taste, Joe would pour off the dark brew, open
up the kitchen window of his home in the elm-tree-lined Packard Ave. neighborhood of Ann Arbor, and dump the coffee
grounds into the bushes below the window, as if he were still

in some Army mess tent in the jungles of Luzon. The grounds made good fertilizer for the bushes, to boot. Having graduated from Army cooking school in the '30s, Joe also defied civilian logic by taking charge of all baking in his household. Whenever Joe baked bread, my mother remembered, the kitchen was strictly off limits, even to Anna.

Although Joe was prepared to leave the military for Anna in 1909, some of his earlier-ingrained Navy and Marine Corps ways came with him. Having spent most of his Marine Corps days as a clerk, Joe had become a stickler for precise accounts and records.

As I sit at my desk with my back to the wall of pine trees that still stands between my front porch and Lake Michigan, I am thumbing through one of the few remnants of Joe's meticulous record keeping. Joe and (in some years) Anna kept all their day-to-day transactions in little, black notebooks. The notebooks got a bit jumbled in the move, and I totally mixed them all up last month when I accidentally knocked the pile of them off my desk while writing a *Gazette* story on deadline. A little bigger than a checkbook, but still small enough to carry around tucked into an inside coat pocket, the Becker account books are both mundane and revealing at the same time.

Anna seems to have been the more business-like of the two accountants in the family, though. The first notebook I pick up is in Anna's hand and seems to cover the end of September 1943 to early September 1945. Joe was still working then, and it makes sense that Anna would have kept the books because Joe — a full-bird Army colonel by then — was Commanding Officer of the Armed Forces Induction Center in Detroit. In an unusual arrangement, Anna and my father (a young teenager at the time) continued to live in Ann Arbor, Michigan, while Joe worked in Detroit and Chicago, commuting by train.

Wartimes were tight, with Anna's book seldom showing more than $50 on hand and sometimes as little as a couple of bucks in the house. Even my dad, who was only fourteen years old in the fall of '43, pitched in by making loans to the house account when he could — although it looks like he was always repaid when the balance was back up again.

How strange it is to have this level of detail about my grandparents' and my father's lives, and yet not know the answers to some of the big-picture questions I have about them. For example, I know to the penny how much money Anna spent on October 7, 1943:

Oct. 7 — To John	*$1.00*
gasoline	*1.89*
Gordon Burrows	*.88*
lunch	*1.18*
watch ribbon	*.25*
tip	*.25*
record	*.55*
Bal.	*$43.89*

But I don't know exactly what Anna's voice sounded like when she talked to Joe on the telephone. I don't know if my dad was eagerly waiting to enlist in the Army as soon as he finished high school, or whether he secretly prayed every night that the war would end before he turned 18. And I don't know if Joe simply got lost in the despair of losing Anna when he redrafted his will after her passing in 1956, or if he had a clear-sighted reason for leaving the fate of The Shack in the limbo of life tenancy instead of simply given it to John and Vicki outright. And I don't know if Joe and Anna's marriage was a true love affair or simply a durable alliance.

These little, black notebooks may not hold the answers to these questions, but they might hold some clues. Every once in while, the books wander from strict bookkeeping into the territory of personal journaling. For example, on Feb. 3, 1944, there is any entry below "cash on hand — .94" that reads, "Vincent passed away noon Thursday Feb. 3rd, 1944. Funeral Feb. 6th 2:30 PM, Petoskey."

Vincent Johnson or Vint, as family and friends called him, is Anna's younger brother. He is something of a shadowy figure to me — a ladies' man, a dandy, childless (at least officially), and a marginally successful wholesale grocery salesman and stockbroker who lived "in sin" with Astrid, his Danish girlfriend, for nearly a decade before marrying her just a few years before his death. Yet, here he is — an entry in the family accounts — no shadow to Anna, I'm sure. There are a few pictures of Vint and a handful of letters from him, but I don't know that much about him. Yet Vint is a constant reminder of how easily a life can fade from the collective memory of the living. Perhaps someone ended up with the records of his life, but I may be one of only a half dozen people left in the whole world with any knowledge of him at all.

Vint makes me appreciate how rare it is to be able to know my grandparents and the people I came from. Most people my age barely know their great-grandparents or grandparents any better then I know Vint. I think we Americans, especially, spend so much time looking to the future and moving from place to place that it's easy for us to lose sight of where and who we came from. I moved back to a spot where the past has converged with the present, and I just happen to have some spare time to explore it. I'm just lucky, I guess. Most people never even get the chance to look back over their shoulders. Not until we are older and quieter do we usually tend to turn around in earnest. By then, however, the past is usually too far back to see clearly. The old papers have long since been thrown out, our father's and mother's friends have mostly passed on, and we are left with a cold trail.

Fortunately for me, however, there is still plenty of material on Joe and Anna to mine. By the time Joe retired from the Army after WW II, he resumed the duty of keeping track of the family finances. Joe began adding meteorological data to his daily financial entries, and by the '50s, the black books became more of a staccato account of each day's doings and less of a financial record at all. Joe's flowing cursive is still elegant-looking, despite arthritis, but the books take work to decipher. I could easily spend a week just reading through these, but it is with Joe and Anna's earlier married lives than I am currently occupied. Although I wander through the '40s and '50s for while, there is one little, black book, in particular, that I'm after. It covers August 1909 to September 1910. I noticed this anomaly last month when I first looked through these records, and I've puzzled over it ever since. There must have been some reason this book was saved, and I have a hunch that it had something to do with the brief letters that are tucked into its pages and a pair of shoes for Anna.

Chapter 27

Nov. 1, 1909

My Dear Anna —

You looked so peaceful as you slept this morning that I did not want to wake you. Made a fine breakfast of leftover cornbread and apple butter. Taking the 5:30 train this morning because I have a lot of territory to cover this week. The new shoes you bought last Thursday are quite becoming on you, but you will have to return them until we see what kind of sales I can make this week. Remember, there is no way I can keep track of expenses when I'm on the road unless you plan for them ahead of time. Here is $15.26 to get you through the week. I'll be home Friday night or Saturday morning.

Lovingly,
Your Joe

What Joe didn't mention in his note was that the hosiery business wasn't panning out quite the way he had hoped. Joe wasn't having any trouble making sales. The trouble was he was making too many sales. The Culpepper Women's Apparel Co. of Warren, Michigan, had never seen a new salesman make such a meteoric rise in such a short time. Joe not only commanded the respect of the male merchants he sold to, but he had an easy charm that disarmed even the most suspicious female shopkeepers and clerks.

Joe was a confident, natural salesman and he had broken Culpepper's sales records in both of the first two months he had worked for them covering Michigan, Illinois, Indiana, and Ohio. Joe's commissions and the money he had saved from Panama allowed the newlyweds to furnish their rented house in Ann Arbor comfortably and with a bit of style — a new upright piano for Anna and her students in the parlor, a velvet upholstered rocker and smoking stand for Joe in the den, and glass-paneled bookcases on each side of the brick fireplace in the living room.

Joe's bosses back at Culpepper, however, figured that such a lucrative territory must be too big for one man, so they cut Joe's territory and (consequently) his income in half. To make matters worse, a nephew of old man Culpepper got Michigan and Indiana (where Joe had established dozens of new customers). Joe would find new prospects in Illinois and Ohio, he reasoned, but he wasn't sure how to make up for all the lost time he would spend leapfrogging back and forth over Michigan and Indiana to get to his disjointed territory.

Joe wasn't trying to hide anything from Anna on the cold, wet Monday that he set off for another week of drumming up business, but he wanted to come up with a couple of solutions before he presented her with the problem. Anna had quickly fallen in love with the university town they had chosen to start their new life in. Some of her students were the children of professors, and there were regular concerts and art exhibits to attend. Anna had already found a church to join, and she liked having things to talk about other than logging, snowdrifts, whitefish, and deer hunting. Her new Ann Arbor friends, however, admired Anna's rugged, North Woods upbringing and marveled at her ability to live in two worlds at once. The last thing Joe wanted to do was uproot Anna again, just as she was making a new home for them.

Many of the traveling salesmen Joe had met in the last couple of months represented several different companies, so Joe planned on taking a side trip to Cloquet, Minnesota, to apply for a sales job there. Although the Culpepper job allowed Joe to return home most weekends, Joe was willing to represent more companies and travel farther afield if he could earn enough commissions to maintain their new home. Having taken Anna from the only home she ever knew in order to be closer to the major train routes, Joe was determined to find more work to make his Illinois to Ohio trips worthwhile.

The following Friday evening around suppertime, the Chicago-Detroit Express pulled up to the Michigan Central Depot on the north side of Ann Arbor. Joe collected his suitcase and his small trunk, now filled with samples of hosiery, matches, and coffee. Although it would be several weeks until he would get paid for his work, this had been a good week. Not only had he found new customers for Culpepper, but he had secured additional positions representing the Diamond Match Company and the McLaughlin Coffee Co. Although he had traveled to Cloquet, Minnesota to land the matchstick job, he had met a man on the train between Milwaukee and Chicago who hired him on the spot to sell coffee-bean orders to the hundreds of cafés and restaurants sprouting up alongside the Midwest's web of railroad tracks.

Gray clouds had been drizzling on and off all day in Ann Arbor, but Joe was smiling as he left the massive granite-block depot at the bottom of the Huron River valley and climbed the cobblestone streets on the side of the hill. Joe hustled up Elizabeth Street as though he was heading to the University of Michigan's main campus, but cut left on Lawrence St. for a block before reaching Joe and Anna's first Ann Arbor home on N. Thayer St.

The days were getting short. Even though it was only a bit after 6:00 PM, the sky above was pitch black. The new electric street lamps lit Joe's way, though, with a comforting electric hum, and he was careful to keep his polished leather boots out of the puddles that were forming in the gutters. There was no light on, however, inside Joe and Anna's snug little house. There was a bulb burning over the front porch, but all was dark inside. All seemed to be in order as Joe mounted the wooden steps to his front porch. Anna's mop was hanging on the wall still dripping and the empty milk bottles were carefully placed at the edge of the stoop for the milkman, but all was quiet. Joe set down his bags and reached for the door, but found that it was locked. As he dug through his coat pockets for the house key, he both knocked on the glass-windowed door and called out for Anna, but there was no reply.

Joe figured that Anna must have gone out to dinner with friends, which was fine since he hadn't expected to be home so soon. Once he got in, dropped his bags, and turned on the light in the parlor, he headed straight to the kitchen table, which was the usual place for Joe and Anna's notes to each other.

Fri. Nov 5, 5:15 pm

My Dear Joe —

Sorry I could not be home to greet you. Mother slipped on some ice on the sidewalk and hurt her ankle (nothing too serious she says) and is having trouble looking after Father who is laid up in bed with influenza or something like it. I am spending the weekend in Blue Harbor until they are better, though.

I left you a plate of cold fried chicken and mash potatoes in the icebox. You can heat it up on the stove if you'd like. I returned the shoes and left you my income from music lessons, so there is plenty of cash ($25.53) and food in the pantry.

Don't take the train up to join me as Vincent was planning to stop by Saturday evening for dinner. He's on his way home to Blue Harbor from a business trip, and he wrote me to ask if he could pay us a call. I wrote him back "yes" earlier this week, but I didn't know about mother then, and now it's too late to reach him because he's traveling. He'll be off again Saturday night to visit one of his girl-friends in Grand Rapids, but ask him to get home to Blue Harbor by Sunday night so that somebody will be here to look after Mother and Father. I'm sorry to leave things in such a rush. Maybe you two brothers-in-law could go out to dinner on the town. I'm sure that would suit Vint's tastes better than my cooking anyway.

I know you will be gone by the time I get home, and I hate to miss even a moment of our little "weekend getaways at home," but we will just have to wait until next weekend. I do, however, wish to discuss some financial matters with the "Marine Corps Paymaster" when we get back. Just remember, Joe, a woman is not the same as a soldier and will have unexpected expenses from time to time. Perhaps we need to make some adjustments to our current book-keeping methods.

The train is almost here, and I must dash.

Lovingly yours,
Anna

We tend to think that the debates about home, career, and money are peculiarly modern problems between men and women, but I can see between the lines of Joe and Anna's little black notebook that men and women have been working on these issues for a very long time. Whether Anna waved banners in Women's Suffrage marches down the streets of Ann Arbor or not, she was on the frontlines of the movement — not only continuing her music teaching career after marriage, but into motherhood, as well. In 1909, Anna wouldn't even be allowed to vote for another nine years, but she could make a living, keep house, and balance the family finances at the same time.

Just as Anna was coming to terms with Joe's adventurous streak and exotic travels (some of the very qualities that attracted her to him in the first place), Joe was having to come to terms with Anna's strength of character and natural competence — some of the same attributes that first attracted him to her. I don't entirely know how gracious or how rough this process was, but I do know that the process would last for almost two more decades. Were there fists banged on tables, dishes thrown across the kitchen, long debates in bed, or just these civil letters? I may never know.

From the little, black notebook I can see that Joe did wait for Vint, and they did go out to dinner (*$2.50*) Saturday night, but Joe spent part of Saturday afternoon Nov. 6th shopping. Anna bought the shoes on Oct. 28 — *"shoes for Anna -$4.25."* She returned them on Nov. 1 — *"returned shoes +$4.25."* But Joe bought them again on Nov. 6 — *"shoes for Anna -$4.25."* There is one last note tucked into the pages of the little, black book.

Nov. 6, 1909

My Darling Anna,

Since I have been banished from the North for the week-end, I am sending your brother as my emissary bearing gifts for you and Jim, and Dianna. The shoes you will recognize, and I hope you will accept them with my apologies. I should have known better than to doubt that my Anna Girl has things well in hand here in A.A. The honey jar is for your folks, so keep your fingers out of it.

I hardly know what to do with myself without you here. It's only been a day, but I am knocking about the house like a lost sheep. I had an excellent week of drumming and I have much news to tell you and matters to discuss. Unfortunately, I will have to be gone for two weeks and won't see you again until the 19th or 20th. Rather than tell you all in this note, I shall wait for you here at home on Monday morning, so that we can have lunch together and a nice visit before I shove off for Toledo. I will try to stay out of trouble until my pretty shepherdess arrives to put me back on the straight and narrow.

Love and Kisses to You,
Joe

A dark cloud had appeared on the newlyweds' horizon, but passed almost as quickly as it came. It wasn't the first storm cloud and it wouldn't be the last, but something had changed. Two strong and determined individuals were becoming a single couple. Instead of facing every ill wind that blew between them with stiffened limbs and unblinking eyes, they were learning to bend in the breeze and reach out to each other for support when the crosswinds threatened to blow them apart. I detect that there was more hurt and anger beneath the pages

of these quaint notes and records than what shows on the surface — Joe worried about his ability to support his wife and
home in the civilian world; Anna left alone for weeks at a time
to keep house and teach music, yet frustrated when she wasn't
given the power to make a simple financial decision on her
own; nervous anticipation before each of Joe's weekends at
home, and quiet despair each time he had to leave. Civilian life
for a traveling salesman and a music teacher wasn't easy.

But they were learning. The little, black notebook entries
starting on Nov. 8 show Anna's handwriting added to Joe's.
Although Joe would add his own traveling expenses and
pocket money to the books every couple of weeks, the transactions show that Anna and Joe figured out a way to share the
purse strings. There is one final entry for Monday, Nov. 8 in
Joe's handwriting, though, that sheds additional light on the
incident of Anna's shoes.

After receiving a telephone call from Anna's mother with
the details of Anna's arrival, Joe met Anna at the train station
Monday morning and carried her bags home. His news was
bittersweet. Even though he had found new work that would
actually improve the family income, he would have to be gone
on longer trips more often. Anna's news, however, recorded for
posterity's sake, trumped Joe's career changes. Beneath *"baked
goods .08"* and *"paper .05,"* Joe wrote:

"Anna is quite certain — We are going to have a baby!"

~ PART 8 ~
EL PASO, TEXAS

Chapter 28

HENRY RICHARDS IS one of my dad's oldest friends from Ann Arbor, and, coincidentally, he now lives in Blue Harbor. Henry took an early retirement from Texaco about ten years ago at the end of Jimmy Carter's oil crunch, and he began a second career as a realtor with Stevens Real Estate in downtown Blue Harbor.

Henry spent a few summers Up North with his family in his teens and used to hook up with my dad for canoe trips and other adventures. Henry and his wife Carmen were quite happy to settle here after one of their daughters married a local veterinarian. Henry and Carmen are good Catholics and they have nine children, all of whom are grown. They already have about a dozen grandchildren, and the Richards' birth rate is climbing. Like Patty Kensington, Henry is one of my few living links to the Colonel and Anna, and especially to my father.

On this fine Tuesday morning in late May, Henry has agreed to spend some time helping me with a story I'm working on this week for the *Northern Michigan Gazette*. My editor, Sean Cooper, already came up with a great headline for this feature: "Forgotten Farmsteads." In this land of million dollar cottages, planned unit developments, and other land grabs, the number of abandoned farmhouses and other shacks out in the country strikes me as a bit odd. While it's understandable that the attention of the folks with the big money is on waterfront and view properties, there is something sad and mysterious in these forlorn structures that dot the countryside just out of sight of the lavish summer homes and condominiums.

I had a hunch that each of these dilapidated houses holds some story, and my preliminary research has turned up some intriguing tales. One stone house up near Cross Village with no roof turns out to have never been completed. According to a guy I interviewed up the road a bit, the former owner was a farmer and schoolteacher back in the '20s. He was in the middle of building a new house for his bride-to-be when he got in trouble for doing something he shouldn't have with one of the girls in his class. He got sent to the slammer instead of getting married, and never came back.

According to Ralph Kowalski, the owner of a restaurant in Cross Village, some Polish settler built a farmhouse that is now half fallen down and lies a couple miles south of the village. Ralph doesn't know much about the guy, except that he was a hell of a good mason. Ralph said the guy sculpted faces out of concrete and set them into his stonework. There are faces stacked up amongst the stones of the half-fallen down farmhouse. And this same guy must have been the mason on Ralph's old restaurant because there are similar faces set into the stone wall leading down to Kowalski's basement. Ralph doesn't know how the old farmhouse came to be abandoned, but he thinks some Indians were the last ones to live there. They left because the place was haunted, according to Ralph.

Henry Richards may not be able to help me confirm the existence of "bad manitous" south of Cross Village, but he has agreed to show me some plat books and teach me how to track down the current owners of the forgotten farmsteads I've located.

While we are at it, though, I'm hoping to mix a little *Gazette* business with some personal business. I can't seem to ignore the "insta-forest" out in front of The Shack any longer, and I'm hoping Henry might have some ideas for what I can do about it. I finally got a hold of Homer Robertson on the phone yesterday. He was polite, but he didn't seem too interested in reaching a compromise on the pine-tree wall before he gets potential buyers lined up for the lots near my house. The best he could do was to say that he would talk to the eventual owners of the lots in the meadow and see if they wouldn't mind trimming back some of the trees to restore some of my view. He was surprised that I found the tree screen so objectionable. Some of his partners had wanted to put up a 10-foot-high, stockade-style fence, but Homer thought I would like the trees better. He had always liked the old Shack, he said, but his financial backers told him that it just wasn't in keeping with the architecture and feel of Four Fires North, the name they are giving to Vicky's half of the property.

Homer cordially referred me to his lawyer if I had any more questions about his development rights as outlined in the purchase option with Aunt Vicky. I held my tongue and tried to remain businesslike in expressing my objections, but visions of monkey wrench sabotage danced through my head as I said goodbye and hung up the phone. If they won't take down the pine-tree wall, then a couple of road-kill-flinging catapults and some searchlight towers with The Clash blaring from speakers might just get my message over to their side of the green screen. I try to push these thoughts to the back of my brain as I walk into the old storefront that now serves as headquarters for Mr. Stevens' team of realtors.

"Come on in, Nick, and have a seat," Henry says, ushering me into his second-floor office after the secretary leads me through the recently renovated realtor digs. Henry has a wide-open, sidearm handshake that almost looks like he is about to slap you five. His distinctive handshake almost threw me the first time I visited Henry when I moved back to Michigan in

January, but I'm ready for him this time, and his warm, gray eyes look deep into mine as our hands grasp. I've probably only seen this guy a half dozen times in my life (mostly when I was just a kid), but he has a way of making me feel like one of his own sons. As I slip comfortably into the padded leather chair across from his desk, however, I also notice Henry wistfully lower his eyes to the floor for a second as he settles into his high-backed, black executive's chair. I realize that there is enough of Henry's departed best friend in my face to tinge these warm reunions with a touch of sadness.

"So, you want to talk about old shacks," Henry says. "It doesn't surprise me that you might have an affinity for them. I suppose that runs in your family."

"Thanks for seeing me, Henry," I start in. "I know this newspaper business won't get any of your houses sold, so I'll try not to take up too much of your time."

For about twenty minutes we run down a list of forgotten farmsteads that I've noticed while driving around northern Emmet County. Henry helps me locate them on the plat book and we start to pull together a list of owners. He adds a couple of other ones he knows about, tells me how to check them out down at the County Register of Deeds, and even provides some good quotes and background for my story.

"A lot of these old places used to belong to Indian families, Nick. Unlike some states where the U.S. government simply sent in the Army to drive the Indians off their traditional lands and stick them on reservations, the government in Michigan mostly took the lands away from the Odawa and Chippewa in subtler ways," Henry explains.

"As I understand it, the lands were held in trust according to the treaties until the 1870s. Then, the government deeded all of the tribal lands to individual tribal members. The only thing was that most Indians simply didn't understand the white man's concept of land ownership and property taxes. The government started charging the Indians' property tax just like everyone else in Michigan, but half the time the Indians didn't even know about the taxes. Their taxes would go unpaid and their lands would end up in tax auctions where loggers, railroad companies, and resort developers could snatch them up for a fraction of their real value. In many cases, the Indians would continue to live in their farmhouses and shacks until the so-called legal property owners showed up with the sheriff and an eviction notice. In one of the worst cases back in the '20s, a sheriff and his posse burned down and murdered or ran off an entire village of Odawas who had lived peacefully on the shore of Burt Lake for centuries."

I pepper Henry with a few more questions about Indians, old shacks, and corrupt real estate transactions of bygone days, but it is Henry who brings the conversation around to more recent and more personal events.

"Look, Nick, I'm happy to help you with your story," Henry says in the middle of one of my questions about the Burt Lake incident, "but I wanted to see you today to ask you a couple of questions about your own family's property."

I set down my pen and notebook. "Fire away, Henry."

"I'm not asking this as a realtor, and I'm not trying to get you to send any business our way, but I hear bits and pieces of information about the Becker property now and then because I'm a realtor, and I think your dad wouldn't mind if I stuck my nose into your family's business a bit.

"I've heard about some kind of purchase option deal that your Aunt Vicky made with Homer Robertson for $75,000. And I've heard that Robertson has already cut roads and started developing part of the property," Henry says as I nod my head in agreement. "What I don't get, Nick, is how any of this jibes with your grandfather's will. Years ago your dad told me the whole story of how the Colonel only left him and Vicky life tenancies, and that the whole thing was to go the State of Michigan as a nature preserve in honor of Anna if there were no grandchildren."

"Yeah, that's the gist of the Colonel's will," I say. "Apparently, Cy Cushman found some way around the Colonel's will that set all of these deals in motion."

"Well, my question to you, Nick, is just how did your dad and Vicky get around the Colonel's will? I sure don't remember your dad telling me about any hearings in the Washtenaw or Emmet County probate courts to reverse Joe's will. Years would go by when I didn't hear much from your dad, but it seems that he would have told me if something as major as all that happened. If Cushman did get around the will, how did he do it and why is the State of Michigan still involved if the will is no longer in effect?"

I open my mouth to address Henry's questions, but I realize that I don't really have any answers for them. "I… I guess I don't really know, Henry."

"I spent a few summers out at The Shack with your dad and his folks, so he always used to give me little updates on the legal problems he was having. That life tenancy thing was always an unmovable obstacle for John and Vicky for as long as I knew your dad, and then, after he's gone I start hearing about how Vicky is trying to sell her half of the property. Even after she passes on everybody acts like she has clear title to that land, instead of just being a life tenant. Cushman is a smart guy and good lawyer, but I just don't get how things went from such a legal logjam to Robertson cutting roads and planting pine trees on your land. As I understand it, Joe's estate should still hold title to the land — not your father's estate or Vicky's estate."

Henry's questions aren't as startling to me as the fact that I don't have ready answers to them. My sister, my mother, and I just assumed that Cushman figured out a way to get around the Colonel's will. That all happened years ago. We have been so focused on fighting the township over that one acre down on the beach and preparing for the next battle with the state, that we may have simply lost sight of a bigger issue. Come to think of it, I have no clear idea why the Colonel's will isn't still in force.

"Nick, I may be totally off base here. Cy Cushman may have worked something out years ago that I just never got wind of. And I'm not accusing anybody of any wrongdoing, but I just thought I should ask — especially after I saw Cushman and Homer Robertson playing golf together last week."

My left eyebrow practically shoots into the air. "Huh?"

"I did a little quiet, investigative reporting myself, Nick, and it seems that Cushman and Robertson are very old friends. Cushman doesn't have anything to do with Robertson's business now, I'm told, but Cushman was one of the original financial backers for Robertson's Four Fire Estates development."

"Holy, crap! I had no idea," I say, rubbing my eyes to get a clearer picture of what I'm hearing. "Does that mean that Cushman probably helped to hook up Robertson with this purchase option deal in the first place? And now he's representing our family? Isn't that kind of a conflict of interest?"

Dark and duplicitous, yet vague implications start to form on the fringes of my wild imagination. Perhaps my suspicions about everyone else knowing more about my own family's legal matters than I do aren't as paranoid as I thought.

"Let's not get ahead of ourselves. Have a jujube. I mostly keep them around for my grandkids, but they are still my favorite candy," Henry says, offering me a bowl of the little multi-colored sweets that get stuck to your teeth if you don't know how to roll them around your mouth without biting down too hard.

I take a small handful and immediately embed a few of them into each of the only two teeth in my mouth with fillings.

"I'm telling you this, Nick, because I want you to be careful," Henry continues. "This is a small town and just about everybody knows everyone else's business. Even my boss, Tom Stevens, is the brother of Graham Stevens, the attorney your family was fighting with in court over the township park. It's almost impossible to avoid these connections. It could simply be that Homer and Cy are just old golf buddies and their personal and prior professional relationship has nothing to do with your family's property. I must ask you, however, not to repeat what I've said here today about your property. I still have to do business with people who do business with Robertson and Cushman, and it would not do me any good if it got around that I was sticking my nose into other people's real estate deals.

"I understand, Henry. As a reporter, I always protect my sources, and as your best friend's son, you have my word."

"The situation with the Colonel's will could be as straightforward as you say, but if I was in your shoes," Henry says. "I would want to know just how the title transferred from the Colonel's estate to John and Vicky's estates. When you go to the Register of Deeds to research your newspaper article, start a title search on your own family's property. It should all be there."

"OK, I think I've got it."

"Do you have any of your dad's old papers on the property?"

"Yeah, and some from Mom, too"

"Well, pull those all together, so you can figure out exactly what Cushman did to get past that will. I may not be able to help you out publicly, Nick, but I will be happy to look at and interpret whatever you dig up. As capable a reporter as you seem to be, I think you will be able to put this puzzle together discreetly, without raising the wrong eyebrows. If everything is on the up-and-up you can bring this property thing to a peaceful conclusion without making a bunch of false accusations. If something does smell fishy, you're going to want to find the source of that stink before anyone has a chance to clean it up."

Chapter 29

LATER THAT MORNING, I'm strolling through the county building in Petoskey heading for the Register of Deeds office. I open the door from the stairwell into the downstairs hallway and almost run straight into Cy Cushman.

"Well, hey, Nick, what a surprise. What brings you to the courthouse?"

The Emmet County Building is not only home to the Building Inspector, the Registrar of Deeds, the County Clerk, the County Treasurer, and a host of other county potentates and their staffs, but it houses all three county courts and their officers (Probate Court, District Court, and Circuit Court). This is home turf for Cushman, but I'm starting to know my way around pretty well myself through my work for the *Gazette*.

"Uh... Oh, hi, Cy," I say, trying not to look suspicious. "I'm just on my way to the Register of Deeds office." I pause momentarily to see what effect this tidbit of information has on Cushman. He manages to keep a smile on his face, but I notice a slight darting of his eyes back down the hallway towards the Register of Deeds office. "Workin' on a story for the paper about abandoned houses in the north end of the county."

"Sounds interesting," Cushman says, his eyes settling back on me. "What's that all about?"

I give him a quick rundown of the story and he seems to relax a bit, but then starts fidgeting with his gold pocket watch, as if suddenly remembering an appointment. He flips it open, and he quickly loses interest in my story.

"I'll be damned," he says, "my watch stopped. This thing has kept perfect time for years. I must have forgotten to wind it. Say, Nick, what time have you got?"

"I've got 10:32," I say looking down at my black Ironman sports watch.

"Oo, I've got to run. I'm supposed to be in the judge's chambers two minutes ago," he says, mounting the steps to the upper floors. "Sounds like a great story. I'll see you in the newspaper, if I don't see you in person first."

"It should be in Sunday's paper," I say.

"Oh, one other thing," Cy says looking down on me from the stairwell landing. "I've been in touch with the Michigan Attorney General's office. They said they are looking closely at their claim on the property this week, and should render an opinion by next week. I'll give you a call as soon as I hear something. Gotta' go. See you later."

"Catch ya' later, Cy."

The Register of Deeds office is just down the hall and around the corner. The office appears to be deserted when I step through the frosted-glass door, but the sound of rustling papers in an adjacent room lets me know that I am not alone. An attractive, middle-age, blond woman in a fitted, gray skirt and tailored, white blouse breezes into the office and sits at her desk, trailing a swirl of perfume that reminds me of the formal gardens at Versailles. She is fingering a string of pearls around her neck and is so engrossed in the papers she is holding in her other hand that she doesn't even notice me until I set my camera bag on the counter. She looks up from the counter straight into my face with a slight start.

"Oh, excuse me. I didn't hear you come in," she says, dropping her necklace. "What can I do to help you?"

I introduce myself and even give her one of the new business cards that Sean Cooper had printed up for me. Cooper settled on the title of "Northern Counties Correspondent" to describe my regular freelancer status. It sounds pretty good, but the pretty lady doesn't seem too impressed. I tell her about the story I'm working on, but I'm not sure if she is listening while she shuffles the papers on the counter. I've got all of the necessary property descriptions, I tell her, and I'll do the work myself, if she just points me in the right direction.

"Well, normally, you have to fill out this form to request each individual record," she says, "but it looks like you've already done your homework and the office is pretty quiet right now, so why don't you just come behind the counter here, and I'll show you how to find your way around the record room. I'm Joanne. I'm the Registrar of Deeds."

As soon as I step behind the counter and into the office, Joanne's demeanor changes almost instantly. She smiles and says, "you could be on to a very interesting story there. It's not too often that the press comes digging around down here. I've seen a few of your articles in the Traverse City paper. You do nice work. The *Little Traverse Times* will send down some young kid who looks like she is just out of high school and doesn't even know what to ask for, but they never look much beyond the day's headlines. This may take you a little longer, but these old records have plenty of tales to tell."

She shows me the files, the microfiche, and how to use the microfiche reader, and I start digging into the list of forgotten farmsteads. "I'll be right out here at my desk if you need anything else, she says with a smile." Looking over the register book, I can't help but notice her well-toned right leg as she sits down at her desk, letting a breezy slit up the side of her skirt fall open. Without looking up from her papers, her hand flutters over the folds of her skirt to cover up her leg, but the slit falls right back open a second later and she doesn't do anything more about it.

I can't really tell if Joanne is flirting with me or just being friendly, but her long, blond hair and elegant scent actually make me think of Libby Hampton's bouncing pony tail and her wildflower-soap smell. Libby has me spacing out for a few minutes until I am able to refocus on the old register book in front of me. About an hour later, I have a pretty good list of addresses and phone numbers of the current owners of the forgotten farmsteads. There's just one more deed to check before I go.

With the property description of the Becker parcels, I quickly locate the drawer for the microfiche that holds the deed history to our property. When I pull the drawer open, though, there is only an empty slot where the record should be. I double-check the drawer, but can't find the roll I am looking for.

"Excuse me, Joanne," I say, sticking my head out of the record room into the main office. "There seems to be a roll of microfiche that I can't find. Could you help me find it?"

I show her the drawer and the empty slot where the film should be. "That's funny. Someone must have forgotten to put it back," she says. "Oh, wait a minute, I know where it is."

She turns to the top of a filing cabinet where there is a wire in-basket labeled "Re-File." There are five or six of the light blue microfiche-roll boxes piled in there. "Here it is," she says. "Sometimes some of the regulars who do title searches come in here but don't have time to put everything back right away. I usually don't check this until after lunch. One of the gals who works for some attorneys was in here earlier this morning."

"No problem. This is the one," I say, loading the roll onto the reader spindle. "You wouldn't happen to know which attorneys the woman works for, do you?"

"Oh sure. She works for Schanski & Cushman."

"Thanks."

My spidey senses are tingling as I scroll through the microfiche roll to find the Becker records. Is it just a coincidence that Cushman's paralegal was probably the last person to check these records? What could she possibly have been looking for, if she was looking at the records for the Becker property at all?

Having just researched the "Forgotten Farmsteads" of northern Emmet County, I'm starting to get the hang of working with these records. When I finally come across the deeds for my family's property, though, the trail is still a bit tricky to follow. Winding the reel back and forth, I find two starting points. In 1852, United States President Millard Fillmore granted part of what is now the Becker property to William Pa-me-chi-ga-bo-we. The other main portion of the property was granted to John Mawachewesheway by the United States in 1872. From these starting points, ownership of the land flows from one Odawa to the next for the rest of the 1800s, but the land is divided into smaller and smaller parcels. By 1902, half a dozen Odawa families are living at the west end of Stanton Road on parcels ranging from five to thirty acres. All of those piles of stones out in my woods were not the work of one farmer, but the result of dozens of pairs of hands trying to bring food to their tables from the fields left behind by the clear-cut logging. Keways, Sagimaws, Nagonashs, and Nogesics formed an Indian neighborhood of rectangular plots out of land that their parents considered just one big tribal community stretching from Blue Harbor to Cross Village. Out of curiosity, I look up some of these Odawa names in the phone book to see if descendants of these families still live in the area. Only one of these family names appears in the white pages, but the spelling is a little different. I wonder where they all went.

As my title search takes me further into the 20th century, more European names appear in the register. Mengers, Wards, Orrs, and even the Stantons who are the namesakes of the road I live on show up in the records. It looks like Joe and Anna weren't able to buy all 105 acres at once, but by the late '20s, the Becker property (as I know it) is on the books.

There is little title activity in the records for the next three decades as my grandparents travel across the country and around the world following Joe's orders.

Nothing shows up in the Register of Deeds until 1956 after Anna's passing and the close of her estate. Anna's will and probate records are entered into the Register of Deeds giving Joe clear title to the land.

And then, things get more interesting. I expect to find some extensive (or at least definitive) record of how title passed from Joe to John and Vicky, but there is only one relevant document. It appears to be part of Joe's probate court file — something called an "Order Assigning Residue of Estate." I've heard about this kind of document before from Cushman's explanations of what will happen with Dad's estate once the debts and assets are balanced. After all of the outstanding bills, taxes, and debts are paid off and subtracted from the total value of the estate, and the judge approves of how the estate has been probated, he signs this type of an order to release whatever is left over (i.e., "the residue") to the heirs or whomever is named in the will. I have to re-read this single-page document a couple of times to understand what it is that bothers me about it.

ORDER ASSIGNING RESIDUE OF ESTATE
STATE OF MICHIGAN
The Probate Court for the County of Washtenaw.

At a session of said Court, held at the Probate office in the City of Ann Arbor, in said County, on the 3rd day of January A.D. 1958

Present, Hon. John H. Lincoln, Judge of Probate.

In the Matter of the Estate of JOSEPH L. BECKER, Decease.

January 3rd 1958 having been appointed for hearing the petition of William F. Farmer, Jr., Executor of said Estate praying that the residue of said estate be assigned to the Devisees and Legatees of said deceased...

The windy legal jargon amounts to John and Vicky getting $500, Joe's house in Ann Arbor, and the farm in North Shore Township.

It further appearing that John J. Becker and Victoria Anne Becker Rolland are sole Devisees and Legatees of said deceased.

It is Ordered, That such residue of personal estate and real estate of which said deceased died seized, be and the same is hereby assigned to the said John J. Becker and Victoria Anne Becker Rolland according to law, to each the following part or proportion thereof, to-wit: in equal one half divided thereof.

John J. Lincoln
Judge of Probate

Filed Jan. 3, 1958
Eloise Schreiber
Probate Register

Prepared and filed
By: William F. Farmer, Jr. Atty.

There is a stamp at the top right corner of the document indicating that this piece of paper was recorded in the Emmet County Register of Deeds on September 10, 1965. Other than that, the only other recent document in the file is a 1971 utility easement from when the Rural Electric Co-op brought in electricity to the cottages on Lower Beach Trail at the base of the bluff.

I guess what bothers me about this "Order Assigning Residue" and the rest of the file on the property isn't so much what is there as what is not there. There is no mention of any "life tenancy" in the order or anywhere else in the file. It reads as if Dad and Vicky have had full title to the land since 1965.

What's the significance of that date? I was born about nine months before this record was entered and my sister Sally was already three years old by then. Did we have something to do with this inexplicable record appearing in Emmet County? Even from what little my mother has been able to tell me, Dad and Vicky were still trying to get around Joe's will in the 1970s. In 1965, Dad was finishing up his first tour of duty in Vietnam, while the rest of us lived in Ann Arbor to be close to Mom's family. I don't get it.

I show Joanne what I've found and what I'm looking for, but she assures me that I have found all of the information that her office has on the matter.

"What if these records are wrong?" I ask her. "What if someone made some error? How would I go about correcting it?"

"Well, it's entirely possible that there could be a mistake in the records, but you would have to hire an attorney to have any changes made," Joanne explains. "People can't just come in and say that the records on file are all wrong. Last year, for example, we had a very angry man come in and demand that he be given the deed to his ex-wife's house. The records clearly showed that the woman held the title to the house, but he said it was his house no matter what some paper said. We had to call in the sheriff's department after he refused to leave."

"Don't worry. I'm not looking for trouble," I smile and hold up my hands in surrender. "You've been very helpful, and I really appreciate it."

"In your case, the register has an order signed by a judge. As long as that is a legitimate document, then it is law. Only a new order signed by that judge or another judge who has jurisdiction could change it."

"That sounds like the long road," I sigh. "Are there any shortcuts a resourceful guy like me could take to finding out what really happened to the title on this land?"

"Without the complete probate court record on your grandfather's estate, it's hard to tell what changes occurred during the probate process. If you have the time, I suppose you could make a trip down to Ann Arbor and get a look at the complete Washtenaw Probate Court record of the estate."

"Sounds like a good idea. Thanks."

Chapter 30

THE REST OF my week is spent trying to write enough stories to afford a quick trip down to Ann Arbor by next week. I ran the result of my title search at the Emmet County Register of Deeds by Henry Richards, and he is as confused as I am about the absence of information on John and Vicky's life tenancies. He agrees that a trip down to the Washtenaw County Courthouse isn't a bad idea. I promised to make copies of the whole file and bring them back for his perusal.

Although I am on my way to setting a personal-best record of writing seven stories in five days for the *Gazette*, I'm also burning the midnight oil sorting through Dad's old files on the property, as well as an envelope that Mom sent me from Florida of all the stuff she has. Mom calls me Friday night after the rates go down.

"Hello, Sweetie. How is everything Up North? Did you get my package?"

"Yeah. Thanks, Mom. I haven't had a chance to do much more than just rifle through it, but it looks like it could come in handy."

We exchange news on the weeks that we are having, and I get updates on my Christian Scientist aunts, uncles, and cousins spread across the country like dandelion seeds scattered by the wind. Mom and her two sisters form something that Sally and I call the Whittier Triangle. All three Whittier sisters live thousands of miles from each other, but the three points of the map they inhabit makes a triangle that covers most of the United States and all of our lives. The Whittier sisters don't approve of gossip, but their network of information provides a welcome service to all of their children and grandchildren who like to keep in touch with each other, but rarely get a chance to actually see one another.

Mom is getting used to mixing family-news updates with family-history fact checking. I know that she doesn't like to dwell on the past, but I don't think she minds setting the record straight wherever she can. A couple of weeks ago, I had talked to both Mom and Luanne Wilson about the alleged $75,000 trust fund that Cushman thought Aunt Vicky had set up for Sally and me. It was the first that both women had ever heard of such an idea. Luanne says Vicky got the money from Cushman and put it to immediate use paying medical bills and doing some repairs on her pool. She was still living off the interest from the rest of the money when she died. Mom says that Dad was happy to see Vicky get some benefit from the land while she was alive.

I explain my recent visit with Henry and the results of my title search to Mom.

"Hmm, did you say 1965?" she asks.

"Yeah, that's when this order got entered into the Emmet County Register of Deeds."

"I think I may have had something to do with that."

"Really? Do tell."

"Your father was in Vietnam, and he asked me to look into building a little cottage down on the beach. We just wanted some place for him to come home to after a long, difficult year. He had spent part of his tour out in the jungle and the last part strapped to a desk in Saigon. My mother (your Nana) and I spent a glorious couple of weeks up here scouting things out. Nana was the architect in the family and together we decided on a cute, little A-frame design that we could call home."

"Whatever happened to that idea? It sounds great."

"Well, we couldn't get a builder to go ahead with it until we got a mortgage, and we couldn't get a mortgage because the Register of Deeds showed the property as still belonging to the Colonel's estate. Aunt Vicky and a lawyer friend of your father's strongly urged me to take that Probate Court Order from Ann Arbor and have it entered into the records in Emmet County to establish their life tenancy rights. So, that's what I did. Was there something wrong with that?"

"I don't think you did anything wrong, but there is something wrong with that order. It doesn't say anything about Dad and Vicky being life tenants. It just looks like somebody got the Washtenaw judge to assign full title to them."

"That can't be right," Mom says, her voice taking on a more business-like tone. "Vicky was quite insistent that we couldn't do anything with the property because she and your father were only life tenants. Your poor father was always coming up with ideas to improve the property or put it to some good use that might help defer some of the exorbitant property taxes we had to pay on that land. In fact, Vicky had stopped paying the property taxes at all after Uncle Rollie died in 1960, and we had to pay them ourselves. Vicky was a real stickler for abiding by the Colonel's will."

"So, do you mean that she was the one who pulled the plug on the A-frame idea?"

"Not really. When it came down to it, we just didn't have the money to build."

"You had that order entered, but you don't know how Dad and Vicky were able to get around Joe's will."

"I'm sorry, honey. I read through all those papers carefully, but it still doesn't make any sense to me. When your father went back overseas after we left Fort Sheridan in '76, he handled all

of that business himself. There must have been letters back and
forth to Cushman and Aunt Vicky, but I was mostly out of it by
then. I'm sorry I can't be of more help."

"Maybe Luanne Wilson can help us out again."

"Oh, that's a great idea. Why don't you give her a call right
away? Just remember that there is only one Divine Mind guid-
ing, guarding, and governing this whole business. Nothing can
be lost in God's Kingdom, not even a piece of information."

"Thanks, Mom. I'll give Luanne a call right away. Good
night."

"Good night, dear."

———

With a bit of God's guidance, I manage to catch Aunt Vicky's
old friend Luann Wilson on the phone just before she steps
out into the hot Tucson sun for dinner and bridge night at her
friend Midge's house. I start to give her the rundown on what
I'm looking for, but I can tell she's in a hurry.

"Look, Nick, I've got to run, but I'm already a couple steps
ahead of you. I don't know the specifics about the Order
Assigning Residue of your grandfather's estate, but I just made
copies of everything Vicky had on the property and sent the
originals to you in a box. I shipped it UPS on Wednesday and
it should get to you by next week. I figure that the sooner you
guys in Michigan get things wrapped up with your dad's estate,
the sooner I can get Vicky's estate wrapped up here. Everything should be in there. Just give me a call if you hear anything, okay, hun?"

"You're a keeper, Luanne. Thanks. I'll call you next week."

"Hang in there, kiddo. Bye."

Chapter 31

SATURDAY DAWNS WITH a gentle rain soaking the new green of the leaves and grass around The Shack. I stay in the old iron-frame bed for another hour dozing and listening to the soft shushing sound — fine drops of rain on the leaves and roof. I realize that it has been almost six months since I last heard the sound of rain on living leaves back in Boston. It has been a long winter and a fitful spring. Even though it snowed only two weeks ago, summer is now on its way.

After a whirlwind of freelance articles and sorting through Mom and Dad's records on the property, I can't wait to get back to Joe and Anna's story. Theirs was hardly the simple life, but I still find it somewhat comforting. In light of my recent title-search discoveries and the resulting unanswered questions, it is tempting to jump around in the Becker records. Something, however, tells me not to waver too far from the chronological path. Anna's letters from her 1931 voyage to the Philippines revealed much of her earlier years to me, and I have a hunch that Joe and Anna's distant past holds answers to my present predicaments. I'm not sure just where and when these answers lie, so I am trudging along letter-by-letter, clipping-by-clipping so that I don't miss something important.

After a couple of years in Ann Arbor, Joe and Anna were able to buy the house they had been renting since 1909 on N. Thayer St. Of course, "buying a house" meant trading in their monthly rent payments for higher monthly mortgage payments. When Joe's income took an unexpected dip again in 1913, he had to find additional companies to sell for. Despite Joe's best efforts, he had to uproot Anna temporarily because of his work. Joe and Anna rented out their Ann Arbor house and moved to Cambridge, Ohio, from about mid-1913 to late 1915.

This two-year foray into Ohio was the beginning of Vicky's years in Blue Harbor being raised by her grandparents. It looks like these Up North stays started as short trips to see Grandma and Grandpa, but got longer and longer. Perhaps "Little Vixie," as the family called her, was taken to live with Dianna, James, and Uncle Vint in Blue Harbor so that Joe and Anna could get settled into new jobs and a new house. It would be eight years, though, until Joe, Anna, and Vicky were able to live together again as a complete family.

While Joe and Anna struggled with the ups and downs of a salesman's wages, Joe came up with sideline work that might offer the young couple some financial stability in troubled times. On January 24, 1914, Joe enlisted as a private in the Ohio National Guard. Europe was poised on a knife's edge between war and peace, and Mexico was trying to recover from the latest army coup. President Woodrow Wilson refused to recognize the government of Mexican coup leader Gen. Victoriano Huerta, and tensions along the Mexican border were high.

Joe had been out of uniform for about five years, and what little additional income the Guard brought him was nothing compared to the satisfaction he gained from weekend and summer service. The uniform fit Joe quite well, and the life of a National Guardsman suited Joe even better. Joe could keep his hand in the military business while still working the rail lines as a salesman. By April, his own men elected Joe captain of Company E, 7th Infantry, Ohio National Guard, and his promotion went through before the company set off for the regiment's annual encampment at Zanesville, Ohio. Joe was able to bring Marine Corps training and discipline to bear on his infantry company and had them in good order before the encampment got into full swing.

I imagine that there were some pointed discussions over the kitchen table between Joe and Anna about Joe's return to the uniformed services. The money troubles the young couple faced were serious enough to drive them farther away from family and the Michigan towns (Ann Arbor and Blue Harbor) that they both loved. The military was no goldmine, Joe told Anna, but it had always provided reliable income. Anna couldn't get past her memories of the years she had spent waiting for Joe while he served in the Marine Corps thousands of miles away, and she did not like to think about what would happen if war actually did break out.

It's just a hunch, but I believe Joe wanted to join the Regular Army full time, and the Ohio National Guard was something of a compromise. The whole idea seemed foreign and drastic to Anna, but Joe had good reason to believe that Army life could actually bring the Becker family back together again. While Joe did yearn for action, he also longed to share with his wife and daughter something of the world he had seen in Barbados, Erie, Cuba, and Panama. There was more to life than little Midwestern towns and endless miles of railroad tracks. Joe had seen the tidy and pleasant Army forts of the Canal Zone, with white painted rocks lining the pathways, sturdy wooden quarters for soldiers with families, and the adventures of discovering what was beyond America's borders. Even the bustling military bases he had seen stateside seemed to offer a lot more for a soldier and his family than the worn-out little house they could afford to rent in Cambridge. Joe may not have voiced all of these thoughts to Anna. Instead of charging head-on into Anna's objections, Joe flanked them by joining the Ohio National Guard.

Joe didn't mind the work of selling coal, matches, coffee, and (most recently) men's work clothes, but it didn't seem to be getting him any closer to making the kind of money that would reunite the family and allow them all to spend more time Up North. Joe savored every trip that they had ever made back to Anna's hometown, but nowadays he rarely even saw the little home that he and Anna had in Ohio. On the back of one blurry photograph of Joe and Anna in Cambridge, Anna has listed Joe's "vacation days at home." In the space of three months, Joe was only home for five days.

Heading off to Zanesville for a week each summer didn't improve the situation, but Anna couldn't help but notice how her husband seemed to thrive in uniform. She carefully clipped several copies of the *Cambridge Daily Guernsey Times*:

COMPANY E COMMENDED BY OFFICERS

Cambridge Boys Returned From Camp Last Night

SEVENTH REGIMENT ENCAMPED FOR WEEK

*Local Men Conducted Themselves with Credit
and Received High Approbation*

Cambridge boys made a proud showing at the annual encampment of the Seventh Regiment, Ohio National Guard, which closed at Zanesville yesterday, the first which Co. E., of this city, has attended. The local soldiers returned to Cambridge last evening. None of the older companies secured a better rating than the local one and its showing was such as to draw personal commendation from Adjutant General Wood and from Col. Knox, the commander of the regiment.

With the other companies of the regiment the local guardsmen went to Zanesville Sunday of last week and pitched their tents on the fair ground. Their camp was ready by noon. In the afternoon a dress parade was held. Monday morning Co. E., it was stated yesterday, was the only one reporting at reveille roll call on time, and throughout the encampment they won commendation for good behavior and military appearance.

On Wednesday the company was on guard duty, Captain Becker being officer of the day. Friday and Saturday sham battles were arranged, Co. E. being on the defensive each time. On Friday Lt. C.A. French was in charge of the advance patrol of the "Reds," defending against an attack by the "Blues." The defense lost, the "Blues" having taken positions before going to their designated starting place, but on the following day the defense was successful.

In inspections on Saturday and Sunday to the local company the following marks were given: On quarters "very good;" sanitation condition, "excellent;" equipment, "very good."

Yesterday afternoon the adjutant general stopped in the company street and complimented the officers on the excellent showing of their company.

There were no accidents during the encampment and good health was enjoyed by all the guardsmen. As a result of a court martial a member of the McConnelsville company was drummed out of camp yesterday morning. He was charged with having struck a commissioned officer who had attempted to quell a dispute between the man and one of the non-commissioned officers of the company.

Despite Joe's success on the Ohio training grounds, Anna longed to return to Ann Arbor, and they did so as soon as they could afford to. Joe had to resign his commission in the Ohio National Guard on April 9, 1915.

Their Ann Arbor renters had to leave town before their lease was up, and Anna jumped at the chance to move back to her own house on N. Thayer St. The move forced Joe and Anna to regain their financial footing yet again, and Little Vixie had to remain with her grandparents. For Joe, however, the family's domestic issues paled in comparison to the growing possibility that America might get into the fight "over there." Joe had a hard time ignoring the fires of war and chaos smoldering across the Atlantic and South of the Border. At the age of thirty, on June 12, 1916, as many Americans were wondering how much longer they could stay out of the war in Europe, Joe figured out how to get back into uniform and into the fight. Joe became a private for the third time — this time with Company I of the 31st Infantry Regiment of the Michigan National Guard.

The timing of Joe's enlistment was too close to the events that the Michigan Guardsmen were about to get swept into to be coincidental. Within weeks, Joe's enlistment would take him many times farther away from Michigan than the 300 or so miles that separated Joe and Anna from their young daughter. I can only speculate on the mixed feelings that Joe had as he re-entered military service. On one hand, he was tired of the endless separations he and his family had endured because of his sales travels. On the other hand, he must have known that the Michigan National Guard was, at best, a long road to bringing his family back together again. The implications of the recently signed Defense Act of 1916 probably didn't escape Joe. The new law put the states' National Guard units under federal service in ways that militiamen had never before seen. From his Ohio Guard days, he knew that he was built for the military life and that he had a lot to offer the farm boys, shopkeepers,

and bankers of the National Guard who might soon find themselves in harm's way. For more than half his life he had been
preparing for the dire days that appeared to lie ahead, and he
wasn't about to watch them from the sidelines. Joe followed his
instincts and trusted that Anna and Vicky would benefit from
his decision in the long run.

Nonetheless, Joe and Anna's choices must have been hard
on Vicky. Vicky was about a month and a half away from her
sixth birthday when Joe joined the Michigan National Guard.
Vicky had spent so much time away from her mother and
father that she probably just accepted the situation as normal. But the effects of the separation did not go unnoticed by
Dianna, James, and her Uncle Vincent. Vicky did not grow up
without love, but she did grow up with people feeling sorry for
her. Anna's brother Vint provides a glimpse into the attitudes
surrounding Vicky's childhood.

A letter from Vint, postmarked July 13, 1916 is addressed to
Anna and Vint's mother Mrs. Jas. Johnson. The letter and enve-
lope feature a drawing of the New Hotel Mertens in Grand
Rapids, Michigan, which proprietor Chas. M. Luce touts as
"Absolutely Fireproof," only "75 steps east" of Union Station,
and with a "European Plan."

Dear Mother & Dad:

*This is certainly an awful hot day; I have never suffered so
much with heat in a long time.*

*Don't let a thing slip by to make Vicky's party nice. Have
everything she wants, buy some little baskets of Bill Darling's & fill them with candy, give them lots of ice cream
and make it a party she will remember as long as she lives.*

*Go cross to the Bakery and have Frank make a nice cake
or else get a package of cake flour and make it your self*

*have candles on it and let Vicky blow them out. If its real
hot out have lemonade.*

Take this $5 and what ever you buy have it nice.

*Love,
Vint*

Beyond Vint's letter, I don't have much else to go on to build
a clear picture of the exact circumstances behind Vicky's continued separation from her family. I can only assume from her
later life that cake and lemonade did not satiate the hunger she
must have had for her parent's presence and affection.

What I don't know about the Becker's private lives in the
years leading up to 1916, however, is compensated by what I
do know about Joe's budding professional military career. By
mid-1916, Joe's personal experiences begin to skirt the edges
of the history books he would collect in later years. Occasionally, Joe's life would even intersect the historical narratives
that were written about the times and events he experienced
firsthand.

In the wee hours of March 9, 1916, anywhere from 300 to
1,000 Mexicans of Pancho Villa's renegade army crossed
the U.S. border into New Mexico and attacked the town of
Columbus, killing eighteen Americans (ten soldiers and eight
civilians) and wounding another eight. The raid was carefully
planned with Villastas surrounding the houses that lodged the
officers who were scattered throughout the treeless and dusty
town. Villa's men looted homes and businesses and burned
down several buildings in the center of town. They even ran
off with about 100 Army horses. Despite being cut off from
most of their officers, the U.S. Army units headquartered and

bivouacked on the southeast side of town quickly rose up from their guard posts and tents to repel the raiders with rifles, pistols, shotguns, and new machine guns they had only recently broken in.

Villa had been a friend of the United States and opposed the corrupt and anti-American regime of Mexican President Venustiano Carranza, who had come to power in 1914 after U.S. President Wilson helped to topple the Huerta government. Gen. Francisco Villa, a former bandit leader, had helped bring Carranza to power, but quickly came to oppose him after Carranza placed his personal ambition above the cause of the Revolution that Villa had thought they were both fighting for. In 1915, after Wilson let Carranza's army use American soil and railroad tracks to outmaneuver and trap the main body of Villa's army at a place called Aqua Prieta, Villa vowed revenge.

Some say Villa's forces attacked Columbus to force the U.S. to become more directly involved in Mexico and bring down Carranza, others say Villa was actually on his way to negotiate better relations between Mexico and America with President Wilson. What is clear is that the attack was the last straw in a series of border harassments and assaults on Americans both in and close to Mexico.

As one of Joe's history books (*Chasing Villa: The Last Campaign of the U.S. Cavalry* by Col. Frank Tompkins) explains, the immediate reaction from Regular Army units stationed on the border and the later response from Washington was swift and lethal:

> *Following initial disarray, the Army garrison fought back and after some two hours of street fighting succeeded in driving Villa's troops from the village. In the process, the 13th Cavalry with rifle and machine gun fire killed an*

*estimated 62 Mexican attackers and wounded another 25
or so.*

*In Washington, a stunned Wilson administration ordered
a so-called "Punitive Expedition" to invade Mexico,
disperse Villa's guerilla band and, hopefully, capture or
kill Villa. Brigadier General John J. "Black Jack" Pershing was given command of the pursuit and a mere six
days after Villa's raid led his troops across the border in
northwestern Chihuahua. During the following thirteen
weeks U.S. Army Cavalry penetrated more than 400 miles
into Mexico, engaging in two fire fights and several smaller
skirmishes with Villista contingents, and two major
clashes with hundreds of troops of the Mexican government of Venustiano Carranza.*

Villa may have been a villain to the Carranza government,
but he was *their* villain. Neither the Mexicans who opposed
Villa nor those who supported him took to the idea of American troops riding around Mexican soil to take care of (what
they considered) a Mexican problem. While some Mexicans
helped the cavalry troopers try to find Villa, most did not. The
Carrazista soldiers and officers garrisoned in Chihuahua at
first feigned cooperation, but misinformation soon blossomed
into outright hostility against Pershing's expedition. By late
spring, Villa was seriously wounded and on the run but still
nowhere to be found (despite several devastating blows to his
forces by both U.S. and Carranza soldiers). Tensions between
Mexican and U.S. Army units were nearing the breaking point.
The Punitive Expedition and its clashes with Carrancistas
were on the verge of causing declarations of war between Mexico and America. With the Regular U.S. Army stretched thin
in Mexico, Washington called up National Guard units from
across the country to defend the border against spill over from

Carrancista-U.S. Cavalry clashes and against the chance of general war breaking out with our southern neighbor.

On June 19, 1916 (just one week after Joe had enlisted), the Michigan National Guard was called out for service on the Mexican border. Anna hurriedly dug Joe's favorite cavalry boots out of the closet to complement his new, green Michigan National Guard uniform, complete with campaign hat. Joe was still an infantryman and the boots weren't regulation for enlisted men, but Joe refused to go back to the standard-issue leggings after his Ohio National Guard captaincy allowed him to buy tall black, leather riding boots.

Joe's spit-polished boots, his maturity (he was now thirty years old), and his military bearing made him stand out from the other guardsmen who gathered at the armory in downtown Ann Arbor. Before the regiment even arrived in Texas, though, Joe's superiors honorably discharged him from his enlisted rank of private and appointed him as a 2nd lieutenant.

Company I gathered at the state mobilization camp at Grayling, Michigan, where it met up with the rest of the 31st Michigan Infantry Regiment. There, the regiment was mustered into Federal Service and packed into day coaches for the train trip to Texas.

Camp Cotton
El Paso, Texas
Co. I, 31st Mich. Inf.
July 15, 1916

My Dearest Anna,

Greetings from "El Paso del Norde" as the old Spaniards used to call this place. Relieved to hear that you got my little notes. Am in receipt of your letter of June 27. We Michigan boys raced down here so fast that I had little opportunity to write you a proper letter, but now that we have settled into camp life I can write you a real one. This border service has proved to be a standard "hurry up and wait" Army operation. There was a big rush to get here, but now that we are here, things have slowed down considerably.

Camp Cotton is right near the Rio Grande, and our tents are pitched only about three hundred yards from the Mexican boundary line. Once we set up camp, Capt. Wilson and I got to work getting our boys into shape. Most days spent on close order drill, marching to get the men into condition for actual campaign service, with schools and athletics in the afternoon.

The men have taken to calling me "Smokey Joe" when I am not in the immediate vicinity. I'm told this not only refers to my trusty pipe, but to the heat I sometimes bring to bear on the men during training. Some of the men still think this is some kind of camping trip, but I am trying to prepare them for actual hostilities. We are quite safe here with such a concentration of soldiers, but stand prepared to support Pershing's forces across the border if the need arises. Nicknames for officers are quite common, and I could certainly do worse. Some men call Gen. Pershing "Black Jack," but this has nothing to do with cards or clubs as I first imagined. Apparently, this is a milder version of the "N_____ Jack," which Pershing got from commanding colored troops earlier in his career.

The men are holding up quite well considering the alien nature of this part of the country. Our drill ground is called the "Mesa," and the boys have never seen such an endless stretch of sandy wasteland. It's about a three-mile hike from camp, and we march out to it at 7 AM every morning. For these men from our beautiful North

Country, the Mesa came as quite a shock. The drill ground is covered with every known variety of cactus and mesquite bushes; horned toads, snakes and lizards, and tropical insects infest the entire place.

During the day, it is very hot, but what is surprising about this place is how cold it gets at night. I have seldom felt colder in the depths of our midwestern winters. On some of our longer hikes we have encountered bottomlands with doby mud. This mud forms a sticky and slippery mass and clings to our boots in large, heavy chunks that makes walking almost impossible. Complaints were heard throughout the company at first, but already the men (including your own Joe) are becoming hardened to the work and accustomed to the surroundings.

My Spanish is also coming back quickly. I felt a bit rusty at first, but have gotten right back into the swing of things. Few guardsmen speak the language, so I am occasionally called upon to speak with the locals. Yesterday, I even met with representatives from Juarez, the Mexican town across the river, to discuss the possibility of securing fresh food supplies from them for our company. These negotiations went well and we were able to buy flour for tortillas, corn, and frijoles. The men have really taken to the local food.

Well, I've got to get ready for a big day tomorrow. Please make sure Vicki gets the enclosed post card when you see her.

Love to you,
Joe

While Joe may have been gaining a reputation as a tough drill instructor amongst the Michigan National Guardsmen, he was a tender daddy in his daughter's eyes. On the back of a color-tinted postcard of an El Paso Street in 1882, Joe writes to Vicky:

Hello Little Vixie Baby Girl: This picture shows how El Paso, Texas looked a long time ago before even Daddy was born — I will send you with next letter to Mother a card showing how it looks today.

Love and kisses for you and mother.

— Daddy

Anna's letters to Joe are mostly business, peppered with longing for him to come home. While some of the companies that Joe represented as a salesman continued to send Joe's salary to Anna, some did not. In fact, Anna had reason to believe that some of Joe's sales jobs weren't being held for him while he was off serving his country. There was talk on the border of sending fathers whose families relied on their support back home, but Congress appropriated $2,000,000 to alleviate the situation. No doubt, Anna received a share of this money, which came as a great relief.

By the fall of 1916, it was clear that the chase for Villa was essentially over. There were still occasional skirmishes south of the border between Carrancistas and Pershing's Punitive Expedition, but Washington's desire to avert full-scale war with the Carranza government pulled Pershing back in closer to U.S. territory. The expedition pulled back so far that Villa, who had recovered from his wounds, rallied his troops in the State of Chihuahua, and began to oppose the Carrancistas with greater strength than ever before. Pershing's forces, bottled up by Carrancistas in the northern part of Chihuahua and held in check by Washington's efforts at diplomacy, could do nothing but stand by and watch, as the situation got worse. As the likelihood of an actual invasion from Mexico diminished, however, the guardsmen who had so gladly rallied to protect their country wondered what they were still doing in Texas and grew restless to return to their families and usual occupations.

Only a sample of Joe and Anna's correspondence from this period has survived the years, but I have enough pieces to flesh out a family crisis that would bring Anna to Joe before Joe returned home from El Paso. Anna had a slightly older cousin named Effa who had grown up in Blue Harbor with the Johnson family after her parents (the Jacksons) left Michigan to follow the logging boom north and then west. Effa had stayed in Blue Harbor for love, it seems, and married a man named Bart Hicks, who soon swept her away to southern California. After several years of marriage, the only joy of which turned out to be a son named George, Effa was in need of rescue and Anna led the charge. Ironically, this family crisis would bring Joe as close to the action of the Mexican Punitive Expedition as he would get.

Amid a handful of letters leading up to Anna's train trip to El Paso, I can pick out a few details, but the exact nature of the crisis is a bit hazy. Effa was "hospitalized" with "broken ribs" and "a bruised and lacerated face." Bart Hicks was "nowhere to be found" but had "filed for custody of the boy," claiming that Effa was "a drunkard and negligent in her maternal duties."

From these hints I'd say that Bart turned out to be a real scoundrel, beating his wife and abandoning his son, while filing for custody out of sheer spite and besmirching Effa's character in order to draw attention away from his own abusive behavior. I wouldn't be surprised if Effa did develop a drinking problem after so many years of heartache from the man she had loved. The Jacksons were unable to intervene, so Aunt Dianna and cousin Anna decided to take matters into their own hands. The plot was hatched in Blue Harbor for Anna and Joe to swoop in by train and sweep Effa and little Georgia out of their California nightmare and back to Michigan for recovery and safekeeping. Joe discreetly arranged for a few days of leave to help out. Anna was to rendezvous with Joe in El Paso, where they would go on together to Los Angeles. Anna's last letter to Joe arrived just before she did.

Oct. 2, 1916

My Dear Joe,

This letter may not reach you in time, but I should arrive by train on the ninth by way of Dallas, Texas. I don't know exactly when the train gets in, so I will get word to you when I arrive and wait for you at the hotel that you picked out for me.

Aunt Elizabeth is in constant touch with Effa's friend Celia, who assures us that Effa is doing much better. Released from hospital two days ago. She's getting around all right, and should be ready for the trip back north. The sooner we get her away from there the better.

I'm so relieved that you will be able to go with me. I don't think we will run into that despicable Bart, but I feel better just knowing that I will see you soon and we can spend a couple of days together, even if it is on this ugly errand. Thank Capt. Wilson again for me.

Lots of Love, Kisses,
Anna

Anna's train was over two hours late pulling into El Paso. After five days' travel by train and the mixture of anxiety over Effa and the excitement of seeing Joe, Anna felt like she had walked the entire way from Ann Arbor when she arrived in Texas. The dust was everywhere and Anna could feel grit between her teeth as she gathered her bags and left the train.

Joe met Anna that night at the hotel, and there is certainly no written record of their reunion, but I trust it was a pleasing one. Anna was not the only wife or girlfriend who came to El Paso to be with their guardsmen husbands and boyfriends. Some Regular Army wives even lived in town to be near their men. Gen. Pershing, however, who had lost his wife and three daughters in a fire in 1915, was not keen on the presence of women near the battlefield. Pershing felt the women made it harder on the men who could not be near their wives and sweethearts, and was bad for morale. As a guardsman, though, Joe had a bit more flexibility.

Joe and Anna boarded the train to Los Angeles the next morning on Oct. 10th. The train was packed with soldiers, salesmen, civilians, and Spanish-speaking Americans. Looking over the heads of the crowd at the station, however, Joe had noticed a family leaving one of the private cars and, holding on to Anna's hand, he maneuvered his way into the closed compartment, just as the family left. Two vaqueros slouched in the opposite bench of the compartment, apparently asleep under broad-brimmed sombreros that covered their faces. A few morning rays from the sun slipped in from the open window at a sharp angle, even though the back end of the train blocked most of the already-hot light from completely filling the compartment. Anna closed the window, remembering the clouds of dust that had blown in on her the last time the train pulled out of the station at Dallas. As she set her bag down beside her, a smaller cloud of dust rose from the upholstery of the chair. One of the vaqueros snorted in his sleep as Joe and Anna settled into their seats.

Joe and Anna dozed off themselves after the train started rocking and creaking its way west. They awoke an hour and half later as the conductor passed down the narrow corridor outside the private compartments shouting, "Next stop, Columbus, New Mexico! Columbus, next stop!"

The vaqueros were already awake and gathering together the saddlebags, bedrolls, and rifles they had stashed on the rack above their seats.

"*Buenos Dias, Señor, Señora,*" said one of the men, who was slinging two bandoleers of ammunition across his chest.

"Good morning," Anna said.

Joe slipped into his sturdy Spanish, asking the men something that Anna didn't understand. She wondered if these two were agents of Pancho Villa, but Joe recognized the man's gold-toothed smile and Indian face. He also noted the U.S. Army saddlebags and standard-issue .30-caliber, 1903 Springfield rifles. Not until the two men left the compartment did Joe remember where he had seen them before. They were two of the Apache scouts attached to Pershing's expedition, and Joe had seen them at the head of a cavalry troop that came into Camp Cotton for re-supply last week. Usually they were dressed in Army uniforms, and Joe could only guess at the kind of clandestine activities they might be up to dressed as Villa's men.

Joe was in the middle of explaining this to Anna and pointing out the significance of Columbus as the scene of Villa's raid when a petite young woman in a wide-brimmed summer hat and short, black hair entered the compartment.

"Is this seat taken?" the woman asked with a smile.

"No, help yourself," Anna smiled back, "you're welcome to it."

Holding on to the compartment door, the woman turned and called back down the corridor. "Georgie, I've found some seats down here. Come on down, dear."

As the woman held the door open, a tall, hatless soldier stepped into the compartment. His head and ears were wrapped in clean bandages, and there was something odd about his face that made both Anna and Joe rise from their seat to see if they could help him.

When Joe saw the single silver bar of a 1st lieutenant outranking his 2nd lieutenant's gold bar, Joe snapped off a salute before offering to take the man's bag.

"Oh, hell, I'm all right, Lieutenant. Don't trouble yourself," the bandaged man blurted out in a sharp, high voice.

The high, reedy sound of the man's voice was unexpected considering his height and stature, which easily matched Joe's wide-shouldered, six-foot-two frame. As Joe and Anna settled back into their seats, they couldn't help but stare at the man's head. His face was bright red and Anna was the first to notice that he had no eyebrows or eyelashes. His head was mostly covered in bandages, and what little of the scalp that was visible showed patches of singed, blond hair.

As the couple settled into their seats, Anna introduced herself to the woman across from her, who said her name was Beatrice Patton.

"And this is my husband, Lt. George Patton," Mrs. Patton said, patting her husband on the knee.

"What a coincidence, we're going to California to see my little cousin whose name is Georgie, as well," Anna said.

George Patton smiled lovingly back at his wife, while Joe and Anna introduced themselves and tried not to stare at the brow-less, lash-less, red-faced man across from them.

"We're heading back to California, too," George said with a quick smile that seemed to actually hurt his inflamed face. "How fortunate we are to share the journey with such a fine couple from Michigan." He paused. "Well, now that we've all been properly introduced, let's get this god-damned bandaging thing out in the open. I couldn't help but notice you staring at me, Mrs. Becker. I don't damn-well expect you were admiring my good looks, either. So go ahead and ask me whatever you want."

"George, you don't have to swear," Bea said, taking his hand.

"You're damn right, dearest, you stop me as soon as I get going."

"Oh, George," she said with feigned exasperation.

"You must have just come from Mexico," Joe guessed. "But I didn't know the 8th Cavalry was down there."

Joe had been teaching Anna about military insignia so that she could navigate her way through Army life, and she was catching on quickly. She noticed the sets of crossed swords with the number "8" connected to them pinned on each of the Lieutenant's jacket collars. A silver bar was on each shoulder. And the initials "U.S." were pinned to his collars where the stiff, green material closed at the throat.

"The 8th isn't in Mexico, but I am," Patton said. "I'm on detachment for special service with the expedition. I'm on Pershing's staff. How 'bout you, Lieutenant? What are you Michigan boys up to?" Anna noticed that the initials "MICH" were pinned to Joe's collars where the "U.S." was pinned to Lt. Patton's.

"Just watching the back door, and trying to keep you Regular Army boys from getting into too much trouble down there," Joe replied.

"You got that right, soldier. We went in after a measly bunch of bandits, and now the whole damn country is practically up in arms against us. And now that bastard Villa, who we practically had by the nose, is running around down there kicking the Carranzas in the ass while we sit there waiting for our weasly politicians to finish having tea with the Mexican delegation up in Connecticut. The whole thing just makes my ears burn even more. If it was up to me, we would shoot the guts out of any sombrero-headed son of a bitch who shoots at us and be in Mexico City by now."

"George, calm down, you're only getting redder," Beatrice said, as her husband's face turned from pinkish red to angry crimson.

"You're right, Little Bea, there's no use getting all worked up, when Washington just wants us to sit there," Patton said. "Hopefully, we will all be able to go back home in a couple of months."

"So how did you manage to end up all bandaged up like that," Joe said. "I haven't heard of any action down there in a while."

"Well, I wish I had gotten this on the battlefield, but I did this to myself in my own damn tent," Patton said. "After getting shot at by Villistas and Carrancistas for months without getting a scratch, I managed to squirt gasoline from my lantern all over my head after coming back from the movies a couple of nights ago. I over-pumped it after it failed to light, but of course it managed to catch just as the gas started squirting out. It was like watching the Fourth of July fireworks up real close. You just haven't seen anything until you've seen flames coming off your own face."

"How horrible, what did you do?" Anna asked, genuinely concerned.

"There was a horse trough just outside my tent and I thank God for the presence of mind to run out of there and put myself out in the trough. It could have been a lot worse if the water hadn't been so close, but I'm sure Providence did not want me to die for something so stupid. I'll die on the battle-field, as any good soldier should."

"Now I know who you are," Joe chimed in. "You're that lieutenant who got Cardenas just before the Guard got called down here."

"Yeah, that was me."

"Anna, you're looking at a genuine Army gunfighter here," Joe said, leaning over to her. "Back in May, if I remember it correctly, the lieutenant here and a small scouting party surrounded this Cardenas fella, who was Villa's bodyguard. As I understand it, Cardenas and a couple of his men came roaring out of this hacienda on horseback towards the Lieutenant and his men with guns blazing. Is that how the story goes, Lieuten-ant Patton?"

"You can call me George." Patton's eyes burned even brighter than his scarlet face and head as he enthusiastically picked up the story. Anna was both drawn in by the wicked smile on his face and slightly uncomfortable from the obvious delight this Army officer had in recounting his tale of bloodshed. "I only had a six-shooter and I always keep one chamber empty like any good cavalryman, so I only had five shots. I wasn't sure if they were Villa's men or Carranzas', so I held my fire as three riders came flying at us from out of the gate. They took one look at me and my scout and turned around to escape around the other side of the building. I had already planned for this and had a couple troopers ready to take them out. Seeing the superior numbers on that south side of the building, the riders turned back towards us and started firing away at twenty yards or less. I fired back five times with my new pistol and one of them ducked back into the house. I found out later that this was Cardenas himself and that I had put a hole in both him and his horse. As I reloaded my pistol, another of the Mexicans dashed by on horseback, not ten yards away. I shot the horse out from under him, and the four guys from the south side of the building shot him up into pieces as he tried to get back on his feet. The third Mexican had ridden about 150 yards away, when the troopers shot him and killed him. A couple of my men ran down to search the body and saw the first guy who had ducked back into the house trying to escape down a stone wall. Our boys hit him a couple more times in the right lung, but the bastard still ran about 500 yards and fired off another thirty rounds before he stopped. That guy turned out to be Cardenas. Cardenas held up his left arm to indicate surrender, but when another one of my scouts went over to him, Cardenas dropped his arm and opened fire. The scout shot him through the head, which is exactly what the duplicitous yellow-belly deserved."

"Good heavens, what an ordeal," Anna said, amazed. "Have you been in lots of fights like that?"

"That was actually my first real shootout," Patton said with a slight nod. "War's a bloody business, but I guess you just get used to it. My hands started shaking for a minute after it was all over, but then I saw these four Mexicans just outside of the house. They were skinning a cow when we first came around to the front, and they kept skinning that cow through the whole thing, just like gunfights were an everyday occurrence for them. They didn't stop until they were finished."

"We're just all glad Georgie wasn't hurt," Beatrice said. "We call it his 'big day as a lion.'"

While Joe asked a few more questions to reconcile the newspaper accounts with George's own story, Anna got quiet and looked out the window at the strange landscape unfolding before her eyes. Dark rocks jutting out of the sand, cactus, long-horned cattle, and endless plains of sagebrush passed by the windows of the train. She was stirred by what she had just heard and what she was seeing. So this was what Joe wanted? What kind of life would she find for herself and for Vicky if Joe made a career of the military? It was oddly beautiful here in the desert, but it seemed dangerous, too.

Just then, Beatrice, who had stopped listening to George's account of strapping the bodies of the Mexicans onto his car and driving into camp with them, noticed Anna's far-off gaze. Beatrice leaned towards Anna and put her hand on her knee.

"Are you new to Army life?" Mrs. Patton asked in a soft voice.

"Yes and no, Mrs. Patton," Anna replied. "Joe was in the Marine Corps and then worked for the Isthmian Canal Commission in Panama when we were courting and first married. I have some idea of what it is like to keep the home fires burning, but I've never lived on a military base. I've only known civilian life firsthand."

"I knew Georgie when he was at West Point, but I didn't get primed for Army life until we married six years ago and moved into our first house at Fort Sheridan, Illinois. At first, I didn't know what to think, Mrs. Becker. The first morning I was there, I heard footsteps on the porch and found a paper in the mailbox that declared that the sun was to rise at such and such a time and set at such and such a time, by order of the post commander. I was quite startled that this Army was so powerful that even the sun conformed to its orders."

Anna giggled at the thought and looked up into Beatrice's delicate, warm face. "I've certainly seen how military orders can empty a town of half the men at the drop of a hat," Anna said. "Joe really wants to get back into the military full time.

I know he is very good at what he does in uniform, but don't you miss your family and having a home you can always go back to?"

"You know, Mrs. Becker, we actually get to see our families more than we would if we lived in one place. My family is in Massachusetts and George's family is in California. The Army keeps us moving so much that we get to work in plenty of visits. And we end up in such interesting places that our families come visit us. And the best part is that you start to develop a wider family of friends that you keep running into every few years."

"You must mean the other Army wives and families?" Anna asked. "A few of us women in Ann Arbor whose husbands are away have started to get together every week for meetings and it has been a comfort for me."

"When I moved to Fort Sheridan, I kept to myself at first, but these Army wives kept coming to check on me and tell me stories. The stories, like some of George's, seemed gruesome at first. One poor woman told me how she sat for two days on the stern of a tugboat in the Yalu River watching corpses floating by, praying her husband's was not amongst them. One young bride, who was a major's wife, had to nurse an entire garrison afflicted with dengue fever. At first, I thought these women possessed some kind of super-human loyalty and devotion, but gradually I realized that these wives of the Old Army were trying to instill in me a store of courage, which is the legacy of every Army woman and which we hand down from one generation to the next."

Anna nodded to Beatrice. "You've given me some food for thought, Mrs. Patton. It may just be this desert air, but I think you've helped me see things a bit more clearly. Thank you."

Anna looked over at Joe, who was in the midst of discussing the merits of the old Army saddlebags over the new ones with Lt. Patton. Both men had discovered they were about the same age, although they came from such different backgrounds. Patton was off to recuperate from his accident and help his father, who was running for the United States Senate, while Joe's father was still back in Ft. Atkinson shoeing horses and fixing farm tools. The two men swapped stories and talked military affairs and politics half way across New Mexico, unaware that something profound had just passed between the two women at their sides. Anna had always had backbone, but on the El Paso-to-Los Angeles train, Anna gained the courage of knowing that even beyond the circle of her family, she did not have to be alone.

PART 9

WACO, TEXAS

———

Chapter 32

I'VE BEEN BANGING out a bunch of stories for the *Northern Michigan Gazette* in order to get some money together for a quick trip down to Ann Arbor to check out the Washtenaw County Probate Court record for Joe's estate. It's only the first day of June, but it feels like summer already. Earlier this week, the package arrived from Luanne with all of Aunt Vicky's files on the property, so I have been almost as busy reconstructing the past as I have been reporting on the present.

Vicky's files have proved both enlightening and unsettling. With all of these stories swirling around in my head (Joe and Anna on the eve of war in 1916; new revelations about Vicky, Dad, and Mom from the '60s; and today's latest news about a semi that went off the highway and ended up with its nose submerged in the Indian River), I decide to get some fresh air and exercise with a walk to my mailbox. The mailbox is a half-mile away at the intersection of Stanton Road and Shore Drive, so getting the mail makes a nice one-mile roundtrip.

Walking down my driveway, through a tunnel of trees, and over the roller-coaster hills of Stanton Road, I am surrounded by the possibilities for this property that I found amongst Aunt Vicky's papers. While both my parents were good record-keepers, Vicky's files contain not only the stuff she received, but also carbon copies of possibly every letter she ever wrote. I'm beginning to get a pretty clear picture of what happened to the property after Joe died.

Though Vicky would make it back to Blue Harbor only once in her adult years, my dad was drawn back down this dead-end, dirt road throughout his life like a pilgrim returning to Mecca. Despite the limits of life tenancy, Dad was always looking for ways to make this place sustain itself so that the property taxes didn't outpace his ability to pay them. He had lots of ideas: a KOA campground, a nature preserve as Joe had envisioned, even the romantic notion of returning the land to the Indians. Except for occasional upkeep and a few small timber harvests, though, Dad's ideas never quite got off the ground. And if they did, Aunt Vicky had a way of stomping them back down to earth. Dad's plan for building an A-frame down on the beach, for example, looks a lot different in the faded black-and-white of old carbon copies than the version Mom told me about last Friday on the phone. Vicky may have stopped paying taxes on the property altogether by the early '60s, but she was, nonetheless. able to keep a relentless grip on the place.

Several letters that are sitting back on my desk have left an irritating scratch in my memory. I am beginning to see a side of Aunt Vicky that explains her distance from her brother's young family.

May 5, 1961
Victoria E. Rolland

6528 E. Calle Mercurio
Tucson, AZ

Dear Janice and John,

I haven't written before this as Rollie and I have been laid up with miserable colds. The past few days we have begun to feel more like human beings again and are regaining some of our zip. April was just a lost month for us and we had to force ourselves to do even the most necessary things.

We did quite a little sightseeing when our guests were here, particularly with Doc Jones. We drove to Tombstone and saw Boot Hill, to Nogales where we had lunch in The

Cavern, an old abandoned silver mine. It is quite a place and when you come we will have to go there. Boot Hill is just as you would imagine it and so is Tombstone. One of the epitaphs there read: "Hanged Legal." Another, "Two Chinese, Shot by Mistake." Between Tombstone and Nogales is really beautiful ranch country where you can see cowboys riding the range.

I am enclosing a check for my share of the expenses incurred by your tree-cutting, survey project Up North. You will recall that I told you that I was not in a position to share in the expense of the tree cutting. In the future, John, I ask that you keep me informed about any business pertaining to the North Shore Township property. Any agreement entered into about that property, such as tree harvesting, etc., should be with full and previous knowledge of both of us as life tenants, and contracted under both of our signatures. Any business at all pertaining to the property should be between us only as the two life tenants. Rollie has no part of it, and should not write you about my interest there, and I feel the same way about a third party who has no part of your or my life tenancy, writing to me about these matters. Business should be under your signature and mine and between us. I am speaking strictly from a legal, business point of view. You and I are the only life tenants, no one else. Any business about that property is properly only your and my concern.

Do plan on coming down here. It would be wonderful if you and Janice would come for Christmas. How long a vacation do you have now? Come whenever you can and stay as long as possible. This is your home in Arizona, too. Wish you were here to join me for a dip in the pool. Once you are in the water it is fine and makes you feel like a million.

Love to you both,
Vicky

It's one thing to hear Aunt Vicky chide my thirty-two-year-old father like an errant little brother, but it troubles me to hear Aunt Vicky treat my mother as a "third party who has no part" in family business — especially, as it turns out, since my mother did have significant legal rights through marriage.

By the time I came around at the tail end of 1964, Aunt Vicky had given up on paying her half of the property taxes, letting her brother shoulder the entire burden while she claimed economic duress from her poolside patio. It is probably only because of my mother's kind and forgiving heart that the later A-frame-cottage episode didn't turn into a civil war amongst the Colonel's descendants.

It was near the end of Dad's first tour of duty as an advisor in Vietnam in 1965 that he shared his dream for the property with Aunt Vicky.

27 June 65

Dear V and R,

Remember me? I am still here, finally back in the engineers, and I can hardly believe that I only have two more months of this nonsense.

The goings on over here are incredible to say the least. I would say that most of what you read in the papers is some how just a little bit not like what really happened. At least that's my interpretation from the clippings I get from Janice.

At any rate, the purpose of this here letter concerns the Blue Harbor property. First of all I would like for you to send the (all of the) deeds and titles to the property to Janice ASAP.

I decided last summer that one way or the other an A-frame on the beach was the only solution. Janice and I

*decided it would best fit in between the Powers and Rowe
places. In May, Janice and Mrs. Whittier made a recon of
the area, and talked with some builders. It now looks that
I might be able to come home to a reasonably nice A-frame
if we get the deed and all property titles, and a mortgage.
The latter, is proving no small task.*

*Janice, armed with full power of attorney for me, went to
the Emmet County Court House, and wasn't able to come
up with any of the documents a builder would require. The
property is still listed under Joseph L. Becker, too! Therefore, please send the documents, or a legal copy to Janice.*

*I don't know yet the exact date I will depart from VN, but
I should have some orders soon. Janice plans to come to SF
to meet me, and we have given some thought to stopping
by Tucson. More about this later. We won't bring the wee
ones with us.*

*I trust all is well with you and Rollie. I suppose you know
about Patty Kensington's father passing away last Dec. I
understand Patty and family are moving to BH for good.
Charlie has some sort of insurance business cooking.*

*Love,
John*

Dad's letter from Vietnam to Aunt Vicky was quickly followed up with reinforcement from Mom, who had just
returned from the aforementioned foray Up North to carry
out Dad's A-frame orders.

Thursday, July 1, 1965

Dearest Vicky,

*I am hoping that John has finally found time to write
you about his plans for the cabin down on the water on
the Blue Harbor property. Because I have his power of*

attorney, he has asked me to do all I can to get this project started, which we have both been dreaming about for years.

I am still trying to find someone to give us a mortgage on the proposed little A-frame; one bank in Petoskey has indicated its interest, so I hope we can do business. I was Up North the week before the end of May, to do what I could. Mom, who is the architect in the family, went with me. We had a wonderful time, and thought how much fun you would have had with us. The weather was utterly gorgeous and warm — it was a lovely, lovely time.

I hope you are planning on being home around the end of August — we surely ought to be bursting in on you, if that's okay. I am really getting excited, although it's too early yet to completely let off steam.

Do you remember Lt. Col. Belini, John's Bn. Commander who had dinner at your house? He is heading for three years at the Pentagon, which he detests. He had thought he might get a District Engineer job, and looked forward to that. They will probably buy a house there; because it is quite certain that he will draw a hardship tour after his Pentagon tour. I asked Bill Morton why Col. Belini didn't want the Pentagon — he said Lt. Cols. are a dime a dozen there, and they often end up carrying coffee — or else work 80-hour weeks and fight the traffic. (It's still better than VN.)

My family is renting a cottage near by on Base Lake for the month of August. There are beds all over the place there — we have done this before — and the children and I will probably spend at least a week there. Then, when I fly to San Francisco to meet John, Mom and my sister Mary will take care of my two kidlets as well, which is certainly fine for them, and such a nice place to be.

Just last weekend, I flew to Boston for my annual Association meeting — went with my brother-in-law and

sister, in Harry's own plane, and he at the helm. It was a
delightful trip, the flying — but we had the craziest time in
Boston, in the huge new Prudential Center — we thought
this would be a real treat. Unfortunately, a convention
of S.P.E.B.S.Q.S.I.A. — Society for the Preservation
and Encouragement of Barber Shop Quartet Singing in
America — was in full swing. Despite our reservations, we
spent the first night in separate living rooms, huge and very
ornate things, with little lavatories in them — no beds,
no bathtub, no phones. Friday morning we were moved
into our own rooms — but the really nutty part was that
the singing went on in the lobby, in the restaurants, in the
elevators, in the halls and in their rooms as they partied
until 3 AM every single night we were there, until Mary
and I felt as though we had been through the wringer by
the time we flew home Sunday. To top that off, I found my
door open one evening, and a man going through my extra
pocketbook! Then I heard also about the bombing of the
restaurant in Saigon which upset me further, as I knew
it was a favorite place of John's. As it was, I learned from
him via tape this week, he was duty officer for all of Sup-
port Command that night, and the results of the bombing
kept him up all night.

We all send you much love. I imagine you are in your pool
often these days — and in the house the rest of the time.
Write soon, because I love to hear from you.

Love –
Janice

P.S. Forgot one very important point. Do you have the
deeds to the Blue Harbor property? If so, could you please
send them — we can't build without that proof of owner-
ship. If you don't have them, do you know where they are?
Many thanks, always.

Aunt Vicky responded with a letter to both Dad in Vietnam and Mom in Michigan. Her reply was swift and final, but it sure seems odd considering the way things look now. The A-frame on the beach was not to be, but somehow Vicky's sale of the property is about to become a reality.

July 6, 1965

Dear John and Janice,

It was good to hear from you both, even though John was mostly "business." I was beginning to wonder if you remembered me, John, not having had even one scratch from you, Christmas included, since you were here a year ago June with your five friends.

The thing, I believe, to do is for John to instruct Dad's old attorney, Bill Farmer, to register Dad's will with the Emmet County Recorder in order to establish our legal status as life tenants of the North Shore Township property, and to clarify ownership. Since John and I are life tenants only, and do not own the property, according to the terms of Dad's will, we have no jurisdiction over the title, and the title cannot be conveyed until you and I have expired. I thought you understood this, John, but apparently there is some confusion in your mind, else you would not have been surprised to find that the property is still registered in Dad's name.

It couldn't be in our names because we are life tenants only, and have, as Farmer explained, reasonable use of the property as long as we live. As long as either John or I are alive, the title to the property will remain in the name of Joseph L. Becker. The deeds, which are in my safety deposit box, would be valueless to you in your present negotiations with the bank for a mortgage. Naturally, the deeds are in

*the name of Joseph L. Becker, and we cannot alter owner-
ship. After we are gone, the title will pass according to the
will.*

*Any responsible contractor will insist on knowing who
has title to the property. Therefore, before attempting any
building or timber cutting, you should have Dad's will
registered in Petoskey. Neither of us can properly obligate
the property without the other's permission.*

*All you have to do is to read Dad's will, a copy of which I
am sure you have. It is all simple and clear, and spelled out
in Article III.*

*However, if you find you can build a cabin on the beach, I
wouldn't stand in the way.*

*Any negotiations for anything regarding that property
must be in the names of John and me as life tenants only.
Do consult with me before any obligations are incurred.*

*These are the facts, and we can't get around them, so
please don't think I am trying to be difficult.*

*From all the new reports it appears that John may be dis-
appointed in being able to return to the States when you
expect. We heard McNamara say last night on TV that
present tours of duty out there could well be extended.*

*Rollie and I are looking forward to having you and Janice
stop off here in Tucson come September. We'll give the pool
a workout. Take care!*

*Love,
Vicky*

So, Mom *was* the one who entered the Order Assigning Residue in the Emmet County Register of Deeds, but that step got
my parents no closer to having an A-frame on the beach. Dad

returned from Vietnam without having a little dream home to welcome him back. It wasn't the first time things didn't go his way, and it certainly wasn't the last, but his return was not without its rewards and joys. He was reunited with his pretty, petite wife. He survived his first tour of duty in Vietnam. He still had the old Shack to call home. And then there was this beautiful new baby boy for him to get to know.

Two and half decades later, I guess I am still trying to know my father in return. I guess that's one of the reasons why I'm here. He wanted more than the occasional visit to The Shack. He wanted a life here. He never really got that chance, but maybe I can make some kind of life at the end of this dead-end dirt road after all.

———

The paycheck I hope to find in my mailbox should get me to Ann Arbor for some answers.

I take a slight detour off Stanton Road to escape the hot, spring sunshine beating down on the back of my neck. I climb the hill at the eastern edge of the old rye-grass field beside Stanton Road and slip into a cool island of trees at the corner of Stanton and Shore Drive. This used to be the old Weaver place. They were still around when I was a kid, but one summer we drove Up North to discover the house and barn burned to the ground. All that remains is the cement basement walls of the barn, overgrown piles of blackened debris, and clusters of lilac bushes that are as tall as the nearby fruit trees and cover almost as much ground as the house they used to decorate. It's just another lost farmstead, but not forgotten as long as some of us remember it. I'm only twenty-four years old and somehow I've become a keeper of memories—memories of places that used to be and of places that only existed in my parents' dreams.

Fire may have been the end of the Weaver's dreams of holding on to the farm that their fathers established on this land, but other factors seem to have kept my father and mother from the life they envisioned for themselves down on the shore of Lake Michigan.

The fragrance of new lilac blossoms follows me across the old Weaver place as I reach my mailbox at the intersection of Shore Drive and Stanton Road. Stuffed between an L.L. Bean catalogue and a couple of *Monitors* is the check from the *Northern Michigan Gazette* that I've been waiting for. My latest burst of stories has paid off — $450 ought to pay some bills and get me to Ann Arbor in style.

As I stuff the check back into its envelope, a letter slips out of its hiding place between the two-day-old pages of *The Christian Science Monitor*. It's from my friend Libby Hampton. For a moment, I can't decide whether to rip the letter open and read it on my walk back to The Shack, or stuff it in my back pocket to savor her words in private at home. I decide to save it, but hustle straight back along the hot and dusty track of Stanton Road, over the roller-coaster hills, and up the drive to the house.

> *Tuesday May 30, 1989*
>
> *Dear Nicholas Nickle-Boy,*
>
> *Hello Sasquatch of the North Woods. Your description of taking your first dip of the year in Lake Michigan was a lot more chilling than enticing. It was cold enough just watching you goof-ball boys jump in Lake Superior on our trip. You'll have to warm things up a bit before you can get a Virginia girl like me in that Great Lakes water. BRRR!*
>
> *I enjoyed your letter last week. The work you are doing for the newspaper up there sounds wonderful. If those*

pea-brains down at the Gazette don't hire you full time, it will be their loss. Although I haven't read your articles yet, I know from spending that week with you that you are a thoughtful, caring, hard-working young man, Mr. Becker, and I'm sure you will go far.

As for me, my life is still hopelessly up in the air, but a few things have hit the ground — Craig, for one thing. He came to visit me as soon as I got back to Bloomington. I'd been waiting to finalize my plans for the summer until he made up his mind on his plans. He was either going to spend the summer at the family cottage up in Blue Harbor or he was going to work for his father's company in Los Angeles. I've been accepted to two great summer programs for high school biology teachers — one in Michigan and one in California. It turns out Craig is going to spend the summer traveling around Europe with his cousins, instead. He invited me to tag along, but he knows that I have to complete a summer field study for my master's program.

I have since resolved my relationship with Craig. We are just going to be friends. In getting older and wiser, I've gained a better insight into what kind of person Craig is — he's too shallow… period. The End. Bleck!

Not to give you any ideas, Mr. Becker, but you mentioned in your letter that you might be going to Ann Arbor in June. Any chance you might be there between the 5th and 6th? I'll be there for an orientation for the summer field study program I'm taking this summer through the University of Michigan. I'm going to be helping a professor study the piping plover. I don't exactly know where I'll end up after the orientation, but I know that plovers like to nest in the dunes along Lake Michigan.

Sorry I didn't mention this Michigan possibility sooner, but I just needed to make up my own mind about my relationship with Craig and what would be best for my teaching career. The last thing I needed was a cute North Woods Sasquatch beckoning me to come to Michigan to be near him — although it would be fun to study the foraging characteristics and habitat of such a fascinating creature.

Give me a call before I leave Indiana on the 10th. I would love to see you again. Bring pictures of our trip. I have some classics of you and Pete with your mouths full of Ramen noodles. I hope your table manners are better in town than on the trail.

Take Care and call me,
Libby

Chapter 33

IT'S TAKEN A couple of days, but my pulse has almost returned to normal since reading Libby's letter. Of course, I called her right away, and we are set to meet next Monday for lunch at noon at the heart of the University of Michigan campus where the two main paths of the "Diag" make a big X. The Courthouse is only a few blocks from there, so I can dive right into the Colonel's estate file after Libby gets back to her orientation.

Although I am having some trouble concentrating, I'm hoping that Joe and Anna can keep me from going crazy before I drive down to Ann Arbor Monday morning. It's raining now and the radio says it will keep raining through Sunday, so I don't mind spending most of my weekend behind my desk.

The particulars of Joe and Anna's relief mission to California are not recorded in the surviving correspondence between El Paso and Michigan. What is clear, however, is that Effa and little Georgie were safely returned to Blue Harbor, where (Anna reported to Joe on November 14, 1916) they "are settling back in nicely."

For Joe and the men of the Michigan National Guard garrisoned in El Paso, the heat of a Southwest Texas autumn quickly turned to the frequent flurries of a border town winter.

Camp Cotton
El Paso, Texas
Co. I, 31st Mich. Inf.
Jan. 1, 1917

My Anna Girl,

Your old Joe has helped to lead his boys to victory! We played our regimental championship game today against the 8th Artillery team at a nearby high school stadium, and whipped the pants off of them. It would be too boastful to tell you the final score, but let's just say that the boys of the 31st were simply too fast and skilful for the artillery fellows. Capt. Wilson, Lt. King, and I made a fine coaching staff, with Wilson as head coach, me handling the linemen, and King sorting out the backfield. When we get back to Ann Arbor and civilian life, we will have to see if the Wolverines have any openings on the coaching staff.

We northern fellas have kind of enjoyed the cold turn that the weather has taken, but much work has gone into winterizing our tent city. Lumber was brought in to build floors and walls for the tents, and we've had to use the newly acquired sibley stoves almost every night.

The men have been fairly well occupied with few complaints, but the possibility of any active service after Villa or against the Carrancistas has clearly passed, and we are all eagerly awaiting orders to return home.

Give my regards to Effa and Georgie, and tell Little Vixie that her Papa misses her dearly. I'll send her another post-card tomorrow. We'll be back in Michigan in no time.

Love,
Your Joe

Many important milestones in my grandparents' lives appeared beside the platforms of train stations. On February 4, 1917, Joe was mustered out of federal service at Fort Wayne, Michigan, and hopped the first train home to Ann Arbor where Anna met him at the station. She arrived just as Joe's train was pulling in. She was still short of breath and rosy-cheeked from hurrying down Thayer Street to the depot. Anna still clutched the crumpled telegram announcing his return home in her left hand as she threw her arms around his neck and kissed him right there in front of a station full of strangers and other families come to meet their returning guardsmen.

Little Vicky, who had been brought back home to Anna in anticipation of Joe's return, was smiling and crying at the same time as she hugged Joe's thigh. Then he lifted her up into his arms and smothered her in hugs and kisses.

———

The next milestone appeared two months later as Joe returned from yet another sales trip throughout the Midwest. He arrived in Petoskey with just enough time to pick up the *Petoskey Evening News* before catching the "Dummy Train" around the bay to Blue Harbor. Joe was planning on spending a few quiet days with Anna and Vicky at Anna's parents house, but the front-page headlines of Friday, April 6, 1917 altered Joe's plans and those of millions of American families.

AT WAR WITH GERMANY

Resolutions Passed at 3 O'Clock

Interned German Ships Seized in All American Ports at an Early Hour This Forenoon

WASHINGTON, APRIL 6 — The United States is at war with Germany. The State of War Resolution, which passed the Senate Wednesday night, having been passed by the House at three o'clock this morning by a vote of 373 to 50, with 9 abstaining.

The resolution was passed after a seven-hour debate in which democratic leader Kitchin prolonged the discussion.

Congresswoman Rankin, of Montana, voted against The State of War Resolution, but when she answered the roll call she said "I want to stand by my country but I cannot vote for war."

Speaker Clark signed The State of War Resolution and the House adjourned until Monday. The House broke into cheers when the result of the vote was announced.

GERMAN SHIPS SEIZED

BOSTON, MASS., APRIL 6 — Five German ships interned here were seized this morning. Their crews dispossessed by American customs officials. The North German Lloyd liner Willehad, interned in the harbor at New London, Conn., was also seized this morning.

German ships interned at southern and western ports, at Panama, Honolulu, Manilla, and other Philippine ports will also be seized.

"STATE OF WAR" DECLARED

The following is the text, complete, of the resolution adopted at three o'clock this morning by the House of Representatives at Washington, previously approved by President Wilson and Wednesday night adopted by the Senate and which has thrown this nation into the conflict now raging in Europe.

"Whereas the Imperial German Government has committed repeated acts of war against the Government and

*the people of the United States of America; Therefore be it
Resolved by the Senate and the House of Representatives
of the United States of America in Congress Assembled,
that the state of war between the United States and the
Imperial German Government which has thus been thrust
upon the United States is hereby formally declared; and
that the President be, and he is hereby, authorized and
directed to employ the entire naval and military forces of
the United States and the resources of the Government to
carry on war against the Imperial German Government;
and to bring the conflict to a successful termination all
of the resources of the country are hereby pledged by the
Congress of the United States."*

Joe was not surprised by the news. Germany's decision to
wage "unrestricted submarine war" against any ships (belliger-
ent or neutral) along a vast swath of the eastern Atlantic had
nearly brought America into the Great War back in '15. The
loss of American life, however, did not end with the sinking of
the British passenger liner *Lusitania* back then. Just last year,
the French steamer *Sussex*, was sent to the bottom along with
more American lives.

Joe, whose father had left Germany because of the Kaisers'
reckless willingness to throw away Germany's sons for their own
personal gain, had no faith in the word of the German Imperial
Government. Joe knew it was only a matter of time before Germany would resume its cowardly policy of sinking civilian ships
and America would join the war. The United States had been
pushed far enough and it was time to push back.

Waiting on the ice-covered Petoskey platform for the
"Dummy Train" to pull backwards into the depot for the half-
hour ride to Blue Harbor, Joe did not join the young men
who jumped up and down and patted each other on the back

when they first heard the war news. Joe had been preparing himself and boys such as these for the likelihood of war for more than a decade, but now that war was actually here, he did not feel the glory and excitement that he saw in the Petoskey boys' eyes. Instead, he saw the months of toil and training it would take to turn boys like these into fighting men. Joe noticed one wide-grinning, lanky fellow in a black-and-red-checked Mackinaw coat who was talking with the friends who had come to meet him.

"By God, I'm enlisting first thing tomorrow morning," the young man said. "Those Huns will wish they never even heard of America by the time we get through with 'em."

For a moment, Joe imagined this boy standing at attention in his first new uniform. This thought was quickly replaced by a darker vision. For a few seconds, Joe saw him face down in the mud of some dark trench with both legs missing. Joe had to shake himself from his vision as the "Dummy Train" arrived.

Once seated comfortably inside the well-heated passenger car that was the front of the train, Joe couldn't help overhearing two local businessmen discussing the war.

"Ralph, I don't know what you're getting so worked up about," the older man in the English cap and navy blue overcoat said. "I doubt if any of your boys will end up over in France. I hear that at most this war will just mean that our navy will help out the allies more."

"Maybe so, Chauncy," said the round-bellied Ralph, "But did you see the article in this evening's paper on Michigan's manpower. Somebody already totaled up the number of Michigan men of military age at 700,000. I gar-entee that at least some of our boys will get shipped acrosst the Atlantic and end up in France."

After all the years in Michigan, Joe's ears still couldn't help picking out the few unusually accented words that occasionally appeared in Michiganders' otherwise thoroughly Midwestern speech. Joe wondered how these little differences could exist only a hundred miles away from where he grew up. A "guarantee" sounded like it had more to do with the long-beaked, sharp-toothed gar he had once caught in the Rock River than with the pledge of certainty that Ralph meant. Joe had long since cured Anna of adding a "t" to the end of the word "across," but it still amused Joe when he heard it.

"Aw, hell, Ralph," Chauncy said. "If you're so worried about your boys than why don't you enlist yourself? It says here that they take fellas up to the age of forty-five. You still got a few years to go before you're too old."

"Well, if they're looking for fat, middle-aged grocers, I'll be the first to enlist, but I don't think I'm exactly what they want. Why don't you lie about your age, I'm sure those dirty Huns will run back to the Rhine when they see your old, ugly Irish sourpuss comin' at 'em."

Both men shook their newspapers open and stuck their noses back into them.

Joe had studied the course of the war in Europe closely. He'd even purchased a map of France back in 1915, which he marked up with pencil from time to time to keep track of the changing frontlines. Joe knew that Chauncy's optimism did not fit the reality of the war. More than anything, the Allies needed soldiers, and infantry soldiers at that. Joe would answer the call not so much out of some misguided sense of adventure, but because he knew that Ralph's sons and perhaps even Ralph himself had a lot better chance of returning home alive with the kind of soldiering that Joe knew how to instill in his men.

The worst part would be having to say goodbye to Anna and Vicky again.

That goodbye came just four months later back down in Ann Arbor on the platform of the Michigan Central Depot. It had been a long, drawn-out farewell. Joe was called up for active duty back on June 1, along with the handful of officers and sergeants comprising the leadership of Company I of the 31st Regiment of the Michigan National Guard.

The company of 166 men came from Ann Arbor and the surrounding small towns and farms. The National Guard Armory was only about a fifteen-minute walk from Joe and Anna's house. Once Joe was called up for duty, he and the rest of the company headquarters staff had about three full months of paperwork, recruiting, induction, organizing and packing before August 16th. On that day, they boarded a train that took the company and its two freight cars full of equipment up to Camp Grayling, the Michigan National Guard base.

As the company's only first lieutenant, Joe was second-in-command under Captain Holland, who had thought it best for the officers to billet at the Ann Arbor Armory until all preparations for mobilization were complete. The officers and sergeants had taken turns with overnight furloughs, and Joe had seen Anna only about once a week since returning to uniform. Despite Joe's years as a traveling salesmen and longer absences as a soldier, Anna had never grown entirely accustomed to his departures. She no longer, though, let the anxious of the inevitable goodbyes spoil the times that they did have together. While she still secretly longed for a more settled civilian life, Anna realized that she was honing the skills of an Army wife.

With this realization, Anna decided to sort out her general fears about Joe's soldiering career choice and separate out the fears that she could do something about from the fears she had little or no control over. She could not control what might happen to him over in France, but she could do something about her fear that she would see less and less of him as he wore a uniform more and more often.

As the company and their families waited for the Camp Grayling train to hook up with the regiment's two freight cars, Joe noticed that Anna was particularly quiet as they stood on the main platform that hot August afternoon.

"Mrs. Becker, you are uncharacteristically quiet this afternoon," Joe said in the playfully formal tone they used to address each other in public. "Is there something you would like to say before the train arrives?"

Anna looked up into Joe's eyes, and he could see that it was not sadness that quieted her so, but something calmer.

"You are looking sharp today, Lieutenant Becker," Anna said, brushing a piece of lint from the shoulder of his green-wool tunic. Joe had been promoted to first lieutenant earlier that summer, and Anna thought the silver bar on his shoulder suited him. "It makes it hard for a girl to say goodbye, but I was thinking that I'm not so sure that I am going to let you go on this little camping trip without me."

"Oh, really? What do you have in mind, my dear?"

The twinkle in Anna's eye sharpened to a thoughtful gaze. "I just want you to know that I have been giving this military life some serious thought lately. Of course, I wish there was no war and you didn't have to leave, but I want you to know that I send all of my love with you, wherever this takes us."

Joe stood in silence for a moment just looking down into Anna's face. "Thank you, darling. That means a great deal to me. I know this life isn't exactly what you had in mind for us. It's probably harder to be the one who stays behind than the one who is called away. But I want you to know that no matter how far away they send me, I will always be working my way back to you."

A tear pooled up in the corner of Anna's eye as she looked into the handsome face beneath the brim of Joe's campaign hat. "You'd better be," Anna said wiping the tear away with the white handkerchief Joe handed her. She swatted him lightly on the chest with the handkerchief for making her cry, and laughed to pull herself together again.

"Anyway, some of the other wives and I have made some inquiries and discovered that there are no Michigan Guard rules to prevent us from visiting our husbands in Grayling or wherever they send you before you sail for France. Apparently, the Michigan commanders aren't as heartless when it comes to spouses as that General Pershing was down on the border. Mrs. Volland's brother has a hunting cabin up near Grayling, and she has offered to let the officers' wives stay there when we can come up to visit. So, I will be seeing you from time to time, if that's all right with you."

"You are full of surprises, Mrs. Becker." Joe wrapped his arms around Anna pulling her to him. "You couldn't have come up with a better bon voyage present if you spent fifty dollars at Potter's Tobacco shop. I will be delighted to see you whenever they let me."

"Have you heard anything about where they'll send you after Grayling?" Anna asked readjusting her hat and blouse after Joe's enthusiastic hugs.

"I just got word this morning. It's still just regimental rumor, but we are heading back to Texas this fall."

"Back to El Paso?" Anna asked.

"Probably not. The Army has a place on the outskirts of Waco called Camp MacArthur. The construction quartermaster from another Guard unit is already putting together a crew to head down there to build the camp."

"Well, I guess I'll be seeing you in Texas, too, then," Anna stretched up on the tip-toes of her new white shoes and kissed Joe goodbye. "Take care of yourself, Lieutenant Becker."

"I will, Mrs. Becker. Give Little Vixie a kiss from her Papa when you see her Up North, and I'll keep an eye out for you as long as my boots are still on American soil. Goodbye, my dear."

Chapter 34

JOE AND THE Michigan National Guard spent the rest of 1917 gearing up for war, but Joe and Anna spent those months in peace with each other. The photographs left to me from that time illustrate a marriage in a relative state of grace. America's entry into World War I suspended enough of "normal" civilian life that Anna felt free to step out of her typical duties as a mother, piano teacher, and church organist to throw herself into the job of soldier's wife.

In the photos, Anna appears everywhere with Joe. She is beside him and his canvas-tent home on a foggy late-September day at Camp Grayling. There she is feeding a tame whitetail deer that some of the men in Joe's company kept before leaving for Texas. She stands tall and self-assured amongst the wooden mess halls of Camp MacArthur in Waco in her stylish black wool dress and jacket with matching patent-leather pumps. There is even a photo of Joe and Anna snuggling together for a picture in some tourist-attraction Texas cave.

Anna's attention and affection in the months leading up to Joe's departure for France proved to be an effective inoculation against the animosity and even hatred that Joe received from the men under his charge during the Waco training. According to one newspaper account, Joe –

> "... was the most unpopular man in the company. Having had regular military training, he was a strict disciplinarian, and to the members of his company, most of whom

considered Army life more of a joke than anything else, his ideas of discipline were, to say the least, irksome."

Joe's specialty was bayonet training. One of Joe's "irksome ideas" was to use goats instead of sandbags to train the men in the proper use of the bayonet. Many decades later, Joe's half brother Arthur recalled (in a family biography that he was writing) some of Joe's cold reasoning on this unusual training technique.

My brother Joseph was credited with several military innovations throughout his career. He was a pioneer in adapting native Philippino pack saddles for Army pack mule teams, as well as adapting Philippino river crossing techniques to military purposes. His knowledge and advances in this field played a significant role in the recapture of the Philippines during the Second World War.

During the First World War, Joseph brought a new level of realism to bayonet drill instruction by using goat carcasses for practice. While the men grumbled about this technique at the time, it proved most effective once the regiment reached the action in France. I asked him about it years later, and my brother explained it to me in a letter.

"In addition to getting the men accustomed to the crude realities of combat, they needed to get the feel of penetrating a living being for their own protection. The practice bags simply could not convey the potential dangers of thrusting a bayonet into a man, turning the blade, and then extracting the blade. A soldier is lucky if his initial thrust does not get stuck on the enemy's bones. We had to teach the men how to get clear of the enemy by using the foot to push off. The goat carcass was ideal for simulating this snagging effect on the weapon. Later in the war, we bayonet instructors learned of numerous casualties among

*the infantrymen who had only been trained on sandbags.
Many were killed while trying to free their bayonets from
the first German they encountered. Unfamiliar with how
to counter this snagging effect, these boys became disarmed
for all intents and purposes and either abandoned their
weapons or died trying to extract them."*

Joe's clinical approach to bayonet instruction may have
seemed cold and hard to his men during training, but as the
same article that called Joe "the most unpopular man in the
company" reported, that sentiment did not last.

*"... as soon as the men got into the game in France, and
began to realize that Lieutenant Becker knew what was
best for them, their attitude toward him speedily changed,
and he is now the idol of his men."*

What was best for seven-year-old Victoria Becker was a
question that both Joe and Anna struggled with. Anna's decision to be with Joe as much as possible left Vicky back Up
North with her grandparents and Uncle Vincent in Blue Harbor yet again. My best guess is that my grandparents thought
that Vicky's schooling was more important than keeping her at
Anna's side in Grayling and Waco.

Vicky fared well in school and a bit of her life is preserved
in her first letters to her parents. Already writing in cursive by
the age of seven, Vicky did her best to please her parents from
afar. Grandama Dianna and Grandpa James kept their granddaughter well-fed, and neatly clothed with billowy bows tied
in her hair. And Uncle Vincent continued to dote on Vicky
with presents and treats, but Vicky's simple childhood letters
reveal the beginnings of a family dynamic that persisted for the
rest of her life. Vicky no doubt adored her parents and missed
them deeply, but she was beginning to learn which heartstrings
pulled at love and which ones pulled at guilt.

Blue Harbor, Mich

Dear Daddy,

I had a letter from mother today I had a merry Christmas and new year I go sledding with Ethel Bulock. I thought I would send you my school work so you can see what I am doing in school I have not been late since I started last fall I like to be early I am going to a party up at Josephine Darling's today 3-5 Did you know I had a redcross doll I made a little middy for redcross I made her a little knitting bag say Daddy I'm getting to be a fine little sewer Uncle Vincent went to the basketball game last night and while he was there we had the worst fire in town the fire was just across from Stein's store Grandpa got some little overshoes with two buckles for Christmas grandma made me a good heavy coat and knit me a sweater I go to the picture show every Saturday night I hope you will keep well so that I can see you when you come back from war Poor mother must be lonesome when she can't see you we have lots of snow up here grandma has a new skirt lots of XXXXXXXXXXX with much love good bye Daddy from Vicky Becker

Blue Harbor Mich

p.s. I got the little gloves and little dishes but the dishes were broken

~ PART 10 ~

ABOARD THE *PRESIDENT GRANT,*

SOMEWHERE IN THE ATLANTIC

———

Chapter 35

"HAVE YOU EVER heard of a place called Sturgeon Bay?" Libby Hampton asks, coyly peering out over the top of her Prickly Pear Southwest Café menu. "Not the one in Wisconsin, but the one in Michigan?

I'm taking her out to lunch along Ann Arbor's Main Street. Henry Richards — a native of the city that is home to the University of Michigan — recommended this place to me before I drove down here, and Libby seems to like it so far.

"Are you kidding? That's like twenty-five minutes north of my house. Why do you ask?" I reply, trying not to show how giddy I feel under her charming gaze.

"Well, that's where we'll be studying the piping plovers. Professor Miller said we'll be staying at the U of M Biological Station in Pellston, but spending most of our day among the dunes at Sturgeon Bay."

"Pellston is only about twenty-five minutes east of The Shack," I say. "How convenient."

"I wouldn't get too excited, Nick," Libby cautions. "Our schedule sounds pretty grueling for the first few weeks. We will be practically on guard duty monitoring the plover nest sites and trying to keep beachgoers and their dogs away from the nests. We might have a little more free time after the chicks hatch."

"I'll be pretty busy, too — lots of stories to write, and there's all this legal garbage to deal with," I say with feigned grumpiness. "But I can tell you one thing for sure — if you're going to be that close to me, I'll find a way to come see you," I say as my unconvincing frown turns to a smile. "Even if I have to dress up in a mama piping plover suit, I'll find some way."

"I'd like to see that," she says, "but I don't think you'll have to go to such extremes. We get one full day and one evening off every week. I don't know what the schedule will be, yet, but I think I can squeeze you in, if you can find the time for me. I would love to see what that old shack of yours looks like in the summer. I bet it's beautiful."

"I'm sure it will only look prettier with you there," I say, looking down into my menu, slightly embarrassed at my cheese-ball comment.

I steal a glance and see that Libby is blushing even as she shakes her head and rolls her eyes at me before perusing her menu. Although I am feeling pretty savvy in khaki pants, blue-checked dress shirt, and brown penny loafers, I have definitely been out in the woods too long. Libby is wearing a light blue sundress with a new yellow Michigan sweatshirt draped over her round shoulders. Her New Balance running shoes and white socks remind me that she was a runner in college, and I wonder whether I will ever be able to keep up with her. Since we were reunited on the Diag in the middle of the U of M campus a half an hour ago, the mere sight of her and the soft, playful sound of her slightly southern voice have filled me with delight. I think I'll take up running again when I get home.

"Let's order," she says, "I'm starving."

After walking Libby back to campus and saying goodbye (I got to kiss her and she kissed back), I'm at the Washtenaw County Probate Court Clerk's Office waiting for the clerk to retrieve the complete record for the Colonel's estate. I'm flipping through the bits and pieces of Joe's estate file that I have from Aunt Vicky's and Dad's records, and trying to put together what I already know with what I expect to find in Joe's probate file.

It all comes down to the Order Assigning Residue that Mom entered into the Emmet County Register of Deeds office back in the '60s. Henry told me to follow the line of title. Following Anna's death in 1956 and Joe's death in 1957, the title to the Blue Harbor property legally belonged to the Estate of Joseph L. Becker. Since Dad and Aunt Vicky were only life tenants they did not have title to the land. The title should have stayed with Joe's estate until both Vicky and Dad passed on, at which time it would have passed to my sister Sally and me—or the State of Michigan if there were no grandchildren to inherit the property.

Somewhere in the last three decades, however, somebody managed to get the title changed from Joe directly to Dad and Aunt Vicky. I suspect that Cushman must have petitioned the court to obtain full title to the Becker farm for Dad and Aunt Vicky. It would be easy to just ask Cushman about this directly, but my instincts tell me I had better get my facts straight before I ask Cy about it. I hope it will all become clear in the next few minutes when I get a look at the complete file for Joe's estate.

The probate clerk calls my name to the counter and hands over the legal-sized folder containing all of the records connected to Joe's estate. I've been doing a little bit of work with these kind of court records for some of the stories I've been reporting on, so the order and steps of the estate process aren't all Greek to me.

Joe's lawyer, William F. Farmer, put a legal notice in the Ann Arbor News informing any and all parties to the estate of the pending hearing. He sent off a notice in the mail to Dad and Vicky since they were the only ones specifically named in the will, and then Vicky and Farmer attested to the validity of Joe's last will and testament and to the fact that Vicky and Dad were the only legal heirs. There are forms for dealing with the $5,000 life insurance policy Joe took out on himself; forms for giving notice to any of Joe's creditors, etc., etc.

As I slowly read and flip through each page of the file, all seems to be going exactly as Joe planned it in his will. I flip towards the end of the file looking for anything dated after 1957 or something with Cy Cushman's name on it. Except for a 1981 letter from Cushman asking for certified copies of the entire estate file, all looks exactly the same, neatly typed on the same fill-in-the blank legal forms published by some Kalamazoo "law blank makers." There is no later petition to overturn Joe's will and assign full title to Dad and Vicky. There are only the papers handled by Joe's lawyer and a few later requests for copies of the file.

This can't be!

I flip back to where I left off and continue to read as the probate of Joe's estate unfolds just as he planned. His house in Ann Arbor and the property in Blue Harbor are about $25,000 each, according to the 1957 appraisals, and all his worldly possessions only amount to about $500. There is a little bit of cash here and there, but almost all of it goes to pay off the handful of debts and expenses Joe's estate has incurred since his passing. Somewhere near the middle of the file, I come across the original "Order Assigning Residue of Estate." It's the same form as the one filed in the Emmet County Register of Deeds. It gives Dad and Vicky $500 and the two properties (Joe's Ann Arbor house and the 105-acre farm Up North) to split equally. There is There is simply no mention anywhere on this form of the life tenancies so carefully spelled out in Joe's will, which is also included in the file.

I double-check the will in the file with the copy of the will I have from Aunt Vicky's files. They are the same.

> ... *Such property as I may own at the time of my death in Emmet County, Michigan, I give and bequeath as life tenants to my issue, with right of survivorship, and with the remainder to my grandchildren, if any, by right of representation.*

My brain is clicking and whirring. If Joe's will was never changed or overturned then Joe's wishes for the farm should still be in effect. That means that as Joe's only grandchildren, Sally and I should not only get Dad's half of the property, but Aunt Vicky's half, as well!

The whole 105 acres should belong to we living Beckers. This means that Homer Robertson's plan to turn half of the Becker farm into a new phase of his upscale resort development just went up in smoke. This means that Aunt Vicky's friends and favorite charities back in Tucson will be splitting up tens of thousands of dollars, not hundreds of thousands. This means that Cushman has some serious explaining to do.

With the complete estate file in front of me, I can see how this happened. Within the context of Joe's entire probate record, the Order Assigning Residue doesn't seem out of sync with Joe's will and the rest of the estate proceedings. In the blanks of the Order Assigning Residue, Joe's attorney simply listed the legal descriptions of the two properties without specifying that Dad and Vicky only had life tenancies to the Blue Harbor property. Taken on its own, however, it looks like the order gives both properties to them outright. It all boils down to what lawyers might call an error of omission.

Mom innocently entered the order into the Emmet County Register of Deeds office in the '60s to show that Dad had a life tenant's interest. Some lawyer, however, took one look at the order and probably told Dad and Vicky that they didn't have to worry about Joe's will anymore. This signed court order in my hands is basically flawed when it comes to the Becker farm, but it has been used to undo Joe's final, careful plans for the property and people he loved.

Somewhere in Dad and Aunt Vicky's undaunted effort to get title to the Blue Harbor land, however, somebody (and maybe everybody) forgot about Joe's grandchildren. How in the hell did that happen? Aren't courts (and parents, for that matter) supposed to look out for the interests of minors? Sally and I were both adults by the time Dad and Vicky died, but it looks like this slippery paper shuffle was underway long before we graduated from high school. Because of a single flawed legal document, Sally and I almost had $375,000 taken right out from under our noses.

Beads of sweat are popping out of my forehead as I sit in the probate clerk's office. A slight wave of nausea sweeps through my system. What I have uncovered has left me angry and sad at the same time. I'm angry enough to fight for what rightfully belongs to the surviving Becker family. But I am saddened by the fact that I now have to do so. Part of me is ready to rise in rebellion, but another part of me sees the awkward position Sally and I must fight from.

Cushman's words from last month's lunch meeting still echo in my ears: "two spoiled kids trying to get Daddy's land with the state fighting for public access to Lake Michigan and a refuge for wildlife." I am quite certain that Sally and I would be in the right to reclaim Vicky's so-called half of the Becker farm. But that fight puts us at odds with the Humane Society of Tucson, a couple of Vicky's other charities, her friends like LuAnne Wilson, a lawyer who I thought was on our side, and apparently all other wildlife lovers and public beachgoers in Michigan. Moreover, we would have to demonstrate how my own father and aunt basically screwed us over (either intentionally or otherwise) to get what they wanted.

None of this makes my poor mother look very good, either. She's usually a pretty shrewd businesswoman.

After the divorce, she was out of the loop when it came to the Blue Harbor property. She gets a share of the land according to the divorce settlement, but I don't think she has seen as much of the legal papers as I now have. The last thing I want to do is drag her any further into this mess. Hell, if Aunt Vicky had only asked us for some money from the property, Dad and the rest of us would probably have given it to her anyway. The way things have shaken out, however, stinks. If I don't fight, Joe's will is broken, a bunch of people in Arizona who we barely know get half of our family farm because of a mistake in the paperwork, and a significant legal error (and possibly some intentional malpractice) goes unrectified. I just can't let that happen.

The rest of my afternoon is spent working the phone from my room at the Motel 6, just south of Ann Arbor. Mom says not to judge Aunt Vicky too harshly. "She had an unhappy life, but that was still a pretty rotten thing to do to her own flesh and blood." Mom says she will try to help however she can, but she's in the middle of her intensive training to become a Christian Science nurse. It sounds like her mother-bear hackles have been raised, though, and she is going to get right to work praying for this situation to be healed. "We can expect nothing less than Truth to triumph," she says.

When I reach Sally at work and explain what I've found out, she is in favor of more direct action. "I'm going to dig up that old hag and give her a piece of my mind," Sally says. "All those years she spent making us feel like no-account ingrates when we didn't send her a Thank You note the day after Christmas — all those years she gave me crap about getting sunburned at Dad's funeral — and you're tellin' me that whole time she was basically working to rip us off? No wonder she never liked us. We were standing in the way of her getting at a bunch of money she wanted even though it wasn't hers to take. What ch!"

Sally is a good one to have in your corner in a fight. She actually gets a bit teary on the phone, but her resolve is clear. She gives me the go-ahead to talk to Cushman on her behalf and "rip him a new one, if he had anything to do with letting this happen."

As kids, I usually seemed to find myself somewhere between appeaser and peacemaker in the midst of the struggles between my father and Sally. I tried to remain a neutral Switzerland to their Turkish-Greco struggle, but most of the time I didn't want anything to do with their combative natures. I was happy with my snow-capped peaks and Edelweiss. I was glad to see them begin to come to terms with each other after they stopped living under the same roof. But now, I find Sally's martial spirit somewhat refreshing, and I am determined to unleash my inner-Sally voice. It's time to stop worrying about manners and start focusing on what is right.

After a few more calls, I have managed to locate Joe's old attorney. His son, who has carried on the family law practice in Ann Arbor, was nice enough to give me his Dad's phone number even though I forthrightly let him know that I was not happy with his father's work for my grandfather.

Bill Farmer is in his late eighties and retired to South Carolina many years ago, but I manage to catch him at home. Farmer is a bit guarded on the phone, and he should be. I'm not even a lawyer, and the terms "legal malpractice" and "malpractice insurance" are already bouncing around the back of my head as I'm talking to him. Nonetheless, he remembers the Colonel quite well, having lived in the same Packard Ave. neighborhood during and after the Second World War, and he remembers handling his estate. Farmer, who seems quite lucid, doesn't remember the details of the estate paperwork and my attempt to describe the faulty Order Assigning Residue seems to lose him.

"What I do clearly remember," Farmer says, interrupting my feeble attempt to describe the paper trail, "is that Colonel Becker set up those life tenancies because he didn't want your father and your aunt to sell the property off after he died. He wanted it to either remain in the family and go to his grand-children if John and Vicky ever had kids or go to the state as a wildlife refuge and memorial to his wife Anna.

"I remember setting up the life tenancies in the will so well because that was the only time anyone ever requested such a provision in any will I ever worked on," Farmer says. "I had to do a little bit of research on them to get it right."

"So, you think that Order Assigning Residue was just a mistake?" I venture to ask.

"I don't know if there was any mistake, but I can certainly tell you that if your father and aunt got clear title to the Emmet County land as you say, then they would have had to have overturned the Colonel's will to do so. If there is no record of that happening in the Washtenaw County Probate files, then something isn't right. You are correct in your understanding that once a court order is signed by a judge it becomes law, but if that order is somehow open to multiple interpretations, then there may be additional issues that need to be determined in a court of law."

I thank Farmer for his time, and he offers to look at the documents for me if I have any further questions. I smell a couple of rats, but I don't think the smell is coming from South Carolina. If Farmer's work for Joe was flawed, it was certainly an honest mistake. The rat stench seems to be coming from Aunt Vicky's grave in Tucson and Cushman's office in Petoskey, but I fear that my own father may have inadvertently played a part in giving away his children's inheritance to his sister. I'll have to sort out Dad's role in all this at some point, but I realize that there was about a year after my father's death when Vicky and Cushman were left holding all the cards. They could have and should have shown those cards to Sally, my mother and me, but they never said a word about the troubling Order Assigning Residue or Joe's will. We may have been mistaken in our understanding that Joe's will was no longer an issue, but neither my father's sister nor his attorney did anything to correct our misunderstanding.

I'm going to find out what Aunt Vicky and Cy Cushman did to try to rip us off, and I hope it is not too late to prevent them from doing so. I'm ready for a fight, but my reporter-ingrained objectivity tells me that Dad's part in all of this throws a wet blanket on any righteous indignation I may feel. After all, if Dad struggled all those years to get clear title to half of the land, he was also working to free up the other half for Aunt Vicky. I'm sure Dad never expected to die before Vicky. Perhaps he secretly expected to end up with the whole thing for himself and his family. Mostly, though, I think he just lost sight of the big picture in the midst of the minutia of his long legal battles over the property.

It wouldn't be the first time that my father lost sight of a big picture that his young son could see, even if I couldn't articulate it. Sitting in this simple motel room just off I-80, I can still see my father waving goodbye to his family from the driveway of our Fort Sheridan quarters.

Maj. John Becker came home from the Corps of Engineers battalion headquarters in his short-sleeved khaki uniform to send us off. He would be going overseas in a few weeks.

I was twelve years old in 1976, and Dad was about to go and finish up the last four years of his Army career back in Germany. Mom was driving our big Chevy Blazer down McCormick Dr. at the start of our journey to St. Louis. Dad's last overseas tour of duty did not require a separation from his family, but he loved Germany and Mom did not like the Army schools for her children. At least that was the story Sally and I were being told. In truth, it was yet another slow-bleeding wound to my parent's marriage. As the youngest and the neutral Switzerland of our family's troubled alliance of independent nations, I was in the dark about many of the particulars of this split. But even as I kid, I knew that this separation did not have to be. I sensed that my parents had reached an impasse, and that there were darker reasons for this trans-Atlantic split. I'm sure I hoped that we would all be reunited one day, but even then I knew that this move would not be good for us as a family.

My sister was sad to be leaving her friends, but quietly elated that she was about to be free from my father. I, too, was sorry to leave my friends (some of the best friends I ever had in our military life). Chris, Steve, Jason, and the other Steve chased us down the streets of the officers' family quarters and across the high, white concrete bridge that spanned the deep wooded ravine near our house, but they couldn't keep up with the Blazer on their banana-seat Huffy bikes for long as they waved and called after me. I remember the whole scene through a watery haze as the tears pooled up behind my thick glasses.

I waved to my friends through the Blazer's back window, but the tears were as much for the man we left in the driveway as they were for my pals. It wasn't just that I was going to miss my father. I cried because I felt sorry for him — sorry that he didn't know how to love better, sorry that he was letting the three people who could have loved him more than anybody drive away.

Chapter 36

IT TAKES ME about four and a half hours to get home from Ann Arbor. My answering machine has three urgent messages to get in touch with Cy Cushman, but he doesn't say why. For a second, I feel like I've been caught red-handed snooping around the Washtenaw Probate Court Clerk's Office, but I can't imagine any way that Cushman could have found out. And so what if he did? Don't I have a right to know my own family's business, no matter how much has been kept from me? I'll be telling Cushman all about what I found down there very soon, anyway. I'm curious, but I don't want to talk to him yet.

Instead, I call an Ann Arbor florist to send flowers and a "thinking of you" card to Libby Hampton at the dorm she's staying at during the orientation. I got a phone number for the florist this morning when I was still down there, but I had to hit the road before the flower shop opened.

The whole way driving up from Ann Arbor, my brain kept churning over what I discovered down at the Washtenaw County Probate Clerk's Office. While driving, I kept trying to turn my mind to more pleasant thoughts like Libby, but I didn't think she would like my imagination getting too far ahead of our next meeting. Although thoughts of her cast a soft light on the blighted scenery around Flint, I spent the rest of the trip from the Zilwaukee Bridge construction mess to The Shack trying to figure out how to prevent Aunt Vicky from reaching out of her grave to rob her next of kin.

Around West Branch, I remembered seeing a stack of letters that Joe wrote to Vicky in the last year of his life. The letters had something to do with Joe's final plans for the Becker Farm, and by Grayling I decided that I would read these letters through before talking to Cushman.

Seated now at my desk, I gather up the Becker family records from The First World War and put them in a stack on the left-hand corner of my desk. I pull the file with Joe's last letters and time-warp my family ahead four decades from World War I to the late 1950s. Although my opinion of Aunt Vicky has taken a decided turn for the worst, Vicky's relationship with Joe only grew stronger in the year following Anna's death. Throughout 1956 and 1957, three or four letters a week flowed between Ann Arbor and Hopkins, Minnesota (where Vicky and Uncle Rollie first lived after Rollie retired from the Army). With my father heading off with his new bride to his first real job as a geologist in Utah with an oil and gas exploration firm, Aunt Vicky was Joe's most reliable touchstone.

Curiously, I have none of Vicky's letters from this time — only Joe's. Although many of the letters were just business, they reveal a great deal more warmth than Aunt Vicky's letters to my mother and father a decade later. He signed his letters "Pa Sha" — as in "oh, pashaw." He used variations on this theme nicknaming Vicky "Da Sha" and finally settling on "Rol Sha" for Uncle Rollie.

Joe had entered his seventies and was still traveling and trying to tend to his own housekeeping and affairs, but he was having his ups and downs — both physically and emotionally. He was learning Latin and took a trip Out West to visit his far-flung Wisconsin relatives. After reading a National Geographic article about the extreme poverty of the Ogallala and Lakota tribes on the Pine Ridge Reservation in South Dakota, Joe was on a crusade sending boxes of used clothing to them. I wouldn't be surprised if many of Anna's clothes ended up on the reservation below the Black Hills, providing some comfort and a touch of midwestern style to the women of Pine Ridge. Joe spent many of his days purging the Ann Arbor house of unnecessary stuff, but he carefully preserved most of the letters, photographs, and records from his life with Anna.

Although he was moving forward, he also worried that he was partially to blame for Anna's unexpected death. He feared that his "mule headed insistence" on making the last leg of a long car trip through a snow storm may have precipitated Anna's sudden illness. In a letter dated February 25, 1957 (almost a year after Anna's passing), Joe wrote: "I keep kicking myself for not staying a day or two in Kalamazoo and thereby not agitating Mother as I did. I just didn't sense how disturbed she was about the hazardous driving."

Vicky's efforts to console her father weren't entirely successful, though.

A2

Thursday March 28, 1957

My Dear Vicky,

Yesterday morning your letter of the 25th reached me. I was so surprised to get it, only having heard from you Tuesday.

All that you say is taken in good part just as you mean it. But no matter how kindly words from any source are meant, they do me little good. You see — after all the years "Mum Sha" and I were together it is difficult to adjust to a different way of life. I am a sort of one track minded individual anyhow and the spirit of Anna will be with me until I breathe my last. Other scenes, places and people do interest me but there can never be such a thing as replacement. I hope you understand. The very core of me is so full

*of Anna that all my thoughts and actions are predicated
on her presence and participation, approval and enjoyment of things with me.*

*I am fully cognizant of the way of life and that there is
an end for us all. As for me — I appreciate companions,
friends and those close and dear to me. A swan or a goose
is inconsolable without a mate. I am too far advanced in
years to find satisfaction and a new life to replace what we
knew. Perhaps in a few years things may be otherwise.*

*As for your questions about the farm, I am still weighing
the options. I can't believe the audacity of those people in
North Shore Township upping my assessment on the farm.
They are probably trying to get even with me about that
little piece on the shore. There is no uniformity about how
they have assessed any of that land at all.*

*How would you feel about turning the whole thing over
to the Michigan Conservation Department as a memorial to Mother? I'll talk to the Conservation man up there
at the earliest opportunity, but they are so vague about
what they would do with the place if we turned it over to
them that I am looking into other means of protecting it.
I would love to see it stay in the family, but the last thing
I want to leave you and John with is the tax bills for the
farm. I can barely keep up with them myself.*

*There is also this to consider. John loves the place just as
you do. If he had a family or even the prospect of children
my inclination would be to safeguard it all for him and
them, as I think you would also. The value of the farm is
quickly rising to match the value of the Ann Arbor house,
and I could simply leave the Ann Arbor house to you and
the Blue Harbor farm to John. What do you think?*

*Do you remember what that old Indian Edmund Shago-
nasee told me when he helped me clear out those tall pines
for the orchard? He told me that he could see that I loved
the sacred land of his people, but he cautioned me. He
said, "It's not just how much we love the land, but how we
love it that makes us part of this wild country or apart
from it."*

*Perhaps this is a problem we had better discuss at length
before I am forced to have a showdown with the tax people
next December. It had always been our hope (Mother and
I) that Chi-noo-ding would remain as an estate in the
family Becker.*

*I will go to the V.A. Hospital next Tuesday AM. Have only
delayed the surgery on my hand because I want to vote in
the election coming up April 1st. All Michigan is getting fed
up with Soapy Williams, democrats and especially with
the Squander-mania everywhere.*

*I think two weeks will be about my limit in the hospital
unless my chest kicks up. Don't worry about my food. I live
well and get all the salt I need.*

Love,
Your "Pa Sha"

There are only a couple more letters from Joe, but this one
pretty much says it all. The V.A. doctors operated on Joe's
arthritic hand with success, and he was beginning to recover.
His concern about his chest, however, proved valid. After
a three-week battle with pneumonia and heart trouble, Joe
passed on. He left his body behind at the V.A. hospital, and
went on to find Anna elsewhere.

Joe's letter certainly puts all of this inheritance crap into
perspective. What is money and land compared to a love that

outlasts death? I don't know if Joe would have put it this way, but I think he left the farm for his family as a way of leaving behind an earthly symbol of his love for Anna. I always thought that the Becker Farm was more of Joe's idea of a retirement place for an old soldier, but now I see that it was more about Anna than anything else.

Not only did Joe have the good sense to adopt Anna's beautiful hometown as the place to spend their summers and retirement years, but Joe picked a piece of property that was a beloved part of Anna's life — "Chi-noo-ding." The Shack is none other than the old Keegonee family home that I read about in Anna's letters. When I didn't see the Keegonee name during my title search of the land at the Emmet County Register of Deeds, I didn't think there was a connection. But now I remember — it was Mary Jane's Auntie's house and she probably had a different last name than Mary Jane.

Looking back over my notes, I see "Margaret Shomin" in the line of names who once owned the Chinooding property. That must be Mary Jane's Auntie. A couple of years later, some real estate speculator named Church snatched up the place. Knowing Joe and Anna's fondness for their Indian friends and Native Americans in general, I imagine that Joe and Anna's purchase of the farm in 1924 was a way of preserving some of that heritage as well as finding a nice place for themselves. I can almost see Joe taking Anna on an unexpected summer drive out into the country north of Blue Harbor to surprise her.

———

In the summer of 1924, Joe, Anna, and Vicky would have spent a month or so of leave visiting Anna's parents up here. Borrowing Uncle Vint's 1921 roadster/pickup with the black canopy folded down between the front seat and the wooden pickup bed, Joe headed up the gravel and sand road that was Shore Drive.

"I have a secret to show you," Joe told Anna as they bounced along the dusty country road that revealed wide stretches of Little Traverse Bay and Lake Michigan beneath the clear, blue sky that Anna had missed during all those years away from home. There was a quality to the light of Northern Michigan that she hadn't found anywhere else in their travels across the country and around the world.

Joe slowed down at the bottom of a hill just south of Stanton Road, and turned left toward the lake down a sandy two-track that went past the Weaver's farm. Anna knew most of the farms and families north of town, but would not have immediately recognized Joe's secret destination. To Anna's eyes, the countryside around Cummings Creek was entirely altered from the world that she and Mary Jane Keegonee knew two decades earlier. The Weavers and their neighbors to the south had cleared and planted hundreds of acres along Shore Drive, and the old forest on the hills between Shore Drive and Lower Beach Trail was just a sea of stumps with dozens of saplings jostling for life in the space that the big trees used to fill. To the north of Stanton Road, Anna could see the still-intact line of cedars that marked the boggiest land and the upper brooks of Cummings Creek, but the uplands were crisscrossed with fence lines to keep livestock in and deer out.

"Where are you taking me, Captain Becker?" Anna asked.

"You don't recognize where you are?"

"I know where Cummings Creek is, but I still can't guess what you are up to," Anna replied as the roadster began climbing the roller-coaster hills. She noticed an old abandoned house at the foot of the hills, and farther up the road she saw a line of tall Lombardy Poplars at the top of the second hill. The poplars shielded a barn and an old house from the north winds that would blow across Stanton Road in the winter. But here in the middle of summer, Anna only noticed the delightful quaking of the poplar leaves in the warm breeze. Along the south side of Stanton Road, Anna could still make out the outlines of neglected gardens and paddocks. The fenced-in pastures were empty except for the tall unmowed grass, clumps of dark-green juniper bushes, and stands of sumac heavy with fuzzy, brown flowers. Beyond the Lombardy-sheltered farm, Anna could just make out the roof of another house, but then Joe turned left up the driveway and past the Lombardy windscreen and into a circular two track. Joe set the handbrake and turned off the engine.

"Does this look familiar?" Joe said, grinning like the Cheshire cat.

It took a moment for Anna's memories of the winter of 1906 to translate into the summer scene before her, but she slowly stepped out of the car without taking her eyes off the simple frame house lying next to the circular driveway. There were a couple of apple trees on the east side of the house, and Anna let her gloved hands slide along the rough-barked trunks as she began to circle the house.

"Chi-noo-ding," Anna whispered as she climbed up the front porch steps. "Joe, this is Mary Jane's old house. Why on earth did you bring me here?"

Anna was a bit puzzled, but turned at the top of the porch stairs looking out from the heights of Chi-noo-ding. There was a wide meadow on the shelf of land between the small hill that the house sat on and the steep slope of the bluff. Queen Anne's lace, daisies, and black-eyed Susans gently waved in the wind. Beyond the bluff, the small waves out on Lake Michigan looked like slow-motion ripples on a puddle, arching into the bay as the shoulders of the wave action caught the shore north of Charlevoix. The North American was steaming out of Little Traverse Bay into the big lake on its way to Chicago, leaving a trail of black and gray smoke that marked the southwest breeze like a windsock. The masts on a pair of racing sloops tilted slightly to the northeast on a steady tack towards Petoskey.

"Because I think Mary Jane and her family would rather you have their old farm than that swindler A.B. Church. We can afford to buy the whole 105-acre place if you want it. I know you like it out here. It could use some work, but those Ottawa lumbermen sure knew how to build a solid shack."

"It's a beautiful house," Anna said before running down the porch stairs, grabbing Joe around the neck, and bursting into tears.

"Why the tears, Anna?" Joe said reaching for his handkerchief. "Don't you like it?"

It took Anna a minute to regain her composure. After considerable eye-daubing and nose-blowing, she looked up into Joe's tan face. "Of course I love it. It's just you, Joe. You never cease to amaze me. Here I was worrying about how far away from home you were going to take us on this next tour of duty, and it turns out you were busy making a place for us to call home whenever we get back. I love it here, and I love you, Joseph Becker."

Anna stretched up on her tiptoes and found Joe's lips beneath his trimmed mustache. Joe and Anna spent the rest of the morning going through the house, barn, and other shanties on the property before loading back up into the roadster and heading into town. They made a down payment on the farm that afternoon with some money they had made from one of Uncle Vint's stock tips. A week later, Joe, Anna, and Vicky entertained Anna's parents from the porch of the house they all decided to call "The Shack."

————

I spend the rest of the afternoon walking through the house and around the property seeing the whole place in a new light. Homer Robertson's insta-forest and the stakes in the meadow don't bother me as much. I'll deal with them later. Looking around, I see the whole place through 4-D glasses. Not only do my eyes see height, width, and depth, but it feels like I can see the expanse of time before me. I can look past the insta-forest and see how wide open the whole area looked after the logging boom. And I'm beginning to see what this place could look like in the future.

I head down to the bottom of the bluff to pick up a trail my grandmother left 83 years ago on a horse named Chieftain. I even bring down her letter to her mother — the one about the sleigh accident when she broke her nose and "lived with the Indians."

Walking along the base of the bluff, I'm looking for a split-trunk cedar tree near the path to the beach. Lower Beach Trail has long-since been widened and the electric company cut a swath of trees along the bottom of the bluff for a power line, but there's still a chance I might find what I'm looking for. If not, I've also brought my swim trunks and a towel for a quick dip in the lake. The water is still pretty damn cold in June, but I've already been in a couple of times.

All of the cedar trees near the trail at the bottom of the bluff have single trunks, and I'm about to give up and hit the beach when I notice a massive stump off to the north of the trail. The stump stands about chest high and is all punky, with rust-colored chips at the top, but there is enough of the base of the tree that I can see a split starting a few feet up from the base of the stump. This crevice, which seemed to form when two separate trunks of the tree started to grow back into one, is wet and mushy and chunks of trunk fall apart in my hand as I poke into it with my fingers. I pick up a hefty tree branch off the ground that has a sharp, hooked end and begin digging into the rotten wood with it. The stump falls to pieces as I sink the stick deeper into the mushy wood. Then, I feel the stick hit something hard. The hard thing keeps me from pushing the stick in deeper, so I instead use the stick as a lever to break off more of the stump. The entire right side of the stump cracks loose and crashes to the forest floor with a small avalanche of rotten wood chips following the big chunk. And there in the middle of the remaining stump is the artifact that closes the circle of a trail that Anna began in 1906 — "a smooth, black rock about the size of a small watermelon."

The rock is just like the one she describes in her letter. It must have disappeared deep into the tree trunk as the tree grew thicker and thicker with each annual ring. It is the rock that marked the bluff path up to Mary Jane Keegonee's house. I must have passed by this stump hundreds of times without noticing anything peculiar about it. But buried inside the rotten wood, like some fossilized dinosaur egg in layers of rock, is the marker that helped save Anna's life in the snowstorm. Without this rock, Vicky and Dad, Sally and I may have never been. Without this rock, Chi-noo-ding may never have become a part of my grandparents' lives. On my way back from my swim, I dig the rock out of the remaining stump and decide to take it back to The Shack. No matter what Aunt Vicky, Dad, or Cushman may have done or tried to do, I have no doubt about where the surviving members of the Becker family belong. I climb the bluff with my ancient artifact, and head home.

Chapter 37

I GLANCE AT my watch as I cross the railroad tracks that run through Petoskey's downtown park. It's 8:50 AM on June 8, and I am on my way to confront Cy Cushman with my Washtenaw Probate Court discoveries. I'm trying to remain calm and remember everything I learned in Sunday School about the dangers of self-righteous indignation and judging others, but I can hear my own pulse as loudly as I can hear the accusations against Cushman that are echoing in my head.

"Best to just remain professional and stick to the facts," I tell myself instead screaming "Cushman is a thief" in the middle of the morning bustle of Petoskey shopkeepers and bank tellers trying to get to work.

Cushman's secretary Donna recognizes me this time and takes me straight into Cy's office saying that they have been expecting me.

"There you are, Nicolas, good to see you," Cushman says, shaking my hand as he guides me to the chair in front of his desk. "We were beginning to get worried about you."

I tell him that I was in Ann Arbor seeing a girl I know down there, and he gives me a knowing wink as I describe Libby and how we met. What Cushman thinks he knows, however, is not the same thing as what I know as I nod back to him.

Cy pulls out his gold pocket watch and flips open the lid, then shakes it next to his ear.

"Hold my calls, Miss Charboneau," he calls out to Donna, then he says, "this thing has kept perfect time for thirty years, but this is the second time it has just stopped for no good reason. What time have you got, Nick?"

"Three minutes to nine."

"Good. That leaves us plenty of time to go over some important issues about the Becker estate."

"Go ahead, I'm listening."

"I have some bad news, Nick," Cushman says handing over a packet of stapled papers with Michigan's distinctive state seal printed at the top of the page (an upright elk and moose holding a shield with a bald eagle above the shield and the state motto in Latin). Dan, our carpenter friend, told me the motto translates to "If you seek a pleasant peninsula, look around."

The letterhead says "State of Michigan, Department of Attorney General, Frank J. Kelly."

"This is the AG office's opinion on the state's interest in your family's land," Cushman says. "Basically, what it says is that the state believes that your grandfather's will still has precedence in determining who the Becker farm belongs to. If you've seen your grandfather's will, you may remember that there was what we call a "right of survivorship" clause in the paragraph concerning the Emmet County property. The attorney general's office contends — and I completely disagree — that the entire property should go to the State of Michigan for the nature preserve that your grandfather specified in his will in case there were no grandchildren to inherit the land."

"But there are grandchildren," I say, mentally trying to outrun the blast from the bomb that Cushman has just dropped in the room. "I don't get it."

"Their argument goes something like this," Cushman continues, "the right of survivorship in a life tenancy situation normally just means that if two people like your father and aunt are given life tenancies in a property than either of those tenancies remains as long as one of the two heirs remains living. In your family's case, that meant that your Aunt Vicky's life tenancy continued even though your father passed on.

"What the state is trying to say is that when your father died before your aunt, Vicky became the sole life tenant of the entire property, effectively cutting off your branch of the family tree because of the "right of survivorship." Since she had no children, there were no grandchildren in a direct line of descendancy from the Colonel to Vicky. The state is saying that since there are no grandchildren through Vicky then the Colonel's contingency for giving the property to the state for a nature preserve in his wife's name comes into play.

"This is only a legal opinion and I will help you and Sally fight it to the end, but I'm afraid this will take some time to overcome. This could add years to the process of settling your father's estate."

I've been fingering the fake brass clasp on the cheap plastic attaché case that I brought to carry the copy of Joe's Washtenaw County Probate record to this meeting. I suddenly realize that I've been clicking the buckle open and closed since Cushman passed the A.G. office's opinion over to me. If Cushman had simply slugged me in the stomach as hard as he could, it would not have been as surprising and devastating as the news he has just given me. I struggle to get my wind back on the inside, but I can almost feel my outsides turning to ice. I sit still for a few minutes.

A couple of minutes ago, I had visions of winning back Aunt Vicky's optioned-off half of our family's land, shedding the light of truth on a web of deception, and securing a brighter future for me and Sally and Mom (and even, perhaps, for a fair-haired, blue-eyed Virginia girl I'm just starting to know). In an instant, I have become homeless, broke, and feel as though I have just wasted the past six months of my life trying to take care of family business. I heard Cushman's optimistic assessment of the case, but there is a certain elegant logic to the Attorney General's opinion that rings truer to my ears than Cushman's overly confident words.

My long silence begins to make Cushman uneasy, and he rises from his desk to pour me a glass of water from the table on the other side of his office.

"Are you all right, Nick?" he says. "Here, have some water."

He hands me the glass, but when I don't take it, he just sets it in front of me on the edge of his desk. "Look, I understand this comes as a shock to you. It was a surprise to me, too. I've never heard of the state interpreting survivorship rights in this way. It's preposterous."

"Is it?" I say, breaking my silence and looking out the window into the park.

"There's something important I haven't shown you yet," Cushman says returning to his desk and riffling through a drawer. "It hasn't seemed relevant to your father's estate, but it is somewhat of our ace in the hole, if I may. Have you ever heard of a probate document called an "Order Assigning Residue?"

"Do you mean this one?" I ask, whipping out the packet of papers from the attaché case, flipping it open to the correct page I marked with a sticky note, standing up, and slapping it down on the middle of Cushman's desk. "I know all about it."

Cushman looks up from his drawer with an expression on his face that reminds me of the porcupine I scared off The Shack porch with a broom last week because it was chewing on the siding. The porky looked only inconvenienced when I stepped out on the porch and shined a flashlight in its eyes, instinctively knowing that its armor of sharp, barbed quills could easily protect it from large predators like me. It casually climbed down one of the porch posts and headed down the porch steps, at first. But when I gave it a crisp whack with the wooden end of a broom, the porky looked back over its low shoulder and started scrambling away in high gear.

"Where did you get that?"

"At the Probate Court Clerk's Office down in Ann Arbor," I tell him flatly.

Cushman looks from the order up over his reading glasses to my eyes and back down again.

"Clearly you've done some homework, Nick. If you've read your grandfather's probate file, then you must understand what this order means."

"Well, I think I do, but what do you think it means?" I manage to ask calmly.

"This is the judge's order that transfers title to the Emmet County property from your grandfather's estate to your father and Aunt Vicky. It's the legal method for conveying whatever is left of an estate to heirs after the debts are paid," Cushman explains.

"How come it doesn't mention anything about my aunt and father being life tenants?" I ask with a note of sharpness entering my voice.

"We don't really know, Nick, that's just the way it came out of the probate process. That all happened decades before your family ever came to me for help with all of the legal problems surrounding the Blue Harbor farm."

"It seems a little odd that you never mentioned anything about this document before," I say a little more sharply than I mean to.

"Look, there's no need to get upset here. I can see where you are going with this line of questioning, but it's not the direction we need to go right now. We need to look ahead, not into the past. Don't you see how this order blows the state's claim out of the water? Someone in your family — I believe it was your mother — had this order entered into the Emmet County Register of Deeds back in the '60s. It essentially gave clear title to both your Aunt Vicky and your father. The whole life tenancy thing was really a moot point all along. And the state can't say that everything went to Vicky because John died first. John really owned half of the land all along according to this order. And since John had you and Sally before he died, then your grandfather had grandchildren to leave the land to. In the worst case, the state might be able to get some of Aunt Vicky's land, but don't worry, you'll get your share."

Cushman can talk a pretty good line, and his words begin to tangle the branches of my unruly family tree into knots. He almost has me wondering if I've got this all wrong until his last few words, which make my jaw clench in anger.

"My share? My share? Do you think that's all I give crap about, Cy? This has gotten way beyond that for me. Sure, I've thought about the money and keeping the house and some land, and I know that Mom and Sally could both really use the money right now, even if they do sell off their share. But this is my family you're talking about. My grandfather tried to do something good, something loving for the family he still had and the family that was to come after him. But for the last few decades everyone — including you, my aunt, and even my own father — has been trying to undo what my grandfather set up. You think my line of questioning about the past isn't the right direction, Cy? Well I've just gotten started.

"Was this order just a clerical error? Mom and I always thought that you had had Joe's will overturned! Why didn't you tell us about this order after Dad died? Did it ever even occur to you that if the Colonel's will was still in effect, then all of the property should be going to me and Sally and mom? If you're our family lawyer, what are you doing letting half of the property get sold off and the money sent to someone who doesn't even own it? Why didn't you say anything? What the hell is going on here, Cy?"

Cy is standing now with his hands on his hips. "Settle down, young man. There's no need to raise your voice. This is no time to buckle under. We just need to stay calm and maintain focus. You're not the only one with a lot at stake in the outcome of this estate. This office has invested a great deal of time and money trying to clean up the mess caused by your grandfather's will. He may have had sentimental reasons for doing what he did, but it has caused a lot of trouble for your family. Look, Nick, we're all on the same team here."

"Are we? I know you're the executor of my father's estate and I know that you had a contingency agreement with my father and Aunt Vicky for the legal work you've done for them, but I don't recall you making any agreements with the living members of the Becker family. Whose lawyer are you anyway? You sure don't seem to be looking out for our interests. Just whose interests are you looking out for?"

"If you're suggesting I've done something improper, you had better tread carefully there, Nick."

"I'm not 'suggesting' anything. I'm telling you this straight to your face. You may not have done anything illegal, and you probably were acting exactly as my father and Aunt Vicky wanted for most of the years you worked on this stuff," I say, looking him squarely in the eye. "But when my Dad died, you and Vicky were left holding all the cards. And when you decided not to show me or my sister or my mother what this Order Assigning Residue was all about, you put yourself on the wrong side of what's proper. You committed one of the easiest sins going — an error of omission. All you had to do was keep your mouth shut and this deal with Homer Robertson would go through and you would finally get your fifteen percent contingency fee off of Vicky's so-called half of the land. It was bad enough that you helped Vicky take what wasn't really hers while she was alive, but after she died and you still didn't say anything you left propriety in the dust."

Cushman's face has turned bright red, and he stomps across his office to slam the door shut.

"I don't really know what you were thinking, Cy, but I know you're not stupid," I tell him. "I'm sure you never lost sight of your bottom line, though. I noticed that your agreement with Dad and Vicky never stipulated how much of the land would be sold after all of the title questions were settled. I bet it felt a lot more secure keeping us in the dark knowing that at least half of the property would be sold by Vicky's estate. If you had told Sally and me that all of the land really should have gone to us, there's no telling how much or how little of it we would have sold. It was probably a lot easier to just keep quiet and stick with the status quo. If you ask me, this whole thing's been a big cluster-fuck. First, the township tries to take part of our land. Then, Aunt Vicky tries to get half of something that isn't even hers. Homer has his hooks sunk into part of the land. You get a nice big chunk of the pie for fighting a battle that I'm not even sure was worth fighting for. And now the state wants to take the whole thing away from everybody. And all because nobody — not you, not Vicky, not even Dad — was willing to abide by the final wishes of a dying old man who left some very specific instructions about an old farm that he loved."

Cushman looks like his head is about to explode, so I sit down and give him a chance to respond before he blows his top.

"Listen to me, young man," he says with an icy new tone to his voice. "You may think you've got it all figured out because you stuck your nose into a few court files and you worked for some big newspaper Out East, but you've got it all wrong. I was doing exactly what I was hired to do — look after your family's best interests. If it hadn't been for me, your poor aunt would never have been able to afford decent medical care, and your father would have gone bankrupt trying to keep up with those rising property taxes. Don't come in here whining to me because some attorney made a slip-up thirty years ago. I didn't come looking for this case; your father came to me. And don't throw that contingency fee stuff in my face. This firm has had to shoulder all of the legal costs for over five years."

"Well, that may turn out to have been a bad gamble on your part, Cy," I say with my words tasting like metal as they leave my mouth. "If what the state says is true, then you just spent five years of your life working for your cut in our land. If the State of Michigan gets it, then there is no sale. And no matter how you slice it, fifteen percent of nothing is still nothing. Through all your legal wrangling, you've not only managed to screw the rightful heirs out of their share of the property, but you've managed to fuck yourself as well."

"I'm not some hick lawyer you can come in here and scream at," Cushman screams back, clearly blowing his stack. "Nobody talks to me like that in my office. I'm a respected citizen in this community. If you hadn't been so busy chasing tail down in Ann Arbor, you might have read the local paper and noticed that I've been nominated to run in the upcoming election for appellate-court judge."

Cushman is still standing across his desk yelling something about how selfish I am being, and how my mother and Sally may still be interested in knowing how the Order Assigning

Residue will save us all. But the furious wind that was filling my chest just moments ago has blown from my sails. I slowly begin to gather my papers and repack my attaché case as Cushman winds down. He still looks pretty ticked off at me, but I can almost see him reeling his anger and ego in for a final go at his defensive strategy against the state.

"Look, Nick, we are all in this together," he says, violently jerking his gold watch out of his vest. I hear a tearing sound and the watch flies up into the air with the links of the gold fob slipping through his fingers. The end of the fob has apparently ripped out of his vest pocket, I realize, as the watch and chain sail through the air catching the edge of his desk. The watch springs open as it whacks the desk and spins to the floor. The glass face shatters as it strikes the iron claw-foot of the globe stand that sits next to Cushman's desk.

"Goddammit, that's just perfect," he says dropping on all fours to pick the pieces off the floor. "That was my grandfather's," he says. As he gets back into his chair and pours the pieces onto his desk, he no longer looks formidable. He just looks old.

"I know exactly how you feel, Cy."

Chapter 38

FIRST LIEUTENANT JOSEPH L. Becker scanned the horizon of the Atlantic Ocean with the field glasses that were tethered to the inside of the lookout basket that was attached to the top of the U.S.S. *President Grant's* forward mast. The view from Joe's high perch was striking. The *President Grant* seemed well sheltered in the middle of a nine-ship convoy. About a mile ahead, the U.S. cruiser *Huntington* floated peacefully at a near stop. It was the only true fighting ship assigned to escort the hodge-podge collection of vessels in the convoy. About a half-mile in front of the *President Grant* and a half-mile behind the *Huntington* was a line of the four fastest boats — the *George Washington*, *Covington*, *De Kalb*, and *Pastores*. These ships, like the rearward line of ships that the *President Grant* was in, were positioned about a half-mile away from each other, four abreast.

Enemy submarines were never far from thought on these crossings, and the ships with the most troops were positioned inside the line of four so that any torpedo attack would likely take out the outermost boats first. Those ships were mostly carrying cargo. All nine ships were painted in the oddest colors and patterns imaginable to camouflage their silhouettes from marauding submarines. The ships varied greatly in size, age, and speed. There was a little two-thousand-ton old tramper and up-to-date ocean liners of twenty thousand tons, which had been pressed into military service. At least two of the ships had been seized from the Germans when America declared war last spring.

It was the regiment's eighth day at sea aboard the *President Grant,* and it was the first time that Joe actually felt that the lookout duty he had earned was an honor and not a punishment. Each of the previous two hour-long watches he had spent in the Navy's 1918 equivalent of a crow's nest had tested Joe's maximum tolerances of dangerous heights and rough seas. A second lieutenant from G Company had slipped on his way back down from the lookout basket during yesterday's rough seas and had swung widely from his safety strap for almost a half hour before the sailors could get him back to safety. He was bruised and battered from repeated crashes into the mast and wire stays, but Joe had seen him at lunch in the officers' mess. Joe had won the coveted lookout duty by being the first of the dozens of lieutenants aboard the transport to assemble his men at the correct life raft station during one of the "Abandon Ship" alarms that were sounded two or three times a day.

The men had grown accustomed to the drill after a week of leaping from their berths in the early morning hours, scrambling to the deck, and forming up next to the life raft that Joe was assigned to command. With nearly half the men suffering from varying degrees of seasickness, though, Joe had had to encourage, cajole, and even threaten some of the men out of their bunks in the first few days at sea. One young farm boy private from Pinckney had even told Joe that he was feeling so awful that he would rather go down with the ship than try to move topside. When the threat of ordering the Pinckney lad to clean the head that was used by hundreds of seasick soldiers who couldn't quite make it to the deck didn't work, Joe convinced the private that he might endanger someone else's life because someone would have to come below to look for him in the event of a real submarine attack. After Joe had got the private on deck, he kept him in the fresh ocean air for the rest of the day running hot coffee back and forth to the sergeants who manned the sentry boxes that had been erected all around the ship to scan the sea for tell-tale periscopes or torpedo wakes. The private had quickly recovered.

By the morning of the eighth day, however, the ocean fell quiet and Joe saw nothing but the ships of the convoy and the flat surface of the water that was nearly a hundred feet below his lookout basket. The convoy had cut engines down to a crawl for the past four hours. It was a quarter to four in the afternoon according to Joe's wristwatch. A couple of hours earlier, the troops had enjoyed a spectacular show as the various gun crews of the convoy engaged in a little target practice on the open ocean. Joe and the other men of the company finally decided that the long halt in the convoy's progress was probably meant to deceive enemy submarines, which may have been lying in wait at a particular spot in the Atlantic based on observations of the convoy's rate of progress and course.

Joe kept his eyes on the sector immediately in front of the *President Grant's* bow, but it took effort to keep his mind from wandering to what lay ahead and to what they had left behind. The bright afternoon sun felt good and Joe took off his helmet and let the light sea breeze flow through his short-cropped, sandy hair. He hadn't heard anything from Anna or Little Vixie since the 126th Infantry Regiment had entrained from Waco, Texas, to Camp Merritt, New Jersey, which was situated just fifteen miles from Times Square in New York City.

The regiment had been under strict secrecy with no mail going out or coming into the camp for nearly a month. There had been some widespread complaints among the ranks about the food, which Joe had quelled by securing for his company some of the best cooks the 107th Sanitation Train had to offer. The stay in New Jersey had been uncomfortable at best.

Measles, scarlet fever, mumps, and other illnesses had swept through Camp Merritt and the temperature outside the barracks had hovered around zero degrees for weeks. Joe admitted to his men that the conditions at camp were not up to standard, but he knew that things would only get worse once the men hit the trenches in France. Still, the men kept their spirits up and even came to look forward to the afternoon hikes of six to ten miles through the rolling hills and woods of New Jersey. Joe had been reminded of the Revolutionary War when Washington and his army traveled some of the same roads — roads that were older than the United States itself. Hiking The Palisades on the shores of the Hudson had been especially beautiful with the landscape covered in a snowy mantle.

What news had reached Camp Merritt had only brought a somber anxiousness to get to France as quickly as possible in order to get in the fight. The Great War to end all wars stopped being a mere abstraction to the men of the 126th just a couple of weeks before leaving the Hoboken docks. The American transport *Tuscania* was sunk by an enemy submarine on February 5th, and thirteen men of the 107th Sanitation Train who had been sent ahead to make arrangements for the rest of the 32nd Division were lost at sea and presumed dead along with the *Tuscania's* crew. Joe could still see the fresh-shaven face of Corporal Metzenbauger who had helped Joe secure decent cooks for Company E. Joe wasn't sure if he ever knew the corporal's first name, but he concentrated on the memory of the corporal's eager, bespectacled face so that he would not forget it. Corporal Metzenbauger was the first soldier to die in the war that Joe knew personally, but he wouldn't be the last.

From atop the forward mast of the *President Grant*, Joe was suddenly snapped out of these reflections by a series of flashes from the *Huntington's* gun turrets. Joe was about to call his observation into the bridge when the first thundering "boom" hit his eardrums. Before he was even able to raise anyone on the phone, the rest of the *Huntington's* port guns flashed, followed by a rolling wave of heavy cracks that Joe could feel inside his chest.

"Foremast watch reporting firing from the *Huntington* port guns," Joe barked into the telephone mouthpiece.

The shells crashed into the sea just a few hundred yards off the *Huntington's* portside, sending a white flume of water fifty feet into the air.

"We see the flashes, Lieutenant," said a voice from the bridge. "Can you tell what they are firing at?"

Joe could just make out a dark dot in the water against the white froth and skyward explosions of seawater. The guns from the other ships of the convoy opened up and began to close in on whatever the *Huntington* was still blasting away at. Joe could just barely hear alarms sounding from the ships ahead of him, and more disturbingly, he could see all five of the ships screws whipping the ocean up as they steamed up from a near-standstill to full speed ahead.

"There's something small in the water ahead, but I can't make it out yet," Joe told the bridge, as he noticed the other ships begin to veer away from the dark spot in the water with guns still firing. The *Huntington* had already pulled away from the object and could only fire with its stern guns, but two innermost ships of the front line were already abreast of the dark spot and firing on the run.

Joe suddenly felt the *President Grant* lurch ahead, almost knocking the field glasses out of his hands as the mast recoiled forward after the initial backward sway. Two huge clouds of black smoke belched from the transport's double stacks as the ship jumped into full speed. The *President Grant's* alarm sounded half a second later, and Joe had to fight the instinct to join his life raft crew down on the starboard deck. He couldn't leave his lookout post, but he knew that Sergeant Pomeroy was up to the task of filling in for him. The "Abandon Ship" alarm was also the call for the ship's crew to get to battle stations, and within seconds of the alarm the *President Grant's* two forward guns exploded with a deafening roar below Joe's feet.

"This is the bridge," came a voice over the telephone earpiece. "The ships of the forward line report an enemy periscope in the middle of the convoy. All lookouts continue to monitor their sectors and call in range reports for any objects you spot. Report any torpedo trails immediately."

The dark object in the water was directly in Joe's lookout sector. He continued to call in range and degree observations, helping to guide the gunners' shells to the periscope. The gunners quickly had the periscope in their sights and began to rain shells down on the turbulent spot in the ocean. Joe felt his stomach flutter as he realized that he was seeing the Navy's understandable, yet cold-hearted tactics for dealing with submarine attacks on convoys play themselves out before his eyes. All of the other ships were scattering away as quickly as possible to prevent the sub from sinking more than one ship at a time. Not only was the *President Grant* one of the slowest boats in the convoy with a top speed of only about ten knots, but pre-arranged orders for how the convoy was to scatter required the *President Grant* to veer off to starboard in a case such as this to prevent collisions with the other ships in the convoy. When the object had first appeared, it was already to the *President Grant's* starboard, and Joe could clearly see that his boat would have to cross the submarine's path quite closely to pass the periscope on the *President Grant's* port side. Despite the bursts of water all around the periscope, it looked like the submarine was holding its position to fire on the *President Grant* at close range.

Joe lost sight of the periscope every now and then in the turbulence of the exploding shells, but the target was getting closer as it appeared to move from the *President Grant's* starboard bow to its port bow. A shot from one of the ship's guns landed a bit behind the object, and Joe thought he saw the object actually bob up and down as the wave from the exploding shell passed it. If it was a periscope, it sure wasn't acting like something that was attached to a submarine. With all of the shells that had fallen within a few yards of the target, Joe began to doubt whether any submarine could have survived such a beating.

"This is the foremast watch reporting. The target does not appear to be a periscope. Repeat. The target does not seem to be a periscope," Joe hollered into the telephone above the roar of the ship's guns.

The height of Joe's lookout basket gave him the best view of the target of any of the sentries on board. Joe heard the order to "cease fire" called out to the gun crews and he strained his eyes to get a look at the target without the froth and flumes of exploding shells. The dark object was still a couple of hundred meters off the *President Grant's* port bow, but Joe could just make out what it was.

"Foremast watch to the bridge. It's a barrel, sir. It is not a submarine. It is a barrel."

"This is the captain," came a voice over the telephone. "Are you sure?"

"Aye, aye, sir. I can make out the iron hoops now. It's just a floating barrel."

The bridge cut the alarm and Joe mopped his sweating forehead with the sleeve of his wool tunic. As the ship chugged ahead, the barrel could be clearly seen floating on the calm surface of the ocean. Joe could hear uneasy laughter and hoots of delight as the barrel passed along the port side of the ship and began bobbing up and down in the wake. Joe thought it was remarkable that the barrel remained intact despite a dozen near misses. A doughboy standing next to one of the forward lifeboats yelled, "You stinkin' bastard," and threw an apple at the barrel, but was a few feet short. The doughboy's display sparked a ripple of laughter down the port side of the ship, followed by a barrage of objects hurdling toward the wayward barrel. About midship, someone hit the barrel with an empty bottle. As the bottle shattered, a roar of applause and cheers erupted from the port side of the *President Grant*.

~ P A R T 1 1 ~

ALSACE-LORRAINE

———

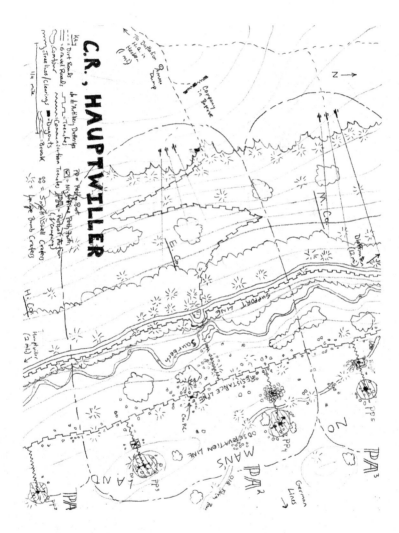

C.R., HAUPTWILLER

Key
- ——— = Dirt Roads
- ===== = Gravel Roads
- ⌁⌁⌁⌁ = Trenches
- ∿∿∿∿ = Contour
- ⌒⌒⌒⌒ = Communication Trench
- ⌢⌢⌢⌢ = Tree Rows / Clearings
- ⌂ = Dugouts
- ⌢⌢⌢ = Brook

1/4 mile

PP = Pillbox Post
⊠ = M.G. Nests, Pits, Posts
PA = Pillbox Action
    (if necessary)
00 = Small Shell Craters
✕ = Large Bomb Craters

To Buttville & Ammo Dump

To H.a in Hedeur (1 mi)

Company in Ravine

Du-Bois-Arm (1/2 mi)

N →

M. Co.

I.

H. Co.

Hauptwiller (3 mi)

SUPPORT LINE

Sourbeeck

RESISTANCE LINE

Co. P.C.

OBSERVATION LINE

German Lines

To Burm-um

NO MANS LAND

PA⁵

PA⁴

PA²

PA³

PA¹

PP5

PP4

PP3

PP1

Chapter 39

NEARLY A MONTH has passed since Cushman and I had it out in his Petoskey office. Before I left, I told him to turn over every scrap of paper that he's ever touched or seen that has anything to do with my family, and then I fired him. He stalled for a week or so, but a whole box of papers showed up by courier a couple of days after I told him how interested some of my newspaper friends would be if they knew how the new candidate for Appellate-Court Judge had been working to undermine an old veteran's last will and testament and screw a couple of young heirs out of land that was rightfully theirs. It wasn't exactly a move out of the *Ethics of Journalism* handbook, but it's only slander if it's not true.

Cushman is still the executor of my father's estate, so he has been sending me letters to keep me apprised of the status of the Becker farm. It's not looking good for the home team. The Attorney General's opinion seems to be gaining ground in the courts, and the *Little Traverse Times* got wind of the story. State and local officials, as well as the regional land conservancy are already starting to make plans for the Anna Johnson Becker Memorial Nature Preserve. At least that part of Joe's dream may come to fruition. Homer Robertson and a few lawyers from the Arizona charities, however, are working side by side with Cushman to defeat this "illegal land grab." Fortunately, the current Emmet County Probate Judge has allowed me to continue living at The Shack until the legal matters are settled.

In the past month, I have been through the full spectrum of my emotional pallet. I left Cushman's office depressed and

devastated; re-ignited my fighting spirit after a teleconference
with Sally and Mom; felt discouraged after failing to find a local
lawyer who was willing to take our case; rose to the heights
of happiness when Libby Hampton showed up at The Shack
for her first day off in the middle of June; and only started to
even out after I picked up my research into Joe and Anna's lives
about a week after the blow up with Cushman.

I haven't given up all hope of holding on to at least some of
the property and I am doing my best to keep on top of the legal
stuff, but after I left Cushman's office I came home and took a
long walk around the property and down to the beach. A bald
eagle soared just above the tops of the red pines. He was riding
the updraft created when Lake Michigan winds run into the
steep bluff along the shore. On the beach, white-gray seagulls
cruised the shoreline, plunging into the waves and coming up
with small fish. I noticed that the birds were doing all right
even though their feet rarely touched the ground. Perhaps I'll
do all right without the Becker land under my feet.

On that walk, I decided that I would make the most of the
time I still have here in this beautiful and soulful corner of
Northern Michigan. I decided to spend every spare moment
getting to know Libby and seeing what we might have
together. In the evenings, I'll keep digging through Joe and
Anna's lives. I may never see their land again, but their story
is mine to keep. If this reporter thing stops being fun, I think I
would like to write about them — maybe a novel. During the
day, I'm sending out resumes far and near and filing a story or
two a week for the *Northern Michigan Gazette*, but I'm not too
frantic about it. I still have my whole life ahead of me, and I'm
not going to let it get eaten away by legal battles and resentment. Joe is actually helping me get some good perspective
on all this. He didn't exactly catch too many breaks in the

early part of his life, but he managed to make something of himself. The struggles I've faced seem pretty puny compared to what Joe was up against as the *President Grant* reached the shore of France on March 4, 1918.

France was full of surprises for Joe and the rest of the men of Co. E — some good surprises and some bad. The first surprise came as the doughboys glimpsed the lush, green hills bordering the channel that led to the port city of Brest. They had left New Jersey in the depths of a frigid winter, and now only twenty days later, it was springtime along the coast of France.

They were also surprised at how long it took to unload several regiments worth of baggage from the holds of the ship. They were anxious to get their feet back on dry land, but had to remain on board for another twenty-four hours until their gear was reached in the holds. Once the 126th Infantry Regiment received their baggage, they were surprised to find that the Navy crew had rifled through every duffle and trunk. The sailors had stolen whatever they wanted, leaving the contents of the baggage scattered about the hold.

The small-scale French trains and boxcars that the men were loaded onto for an 18-hour ride to Saint Nazaire were surprisingly funny to the Michigan guardsmen accustomed to larger American railroad stock. Stenciled across the side of each boxcar was a phrase that would become all too familiar to the doughboys — "40 Hommes et 8 Cheveaux" (40 men or 8 horses). By the end of the ride, some of the Michigan boys wished they were horses. While Joe and his fellow officers expected that their troops would spend much of the first few weeks in France at hard labor in preparation for Gen. Pershing's massive build-up of supply lines for the American

Expeditionary Force (A.E.F.), they were surprised by the scarcity of food in the camps. Joe and several of his trusted sergeants spent every spare moment scrounging for food for the company.

One of those sergeants was Bill Pomeroy, who kept a diary of his experiences in World War I. About a quarter of a century later, he wrote a letter to Joe (who was by then a colonel) recalling their days together in France. The newspaper stories about the advance of World War II G.I.s let loose a of flood of memories from one old World War I veteran to another.

Oct. 1ˢᵗ, 1944

Col. Joseph L. Becker
Army & Navy General Hospital
Hot Springs, Arkansas

Dear Col.:

I just learned that you are a patient in the hospital at Hot Springs. Some years back, as a patient in Hines Veterans Hospital near Chicago, I met some veterans who had also been patients at Hot Springs. They praised the facilities there, especially the hot baths. Let us hope that your ailment is not so severe but what you can still enjoy life, and I wish you a speedy recovery.

Norman (Friday) Findlay, whom you remember as our cook in War I, has sold his place at Arc Lake and moved to a location near Muskegon, Mich. I wonder what he did with his huge supply of canned goods; meat, fruit and vegetables; and with his numerous stoves. He must have made more than one trip with his truck to haul the stuff away. "Friday" was known as a pretty good manager, and wouldn't leave anything useful behind. I must get the correct "dope" from Harry Sanderson.

Last week there was a big article in the news concerning Herman Renker's son, who completed about 60 raids in a big bomber over Germany, and shot down several German planes. You undoubtedly remember Herman as a corporal in our company in War I, who was wounded on the same day as Emil Schloss. Herman has another son serving in the Marines.

Today's papers mention numerous towns in France located in the War I battle-area, where our company served when you were our commander in 1918. There comes to mind Champlitte where we trained; Vaux where we entrained for Belfort after a 25 kilometer hike with full-pack and equipment from Champlitte; Grosmagny, some miles out of Belfort, where we camped for some time, and where, you may recall, that you purchased wine for the entire company, and also paid a Frenchman 75 francs to quit hollering at us because we cut some of the grass in his field to make a clean place for our kitchen; Romagny and Rougemont where we met a French Sergeant with a bragging German prisoner named Graf, while we were on the march to the Alsace front; Guevenatten, a couple of miles from the trenches, where we halted late at night, from which were visible the numerous flares and sky-rockets shot up by the Germans in their front-line trenches, and which lit up the night sky like an enormous Fourth of July celebration, and from which were heard the explosions from artillery firing at the front; and Hecken, where we first went into the trenches on a dark, gloomy, raining night...

————

Joe marched through the early June rain at the head of E Company, his eyes straining to see the edge of the gravel road that led up to the front. His regiment had been in France for three months now, but this was his company's first chance at trench duty. Fat raindrops pelted the wide, round brim of his steel helmet, sounding like a cascade of ball bearings on a tin roof. Though he could barely see the sergeant walking at his side or his company behind him, he could hear them by the continuous harmonic hum of the raindrops falling on their helmets and on odd pieces of metal equipment strapped to packs. He was even starting to tell the difference between one soldier and the next by the slightly different pitches of raindrop percussion on helmets and gear. Despite the dark, Joe never felt his senses so alive. If it kept raining while they were in the trenches, the knowledge of this music of the raindrops might come in handy for distinguishing friend from foe, Joe thought to himself.

Occasional flashes of lightning from the sky and explosions from artillery shells and flares in the distance filled the night with bursts of flat, grayish light that allowed Joe to get a quick look at his own ranks. Some of his men had thought that "getting your marching orders" was just a saying, but in the eleven months since the company left Ann Arbor for Waco, Texas, Joe's men had learned the science as well as the routine of Army life. The order that came a few days ago sending Joe's company and the rest of the 2nd Battalion to the front-line trenches of Alsace-Lorraine left little room for improvisation. The order specifically called for columns of fours with 500 meters between companies and fifty meters between platoons. Company E was leading the way, followed by F Co., G. Co., H Co., the Sanitary Detachment, a Machine Gun Company, and the Wagon Train. When Joe first got the order, he was surprised that his company was to lead the march. He was only a 1st lieutenant. Several captains were marching with the units behind E Company, but Joe had spent the most time going over this same ground in the daylight and touring the trenches with the French officers they were about to relieve.

Two French sergeants were marching with Joe and Sgt. Pomeroy at the head of Co. E as guides, but the last thing that Joe wanted was to get an entire battalion lost in the gloomy night. Before leaving, he had spent hours in his tent committing to memory the road maps of Alsace-Lorraine and the wax-paper trench maps of their sector. Even now, he went over the geography of the war in his head as he walked, starting from the big picture and mentally working his way down to the red dot that indicated the company Post of Command (P.C.) that would serve as his field headquarters for the next couple of weeks.

After four years of fighting, the Allies (France, Britain, and recently the Americans, as well as a host of smaller international and colonial units from Belgium to Algeria) were at a virtual standstill. A nearly continuous line of trenches stretched from the English Channel where British troops held the western-most tip of Belgium to the spot just about ten kilometers south of Joe's current location where the old borderlines of France, Germany, and Switzerland met. To the north, the Germans held most of Belgium and a wide and deep swath of northeastern France. Recent German offensives had driven the Allied defenders back to within sixty kilometers of Paris itself. The so-called "Quiet Sector" that Joe was now walking into was just about the only place along the entire front where the French held formerly German territory. The French push into southwestern Germany had occurred at the outset of the war in 1914, and the lines hadn't changed much since then.

What Joe saw just over the crest of a wooded hill, though, didn't exactly look or sound like a "Quiet Sector." Only a couple of weeks before, a private in Company I had caught a machine gun bullet in the temple and become the first American soldier to fall in action on German territory. The list of casualties had slowly but steadily continued to rise since then.

The dull thud of artillery shells exploding on both sides of the lines was getting sharper, and Joe could begin to see individual shell bursts rather than just wide flashes lighting up the eastern horizon. Talking wasn't allowed in the ranks, and Joe had said little since leaving Guevenatten after sundown. He looked over to Sgt. Pomeroy just as a flare lit up the sky, and saw him smiling from ear to ear. Even in the dark, Joe could tell Bill Pomeroy by the occasional clink of the sour wine bottles he had in his pack. Except for the couple of weeks that Joe had been temporarily in charge of Company A back in April, Sgt. Pomeroy had been at Joe's side nearly every waking hour. Bill spent most of his off-duty hours treating the war as his own personal tour of French wine and spirits, but he had proven himself resourceful and reliable.

Sergeant Pomeroy was a jobsite foreman for a small construction company back in Michigan, and when he gave an order most soldiers had enough sense not to hesitate. Physically, he was quite different than Joe who was tall and fair-haired. Sergeant Pomeroy was squat, dark, and still a bit thick around the middle despite three months of meager food rations. They had known each other since the Mexican Border Service two years ago, and Joe had become accustomed to the contrasting sides of Sgt. Pomeroy's personality and character. On the one hand, Sgt. Pomeroy was one of the crudest men Joe had ever known. He had ways of cussing an errant soldier up one side and down the other that rivaled the Marine Corps drill instructors Joe had encountered back in 1905 at the Philadelphia Naval Yard. On the other hand, Sgt. Pomeroy cared for his men with the tenderness and selflessness of a mother.

Joe had even learned that this man who had only finished the eighth grade was keeping a diary, carefully writing his entries almost every day. Bill Pomeroy wasn't smiling through the rain and gloom because he liked killing and war, but because he was going into battle with men he liked or, at least, cared for.

Joe hadn't seen Sgt. Pomeroy so filled with mirth since Joe had accidentally fallen into a ditch near Grosmagny. Joe came up covered head to toe in mud. Joe seldom swore in front of the men, but he had unleashed a string of oaths to match anything Sgt. Pomeroy could spit out. Joe was furious, thinking that someone had pushed him. The men near the ditch had stood in shocked silence, at first, afraid that Joe might mistakenly lash out at one of them, but Sgt. Pomeroy broke the tension by charging and snapping off a fence post that Joe had accidentally backed into, causing him to slip into the ditch.

"That ought to show the lousy, frog fencepost to keep away from an American officer," Sgt. Pomeroy shouted, pointing at the battered pole as it sank into the mud.

The men broke into the hardiest laughter they had had in weeks, and Joe's fury quickly turned to a few laughs at his own expense once he grasped what had happened. Now, as he marched beside Sgt. Pomeroy into the stormy night, Joe was smiling, too.

"Lieutenant Becker, this is where we leave the main road," Sergeant Deufmont whispered as he and the other French guide walked past a short white post that marked a two-track dirt road that was heading over a wooded hill to the west of Hauptwiller. The trenches were just on the other side of the hill.

Sergeant Pomeroy quietly gave the order for the first platoon to switch into a two-column formation to navigate the dirt road leading up to the trenches. Joe could now make out individual rifle shots coming from the lines, as well as the distant burst of a French *chau-chat* automatic rifle. It was already about 10:00 PM, and the nighttime was the most active period of trench warfare.

Joe replayed the mental picture of the trench maps he had memorized for this area. There was a lot more to these trenches than most of Joe's men had first envisioned. One green recruit had told Joe that he "just figured there was one deep ditch running the whole length of France for the Allies and 'nuther ditch a couple hundred yards away for the Huns." Instead, there was a complex trench system about a quarter-mile deep on the French side, a strip of No Man's Land of up to half a mile wide, with support trenches in the rear and observation trenches out in front of the main trench.

To bring order to this confusing web of trenches, dugouts, communication lines and observation posts, the entire length of the front was divided into individual "Centers of Resistance" — usually organized around and named after a nearby village or forest. For example, the front-line sector that Joe's company was currently picking its way into was known as C.R.,H. (Center of Resistance, Hauptwiller). As Joe and his men were moving into the trenches, the 2nd Battalion Headquarters staff was settling into the village of Hecken about a mile west of Hauptwiller.

For each Center of Resistance, there were small trench sectors called "Posts of Action." These posts were numbered from right to left, so that P.A. 1 was on the southernmost part of the trenches and P.A. 3 was the northernmost sector of the C.R., H. Joe's orders called for his company to relieve the French troops in P.A. 2 of the Hauptwiller Center of Resistance. Each Post of Action encompassed several Petty Posts. A Petty Post (P.P.) was basically a dugout with a network of observation trenches that was out in the middle of

No Man's Land. Each Petty Post was accessed by a narrow, zig-zagging "communication trench" that allowed soldiers to come and go between the main firing trench and No Man's Land without being seen from the enemy lines. The Petty Posts were also numbered from right to left, with P.A. 2 controlling P.P. 3 and P.P. 4.

Although Joe's mental picture of his trench maps was quite good, the muddy two-tracks and paths over the forested heights leading to the main trenches looked all the same in the dark, and Joe was glad to have the French guides with him. Even they had to slow down every once in a while to make sure they were going in the right direction. Joe and Sgt. Pomeroy marked how the French sergeants looked up into the canopy of the trees to get their bearings when the night sky fell quiet and dark.

There was a break in the rain. E Company crossed the summit of the wooded hill and started heading downhill. The next burst of light from a string of German artillery shells landing on the French firing line gave Joe the first real glimpse of the ground he and his men would be defending. A volley of flares from the French lines followed, lighting up the countryside for miles around. Joe was standing on the side of a hill that gently sloped down to a valley with a small brook running through it. The main Allied trenches were on the far side of the brook in a thicket that ran along the edge of what must have been a farm field four years ago. The Germans were dug into the edge of a forest on the other side of the field. It must have been a beautiful valley at one time, Joe thought to himself — not all that different from the Northern Michigan farmsteads that Anna loved to ride through in the summers.

Standing at the head of the column, Joe was just inside a jagged treeline. A few steps ahead, Joe was about to enter a hillside clearing of stumps, fallen timber, and bare trunks that had been pulverized by sustained shelling. In another flash of light, Joe noticed that the road he was standing on was about to descend into a wide and deep support trench that switchbacked down the torn-up face of the hill. The shell craters on the hillside were so interlaced that the slope had been turned into a confusion of logs, rubble, and earth. To his right and as far left as he could see, a wall of still-standing beech trees ran along the face of the hill. The guides stopped and gestured for Joe and Sgt. Pomeroy to join them beside the two-track while the rest of the company remained in the cover of the dark forest.

"This is the maximum, effective range of the Germany artillery, Lieutenant," Sgt. Deufmont said, gesturing towards a dark opening in the side of the hill. "Of course their big guns can reach all the way back to Hecken, but this is as far as their 75 mm field artillery can reach. They used to fire a couple of shells up here every day just to see how the wind and atmosphere would affect their range and accuracy, but I think they don't have bombs to spare with all of the fighting up along the Marne. If you please to step into this bunker, you can get a good look around without being seen before we descend into the valley."

Once inside, Joe's eyes adjusted to the deeper gloom. Sergeant Deufmont was speaking rapidly and quietly in French to one of his countrymen in the bunker, but Joe could only make out a couple of other vague forms in the dark. They were in a log and earth bunker just within the treeline. Horizontal firing slits cut into the walls of the bunker offered a panoramic view of the entire battlefield. Deufmont introduced the two French soldiers who were on bunker duty to Joe and Sgt. Pomeroy, but these artillery spotters quickly slipped out of the bunker before Joe had a chance to practice his French on them.

"We will have to wait until the bombardment dies down before we attempt to cross the clearing," Sgt. Deufmont said. "We only use this road at night. The Germans probably won't see us in this bad weather, but there is no need to risk bringing down a bombardment on our heads while we are out in the open. *Nes pas?* In the meantime, this is the best seat in the house, as they say."

"Sergeant Pomeroy," Joe said. "Tell the men to take a twenty minute break. Starting with 1st Platoon, bring each squad up to the edge of the clearing for a good look around. I want every man in the company to get a chance to see the lay of the land before we head down into the trenches, but keep them quiet and out of sight."

Joe pulled out his field glasses and focused in on the French side of the line. On his inspection of this very sector last week, Joe had been surprised at how many trees were still intact after so many years of fighting. The woods resumed a few hundred yards down the slope below the pulverized clearing. One of the persistent dangers of the Quiet Sector came when German snipers managed to sneak through the lines and up into the trees to fire back down into the trenches. Through the binoculars, he located the huge forked oak tree that a German sniper had been shot out of just last Thursday while he was touring P.A. 2. The sniper hadn't managed to get a shot off before he was spotted and killed, but Joe couldn't help noticing that the big oak stood within range of the dugout that was about to become his home for the next couple of weeks. Joe made a mental note to ring the base of that tree with barbed wire before morning.

From this vantage point, Joe could see down into the trenches. Although Joe was an advocate of Gen. Pershing's "open warfare" strategy of staying on the move and avoiding the kind of hunkering down he was seeing before him, Joe still admired the centuries of European siege mentality that had gone into the modern trench system below. The main "firing line" trench is seven feet deep with a shallower "fire step" running along the side of the trench that faces the enemy. From the "fire step," soldiers could shoot over the top of the trench and even scramble up and over the parapet when ordered to do so. The main trench wasn't just dug in a straight line, either. About every 20 feet, there was a jog in the trench. So, even if the Huns did manage to reach the Allied trenches and climb in, they wouldn't be able to shoot very far. Each traverse in the trench line protects the defenders against flanking fire, Joe thought to himself.

"So, Lieutenant, will we have the pleasure of being treated to this kind of fireworks show every night, you think?" Sgt. Pomeroy said, returning to Joe's side.

"The shells are coming in five at a time every thirty seconds now," Joe said, looking at the glowing hands on his wristwatch. "This doesn't happen every night, but the French say this is pretty routine stuff. The German battery is probably located a half-mile or so behind that forest. Even the French planes have a hard time locating them when they are in action, but the Germans just pick up and move when our guns start to find them. It's the same thing on our side. The latest intelligence says there are about five enemy batteries operating in this sector."

"Where are them petty posts we toured, Lieutenant?" Sgt. Pomeroy asked, scanning No Man's Land with Joe's field glasses.

"Just look for the cluster of shell craters to the right and left of the P.C. dugout."

"Oh, yeah. I see those two zig-zaggy little communication trenches leading out to them from the main trench. The petty post looks deserted, though, sir."

"The French only use them during the day when they can see. They pull back to that other dugout at night. You see it? It's about half way between the main firing trench and P.P. 4. We'll

post a platoon out on the petty post at first light for observation, but we'll have to clear the communication trenches and
check for mines and Germans on our way out there. We may
want to rethink some of the tactics the French have been using.
I'm not so sure it makes good sense to pay the price of re-tak-
ing the same ground over and over every day. We'll see."

The German barrage fizzled out and fell quiet as the rain
began to fall again. Joe slipped his field glasses back into their
case, and rounded up his sergeants. Company E marched down
the hill, through the woods, across the brook, and into the
trenches. The French troops, looking dirty, wet, and exhausted
sat or were lying on the fire step loaded up with all their gear,
ready to move out. Quietly, they rose to their feet and faced
the Americans as Joe marched along the duckboard walk to
the field headquarters. He was glad they didn't salute in case a
sniper was nearby. The French (in their steel helmets with their
small front brims) looked more like miners than soldiers, but
Joe knew that after a short rest they would be heading off to
some of the heaviest fighting of the war.

Company E of the 126th Infantry relieved the 5th Company of the French Army's 4th Infantry Regiment at 11 PM on
June 11, 1918. The rest of the night was quiet, and there was no
change in the battle lines drawn on the maps that the generals
used to keep track of the war in Alsace-Lorraine. But in the
morning, the Germans in Joe's particular sector of the war
would discover that they were no longer facing a battle-worn,
depleted French company. The rest of 2nd Battalion was taking
over the trenches to the right and left of P.A.2 at the exact same
time that Joe shook hands with the French captain that he was
relieving. The American Expeditionary Force had arrived at
this particular stretch of the front, and Joe was determined to
make a good first impression on the enemy.

Chapter 40

ON THE NEXT morning, after a busy night spent coordinating sentries and sending out patrols to the more deserted sections of the trenches, Joe was relieved to see the first faint light of dawn appearing behind the enemy lines. The rain had stopped and the clouds were beginning to break up. Joe sent out a last squad of sentries to make sure that no Germans were hiding nearby. Attacking just as the first rays of morning sun hit the Allied trench lines was a favorite tactic of the Germans, but the sentries returned without seeing so much as a single Hun.

Joe was anxious to have a look at the petty posts for himself, and sent runners to the two platoons that were waiting to move from the night petty posts up to the daytime petty posts, which were deeper into No Man's Land. Joe started heading into the command-post dugout to find Sgt. Pomeroy, whom he had ordered to get some shuteye, but was surprised to find him sleeping on the fire step just outside of the dugout.

He grabbed two cups of coffee from Friday the cook, and tapped Sgt. Pomeroy's shoulder with his boot to wake him.

"Judas Fucking Escariot, who's kicking me?" Pomeroy said as he scrambled to his feet with his eyes still closed.

"A good morning to you, too, Sergeant," Joe said handing him a cup of coffee.

"Oh, sorry, Lieutenant. I must have dozed off."

"I see you are ignoring my explicit orders again, Sergeant. What am I going to do with you, Bill?"

"Well, if you want to discipline me, go ahead and send me back down there," Sgt. Pomeroy said. "I went in the dugout like you said and started reading my skivvies for lice before going to sleep when a God-damned rat the size of a cat jumped on my bare ass and ran across my back. Then, I started noticing that they were everywhere down there. I've worked in sewers that were tidier than that hole."

"I noticed quite a few running around the trenches last night," Joe said. "I think they kind of gave the boys the willies. Most of the grenades and rifles that went off last night turned out to be aimed at rats instead of Germans."

"How do the frogs live with all these rats running around?"

"Apparently they make good watch dogs for gas attacks. Deufmont said that one sniff and the rats turn their toes up in the air. We'll take care of the rats later. Right now, I want you to join me for a morning stroll up to P.P. 4. Lt. Wilcox is already heading out to P.P. 3."

Joe, Sgt. Pomeroy, and Sgt. Deufmont (who was just returning from a patrol) headed north up the main firing trench to the communication trench that led out into No Man's Land. Joe was pleased to see that all of the sentries he had set were alert and scanning both No Man's Land in front of the trench and the woods to their rear. Sergeant Deufmont was half covered in mud, and Sgt. Pomeroy looked him over as they walked up to the communication trench leading to P.P.4.

"How'd you make out last night, Deufmont? Did you find your missing man?"

Sergeant Deufmont said nothing, but shook his head without turning to face Sgt. Pomeroy. Deufmont had not only been left behind to help E Company acclimate to life in the trenches, but he and the French Sgt. Voutan had been ordered to search for a missing comrade who had been left behind by the French 5th Company. Sergeant Pomeroy realized that the two Frenchmen had probably spent hours crawling around out there in No Man's Land trying to find their man or what was left of him.

"Don't worry, Deufmont," Sgt. Pomeroy said. "We'll find him now that we've got some daylight to work with."

Joe passed a couple of sentries standing at the entrance to the communication trench leading out into No Man's Land. Joe noticed a slight twitch of Pvt. Miller's right hand as Joe approached the narrower communication trench, but Pvt. Miller remembered not to salute. The men were allowed to talk quietly now that they were in the trenches, though, and Pvt. Miller offered a "Good morning, sir" instead.

"Good Morning, Miller," Joe said as he entered the dirt trench. The communication trench was much smaller and not quite as deep as the main firing line. It zig-zagged for about three hundred yards out to the night time petty post, which was thinly manned now that most of the platoon had moved farther out into No Man's Land to take up positions in Petty Post 4. Joe had to stoop slightly to keep his head from sticking up above the parapet. Walking along the trench with his eyes nearly at ground level made Joe feel like one of the raccoons he used to see sniffing around the burn pile behind Anna's parents house back in Blue Harbor.

The smell of coffee told Joe that he was nearing P.P. 4 — a wide hole dug in the ground with a small corrugated-steel-reinforced shed in its center, which led down to a well-protected dugout. A maze of shallower observation trenches and firing positions fanned out from the walls of the main hole like the spokes of a wagon wheel. At the hub of this post stood Platoon Sgt. Emil Schloss with a tin cup of coffee in one hand and a bayonet in the other. Emil's family owned a hardware store in downtown Ann Arbor, and Joe had known Emil for nine years. Sergeant Schloss was Joe's nuts and bolts guy, and could fix anything you gave him with whatever he could find on hand. Emil and Bill Pomeroy had known each other their whole lives, and Joe's two best sergeants could often be found trying to outdo each other at the nearest café in their off-duty hours. Sergeant Schloss was using his bayonet as a pointer to show where he wanted the rest of his men positioned on a map of P.P. 4.

"I don't care that you guys already checked it out," Schloss said. "I want two guys right over there keeping an eye on our rear. Mach Schnell!"

Like Joe, Sgt. Schloss's parents had come from Germany, and he spoke the language fluently. There were a lot of soldiers in the A.E.F. who were of German ancestry. Even Gen. Pershing was descended from Prussian stock. Some Guardsmen who came from mostly Dutch or Irish settled areas of Michigan had grumbled about "huns in our own ranks," but it hadn't taken much time for experienced soldiers like Joe and Emil to knock that crap out of their heads. As Sgt. Schloss had told his men back in Waco, "We are Americans, just like you. A lot of us left Germany so we didn't have to fight for the very same bastards who'll be sending the enemy at us. I don't care if the enemy is my second cousin or something. We probably got more reason to fight the Kaiser and his thugs then anybody going over there."

"Have your men reached the advance post, Emil?" Joe said as he relit the pipe he had been holding in his teeth. There was no smoking allowed at night in the Petty Posts, but enough light was filling the eastern sky now that Joe declared it to be day and several other soldiers followed his lead and lit up.

"They should be in place now, Lieutenant. Let me just send up a runner to make sure that the advance post is secured."

"That won't be necessary, Sgt. Schloss," Joe said. "We're heading up there right now. If everything is squared away here, why don't you come join us?"

"Sure thing, let's go boys," Emil said, snatching his rifle and map.

The communication trench leading deeper in No Man's Land was so narrow that two-man firing bays had to be dug into the trench walls every twenty-five yards or so to allow anyone walking the trench to squeeze past the lookouts who watched the flanks for trouble. About half way between the nighttime post and the advanced daytime post, a private stepped out of his firing bay in front of Sgt. Schloss with his finger over his lips.

"Sshhhh, Sarge, you gotta check this out," a freckle-faced nineteen year-old whispered in the pale morning light.

"Step aside, Private, you've got to keep the trench clear," Sgt. Schloss hissed back. "How many times have I got to tell ya, O'Neill? Why are we whispering?"

"Sorry, Sarge, but you need to hear this, and the lieutenant, too," the young man said looking over Emil's shoulder to Joe as he hopped back up on the fire step of the two-man bay. The duckboards in this part of the trench were partially submerged in a mud puddle that looked like it could swallow a man whole if he stepped off the wooden planking at the bottom of the trench.

"Okay, whadda ya got?" Sgt. Schloss said quietly.

O'Neill crouched down on the fire step as Joe and the sergeants gathered around the firing bay as best as they could. Another private stood looking out over the top of a wall of rough planks with his finger on the trigger of his rifle.

"Me and Perkins was just gettin' settled in up here when we hear this noise coming from the other side of these planks, you see? Kind of a scratchin' sound. We was gonna toss a grenade over to make sure it wasn't no Hun, but then we remembered about the missing Frenchmen. It ain't just dirt on the other side of them planks. There's this ditch, but we can't see over the planks to get a good look down in there without going over the top. What should we do, Sarge?"

Deufmont shouldered his way up to the front of the group.

"Where does this ditch lead to, Sgt. Deufmont?" Joe asked.

"This is the old road that runs parallel to our main line. The road is mostly destroyed now, but the old ditches provide some cover," Deufmont said. "It is a good place to slip out into No Man's Land at night, but we have not used this ditch for some weeks now and have kept it boarded up."

"There it goes again," Pvt. Perkins whispered without taking his eyes off of the ditch. There was a faint rustling sound coming from the other side of the planks.

"Pull the planks out, Private," Joe said.

"Yes, sir."

The planks were wedged between two upright pairs of old fence posts. The top plank was so swollen from last night's rain that Perkins couldn't lift them out, even with his bayonet. O'Neill tried to help, but only managed to get his bayonet stuck in between the planks.

"Out of my way, boys," Sgt. Pomeroy said, jumping up on the fire step, as the two privates jumped down. "Clear the deck." He dislodged the bayonet with the butt of his rifle and then grabbed the top of the plank, yanking the entire wall of planks towards him. The inner posts budged a couple of inches, and Bill threw the entirety of his considerable weight and brawn into jerking the wall towards him.

There was a muffled snapping sound as the rotten bottoms of the fence posts broke at the base of the plank wall. Sergeant

Pomeroy flew backward off the firestep, scattering the men below out of his way. He landed flat on his back, driving the duckboards deep into the mud and splattering Joe and the other men with the brown ooze. The demolished pieces of the plank wall and a wave of thick brown mud that had been dammed up behind the wall poured down on top of Sgt. Pomeroy nearly burying him at the bottom of the trench. After the flow of mud from the ditch, another wave of blackish water flowed out of the ditch and cascaded over the firestep, followed by two, then four, and then six more rats that were flushed into the trench by the sudden bursting of the plank-wall dam. Joe and three other men quickly reached into the pool of muck and pulled Sgt. Pomeroy to his feet.

A pair of round, bloodshot eyes opened and blinked from under the coating of mud and filth that dripped off the sergeant. He came up sputtering to clear his mouth of mud. Then Pomeroy caught his breath, and Joe and his men braced themselves for a string of curses to pour out of his mouth. The rats scrambled out of the mud hole and scampered up and down the trench line. Private O'Neill gingerly handed the sergeant his helmet, looking as if he might get his arm bit off in the process.

Sergeant Pomeroy wiped the mud from his face and torso, rapped his helmet on a nearby timber to knock it clean, and waved his hand toward the new opening in the side of the communication trench.

"I believe the way is clear now, gentlemen," Sgt. Pomeroy said in his most civil tone.

After Joe finished helping Sgt. Pomeroy remove the worst of the mud from his uniform, he noticed the fencepost that Pomeroy had snapped off floating to the surface of the mud puddle. Joe wondered how much of Bill's commotion was noticed on the German side of the lines. He pulled the fencepost out of the puddle and tossed it up and out of the trench away from the ditch opening. Before the fencepost hit the ground, a burst of machine gun fire from the German lines caught the post in midair sending splinters and chunks of wood flying over the heads the men in the communication trench.

"That ought to show the lousy, Alsatian fencepost to keep away from an American non-commissioned officer," Joe said with a nod towards Sgt. Pomeroy.

Pomeroy and two other Americans who had witnessed Joe's plunge into the mud a couple of weeks ago had to muffle their laughter.

"I guess we better keep our heads down, eh Lieutenant?" Sgt. Pomeroy said.

Just then a soggy piece of paper poured out of the ditch into the trench on the last trickle of blackish water. Pvt. Perkins picked it up before it flowed over the firestep.

"I can't read it," he said. "Looks like it's in French or something."

Perkins handed it to Sgt. Deufmont. "What's it say?"

Deufmont studied it for a moment as the wet paper fell apart in his hands.

"Much of it is faded beyond recognition, Lieutenant," Deufmont said. "But I can make out the beginning... 'Mon Cherie, Marie-Pauline,'... I believe the French soldier we are looking for had a girl by that name. He was from the same village as me. This is one area of No Man's Land I was not able to reach last night. He may still be out there."

"Let's go," Joe said. "Deufmont, you lead the way. Sergeant Pomeroy, you're already perfectly camouflaged for crawling through the mud, so you take up the rear behind me. Sergeant Schloss, you and your men continue on to the advance post and we will join you there shortly. Privates O'Neill and Perkins, you stay here at your post, but go for help if we are not back in thirty minutes."

"Yes, sir," Joe's men said in unison as they went about their duties.

Deufmont quickly disappeared down the ditch, and Joe and Bill Pomeroy scrambled through the mud on their hands and knees to keep up with him. The ditch was only a few feet deep, but an old gravel roadbed rose a few feet higher on their right so that they could crawl along with the raised roadbed between them and the German lines. Joe immediately realized that the greater danger lay to their left, where Joe's own men might mistake him and the two sergeants for the enemy. He also realized that crawling around in broad daylight in No Man's Land wasn't exactly what a company commander should be doing. As a lieutenant, Joe had grown accustomed to getting the job done himself or with the help of one or two trusted non-coms or a small squad, but now he had over 180 men and a mile of trenches that he was responsible for. Still, when nearly every one of those men was deployed on specific trench-sentry details, only Joe and a few other men were available for unexpected jobs like looking for a missing French soldier... or recovering his body.

It was a slow slog through the mud, and the three allied soldiers could sometimes crawl on all fours, but had to crawl on their bellies where the ditch was shallow. About seventy-five yards along the ditch, Joe saw Deufmont's legs slither down into a large shell crater. As Joe reached the lip of the crater, he saw Deufmont crawling around the edge of the huge puddle at the bottom of the crater. Deufmont reached out and was about to touch his fallen comrade's foot. Joe's weeks of training back in Champlitte instantly kicked in.

"Stop, Deufmont! Don't touch him," Joe yelled out from the edge of the crater.

Sergeant Deufmont stayed his hand just inches away from the dead soldier's foot, and Joe could see the cords tied around the dead Frenchman's ankles and wrists.

"They've mined his body, Sergeant," Joe said. "Can you see any explosives underneath his body?"

"*Oui*, Lieutenant," Deufmont said. "I can see them now. There are grenades, some sticks of dynamite, and maybe some landmines that the dirty boche have piled under him. It looks that if I had touched the body, I would have been blown to atoms. I am much obliged to you, Lieutenant Becker. But what kind of pigs would do such a thing?"

"This is the worst of cowardice, Sergeant, but only desperate men would resort to such measures. Perhaps the Germans have shown us more of their weakness than their cleverness."

"I can see his face now," Deufmont whispered. "It is the man I am looking for, and I do not have to touch him to tell that he is dead."

"We'll have to head back now, Sgt. Deufmont, but we'll get some demolition engineers out here first thing after nightfall to recover the body. What was this soldier's name?"

"He was Private Henri Gerould. He was only a boy when I knew him back home in Lisieux. I don't even know what to tell the captain who will have to write his family. He was last seen heading off to the latrine, and now he has been turned into a bomb. What can you say to that?"

"Well, at least we can give Private Gerould the dignity of a proper burial," Joe said. "Here, let me help you out of there." Joe extended his hand down into the crater and pulled Sgt. Deufmont up the slippery sides of the shell hole. Joe, Pomeroy, and Deufmont returned to Petty Post 4 before the thirty minutes was up.

Later that night, Joe personally tested out a new weapon called a Brant cannon. It fired grenades all the way from the Allied main trench to the main German trenches, providing a distraction for the demolition engineers to disarm the explosives and recover the French private from No Man's Land. The Brant cannon had the desired effect upon the Germans, who thought that their new American adversaries were lobbing grenades at them from within throwing range of their main trench. The exploding grenades caused considerable excitement among the Germans, who sent up a volley of flares and rockets to light up the night sky. The Germans couldn't see any Americans in front of their lines, but the American engineers near P.P. 4 could see Private Gerould well enough to cut him loose from the explosives and retrieve his body.

The next day, the French soldier's body was laid to rest in the little burial ground on the side of a hill on the outskirts of Soppe-le-Bas beside the graves of French and German aviators.

———

It didn't take long for the Germans opposite the Hauptwiller Center of Resistance to confirm that they were facing American troops. Company E was not the first American unit to man the trenches of Alsace-Lorraine, but they received the same reception that the first Yank companies had received at the end of May. Joe's diversionary Brant cannon attack on the night of June 12th also seemed to stir the German's into an unusual frenzy of activity. A page hand-copied from Joe's logbook shows how noisy the "Quiet Sector" could get.

June 13, 1918 –

At 5:00 AM one enemy observation balloon appeared and at 5:30 AM two more appeared. At 6:45 AM two boche planes flew over our lines, and about a half-hour later a French plane was seen flying toward the enemy lines. During early morning, there was some machine gun firing by both sides. 7:00 to 8:00 AM, very little activity by either infantry, artillery or air service. No gas. 8:00 AM until noon, artillery very active on both sides. 11:30 AM, two French planes observed flying low over our company sector. 12:05 PM, twenty-nine high explosive shells fired at Company Headquarters. No casualties or damage done. Enemy artillery fire continues on our right. Some gas shells. Several shells struck within a few yards of 'line of resistance trench,' and one road in rear. Between 9:00 and 10:00 AM, our artillery destroyed some buildings in Burnhaupt le bas. At 1:50 PM, one high explosive shell burst in the air directly over the Company P.C. At 3:50 PM, 43 high explosive shells and 3 duds fell from 5 to 50 yards of P.C. At 2:10 PM, a shrapnel shell exploded 20 yards from day post in P.P. 3, slightly damaging communication trench. Enemy has correct range on P.C. and P.P. 3 — a shell exploding 5 yards to right. Other shells exploded directly over them. Telephone wires broken by bombardment and immediately repaired by Sergeant Schloss. Enemy sniper's post observed in a bush 500 yards away, 135 degrees N.E. of P.P. 4. Message received at 12:55 PM from P.C. on right stating gas shells exploded on right of their sector. Plane seen directly over P.C. at 1:50 PM, at same time enemy shell exploded in vicinity; believed to be enemy plane in disguise. At 5:28 PM, 62 enemy shells landed within 100 yards of P.C. sector on right, heavily shelled at same time. 6:00 to 7:00 PM, heavy shelling to right and left of sector. 7:00 to 8:00 PM, shelling by friendly and hostile artillery.

P.P. 3 and P.P. 4 day positions occupied during night per
order. 8:45 PM, large caliber hostile shells began falling to
left of sector. At 8:30 PM, a working party of one sergeant,
three corporals and twenty-four privates went out in
wire and erected 75 yards of new wire entanglement. At
8:50 PM, a patrol of one American platoon, and French
sergeant, five French corporals and five French privates,
proceeded to point between 55.16 and 56.15 with orders
to attack enemy patrols and take prisoners. At 9:00 PM,
another patrol of one American platoon, and one sergeant,
one corporal and three privates (French) proceeded to
intersection of Seultsbach Creek and Hauptwiller-Burn-
haupt road, with same orders. No enemy encountered by
either patrol and both patrols returned at 3:30 AM by way
of P.P. 4. No casualties.

I suspect that Joe's entry about the orders to occupy
the advanced (day) positions of the Petty Posts may have
stemmed from his own ideas about holding ground. Apparently, 2nd Battalion Headquarters thought the idea worth trying out, and later adopted a policy of occupying the advance
petty post positions on a couple of randomly selected nights
of the week so that the Germans had to think twice about
moving around the Petty Posts at night. An American company a couple miles up the line managed to capture a few
German scouts before word got out that the Americans
weren't necessarily following the French playbook by falling
back each night to safer positions.

I wish I had the rest of Joe's logbook entries to get a better
idea of how he handled himself while in command of a mile of
contested battlefield.

According to a tattered page of Sgt. Bill Pomeroy's published "Doughboy Diary," the excitement of life in the trenches
soon wore off. Artillery barrages and German snipers became

the norm, and Sgt. Pomeroy saved his ink for anything else out of the ordinary. As a sergeant, Bill Pomeroy had more freedom of movement than the typical doughboy in the lines. Joe routinely sent him to the rear to deliver reports to headquarters and to guide food and supplies back up to the front.

June 14 — When off duty in trenches men are supposed to stay in dugouts, but they don't like them either. Too many rats and too damp. Found a map of this sector in a deep dugout. It shows our trenches, also the German's

June 15 — About all we are doing is guard duty in the trenches. Gas alarms sometimes sound but I have not yet smelled gas. We can easily see the German observation balloons, which seem to be close enough to hit with a rifle. It takes more than a few bullet holes to bring them down.

June 16 — Machine guns opened up tonight. Probably just practicing.

June 17 — Went down to Hecken today to eat some breakfast. Our kitchen is just outside of Hecken in apple orchard.

June 18 — Hecken is only a small dump. No wine or beer to amount to anything. Some of the buildings here are ruined from artillery fire.

June 19 — Our men make much racket in the trenches now. Very seldom see a German. Not much firing going on. Lt. Becker and Lt. Wilcox scour the woods looking for German snipers. Alfred Shiplock went to Horse detail. Sgt. Schneider joins the 2nd Platoon. Sgt. Enkeman goes from 2nd Platoon to 3rd. Hurrah!

By Joe's ninth day in the trenches near Hecken, Company E was running at maximum efficiency. The wisdom behind Joe's disciplinary measures was becoming all too clear to the men. Rather than leave the men to loiter around the trenches when they were off guard duty, Joe had implemented a program of rigorous trench improvement, advanced marksmanship training, and the caching of supplies and ammo closer to the lines. It was Joe's thinking that his men should not only have enough supplies to defend their sector, but they should be prepared to advance across No Man's Land and into enemy territory at a moment's notice. The hope for a "break through" in the enemy lines had kept veteran French and British soldiers fighting for years, and Joe refused to be caught waiting for supplies from the rear in case the order to attack finally did come.

This meant that Joe's men had to keep their packs loaded and ready to go at all times. The men of Company E could expect latrine clean-up duty or worse if they were found without a full three-day load of supplies or with the contents of their packs spread all over the firestep.

One of Joe's orders that the men found particularly humorous was "rat detail." Joe had Sgt. Schloss cobble together a couple dozen rat traps made from old ammo crates and barbed wire. Most rats were killed instantly in the traps, but a handful of live traps were used to keep some rats for release out into No Man's Land as targets for both day- and nighttime marksmanship training, or they were kept in barb wire cages spread out along trenches as "gas sentries." The caged rats would die at the slightest whiff of poison gas and alert the men of gas attacks. By the end of the first week, there was a noticeable decline in the rat population in Joe's sector. An unexpected benefit of "rat detail" was that fewer rats meant less lice, which turned out to carry the trench fever that tore through the lines near the end of June. Only a couple dozen of Joe's men caught the fever, which incapacitate a man for three or four days, while other companies saw half of their soldiers come down with the disease and wind up in the hospital.

Joe and his lieutenants and sergeants had successfully drummed this state of readiness into the minds and bodies of the men of E Company, so that on the morning of June 20, E Company was more than prepared to respond to a rumor that slowly spread down the American lines — the Brass was making a surprise inspection of the trenches.

Chapter 41

IT WAS THE last official day of spring, as Lt. Joe Becker and Sgt. Bill Pomeroy retraced the steps they had taken on the gloomy night they first entered the trenches. They had orders to report to 2nd Battalion Headquarters. The morning chill had already burned away, and Joe felt the warm sun on his back as he and his trusted sergeant crossed the last open field before Hecken. Tidy hayfields boxed off by rows of round-topped trees sloped upward to the village that sat on the flat top of a gentle hill. A farmer drove a horse-drawn mower through the last row of thigh-high hay as the two soldiers walked up the road leading to the village.

Although Sgt. Pomeroy had been in and out of Hecken several times since the company went into the trenches, Joe had not seen the tiny village since marching through on the way to the front. It had been too dark to see much more than the darker silhouettes of buildings with steep-pitched roofs. Now in the bright sunlight of day, however, Joe's eyes took a second to make sense of what he was seeing ahead of him. What seemed to be a stand of trees undulating in the morning breeze was actually a camouflage screen set up to hide the main road from enemy observation. Walking around the screen, Joe got his first good look at the village square, which was surrounded, on three sides by rustic, exposed-timber buildings that would not have been out of place in Bavaria. Indeed, most of the civilian inhabitants of Hecken still considered themselves German, in spite of France's four-year occupation of the Alsatian frontier.

The threat of locals spying for the Germans and sneaking information across the front was a constant concern. There was even a rumor of a German shepherd dog who was let loose every night by his owner to slip notes across No Man's Land, but the clever creature was never caught in the act.

At the center of this formerly German village towered a life-size statue of Jesus nailed to the cross. One French and one American sentinel stood smartly at each side of Jesus' feet as though they were guarding him like the Roman soldiers of old. On closer inspection, however, it was the rough-planked sentry box in front of the crucifix that the sentries were guarding.

"Halt! Who is there?" the American sentinel challenged as the two men approached the square.

"Lieutenant Becker and Sgt. Pomeroy, E Company, 126th Infantry," Sgt. Pomeroy replied, giving the countersign for the day.

"Advance," the sentry said, crisply drawing his left hand down to his right side for a rifle salute to Joe.

"You fellas seem like you're on your toes today," Sgt. Pomeroy said. With so many of the men down with trench fever, H.Q. had needed to pull a few men out of the trenches just to keep the sentry boxes manned. This particular private was one of E Company's own men. Although Joe expected his men to follow general sentry duty orders at all times, this private acted as if he had never seen his own company commander. "Anything going on?"

"You can never be too careful around here," the sentry said. "There's word flying around of surprise inspections today. They say some generals like to walk into headquarters looking like some regular bubs off the lines. I recognized you and the lieutenant right off, but I'm just doing my job, Sergeant."

"Carry on, Private."

Joe and Bill walked past the iron fence at the base of the crucifix and crossed the small square. A few white geese and a handful of chickens scattered across the cobbled street as the two men strode up to a white farmhouse that served as battalion headquarters. Joe knocked the dried mud from his boots before entering, but still managed to track dirt into the entryway. A clerk whose head was buried in a pile of papers gestured for the men to sit on a bench across from him.

"I'll be with you in a minute," the young, bespectacled corporal said.

Sergeant Pomeroy was feeling particularly civil after such a fine walk through the countryside, so he waited about ten seconds before preparing to bite the clean-uniformed boy's head off for keeping a company commander waiting.

Joe could see Bill's face redden with annoyance at the clerk. Joe put a hand on Sgt. Pomeroy's shoulder to restrain whatever string of oaths Bill was about to unleash on the boy.

"Why don't we cool our heels for bit, Sergeant?" Joe said.

"Sure thing, Lieutenant," Sgt. Pomeroy said, catching on and putting a special emphasis on "Lieutenant."

The clerk looked up from his paperwork with a start and jumped to attention. "Oh, geez, sir! I'm sorry I didn't see you standing there. I thought you were the couple of sanitation guys that I was looking for." The young man snapped off a salute. "What can I do for you?"

Joe returned the boy's salute (such courtesies were not only allowed away from the front lines, but expected here at battalion headquarters). "We were ordered to report to Major Potter. Could you tell him Lieutenant Becker is here from E Company?"

"Oh, geez, sir. Major Potter's not here right now. Maybe you could come back after lunch," the corporal suggested.

Joe didn't have time to restrain Sgt. Pomeroy's ire this time. "Now listen here you flathead, pencil-pushing punk," Sgt. Pomeroy growled quietly. "You find Major Potter right this second or someone who knows where he is, or I'll drag your scrawny butt back to P.A. 2 and feed you to my pet rats for lunch. You understand?"

"We would appreciate it," Joe added in his kindest tone.

The clerk disappeared into the depths of the farmhouse, returning with first one lieutenant and then another who finally admitted that Major Potter had been called away to regimental headquarters for the morning. By the time Joe and Sgt. Pomeroy had been passed on to a third 2nd lieutenant, someone else found the orders that Major Potter had had typed up for Joe that morning.

The orders were fairly routine: In three days Joe's company was to be relieved from P.A. 2 and sent a few miles down the line to take over P.A. 1 for another couple of weeks. As before, the orders stated exactly when, how, and where the company was to move. After trench duty, a company would typically fall back into reserve positions followed by five days of rest well to the rear of the lines. And then, the whole trench-duty cycle would start over again. Joe couldn't imagine why he had had to leave his men just to pick up such routine orders. Major Potter could have sent a runner to deliver them or someone at 2nd Battalion Headquarters could have called on the telephone line and had Joe send one his men to pick the orders up. What was unusual about the orders was that Maj. Potter had also slipped a hand-written note into the envelope for Joe.

All it said was: "Lt. Becker — Do not leave B.H.Q. until I return. — Maj. Potter"

It was still barely 11:00 AM, so Joe and Sgt. Pomeroy headed over to the company kitchen in the apple orchard behind the farmhouse to scrounge up something to eat and gather the latest military intelligence.

They only needed to see one man for both things. Friday Findlay, the black company cook, not only kept the coffee and beans warm in case unexpected guests arrived from the front, but he and the mostly black soldiers of the supply train were one of the most prolific sources of information in the whole A.E.F. The men who worked the supply train and the company kitchens not only got to move around from battalion to regimental to divisional headquarters more than most generals did, but since nobody bothered telling them much of anything officially, they kept each other informed as best as possible. With only one black company (the 92nd) actually serving in combat, most of the black soldiers of the A.E.F. were restricted to the most menial jobs in the Army. Those jobs, however, took the black soldiers up and down the battlefield. The black soldiers' underground network of information stretched all the way up to the wardrooms of the top commanders. They were careful who they shared this information with, but the lowliest Army mule-skinner could often know of an impending offensive attack long before the soldiers in the lines ever did.

Joe heard Friday Findlay long before he saw him. From beneath the remaining petals of apple blossoms came a low, rolling laughter that Joe recognized as his company cook's. Pots and ladles were clanging in the orchard as Friday and his two cooks were preparing a hot lunch to send up to the trenches. All of Friday's stoves were ablaze as the kitchen crew warmed up heaps of baked beans and grilled hundreds of sausages. Since coming to the farmlands of Hecken, the quality and quantity of food had improved significantly.

"Ten-hut!" Sgt. Pomeroy barked as he and Joe stepped under the canvas awning that Friday used to keep the apple blossom petals out of his food. The men in the make-shift tent snapped to attention and saluted Joe, with Friday giving something like a rifle salute using the long spoon in his right hand.

"At ease, men," Joe said with a smile.

"Lieutenant Becker, Sergeant Pomeroy," Friday grinned. "To what do we owe this honor? Every thin' alright with the food, Lieutenant?"

"A-Okay, Sgt. Findlay," Joe said. "We are just up to see Major Potter, and thought we might be able to trouble you for a bite to eat. We got called up here too early to catch breakfast, and now it looks like we won't make it back to the line for lunch."

"Yes, sir, yes, sir," Friday said. "Dish 'em up a couple plates, Leroy."

Joe and Sgt. Pomeroy dug into the hot food with gusto. It took about an hour to get the meals up to the front, and since neither Joe nor Bill were usually able to dig right in, a hot meal was a rare treat. As Friday and his crew finished cooking up the lunch and loading nearly a ton of food into wagons, Joe chatted with Friday between bites. Since it took a lot longer for the wagon train to pack up and move than it did for the rest of the company, Joe let Friday know about the upcoming orders to move farther down the line. If the cooks got a good head start, then the men were more likely to find a hot meal waiting for them after the march.

"I appreciate the head's up, Lieutenant, so I'll tell you sumpin', too," Friday said as he loaded the last canister of hot beans on to the back of one of the wagons. "I know you and the sergeant here are anxious to get back to the lines, but if the major asked ya' to hang around for a bit, I reckon it's because he's lookin' for someone to lead a tour into the trenches. You didn't hear it from me, Lieutenant, but I hear there's some big brass coming down the road this afternoon. I done heard

Major Potter bring up your name when he was talking to Captain Haley about giving some V.I.Ps. a tour of the front lines. You best be ready for whoever they got comin' down that road."

"I'll do that, Friday, and I appreciate the information," Joe said. "As always, both the food and the conversation have been a pleasure. If you get to the P.C. before I do, tell Lt. Wilcox to have the men at the ready for a big inspection when I return."

"Yessir, Lieutenant!"

With that, Friday and his cooks climbed up on the wagons and headed up to the front lines.

The noon hour came and went without any sign of Major Potter, so Joe and Sgt. Pomeroy used the time to clean themselves up as much as possible. After the lunch hour, the battalion H.Q. crescendoed back to a noisy clatter of typewriters, telephones, and shouted orders between the various rooms of the farmhouse. After checking in with Lt. Wilcox by phone several times to make sure the company was ready for visitors, Joe found himself sitting next to Sgt. Pomeroy across the entryway from the young, bespectacled clerk who was again hunched over his desk copying supply requisitions into a ledger book.

At about 1:15 PM, the corporal of the guard strolled in from the village square mopping his brow. He acknowledged Joe with a salute and sidled over to the clerk.

"Say, Jimmy, can I bum a smoke off of you?" the corporal said.

Without looking up or lifting his pen from the logbook, Jimmy the clerk slipped a cigarette out of his left breast pocket and gave it to the guard.

"Thanks, Jimmy, you're a real pal," the guard said.

"Can't you see I'm working here?" Jimmy said.

"Sure. I was just wondering if we were expecting anybody important today," the guard said. "One of my sentries said a car just blew through the village loaded with officers."

"If anybody important was coming, I would know about it," Jimmy said, finally looking up with a scowl. "It's probably just some regimental brass passing through."

Joe and Sgt. Pomeroy quietly chuckled to each other recalling how well their arrival had been expected earlier that morning.

"Okay. If you say so, Jimmy," the guard said. "I'm going to go stick my head under the fountain for a bit if anyone calls for me. Okay."

"Let's go stretch our legs, Sergeant Pomeroy," Joe said, heading out into the hot afternoon sun that was baking the village square.

A cloud of dust blew around the corner of one of the rustic buildings of the square immediately followed by an open-air staff car loaded with officers. Major Potter, a thin man in his fifties with a sharp nose leapt from the running boards before the automobile came to a full stop. He opened the door for a tall, mustached man wearing leather riding boots, gloves, and the distinctive Sam Browne belt that was officially banned for officers back in the States. On his head, he wore the leather-visored officer's field cap that he had designed for the U.S. Army, and still bears his name. As this older gentleman athletically stepped out of the car while maintaining his proper military bearing, Joe instantly recognized him even before he noticed the four stars on his shoulder. It was General John J. Pershing in the flesh.

"Ten-hut!" Sgt. Pomeroy called out as he and Joe jumped to attention.

General Hahn, commander of the 32nd Division, quickly followed. This simple, two-piece leather belt had stirred quite a controversy in the U.S. Army. It was a wide belt that buckled around the waist on the outside of the uniform, with a diagonal strap that ran across the chest and over an officer's shoulder.

General March who was Gen. Pershing's superior back in Washington detested the belts and ordered them banned back in the States. Some Army insiders interpreted the wearing or the absence of the Sam Browne belt by officers in France as an indication of loyalty. Those who wore them were in Pershing's "open warfare" camp, and those who didn't wear them were loyal to Gen. March's more traditional, old Army ways. Joe, who had worn one since his days in the Ohio National Guard, had long ago decided that the whole belt/no-belt issue probably just boiled down to how fat an officer was.

Colonel Westnedge, the commander of the 126th Infantry Regiment, a French general, and several other aids and staff officers whom Joe did not recognize, followed Hahn out of the car.

"Ah, Becker!" Major Potter shouted. "Just the man we are looking for." Potter hurried over to Joe with a smile on his face, which quickly turned into a frown as he drew near. His voice dropped to a sharp whisper as he approached Joe. "Where are the rest of my men? I telephoned ahead to have the men assembled for a field inspection."

"They don't seem to have received the word, sir," Joe said.

"Dammit!" Major Potter cursed under his breath. "All these confounded telephone lines running in and out of this place and you still can't get a message through when you need to."

"I know exactly what you mean, sir."

"Look Becker, Gen. Pershing wants a company commander to give him a tour of our sector of the trenches. Your boys are in better shape than anybody else, so I picked you to take him and his staff to inspect the lines. I've got to stay here to get the H.Q. ready for an inspection on the general's way back, so I'm counting on you to do 2nd Battalion proud."

"My men are already on the alert," Joe said. "We had word of some V.I.Ps. showing up since this morning."

Major Potter made the introductions. Two disappointed staff officers were left behind to make room for Joe and Sgt. Pomeroy, whom Joe had asked to accompany the inspection party. After a brief pit stop in which Joe could hear Major Potter whipping his H.Q. staff into a frenzy of inspection cleanup inside the old farmhouse, Joe found himself seated in a bouncing car next to the Commander-in-Chief of the American Expeditionary Forces.

"You look familiar, Captain Becker," Pershing said. "Have we met before?"

"It's Lieutenant Becker, sir, and, yes, I was with you two years ago on the Mexican Border. I did some translating for you when you came back to El Paso."

"Ah, yes. The ex-marine from Michigan — I remember. Your language abilities were particularly useful that day. Do you speak any other languages?"

"I grew up speaking German. My French isn't pretty, but it's coming along."

"Good for you, Captain. I may not always remember names, but I never forget the cut of a man," Pershing said.

Pershing's car sped down the country roads towards the town of Hauptwiller. Vehicles could reach Joe's sector by a much longer route to the east of Hecken and then northwest along a dirt road that paralleled the Seultsbach creek that flowed between Joe's trenches and the wooded hills between Hecken and the front. They passed Friday and his wagons on the way back to the battalion H.Q. Joe and Sgt. Pomeroy took turns explaining the sights and recounting their first experiences in the trenches.

Once the V.I.Ps reached Post of Action 2, Joe carefully guided them into the trenches without exposing his guests to enemy observation or fire. Joe's men had cleaned up nicely and they looked sharp without looking like they were trying too hard. Pershing strode quickly along the duckboards, but stopped frequently to chat with the men of Company E about where they were from, what they needed, and what they had learned.

Pershing nodded approval when he discovered the dough-boys' packs loaded with several days of ammo and gear in the event of a break in the enemy lines. He scowled when he saw the rats in the traps, but then smiled and had an aide make some notes when Sgt. Schloss explained the purpose of and beneficial effects of "rat duty."

Ever the tactical instructor, Pershing not only inspected the troops, but also drilled Joe on how Joe's company would use its current position in the lines in the event of a major attack by the Germans. Joe was able to point out sniper and trench mortar positions that he had established in the wooded hills behind the main trench, as well as provisions he had made for the main firing line and petty posts. Joe's answers were met with approval, and the general gave him some pointers on maintaining communications with the other units in the area.

"Above all, never give any ground, Captain Becker." General Pershing said. "We are not going to make the mistake of paying for the same ground twice."

"I understand, sir, but it's just Lieutenant Becker, sir. I'm not a captain."

"I suppose you wouldn't object to my calling you Captain Becker from now on, then?"

"No, sir." Joe said. "I admit it would please me greatly."

"Well, don't put them on now, but I believe you'll be needing these, then." And with that, Gen. Pershing handed Joe a set of double silver bars and Joe became a captain in the United States Army.

~ PART 12 ~
OSWEGO, NEW YORK

———

Chapter 42

I'VE SET ASIDE Joe's World War I papers to spend the Fourth of July with Libby Hampton. She and her fellow University of Michigan piping plover lovers have been keeping twenty-four-hour vigils over the Sturgeon Bay dunes to keep swarms of summer beachgoers from trampling the nest sites. Free-roaming beach dogs seem to be the biggest threat to the eggs and baby birds, so Libby has taken to keeping a package of Snausage dog treats in the cute little black fanny pack that she wears over her cute little bikinied fanny while on beach patrol. Libby's little black bikini with the white trim — to say nothing of her joyful charm and witty repartee — have lured me to Sturgeon Bay on several days that I should have been working.

The professor in charge of the piping plover study, however, has ruled the nesting sites off limits to extraneous friends, relatives, and (especially) boyfriends. I guess one of Libby's field-study colleagues was caught making out in the dunes with a local boy one evening, and they narrowly missed rolling over a new nest in the dark.

I tried bringing my work down to the beach to spend more time with Libby during her breaks from plover patrol, but old newspapers, letters, and clippings don't fare too well in the sun, wind, and sand of Sturgeon Bay. I thought it would be cool to do some interviews from the beach with one of those executive phones you see guys in limos use in the movies, but I'm pretty sure such an extravagance isn't in my freelance business budget. Anyway, who would want to be strapped to a portable phone on the beach all day? Sometimes I get the stupidest ideas.

My ideas for how to spend the Fourth with Libby, however, are pure genius. First, Libby and a few of her friends (Mike, Jill, Lydia, and Melanie) from the U of M Biological Station at Pellston came over to The Shack for a little barbecue before heading into Blue Harbor to take part in the little resort town's biggest holiday of the year. We snatch up enough space on Main Street for all six of us to set up our beach chairs on the curb and watch the most Norman Rockwell-esque Fourth of July parade I've ever seen. Old jalopies polished up to a new shine; a herd of kids on bikes and trikes decorated in red, white, and blue bunting; the American Legion Drum and Bugle Corps; a fleet of fire trucks with sirens blaring; a platoon of kilt-wearing bag pipers from the Canadian side of Sault Ste. Marie, and roller skaters chucking out handfuls of candy to the kids roll by us. Thousands of locals and resorters have turned out for the event. It's a bit cheesy, but a lot of fun.

After the parade, we brave the long lines for ice cream cones, and then return to the Becker farm for a swim down at our beach — at least it is still technically "our" beach until the courts say otherwise. Then, we kick back at The Shack with naps and ice-cold Cokes (or beers for Libby's friends) until evening. I grill hot dogs on my porch as we watch the sun set, and then head back into town for the fireworks, which don't start until about 11 PM due to our long Up North summer days.

Henry Richards, who I ran into during the parade, invited me and my guests to watch the fireworks from his lawn. Henry's old Victorian house is not only big enough to accommodate his large family and the host of grandchildren who come to visit, but it also turns out to be part of the Becker family story. A lumber baron named Higginbotham originally owned it, Henry said.

"Who knows, if Anna wouldn't have married Joe, then this could have been your house," he jokes.

Henry's house sits high up on the bluff overlooking the downtown. The view from Bluff Street — which has been carefully framed by the well-pruned trees that grow on the slope of the bluff — is legendary. The vistas have lured both professional postcard photographers and open-air painters for over a century. Since I had spent all of my Fourth of Julys either working at summer camp or in the newsroom back in Boston, I had never seen the famous Blue Harbor fireworks until tonight.

They shoot off the fireworks from the deck of a big boatyard barge. We are perched high above the water on Henry's lawn, so that some fireworks burst at about eye level above the harbor, while others fly a quarter mile into the velvety dark-purple sky that stretches over the bay. Hundreds of small boats and big yachts float in the harbor and register their approval of the light show with a chorus of boat horns. Libby snuggles closer to me under a scratchy wool blanket as the concussions from the biggest explosions reverberate in our chests.

"Ooooo, look at that one," Libby whispers into my ear, with all the delight of a ten-year-old kid.

"Happy Independence Day, Libby," I tell her as I sneak a kiss on her soft cheek which has been cooled by the night air.

"Hey, knock it off, mister. Can't you see I'm trying to watch the fireworks here," she says as she kisses me back and holds my arm closer.

I follow her gaze out across the bluff and notice that other fireworks shows have started up all along the horizon. Behind the Blue Harbor show and across the bay, Petoskey's fireworks (looking half the size of Blue Harbor's show in the distance) pop and boom casting an upside-down reflection on Little Traverse Bay. To the east, a small-scale show is being shot off from the Bay View Association's dock. And way off on the horizon, we can just see the round tops of the fireworks displays in Boyne City and Charlevoix.

"I guess I'm making up for lost time," I tell Libby. "I never saw much in the way of fireworks at camp, and now we're getting five shows all at once."

I suddenly grow quiet as I realize that this may be my first and last Fourth of July in this little town. Sometimes it's harder to lose something that you're just getting to know than it is to lose something you've known all your life. Libby notices my stillness, and turns to me. I try not to dwell on the pending loss of the family property when I'm with Libby, but she is concerned about me and we have discussed each other's lives and hopes, so she knows what's going on with the court stuff.

"What are you thinking about over there, Nick?" she asks.

"Oh, I was just trying to figure out how many donkeys you could fit on that big blue yacht down there," I tell her as the clouds lift at the sound of her voice.

"Very funny," she says slugging me on the shoulder under the blanket.

"This place has kind of grown on me, Libby. This town — the farm — The Shack — the water — I guess I was just trying to figure out how to get back here after they toss me on my ear."

"I thought that's what it was," Libby says, "and by the way, the answer to your problem is 764."

"What?"

"764 — that's how many donkeys would fit on that boat," she says with a wink.

"Oh, yeah? How did you figure that out?"

"It's a math thing — you wouldn't understand."

"That's for sure — I never made it past algebra two."

"That's okay," Libby says. "With deep brown eyes like yours you should be able to make it on looks alone."

"You like my eyes, huh? Is there anything else you see that you might like? Because I sure like what I see in you."

"Here comes the grand finale," she says. "Just watch the fireworks, flirty."

"I am," I say as I brush back her long, sun-bleached blond hair and lean in to kiss and nuzzle her lovely neck. She continues to "ooo" and "ahh" at the fireworks, but I can tell that her eyes are closed as she tilts her face up to the cool, velvety night sky. I don't have a clue what will happen in the near future, but I'm sure happy with the immediate present.

Well after midnight, we begin to say our goodbyes to Henry, his wife Charlotte, and the other two- or three-dozen Richards family members we've met. Libby's friends are piling into Lydia's white Chevy van for the ride back to Pellston when Libby surprises me yet again. She pulls me aside to a dark corner of Henry's driveway.

"Hey Nick, you wouldn't mind giving me a ride up to Sturgeon Bay in the morning, would you?" Libby asks. "I have to be there by 5:30 to relieve the professor who has been guarding the nest sites all night."

"No problem," I say, "what time do you want me to pick you up at the biological station?"

"Actually, I was thinking about leaving from your place, if that's all right with you. Your place is closer to Sturgeon Bay than Pellston, and I thought I might be able to get in a bit more sleep, if that's okay."

"Uh, um — *okay*? That would be considerably better than just okay," I say, trying to ignore the few heartbeats that I just skipped.

"Don't get any ideas, bucko. I just need a place to crash for the night."

"Oh, of course not," I say. "I was just flustered there for a second trying to remember if I had put clean sheets on the guest bed."

Lydia's van headlights illuminate a skeptical smirk on Libby's face that lets me know that neither of us is fooling anybody.

"All right, then I'll let Lydia know that I don't need a ride."

They say a gentleman doesn't kiss and tell, but when a man falls in love with a virtuous woman, his silent discretion shouldn't leave the impression that more has happened than it really has. I did find some clean sheets for the guest bed and put them on, but Libby and I never made it past the lumpy old sofa that sits in front of the fieldstone fireplace in the living room. I built a bright, crackly fire and kept it going until 2:00 AM, but we found plenty of warmth that long summer night beneath one of my grandmother's quilts as the fire died down. Our clothes stayed on (mostly), and we just kissed, and held, and touched, and felt, and wrapped ourselves around each other like the roots and branches of two trees that grow side-by-side in the oldest part of the forest. Before we knew it, the eastern sky stirred with first light.

Chapter 43

WITH THE EARLY start I got this morning, I have already been to Sturgeon Bay and back, and finished up an article for the *Northern Michigan Gazette* about a World War II veteran who lives over in Alanson and managed to get around the "Sullivan Brothers" rule by serving on the same aircraft carrier as his twin brother in the Pacific. He was a ball-turret gunner in a Navy torpedo-bomber and lived through an air battle over Hong Kong by flying in tight to a cliff that was riddled with anti-aircraft batteries. The Japanese gunners took out two-thirds of this guy's attack wing, but they couldn't touch his plane when it flew close and fast in front of the caves that the Japanese had dug into the cliff for their guns.

With work out of the way by two in the afternoon and Libby not free until about 8:00 this evening, I've decided to spend some time trying to pin down a few answers to questions I have about Joe and Anna and their life here in Blue Harbor. Even though it has been more than three decades since Joe and Anna spent their summers here, I'm surprised that I haven't run into more people who knew Joe and Anna more directly. Patty Kensington and Henry Richards knew Joe and Anna as my dad's parents. Patty and Henry are only in their sixties now, but surely there must be people in their seventies, eighties, and nineties still living here who knew my grandparents or went to elementary school with Aunt Vicky. I have a hunch that if I find "where," then it will lead to "who." I am on my way to find the exact spot where Anna's family lived on 3rd Street at the foot of the bluff that lies behind the downtown. I've had a vague idea of where the house was, but the couple of times that I cruised down that street I haven't had the photographs that I now have beside me on the bench seat of the old red pickup. I've also got the address, so it shouldn't be too hard to find.

Driving down West Hill into town, my first discovery is that 3rd Street is actually divided into East and West 3rd Streets, so I wasn't even looking at the correct end of the street. I take a left onto E. 3rd Street. Blue Harbor proper is one of those towns that is so small that it takes years to actually learn the street names because you can get just about anywhere without needing to know them. Directions given by locals and summer folks tend toward the "two houses down from the Episcopal Church" variety, or the "brick building at the foot of the bluff next to the stairway" type. With this in mind, I pull over to take one more look at the old photos of the Johnson family home and try to orient myself to the angle and fall line of the bluff in the background of the pictures. When I look up, I realize that I am parked directly across the street from the old Johnson place. I didn't recognize it on my early casual attempts because the porch that wraps around three sides of the front in the pictures has been removed. The tall narrow windows in the picture match the windows before me exactly, and then I notice the low, concrete retaining wall where Anna saw Joe playing fetch with her dog Taffy. The house has been through a few modifications, but this is definitely the place.

Ironically, this is a place I have visited several times before. Connected to the old house is a sprawling, one-story addition that is home to Blue Harbor's own weekly newspaper — the *Blue Harbor Resorter*. The *Resorter* not only features Patty's column, but its back issues and staff have provided useful background for a few stories I've written for *The Northern Michigan Gazette*. Miriam Flynn — the publisher's wife, the mother of the editor, and the most reliable source of information at the *Resorter* — is working away at her desk on what looks to be a circulation database.

" Hello, Mrs. Flynn. You're not going to believe what I just figured out."

"Oh, really?" she says. "I'm not that easily surprised, Nick."

"Your office here is attached to my ancestral home."

"I thought you lived out near Cummings Creek, and I certainly don't remember any Beckers living here. What are you talking about?"

Miriam Flynn is only in her late-forties, but she knows the local history and people better than most and more than she lets on. Her family's paper has traded on the comings and goings of the town and the townsfolk for decades. We've already had the discussion about who I'm related and not related to, so Mrs. Flynn already knows part of my local pedigree. The Johnson family's tenure in the adjoining house was before her time, though. I show her the old photo and letter with the address. She and I step out on her sidewalk to compare the photo and the house next to her office before she is fully convinced. We put what she knows together with what I know and our dates seem to add up. The newspaper office was originally added on to the old house as a dry cleaning business, she tells me.

"But I guess the Johnson family could have owned it before then," she says. "Isn't that something? We'll have to write up a blurb in next week's paper."

"That would be fine with me," I say. "My family name could use a bit of good press these days."

She asks me a few polite questions about what is to become of the Becker property, and I fill her in on the big picture, but I don't even know what will become of the legal fiasco. She gives me a quick tour of the old house which is between renters right now and filled with somebody's packed up belongings and building materials for a renovation that seems to be moving through the house one room at a time. Despite the drywall dust and lack of light bulbs, the steep narrow staircase and small rooms evoke the years my great-grandparents spent living here. Anna's mother — Dianna Johnson — held this household together with a wiry strength that is still visible in old photographs of her — especially in her long, worn hands. Late in life, she helped raise Aunt Vicky from babyhood through elementary school. She took in boarders when times were tight, and worked a few days a week at the post office just a block away. She nursed her husband James through a long illness that kept him confined to one of these upstairs bedrooms for the better part of a decade. And she even helped support her son Vint and his girlfriend by letting them live with her until she passed in 1940.

I may not be able to find anyone alive who remembers James and Dianna Johnson, but there is still hope that I can find some more living links to Joe, Anna, and Vicky. Mrs. Flynn gives me names and numbers of some old timers who may have known my family. Most of them are up at the nursing home at the top of East Hill, but one man on the list still lives in his own house. Mrs. Flynn lets me use her phone to make an appointment with the nursing home director and to call Lamar Connor at his place up on Lake Street.

Lamar Conner doesn't hear too well on the phone, but once he catches my name and my relation to Joe and Anna, he invites me up to his place for a visit. It's just a three-minute drive up to the long, ranch-style duplex that Lamar calls home. Just as I begin walking up to his door, though, a minivan pulls up next to my pickup and out steps a middle-aged woman in a blue-floral nursing uniform. I say hello and wait at Lamar's door without knocking to make sure that I'm not interrupting someone else's visit. I guess Lamar is a popular guy. The nurse helps out a tiny old woman with owlish round glasses and a black-lacquered cane. It takes a second for me to recognize this woman outside of the context I usually see her in. It is Mildred Walker — Patty Kensington's mother.

Mildred lives in the other half of Patty's big brown house. I almost always say hello and chat with her when I visit Patty, but she is quieter and more formal than her gregarious daughter, so I have never really gotten to know her well. Patty and I like to talk about my dad, but Mildred always reminds me that she knew my grandparents. I have never been able to get much more than that out of her, so it didn't even occur to me to interview her at length about them.

I suddenly realize that the nurse is unsure about what to do with this stranger standing between Mildred and Lamar's front door, so I bounce back down Lamar's sidewalk to make myself known to them. Once Mildred has her feet planted firmly on the ground, she notices me standing by.

"Nicolas Becker, what on earth are you doing here?" she says somewhat sternly.

I explain the purpose of my visit to both women, and the nurse seems relieved that Mildred knows me.

"I can come back another time, if you would rather visit Mr. Conner by yourself," I tell Mildred.

"Nonsense," she says. "If you're trying to find out about the Becker family, then you've come to the right place. Both Lamar and I knew your grandparents as well as anybody in town. Give me your arm, Nicolas."

"I'll pick you up at 4:30, Mrs. Walker," the nurse says, hopping back into the minivan.

"Lamar and I are just friends," Mildred says as we shuffle down the sidewalk to Lamar's front door. She gives me a look that says I better not get any ideas about them. "There aren't too many of our generation left, and we just like to visit and talk about the old days and what our children, grand-children and great-grandchildren are up to. It's probably not very exciting for a newspaper man like yourself, but you're welcome to join us."

"I appreciate that, Mildred," I tell her. "Sometimes the best stories come from people just like you."

We finally reach the door, and Lamar welcomes us in. Mildred introduces us, and Lamar gets us settled into his living room. Lamar is neatly dressed in matching khaki pants and work shirt, with an overloaded pocket protector weighing down the left side of his shirt. He wears thick, black-framed glasses, but I notice that he gets around pretty good without a walker or cane.

"Lamar is ninety-six, and I'm ninety-four," Mildred starts off. "Lamar was a groundskeeper at the Topaque golf course for fifty years before he retired. My husband was a butcher and we had a store downtown for almost as long. Nicolas, here, wants to know about his family. You remember Colonel and Anna Becker? How did you know them, Lamar?"

"They were friends of my father's, at first. Everybody knew everybody in town back then. My dad was friends with Anna's parents, and he used to drive his old jalopy out to that farm-house of their's for visits in the summer. He used to help the Colonel with odd jobs around the place, but when he got old like me he just liked going out and visiting. He shared the Colonel's love of good pipe tobacco, and they used to just sit out on that porch overlooking the meadow and the lake and just talk. No matter how crazy things got here in the summer with all the resort people, the Becker place reminded my dad of what it used to be like around here."

Mildred is listening with a bit of a scowl on her face. She seems a bit restless on the end of the couch, so I try to bring her into the conversation.

"How did you get to know my grandparents, Mrs. Walker?" I ask.

"I knew your grandparents pretty well, but I probably got to know them through Patty," Mildred says before taking a long pause.

"I want to tell you something about your *father*, though, Nicolas," Mildred says. "All this talk about your family's property in the newspaper and a nature preserve and all that just doesn't make a lick of sense to me. I probably shouldn't be telling you this, but maybe this might help you ... ."

Mildred gathers herself together in her seat and looks up at me over the tops of her thick bifocal lenses. My reporter senses are instantly on alert. Any time someone says they "shouldn't be telling" me something, it's something well worth hearing. The serious tone of her voice makes the hair on the back of my neck stand up and a chill run down my sides. She clears her throat two times.

"When your Aunt Vicky was just a teenager, she had an illegitimate child. That boy was your father. The Colonel and Anna raised your father as their own son, but he was really their grandson. Your aunt is really your grandmother. The Colonel and Anna are really your great-grandparents. The Army moved them around so much that they were able to keep it a secret, but a lot of people here in town knew that your father was really Vicky's son."

Chapter 44

MY HEAD HAS not stopped spinning since I left Lamar's house. Mildred's news nearly knocked me off Lamar's sofa, but neither of the nonagenarians knew anything more. Whoever got Vicky pregnant wasn't from around here. So many questions are bouncing around my brain that I have to pull over at the scenic lookout before Stanton Road to get something down on paper to help me wrap my head around this new reality. I sketch out two versions of my family tree:

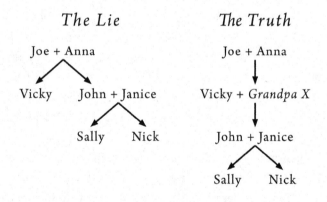

My next thought is that somewhere out there (either dead or alive), Sally and I have a mystery grandfather. I decide to call him "Grandpa X." Secondly, I wonder how this family indiscretion affects me. Am I at greater risk of doing something wrong because Vicky got knocked up? I remember a saying in the Bible about fathers eating sour grapes and their sons' teeth being set on edge. Does this apply to grandmothers and grandsons, too? I think Jesus mentioned the old Hebrew saying only to say that we shouldn't say it anymore, so I don't think I'm doomed to follow Vicky's footsteps. What I do need to follow, however, are the clues that lead back to my father's birth. Before I get too far ahead of myself, I need confirmation and more information. I'm on the phone within seconds of reaching The Shack.

"Hello."

"Hi, Mom, it's me."

"Hi, Sweetie. How are you?"

"Well, actually I'm kind of stunned right now," I tell her. "I just learned some surprising news while visiting Mildred Walker and Lamar Conner."

"Oh, how wonderful. You met Lamar," Mom says, not quite picking up on the urgency of my call. "Isn't he the nicest fellow? There's a great story about him. When I was newly married, your father and I visited Joe and Anna up at The Shack. It was still pretty remote back in those days and everything was still pretty open from the logging days. The Colonel noticed someone driving up Stanton Road toward the farm. He ran into the house and reappeared with a shotgun. It was so unusual to get visitors back then. Then, as this old jalopy approached the driveway, the Colonel's face broke into a big smile. 'Oh, it's just Lamar,' he said and put the shotgun away. I was pretty surprised..."

"Mom! I need to tell you something," I say, cutting her off. "Mildred told me that Dad was really Aunt Vicky's son."

"What? Good heavens. What on earth did she mean by that?"

I repeat Mildred's story and have to take Mom step-by-step through the two family trees that I drew in my reporter's notebook. Once the full picture becomes clear, I hear a quick gasp from Mom over the hundreds of miles of phone lines.

"Oh, dear," she says. "That's what Patty Kensington was trying to tell me so many years ago."

"What do you mean, Mom?"

"It must have been back in the '50s after your father and I first started having marital difficulties."

"What did she tell you?" I ask.

"She said that her parents believed there was always some secret rift between John and Vicky that made things uneasy between them. Patty didn't know what that secret was, but she thought finding out what it was might help me understand your father better."

"Did you ever look into it?"

"No. I just felt that if the Beckers wanted the secret kept, then I should just honor their wishes. And so I never really gave it a lot of thought until just now."

"I wish you had been a little more curious," I tell her.

"I'm so sorry, honey," she says sweetly. "I was just so busy trying to make the present work out with your father that it never occurred to me to dig up the past. And then you kids came along, and I was busy thinking about the future."

I can almost hear the wheels turning in Mom's head, but I don't want to make her feel bad for not sticking her nose into her in-laws business.

"Do you think Dad had any idea that his sister was really his mother?"

"Heavens, no," she says. "In all the years we were married, John never gave any indication that he thought of Joe and Anna as anything other than his parents — and he certainly never acted like Vicky was his mother... *his mother*... that sounds so strange."

"No wonder things were always so weird and uncomfortable with Vicky," I say. "I mean, you'd drive half way across the country to see her, and she was always bent out of shape if we showed up at the wrong time or didn't send her a thank-you note the day after Christmas. She always made us feel like we were doing something wrong, and the whole time she was hiding this huge secret from all of us and basically plotting to rip us off."

"Well, I don't think we should be too hard on her, honey, but this news certainly does explain some things."

"It sure does, Mom."

"You had better give Sally a call, honey," Mom says. "She'll want to know what's going on as soon as possible."

———

A few touch-tones later and I'm on the phone with Sally. I give her the news. After about a dozen "Oh, my gawd's," Sally settles down and prepares for action. She wants more information, too.

"All right," she says. "I'll call everyone on the Whittier side of the family and see if anyone knows anything else."

Sally and I are both thinking that the implications of this startling revelation may go well beyond mere bloodlines, but we agree to hold off on too much speculation until we know more.

———

My next phone call takes my ear and voice all the way to Tucson, Arizona. Luckily, I reach Lu Ann Wilson on the fifth ring. I relay what Mildred told me, and I'm met with silence on the other end of the line.

"Are you still there?" I ask after a long pause.

"Yes, I'm here, Nick," she says sounding more serious than I've ever heard her. "She made me swear that I would never reveal her secret, but now that you've discovered the truth yourself, I don't see any harm in talking about it. I was kind of wondering how long it would take you to find out after I sent all of her papers to you."

"Actually, I just learned it from some old friends of the family here," I say. Then, I read Lu Ann my notes from talking with Mildred and Lamar.

"It doesn't surprise me that you didn't find anything in her papers," Lu Ann says. "There may be something in there, but I doubt if you'll find much of anything. Vicky told me that when the Colonel died she raced off to Ann Arbor to get there before your father. She frantically went through all the papers and old letters and gathered up anything that mentioned her pregnancy or Joe and Anna bringing up the baby as their own. She told me that she burned up any incriminating evidence in the fireplace."

"I've only given a quick look at the papers from then," I say. "If Dad was born on March 10, 1929, then anything from nine months or so before then might provide some clues. Let's see — that would be around July 1928. They were stationed at Fort Oswego, New York when Vicky got pregnant. Do you know anything about the father?"

"There was a boy named Tom, and they were deeply in love — that's all she said. She was only seventeen when it happened."

"Why did she keep it so secret? Even after my dad died?" I ask. Some unpleasant answers to questions like that are already taking shape in my mind, but I would still like to hear Lu Ann's take on it.

"You have to understand how different things were back then, Nick. These days people go on the Phil Donahue show and air their dirty laundry to the whole world, but back then, there was a huge stigma attached to having a child out of wedlock. Such a scandal could not only have ruined Vicky's reputation, but it could have destroyed her father's military career."

"So as far as you know, my dad never knew that his sister was really his mother?"

"Oh, no. He never knew the truth, although I suppose every child has some instinctive connection to his mother. Her parents shipped Vicky off to Braneu College in Atlanta, Georgia, and she never saw that boy Tom again as far as I know. But giving up her son was harder than she would admit to herself. Once, after your father visited Tucson on his way to Vietnam, Vicky told me a story about your father as a baby. He must have only been one or two. Vicky came home from college and met her parents and John on the porch of their quarters on the base. When Vicky went to hold him, though, he slugged her right in the breast. I tried to tell her that little John was probably instinctively angry with his real mother for leaving him for so long, but Vicky just thought he was a rude, little boy. She never forgave him. When she told me the story, your father was probably in his thirties, but there was still so much pain and resentment about the incident in Vicky's voice."

"No wonder they weren't close," I say. "Even when I tried to get to know Vicky better, things didn't go so well."

"I remember that trip very well, Nick," Lu Ann says. "Vicky did not want you to come and start asking a lot of questions about your family. She wanted to get rid of you as quickly as she could, and she was pretty proud of herself when she shuffled you off in less than an hour. But I was ashamed of the way she acted. 'But that's your grandson,' I told her."

"Maybe her secret past made her lose sight of the present that was standing at her doorstep," I say. "Anyway, if you can think of any of her friends that might have known something more about this Tom guy, please let me know."

"I'll do that, Nick," Lu Ann says before we say our goodbyes.

I spend the next few hours alternately digging through the Becker family letters and working the phone. Sally called back to tell me that both of our Whittier aunts and even all of our cousins had heard that there was some Becker family secret involving Dad and Vicky. There had even been speculation that John was Vicky's son, but no one ever made that suggestion to us nor did they make any connections between the rumor and the current legal problems with the land. I bring Sally up to speed on my call with Lu Ann. I can tell that Sally is itching to talk about the wider implications of today's discovery.

"Do you think … ," she says, tentatively.

"Oh, yeah, I'm thinking what you're thinking, but I want to check out more of these letters first. I've got to pick up Libby from the beach in a couple of hours, so give me a chance to find something in writing first. Is it alright if I call you tonight?"

"Okay, Nick, but this could change everything. I mean we can't even call her Aunt Vicky anymore. We should call her Aunt-Slash-Grandma Vicky from now on."

"I know. I know. It's like our whole reality has been shifted. There's a lot to figure out, but I'll call you later, Sis."

"Bye, Nick."

My final flurry of phone calls to Henry Richards and Dad's other friends reveals that Vicky's secret was indeed kept from my father for his whole life. Vicky may not have fooled Joe and

Anna's Blue Harbor friends, but until now she got away with fooling most of the rest of the world.

"About the only thing that I remember your dad saying," Henry Richards tells me, "is that sometimes he felt that living with Joe and Anna was like living with his grandparents. I don't think that he suspected that he was really their grandson, but they were so much older than my folks and the other parents of kids our age that John didn't think they could ever relate to him, especially when he was a teenager."

Dad's friends all have about the same reaction. They are surprised, but the truth I've uncovered makes sense to them. We all wonder what difference it would have made to Dad's life if he had known the truth about his place in his family.

Between calls, I dig further into the family correspondence. The first thing that I find is a gaping hole. A few months after Dad was conceived, the letters between Dianna and Anna, Anna and Joe, and between just about anyone else are missing. This yearlong gap in the record even lasts six months or so after Dad is born. Before and after this gap there is no mention of a boy named Tom, or Vicky's pregnancy, or even of Dad's birth and the decision to raise him as Joe and Anna's own son. I fear that Vicky may have been successful in expunging her secret from the family archives. Even Dad's birth certificate shows Anna and Joe as Dad's mother and father.

Vicky's letters pick up again in the fall of 1929 as she begins her first year at Brenau — an all-girls' college in Gainesville, Georgia. Although she mentions Dad and inquiries after him, her Brenau letters are mostly filled with news of her Alpha Zeta sorority, classes, and her financial needs. She is an industrious and talented student. Her English professors even praise her poetry. Perhaps they can sense a depth of pain and experience that exceeds anything her eighteen- and nineteen-year-old classmates have attained. Knowing what I know now, one poem that she sent home in a letter hints at her lost love and hidden past.

This April

April with mad, swirling sheets of rain
Has come again. The air is heavy
With her incensed presence. Hepatica
And daffodil are looking at the woods
With open eyes. But can April with all
Her green and liquid newness cast away those
Memories of you — Can it be April
With you not here?

A feeling of unrest has come to me with the Spring.
The budding of the leaves and awakening of the fields,
Have given me a vague disquietude.
Perhaps, it is the call of gay, far lands
With broad rolling seas between –
But I think it is only my wayward gypsy heart.

This poem is about all that Vicky is willing to show of her "wayward gypsy heart." I'm about to call it quits for tonight and get ready to pick up Libby when I open a letter from Dianna dated Nov. 8, 1928 — about five months into Vicky's pregnancy. What first catches my attention is a little note in the top, left corner — "Tell Vicky to write me. She is still my Vicky."

Dear Anna, Vicky & Joe,

Your letter arrived this morning. I was sure glad to
get it. You must have had a nice time while in Can-
ada. — awfully sorry I could not be there. Effa wrote
me that she was going to New York for Xmas and would

stop here either going or coming. Glad to have her any time but winter is so dull. Too bad she could not come in summer, however anytime will be all right. Now, about Vicky — don't be hard on her. Governor Green's daughter did the same thing, and they just made the best of it. It seems to be a common thing these days. So you and Joe must not forget who she was before this happened and you must be charitable. If Effa is with you for Xmas, I may be there just to be with Vicky and to treat her just the same — as if nothing but right prompted her. She no doubt feels that she had a reason. You know Alice Simmon's daughter did the same, and she gave up her college and married a chauffeur, yet they make all they can of him. When you write, tell me the young man's name. It seems to me that you ought to have it announced. It always looks better that way. How I wish Vicky could come up here for a while. Now I must close and say good night. Write soon and remember to be kind and charitable.

With love,
Mother

If Joe and Anna had followed Dianna's advice about being more open about Dad's birth and parentage, our family history certainly would have been different. Although I cannot say it would have necessarily been better. Dianna's sympathetic words towards Vicky may have saved this letter from the fire that Vicky lit in Joe's Ann Arbor fireplace just after his death. Dianna — whose post office experience probably taught her to avoid being too explicit in letters — is careful not to record what "happened" to Vicky. But the message between her lines is clear enough to set my mind at rest. Vicky is Dad's mother.

I have just enough time to check a few more letters out and gather up a few things to show Libby. I race out the back screen door with a new hope. The stretchy metal-spring sound the door makes as I open it and the double wooden clap of the screen door shutting behind me — hard and loud with the initial slam then a softer secondary slap as the door bounces back into its worn wooden jambs — has the familiar ring of a home that I may be able to come back to.

My red pickup is barreling up State Road in no time on the way to Cross Village. Northern Michigan has taken on a startling new beauty as the evening sun casts a warm silkiness on the old fields and new forests. Lately, I've been taking in the scenery like a dying man who knows that each time he looks at a perfect birch tree or a backlit breaking wave it may be the last time he does so. Now that I have been recast as the great-grandson of Joe and Anna Becker and the grandson of Victoria Rolland, however, I'm seeing this land as a place for my own progeny.

I can hardly wait to tell Libby what I've learned today, but I still manage to remember to stop at the Gull's Nest Tavern on the way up to Cross Village. I ordered a Mediterranean pizza for a beach picnic with Libby. She's already spent two shifts of her day on piping plover patrol (getting a ride back to Pellston for some R&R and then returning to the beach this afternoon), but I'm hoping she won't mind spending another hour or so to watch the sunset with me over pizza. Ten minutes north of Cross Village, the road Ts. I take a left and the road curves between the last couple of ridges of tree-covered dunes just before it opens up to Sturgeon Bay — a sweeping half-moon of sandy beach, blue-green water and open dunes capped by grass and juniper. I find Libby standing at the water's edge looking out into the water with her right hand saluting the lake as she keeps the lowering sun out of her eyes. Her slender arms and long, pretty legs look even darker than what I saw this morning under the quilts, and her blond hair has almost been bleached to a silvery white by the sun.

Libby is business-like near the professor who glances over at me from within the nesting area, but she slips her hand into mine as we walk down the beach to a secluded sand bowl where she greedily wolfs down two pieces of pizza after picking off the black olives and flinging them onto my piece.

"Were you looking out for Lake Michigan pirates when I just arrived?" I ask her.

"No. But apparently I've caught one sneaking in by land."

"You mean me? What possible qualifications do I have for piracy?"

"Aren't you that rascally boy from last night?" she says, licking the pizza grease from her fingers.

"Yes, that was me, but it turns out I'm not the same man that I was this morning."

"Whatever do you mean, Mr. Pirate?"

I tell her the whole story from this afternoon until now. She listens intently, and I only have to go over my shifting family tree once, drawing the two versions in the sand for her. She asks a few questions, and then I show her Dianna's letter about not being "too hard on" Vicky.

"Nick, doesn't this change everything?"

"I think it does, Libby, but I've been turning this thing over in my head so many times today that I just need to talk it through with you to get it all straight."

"Doesn't it all go back to Joe's will?" she says.

"Yes, it does. The will is the basis of the state's whole claim to the land," I say, picking my way through what I knew and what I know now. "The will made Joe's 'issue' life tenants of the land, but gives the land to his grandchildren. And the state was only supposed to get the land for a memorial nature preserve if there were no grandchildren."

"That's it then, Nick," she says with determination. "If your dad is really Joe's grandson and the only grandchild, then the whole property should have gone to him regardless of Vicky's life tenancy. Shouldn't it?

"I'm no lawyer, Libby, but I think that's right. The state's claim is based on Dad only being a life tenant as Joe's 'issue.' But if Dad wasn't really Joe's son, but his grandson, then it shouldn't have made any difference that Dad died before Aunt-slash-Grandma Vicky. The state says that Vicky's rights of survivorship made her a life tenant over all of the property when Dad died. The Attorney General's whole case rests on the fact that Vicky didn't have any children to inherit the land — which cut us out. But since Dad is really Vicky's son and Joe's grandson, then it all would have gone to Dad. Which I guess means that it all goes to Sally, Mom, and me."

"Oh, my gosh," Libby says. "That makes Vicky even more rotten than I thought she was."

"What do you mean?" I ask.

"Not only did she try to cheat you, your mother, and your sister out of half of something she didn't even have the legal right to sell, but she could have let your dad get all of the land with just a word. If she would have just told him the truth about being Joe and Anna's grandson then your dad probably wouldn't have had any trouble getting clear title to all 105 acres."

"You're right," I say. "She could have saved him all that legal trouble and expense, and the state wouldn't have had any claim on the property. But she was way too far down that road to ever call him up and say, 'Hey, guess what, John? I'm really your mother.'"

"How could anyone do that to their own kid?"

"I don't know, but now that I see all of the puzzle pieces in place, I believe Joe knew exactly what he was doing when he drew up that will," I say as the white-yellow sun ball touches the Lake Michigan horizon. "Joe kept Vicky's secret, but I don't think he liked where that lie was heading. I know that Joe wanted Dad to have the Blue Harbor property and for Vicky to have the Ann Arbor property. But Vicky wanted to make sure she got exactly half of everything. As the value of the Becker farm grew and grew, Vicky grew greedier and waited for a chance to cash in on what she probably felt was her fair share of the family fortune.

"Just look at this will again," I say pulling out a photocopy I stuffed in my back pocket before heading out to see Libby. "It's all right there, isn't it?"

I give and bequeath all my real property to my issue, in equal shares. Share and share alike, except such property as I may own in Emmet County, Michigan. Such property as I may own at the time of my death in Emmet County, Michigan, I give and bequeath as life tenants to my issue, with right of survivorship, and with the remainder to my grandchildren, if any, by right of representation. In the event that my issue leave no surviving issue, then I give and devise my said realty in Emmet County, Michigan, to the State of Michigan, to be maintained and managed by the State Department of Conservation as a nature preserve and memorial to my wife, ANNA JOHNSON BECKER, whose name it shall bear.

"I think Joe created a will that was a last chance for Vicky to come clean about her relationship with Dad. Joe secretly left it up to Vicky to tell Dad that she was really his mother. All she had to do was give up her secret, and Dad could have had all of the land that he loved so much. But Vicky let both Joe and

Dad down. She kept her secret to herself. Dad died without ever knowing who he really was. And the land has almost been snatched away from the last of the Becker family."

"It won't be snatched away now, Nick," Libby says. "I can't believe any court in the land would let the property be taken from you and your family once they know what you have discovered. You did it."

"I don't know if I've done much of anything yet, but I feel like these past seven months are actually starting to make sense now."

"How so?"

"Ever since I had that blowout with Cushman and found out the state was going to take the land, I've kind of been wondering what I'm supposed to be doing here Up North. I mean it's incredibly beautiful here. I mean just look out there at that sunset. But coming here hasn't exactly done much for my career, and until you came along, I haven't really had too many close friends to help me see things through. I tried to sort out all of these legal problems, and they only spiraled down to complete disaster," I tell her, with the last rays of sun slipping down into the lake with an almost-audible 'hiss.'

"But now I think I get it. If I hadn't come to live at The Shack, I may have gotten some great newspaper job somewhere else, but I don't think I ever would have had the time and inspiration to really dig through those old boxes from Tucson. If I hadn't come here and started asking questions, I may never have learned the truth about my father, Joe, Anna, and Vicky."

"So what are you going to do now, Nick?"

"Tomorrow there will still be a lot of work to do — a new lawyer to hire, some more evidence to gather to build a strong case, and I've got a few ideas about the *Anna Johnson Becker Memorial Nature Preserve* that I would like to run by the appropriate people. And then there is a missing Grandpa X to track down. Tonight, however, all I want to do is spend as much time with you as I can before we get to tomorrow. How does that sound, Libby?"

Libby doesn't answer me with words. She slips her hand into mine and gently guides me to my feet and down to the water. The sky above the lake is even more spectacular than last night's fireworks. A five-fingered cloud of streaked pink and orange reaches out to the mainland from the shipping channel between Wagoshance Point and Beaver Island. Libby sheds her sweatshirt and runs out ahead of me into the crisp, clear waters of Sturgeon Bay. I strip down to my boxer shorts trying to catch up to her. It takes us both a few minutes of huddled wading before we dive in, but soon we are both up to our necks — losing ourselves in the luxurious coolness of Lake Michigan and finding ourselves at home at last.

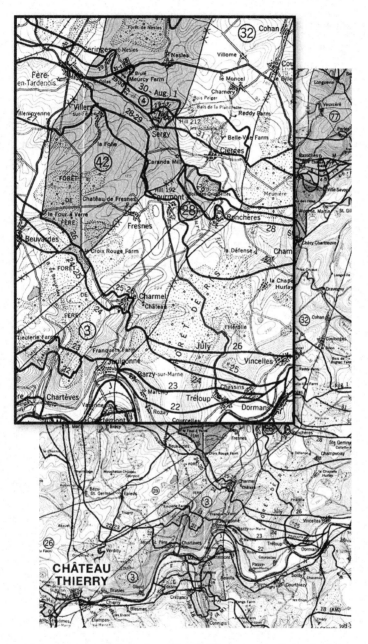

Map courtesy of American Battle Monuments Commission

~ PART 13 ~
CHÂTEAU-THIERRY SECTOR

Chapter 45

JOE FINGERED THE breast pocket of his wool uniform as the 32nd Division convoy bounced over the temporary pontoon bridge that led across the Marne River and into the center of Château-Thierry — an ancient, stone-walled, castle-hearted city just 56 miles northeast of Paris. His pocket carried orders to report stateside to Camp Pendleton, California, in six weeks.

The sun was setting on this hot July 27 Saturday in France as the convoy pulled to a stop. The allied artillery batteries on the outskirts of the city were so close now that he could see individual burst of fire in the darkening sky and feel the concussive thumps and booms in his chest. Joe was trying to picture what Anna and Vicky were doing right now back in Michigan, but the big guns drove such thoughts out of his head. For Joe, every week, day, hour, or minute that passed in France became one less week, day, hour, or minute that he would have to spend with his girls before reporting for duty again.

Joe's surprising battlefield promotion to captain by General Pershing was quickly followed by an even bigger surprise — Joe was being reassigned to command a US Army school for bayonet instruction back home. Joe was no longer an official member of the Michigan National Guard. He was regular army now, and the US Army desperately needed experienced officers back home to train the massive wave of green recruits destined for France. Joe was one of 12 top-rated officers from the 126th Regiment selected for training assignments after Pershing's inspection tour.

On July 18, just before leaving Alsace-Lorraine and getting buried in paperwork and errands at regimental headquarters, Joe introduced his men to their new CO, a lanky South Dakotan named Capt. Frank McGee. McGee had just returned from two months of training for shock-troop assaults, and it was clear that the men of the 32nd Division were about to leave the Quiet Sector for the heavy fighting in northeastern France. Sergeants Pomeroy, Miller, and Schwartz presented Joe with a lion's-head sword that they took off a dead Bosche officer who had led an unsuccessful prisoner-snatch raid earlier that week.

Before heading back home, Joe was on assignment for a few weeks helping regimental HQ prepare for the big move from Alsace to the Château-Thierry sector. Joe's temporary job, however, gave him one big advantage over being a trench commander — he had clearance and access to maps, plans, and orders that gave him a better view of the "big picture."

A few days before Joe bid farewell to the men of E Company, the German High Command had thrown 23 divisions against the French 4th Army just east of Reims. At about the same time, another 17 German divisions attacked the French 6th Army to the west of Reims. The two-fisted punch directly to the face of the French and American troops along the Reims front pushed the allies back on their heels. While the Germans made only small gains to the east of Reims, they overwhelmed the French Sixth Army, pushing the allies back nearly 50 miles in a semi-circle bulge from the original springtime battle line north of the Aisne River. The Germans advanced to within 50 miles of Paris and established a bridgehead across the Marne River. French, American, and Moroccan troops had quickly counter-attacked and stalled the advance on July 17. The allies were already taking back territory when Joe and the 32nd arrived in trucks with Chinese drivers. Enough time, however, had passed to allow the Germans to dig in throughout the sparsely populated countryside to the northeast of Château-Thierry. No one knew how long it would take to push the Germans out of their new salient of resistance. The ensuing counter-attack would come to be known as The Second Battle of the Marne.

Joe thanked the Chinese driver and grabbed his gear. Château-Thierry looked like a massive earthquake had hit it. Across the street to the west, an entire stone apartment block was in ruin with only two walls and a few chimneystacks still standing. To the east, the three-story building that was posted with a sign for the "Billeting Officer" was scarred and blackened in spots, but looked like it might not come tumbling down the moment he stepped inside.

"Glad you could join us, coach," came a familiar voice from across an ornate desk neatly piled with papers and maps in a foyer that was tiled in black and white marble. It was Joe's old battalion commander and the head coach of the regimental football team — Captain (now Major) Al Wilson. Wilson's wire-rimmed glasses were starting to fog up from the sweat pouring off his thinning hair. Even with the sun going down, it was still hot.

"Good to see you, Al... I mean, Major," Joe said with a quick salute. "It looks like you're preparing for a big game," Joe said pointing to the piles of paperwork spread out between them. "What have you been doing with yourself this past month? I haven't seen you since back in Angeot?"

"With this gimpy leg, the army thought I would be more useful organizing convoys, buckets, and billets than trying to stay ahead of a bunch of 18 year-olds in the field. I got booted up a rank and reassigned to the Service of Supply," Wilson said.

"I miss working with our Michigan boys, but I still run into a few of the Ann Arbor fellas every once in a while."

"Most of them are still around. I ran into Buck Markey the other day, and he's still carrying that game ball around in his pack. That kid could easily be playing for the Wolverines right now instead of this..."

"Hey Joe, I just remembered!" Wilson said. "Col. Westnedge's aide told me to send you right up to see the colonel as soon as you reached us. Go to the big building at the end of the street and down into the basement to get to regimental HQ. Just stay on the packed cobblestones out in the streets. The ordinance guys are still finding mines and booby traps all over the place. And here's your billet — it's a square house on Place Carnot. Just follow the map I've included."

Joe didn't want to keep the commander of the 126th Infantry Regiment waiting for long, so he grabbed a couple of rations and headed up a slight incline to the Château-Thierry city hall at the end of the street. Doughboys with picks and shovels were busy filling holes and stacking salvageable bricks and stones into piles on the sidewalks. A couple of sentries and clerks later, Joe found himself standing at attention before his regimental C.O., Col. Joseph B. Westnedge. With broad shoulders and an upright bearing, Westnedge was an outstanding commander known for his unflagging energy and selflessness. He served in the Michigan National Guard during the Spanish-American war in 1898, as a lieutenant-colonel helping to quell the 1911 Jackson prison riot, and as the commander of the 126th since the Pancho Villa affair in 1916.

It didn't surprise Joe that Westnedge picked the most uncomfortable accommodations in the city hall for his command post. In the field, Westnedge spurned the privileges of rank to match the conditions and surroundings that his men had to deal with — even though he usually got less sleep and less chow than the typical private in his regiment. "Colonel Joe," as his men knew him, had a quiet, respectful way of dealing with subordinates and peers alike that Capt. Becker wished he could better emulate when his own "Smokey Joe" side came out.

"Capt. Becker to see you, sir," an orderly announced, as "Colonel Joe" stood over a large map that read "Aisne Department." Westnedge continued to stare at the map for a few moments before looking up.

"At ease. Good to see you again Becker," Westnedge said returning Joe's salute. "How was the drive up from Paris, captain?"

"A bit bumpy, sir. We managed to keep the front of the convoy moving pretty well, but with the traffic heading to and from the front, our men and gear are spread out over 30 kilometers, at least. The last of the men should be here by 2000 hours, but our supply train and the chow wagons are so far behind that I didn't even see them at all today."

"I'll send word to keep an eye out for the end of the supply train and hurry them along," Westnedge said. "The men will want hot meals to get them through the work we have ahead of us. Take this down to the Signal Office on the third floor, corporal" Westnedge said as he quickly wrote up the dispatch and handed it to his orderly.

"Will that be all, sir?" Joe asked.

"There is one more thing, Capt. Becker," the colonel said carefully sorting through another pile of papers on his desk. "Ah, yes, here it is," pulling out Joe's service records. "How's your French coming along?"

"Just serviceable, sir. I can read it pretty well now, and Sgt. Deufmont back in Alsace told me I was starting to sound like a Norman native — a 7-year-old native, that is," Joe said with a smile.

"Well, according to your service record, you have a real gift for language — German, Spanish, and now French. I know that you have orders to get back home, and I wouldn't fault any man who turned down the job I'm about to offer you ... under the circumstances."

"What job is that, Colonel?"

"I need someone with good eyes, a clear head in combat, and "serviceable" language skills to help me keep on top of this offensive, Capt. Becker. As you know, we've been assigned to the 6th French Army. Marshal Foch wants to avoid any chance of language foul-ups in any sector where French and American troops are fighting near each other. We even have a division of French Moroccans on our left flank who mostly speak Arabic. I don't know what he's going to do about them, but he's ordered that all American liaison and scout officers down to the regimental level buddy up with a French officer throughout the duration of the attack. If you accept this assignment, I'll only need you for a week at the most. That should still give you enough time to catch a transport home, take some leave with your family, and reach Camp Pendleton. I've got five of my staff officers returning straight from language school next week, and one of them will relieve you as soon as they check in. In the meantime, I need an officer who can serve as scout and courier for me, and as a liaison with our French friends. I need someone with combat experience who speaks the language and can ride a fast horse. I need someone like you, Capt. Becker. But let me be perfectly clear — I'm asking for a volunteer. I'm not ordering you. The choice is yours, and I've got your transit orders back to the States right here. Only the dates are left blank."

Joe expected that there would be "one more thing" before he could go home. He felt a small lump of frustration in his chest as the Colonel was describing the job offer — "I don't mind going where they tell me, but I wish they would make up their minds," Joe thought to himself. By the time the colonel got to the part about "a fast horse," though, Joe had already quieted those thoughts and had his answer.

"I would be happy to help you out, Colonel," Joe said, "as long as you can get me off the line in time to catch a boat and report for duty in California. I wouldn't want to be late for my first assignment for the U.S. Army, sir."

"You have my word on it," Colonel Westnedge said, shaking Joe's hand.

"That's good as gold for me, sir," Joe replied.

Before the hot night was over, Joe had a horse under him, a French captain named Broussard beside him, and two mounted riflemen-runners behind him as he headed east of the city limits following the main road along the Marne. Behind him, the French and American artillery batteries flashed like heat lightening. Further upriver, the valley turned to the northeast, and Joe's courier detail stopped to watch the fireworks ahead of them. Columns of fire and the light from bursting shells rose above the tree line far off in the distance. Sitting atop a chestnut mare named Sarrasin, Joe felt — for just a moment — a sense of quiet settle in around him amongst the potato fields and farmhouses of the Marne Valley. Then, he gave Sarrasin a light squeeze, and the small scouting party was off to link up with the U.S. 3rd Division somewhere in those exploding woods before him.

Chapter 46

PRE-DAWN JULY 29TH found Joe and his scouting party more than a dozen trips into their back-and-forth assignment of reporting to Col. Westnedge, carrying orders to company commanders, and gathering intelligence from other units. The allies had managed to push the Germans back about 15 kilometers, but the Bosche had heavily reinforced their fallback position along the small stream known as the Ourcq River. The river's steep banks were less than 20 feet across, but they made a natural barrier that the Germans fortified with a host of artillery pieces and machine guns on the hilltops to the north of the river. The 32nd Division, including Joe's 126th Regiment was moving into position to take over the front lines. Joe still didn't know exactly where and when that would happen, but the 32nd Division's turn to take a crack at the Germans was inevitable.

Now, if Joe could just find the 126th Regiment in the dark forest. Foret de Fere was just a dark spot on the French maps between two tiny villages: Beuvardes to the west and Fresnes-en-Tardenois to the east. It had been more than a week since the boys from the 42nd Division had driven the Germans out, and the woods were filled with the unmistakable odor of human corpses, which only seemed to grow stronger as Joe, Capt. Broussard, and Privates O'Neill and Perkins walked their horses, groping their way with their feet, along a logging road that seemed to be heading in the right direction. Broussard, a veteran company commander with a bushy, black beard was proving to be an invaluable partner. His company spent a

year fighting the Germans in the Château-Thierry sector, and
he knew the terrain as well as Joe knew the old Rock River of
his boyhood. Broussard also had a wry sense of humor that Joe
was starting to appreciate.

"In this darkness, the Bosche wouldn't even have to move
to kill us," Broussard whispered stumbling over a tree root.
"They could just stand in place and wait for us to trip into
their bayonets."

The battalion was supposed to rendezvous with an artillery
unit that was already working the Germans lines ahead. The
brilliant flashes and two-note ka-boom from the 75mm guns
left no question as to the whereabouts of the American battery
up ahead in the forest.

"What the hell is that?" Private Perkins whispered through
his teeth. "There's somethin' up here on the road. "Aauugh, and
it smells real dead."

"Hold Up," Joe said as he felt something soft with the toe of
his cavalry boot. "Private O'Neill, go ahead and turn on your
flashlight, but just for a few seconds."

O'Neill flipped the switch to the little light that looked like
a whiskey flask. A faint beam flickered to life revealing a wide
spot on the forest track littered with dead Germans — dozens of them. Beyond the nearest pile of bodies, Joe could see
orderly rows of dead lined up on either side of the road in the
gloom. Sarrasin stomped the ground, stirring up a cloud of
flies that sounded like a nest of hornets in the dark.

"Sacre bleu," was all that Capt. Broussard could get out
before covering his nose and mouth with a sweaty rag he kept
tied around his neck. In four years of war, Broussard had seen
more than his share of death, but he did not like coming upon
death without warning. Without preparation, the eye is often
drawn to the most grisly sights.

"Let's go around," Joe said. "It looks like Graves Registration is taking care of this. Go ahead and leave that light on until we get around them."

Perkins took point as O'Neill lit the way through the underbrush from behind. Joe swept his right arm in front of him to guard himself and Sarrasin from getting sticks in the face. As Perkins angled back towards the logging road beyond the wooded morgue, he suddenly froze.

"Halt, you Heine bastard!" he cried into the gray forest. Perkins snapped his Springfield up to his shoulder. Joe took two steps beside him with Colt in hand and saw a German sitting on a log with a book open in his lap as though reading — just five feet from the end of Perkins rifle barrel. "Hands up or I'll shoot," Perkins said flatly.

The German didn't move.

"What the hell?" Perkins whispered as he eased his finger off the trigger.

"It's all right, private, this one's dead, too."

From Joe's angle, it was clear that this soldier was no longer a threat. As Perkins moved around the log to face the German, he could see that the German's head had been split nearly in half by shrapnel. One side hung over the book, but the other half had fallen over onto his left shoulder with brain, jaw, and skull clearly visible in the electric glow of O'Neill's flashlight.

"Poor schmuck never saw it coming," O'Neill said. "That's the most god-awful thing I've ever seen. Let's get the hell out of here."

"Just a second," Joe said, handing his reins to O'Neill. There was a Bosche coat on the log beside its dead owner, and Joe pulled the book out of the German's hands before covering the body with the coat.

"Let's keep moving," Joe ordered, as he slipped a blood-splattered copy of *Effie Briest* into his satchel.

Joe and his scouts reached a crossroads near the artillery battery as the last of the 126th marched past the guns and farther up into the woods to get out of direct ear-shot of the six 75s that were lined up in a clearing and pounding away at the German lines — some three-and-a-half miles away. A sign pointed west towards Beuvardes, and Joe sent O'Neill and Perkins with the horses back down the road to a temporary pen set up to care for the artillery unit's mules. Sarrasin and the other three French horses were proving to be strong and steady, even under fire, but Joe was mindful to give them a rest whenever possible.

Joe and Broussard followed the tail end of the column of doughboys a few hundred yards in front of the battery, and were surprised to find the men setting down packs and spreading out bedrolls in the thick underbrush so close to the artillery battery.

"This is not right," Broussard, said. "They are too close to the battery."

"I agree," Joe said. "Let's see if we can find Capt. McGee or Sgt. Pomeroy from E Company and get these men moved farther away and into some cover. I don't see any foxholes or dugouts…"

Just then, three cracks from a rifle behind them cut through the night air that was heavily laced with the acrid smoke coming off the 75 mm guns. This was the signal for a gas alarm, and the cry of "Gas Attack" and the clacking the wooden gas alarm rattles rose throughout the woods. Joe held his breath as he pulled his gas mask out from the bag he kept at his side at all times and slipped it over his head, using his thumbs to check for a tight seal around his face. They listened for the telltale hiss of gas shells nearby, but the only shell sounds where coming from the 75 mm rounds flying over their heads towards the German lines. It was another false alarm, and the all-clear signal followed moments later.

"Who fired those shots?" came Sgt. Pomeroy's familiar bark from the darkness nearby. "That's the fifth false alarm we've had in the past two hours. Use your heads, lads. That's just the smell of the powder from own guns. We're probably miles away from the Germans, and the wind's at our backs. If we don't have shells coming down on us and the wind is blowing into the German lines, then we don't have gas," he yelled. "But good work heeding the alarm anyway," he said more softly. "You only have to be wrong about gas just once to end up dead or dying. And just a snort of that chlorine in your lungs or that mustard on your skin will make you wish you were dead."

"Sgt. Pomeroy, glad to hear that you're in good voice tonight," Joe said. "Lungs like yours are a first sergeant's best weapons."

"S'at you, Captain Becker? Even if I could see my own hand in this inky night, I wouldn't recognize you without that new horse of yours. You didn't lose him did you, sir?"

"We left the horses to the rear. I've got to round up the company commanders for a briefing tomorrow morning, Bill," Joe said. "Any idea where we can find Capt. McGee and the rest of the other officers?"

"They're all huddled up together trying to get a battalion C.P. set up," Sgt. Pomeroy said, taking Joe's wrist and pointing Joe's arm in the dark. "Up this way."

Another flashing round of artillery from the 75s lit up the trees around them and the back of Pomeroy's close-shaved head. The sudden light on wide-open pupils etched every detail of the night into crisp portraits... the glare off the glass lenses of a soldier's gas mask as he pulled it over his head, clusters of acorns hanging down from the branches, the white pulp of splintered tree trunks from earlier fighting in the Foret de Fere, and streams of sweat cascading down Pomeroy's neck.

"Did you think about moving the men farther away from the battery, Bill?" Joe asked as they stumbled through the underbrush trying not to step on sleeping soldiers.

"Yessir. Capt. McGee and I were just thinking the same thing. We've got some scouts looking for a better spot in the north end of the forest. You remember what happened the last time we camped near the big guns in Hauptwiller, right Captain?"

"Sure do. How long have those 75s been firing from that position?" Joe asked. "I'm surprised the Bosche aren't shooting back yet."

"It's been pretty quiet so far," Pomeroy said. "I just hope we..."

A new noise snatched the attention of everyone in the encampment. A different sort of shell scream cut through the clatter. This one was clearly inbound and it was immediately followed by the piercing cry of more shells that sounded like the Devil's own choir.

"*Incoming!* Find the dirt! Find some cover!"

The first shell hit the ground just 25 yards in front of Sgt. Pomeroy who was already on his belly squirming to find any sort of depression on the flat forest floor. Half a second later, three more shells blasted the dark away sending a wave of flame, smoke, shell fragments, and wooden splinters flying through the air. Each new shell that smashed into the woods came closer and closer to where Joe was lying. Sergeants screamed for the men to "get down" and "find some cover," but there were no foxholes or trenches to be found anywhere. It was a rolling barrage, which Joe had seen from afar but never up this close. As the line of bursting shells moved behind him, Joe tried to get to his knees to see if Pomeroy and Broussard where alright, but another wave of explosions was on him before he could move, and he was thrown on his back.

"Stay down, Capt. Becker," Broussard yelled, grabbing a hold of Joe's shoulder. "There is nothing you can do until it's over, except get your limbs tore off. Just lie still."

Joe moved his helmet to protect his face, but he could still see a slit of fire and terror beneath the metal brim. The shell that knocked him on his backside felt worse than that 250-lb. linebacker that caused Joe no end of trouble back in his high school football days. He looked at his watch and began counting how many shells were falling per minute to get some idea what they were up against.

"One... Two... Three... Four..."

Even lying on the ground, Joe could feel both the earth-shaking rumble of nearby blasts and the rolling shock waves through the air from the exploding shells. The close ones felt like they sucked the air right out of his lungs, and his ears were already ringing beneath a muffled sound fog that did not dissipate between explosions. Without even moving, Joe's gut felt alternately stretched and squashed like the bellows of his father's forge back in Wisconsin. He closed his eyes against the waves of heat from the closest bursts, and tried to wiggle his body as deep into the forest floor duff as he could, but getting up was suicide. There was no way to help anyone else and nowhere to hide. Shrapnel, dirt, and wood fragments from exploding trees flew inches from his face. All around him, men screamed — some for stretchers, some for their mothers, some cursed the German gunners, and some for God's help. Only a few medics managed to answer the call, but they were soon mowed down by the horrific pounding that fell upon the men of the 126th that early morning in the Foret de Fere.

"Forty-six... forty-seven... forty-eight... forty-nine." Joe reached "fifty" as the glowing second hand of his watch reached the one-minute mark. Joe figured that at least a dozen German guns were pouring their blind hatred into the forest. The repeating waves of rolling shellfire meant that the Germans weren't exactly sure where that American artillery battery was located, but they certainly managed to find some American infantry. It was only a few hours till dawn, but it was going to be a long night anyhow.

Chapter 47

THE SHELLING IN the wee hours of July 29th in the Foret de Fere took the lives of four men of the 126th and took 15 others out of action — some for the rest of the war. Joe, Pomeroy, and Broussard managed to crawl up to the regimental command post in the dark during lulls in the barrage. They delivered orders for all company commanders to gather the following morning for a briefing in Le Charmel. Joe returned to Col. Westnedge with news that the 126th had moved back two kilometers from the artillery batteries (there were a dozen French and US units scattered throughout the forest) to prevent any further unnecessary casualties.

The next day, the division staff and regimental officers (along with Joe and Broussard) met with the French 6th Army staff and reconnoitered the battlefield. By late morning, the 32nd Division took over an eight-kilometer-wide stretch of the front lines from the US 3rd Division.

Although Gen. Haan, the commander of the 32nd, launched an immediate attack on the German positions that had slowed down the men of the 3rd Division, the 32nd had no more luck in digging the Germans out of their hilltop fortifications overlooking the Ourcq River. There was a particularly stubborn line of resistance in the stands of timber along the Ourcq River high ground: Jomblets, Planchette, and Pelger Woods were particularly thorny. The Second Battle of the Marne was no longer a trench-line stalemate like Alsace-Lorraine to the southwest or Flanders to the north. It didn't take a lot of digging, though, to create an impenetrable wall of machine gun bullets and artillery shells that was keeping the Americans at bay in the wide-open country along the Ourcq.

Haan's division tried to punch holes in the German lines along the high ground north of Cierges and east of Sergy, but the results were disappointing at best and deadly at worst. Too many doughboys were getting caught out in open fields under heavy German shelling — with only shell holes for protection against ferocious strafing from well-protected machine gun positions. It was "like throwing snowflakes into the mouth of a blast furnace," one weary lieutenant told Joe as he set off for another frontal assault because of the orders Joe delivered.

But there were signs that the German lines were wearing thin. On July 31st, the day after taking over the front lines, Sgt. Pomeroy led his company into the small village of Fresnes-en-Tardenois northeast of the Foret de Fere and captured an entire squad of Germans who overslept in a barn full of soft feathers. Later, Sgt. Schloss and his men took a brief snooze in the barn, but were soon wakened by an infestation of lice that riddled the feather pile. Pomeroy and Schloss figured the Bosche must have been beyond exhaustion to sleep for long in that lousy pile of feathers.

Even the German aces, which had held almost complete control of the air above the battlefield, seemed to thin out. As E Company took position to the east of Fresnes, a German plane fell to the ground in flames not fifty yards in front of them. The pilot's head appeared briefly above the burning cockpit, trying to escape the wreck. A private asked Pomeroy if he should take a shot and put the guy out of his misery.

"Save your bullet, kid. You'll regret it when you're down to your last few rounds," Pomeroy said. "And the Heine son of a bitch deserves all the misery he can get."

German pilots were adept at dropping hand-held bombs from their cockpits as they flew over allied lines, and were rather unpopular with allied foot soldiers as a result. The dying German pilot slipped back down into his cockpit just seconds before the flames got into his remaining bombs. Pilot and plane were instantly blasted into smoking fragments.

———

Joe spent the rest of July 31st and the ensuing night running dispatches and orders between Col. Westnedge's command post in a Sergy farmhouse and an observation post on the south side of the Ourcq River valley where a telephone connection was set up with Division HQ. Col. Westnedge had personally taken charge of untangling a mess of telephone wires in Sergy and establishing the missing telephone connection between Sergy and Cierges, but it would take hours before they were all hooked up. Joe was in the Cierges observation post around 1:45 AM when word came from Division that the attack orders he had just delivered to the 1st and 3rd battalions of the 126th Regiment had been changed — instead of both battalions attacking at 3:30 AM, 1st Battalion was to proceed as ordered, but 3rd Battalion was to wait until 4:30 AM to avoid getting hit by the artillery barrage that was about to rain down on the Germans in Jomblets Woods.

The road between the two villages was ranged in by German artillery, but "the Four Horsemen of the Dry Lips" as Joe and his thirsty crew were now calling themselves flew across the exposed sections of the gravel road at full gallop, hoping there was enough light to spot any gaping shell holes in the roadbed. Even in the dark, they managed to draw the attention of an enemy spotter, but the brief spasm of shells was too little, too late, and the Horsemen reached Sergy in record time.

Message delivered, Joe stood by in case Regiment needed to get another message through to Division. A small cluster of officers and aides peered through binoculars from a high earthen berm at the edge of Sergy. In the dark, Joe could pick out the familiar voices of Col. Westnedge and Major Wilson, and a few other Regimental regulars, but there was also a contingent of French officers in their midst. In silence, they watched an awesome display of American and French artillery pound the German-held Jomblets Woods for an hour. With fires still burning in the woods from the shells, Joe watched the men of 3rd Battalion leave Sergy spread out in battle formation with gas masks on — disappearing into the smoky night heading east over open fields towards the shattered and smoldering woods a kilometer away. Then, he saw the staccato flashes of first one, then three, then ten or more German machine guns open up on the attacking US soldiers in the dark. Somewhere to the northeast of the woods, Joe could see bigger flashes of light from the German battery, followed by exploding shells in amongst the attacking doughboys. Joe watched helplessly with nothing to do.

"They cannot stop there in the open," a French officer said to Westnedge. "They will be cut to pieces."

Even in the dark, Joe picked up on the officer's commanding tone. Capt. Broussard filled Joe in. It was General de Mondesir, the commanding officer of 38th Corp, the immediate superior officer to Gen. Haan the American commander of the 32nd Division. Gen. de Mondesir had a reputation as a fiery leader who knew how to pick a fight with the Germans.

Joe peered through binoculars at the contrasting gloom and bright flashes out in the field. Joe saw silhouettes of men in the distance cut down by machine gun fire, bodies flung 10 feet into the air from exploding shells, and lines of Germans rushing out to meet their enemies, but for every silhouette of dead and dying Americans, Joe saw a dozen more men rising up from their shell-hole cover and running towards the woods — wave after wave of US skirmishers.

"The German shelling is not having its intended affect, Colonel Westnedge, oui?" de Mondesir said. "It's driving your Americans out of the field and into the woods. Look at them go! They're obliterating the Germans and starting to reach the tree line. *Oui, Oui, Les soldats terrible, tres bien, tres bien!*"

General Mondesir's smile and accolades for the American fighters spread through the group of French officers. "*Les Terribles,*" they cried, and a nickname for the 32nd Division was born.

Over an hour into the battle for Hill 212 (as this modest bit of terrain was called), there were telltale flashes and rumblings from the southeast side of Jomblets Woods. 1st Battalion was knocking on the German's side door while 3rd Battalion seemed to have kicked in the front door. The battle raged on for hours as German machine guns slowly fell silent or turned against their previous owners. Joe kept tabs on the battle's progress as Westnedge sent him back and forth to 2nd Battalion in the rear and the observation post in Cierges to relay status reports.

By the first light of sunrise on Aug. 1, however, there was no sign of life left on the edges of Jomblets Woods. There was sporadic firing from deep within the wood and the deep booming of long-range German guns somewhere off in the distance, but it had been over an hour since de Mondesir had heard anything concrete from the front line, and he was growing irritable at the lack of information. Even the stream of stretcher-bearers slowed to a drip. Had both sides simply wiped each other out and there were only a thousand corpses holding a two-kilometer-wide gap in the front lines? Was the relative quiet of

Jomblets a sign that German reinforcements had slaughtered the men of the 1st and 3rd Battalion and were secretly waiting to ambush the 2nd Battalion that was about to clear the woods? Or had "*Les Terribles*" wiped out the main body of Germans and were now in hot pursuit of fleeing rear-guard troops?

Gen. de Mondesir needed answers. He looked around and saw Broussard.

"Captain, I need you to find out what has become of the attack on Jomblets," de Mondesir commanded. "Take your American liaison into the forest, find out what has become of the 1st and 3rd Battalion, and report right back here immediately. Speed is of the essence. I need to know whether I am sending 2nd Battalion into a cleanup operation or an ambush, so be careful. You are no good to me dead."

So far, Joe's war had been a fairly distant affair, never getting close enough to a living enemy to see into his eyes. It was about to get a lot more personal.

The Four Horsemen of the Dry Lips mounted up and flew across the bomb-cratered wheat field to the southwest of Jomblets. Stretcher-bearers had carried off the wounded, but the field was still littered with the bodies of US and German soldiers. A decapitated doughboy lay chest down in a shell hole, still wearing his loaded rucksack. Sarrasin was weaving between the big shell holes and leaping across some of the smaller ones, giving Joe the ride of his life. He glanced over at Capt. Broussard who was grinning like the Wild Man of Borneo beneath his flowing, black whiskers.

The captains left Perkins and O'Neill with the horses at the edge of the forest. Just a few yards into the woods, however, they encountered even more dead as sunrise began to filter in from their right.

"I see many more Bosche dead then Yanks," Broussard said. "But be careful, these Germans can be deceitful."

Just then, Joe heard voices coming from deeper within the wood. Joe and Broussard crept towards the talking, until they were certain it was English.

"... the hell knows, Brooks? Wasn't this machine gun pointed the other way when we went through here earlier?" a bloodied American sergeant asked a scrawny corporal as they stood over the bodies of two Germans with coats thrown over their faces. The doughboys kept their rifles pointed at the bodies in the foxhole.

"I don't know Sgt. Bailey. I keep getting turned around in these damn woods. It's not like being back home in Cheboygan," the corporal said. "Every tree and bush looks the same to me. And everywhere I look, it seems like I see the field we came in through."

"I say we put a couple of bullets in them just to make sure. A dead Hun can do no harm, and if I hear another one of these Bosche sons of bitches keep firing away at me until they run out of ammo, and then throw up their hands and cry 'Kamerad,' I'm going put a bullet in his head, too."

Joe cleared his throat before stepping out from behind a tree. "American and French officers coming out in the open. Hold your fire! What seems to be the problem here, sergeant."

"No problem, sir. I was just thinking something didn't look right here. The corporal and I were sent back to work this ground over again to make sure there aren't any Germans playing possum or trying to sneak up behind us from the rear. We've cleared out a couple of holdouts, but this tipped over machine gun looked wrong to me."

Joe used hand signals to keep the discussion going while ordering the doughboys to move out of the area: "I wouldn't worry about these two, sergeant. Take us up towards the line."

Joe and Broussard kept their feet planted as they silently drew their side arms while the two American soldiers moved away. A few seconds later, the German "bodies" threw the coats off their heads and reached for the machine gun.

"Hände hoch!" Joe shouted. "Ergeben Sie sich!"

The Germans neither put their hands up nor surrendered, but tried to turn the machine gun on the two captains who emptied their pistols into the heads and torsos of the surprised ambushers. The Germans' screams and groans echoed through the woods and raised the hairs on the back of Joe's neck.

"This 'playing possum' does not seem like a very fun game for the possum," Broussard said. "But you have to admire their nerve remaining still while we discussed whether to kill them or not."

The two doughboys returned to the machine gun nest. "I guess the surprise was on them," Corporal Brooks said. "What do you want to do with the gun, Captain? It'll take all four of us to haul it through the woods on that drag sled over there."

"Spike the gun," Joe said. "We need to move on, but first tell us the situation up front."

Sgt. Bailey said he was with I Company, and had spent about an hour clearing this section of the woods. When he left the front line, the 1st and 3rd Battalions had linked up and were trying to fight their way across 200 yards of open field between Joblets and Planchette Woods.

"The Germans have an observation balloon up behind them and planes all over us spotting for their artillery." Bailey reported. "There is a battery on the road leading out of the Planchette, and if you so much as stick your pinky out from your cover, the shells come raining down."

"Do you know what's happening now?" Joe said. "It seems awfully quiet up there." There was shelling and rifle fire in the distance, but it did not sound close enough to be in the Jomblets.

"No, sir. Just following orders to clear these woods. The place is still crawling with Boshe. A couple of my guys are taking 23 prisoners that we managed to round up back to the rear. Most of the prisoners were pretty shot up or gassed by their own shells, but you should have seen the burley bruiser that Corp. Brooks here got into a scrap with."

Brooks smiled and shook his head before looking down at his toes. "Size don't have nothin' to do with it, didn't I tell ya, Sarge?"

Bailey continued: "They both come around a big tree so fast they nearly ran into each other. I heard two shots ring out from their rifles and ran to help, but they were into a bayonet battle by the time I reached 'em, and flinging around so fast that I couldn't get a clear shot at the German who was grinning like a big old tomcat that had cornered a mouse. But every time that German tried to get in a good thrust with his bayonet, Brooks here would parry, dance around him and get in a couple good licks. Brooks slashed the big guy's knuckles, found an opening, and drove that bayonet into that Bosche up to his gun sights. The German wasn't smiling anymore, and then Brooks yanked the bayonet out so hard that Brooks somersaulted backwards twice. The Bosche never got up again."

"Good work, corporal," Joe said. "I'll let Col. Westnedge know personally... Brooks, I Company, right?"

"Thank you, captain."

Joe and Broussard left the two men to their work, and heard the abrupt thumps of grenades destroying the heavy machine gun. It was easy to find the front by following the trail of bodies and devastation that littered the forest floor. Soon, they could see the north edge of the forest, which was studded with foxholes and shallow trenches with tree-limb covers. The American line here was only a half dozen men deep, but stretched to the right and left as far as Joe could see in the dim woods. The American soldiers lay quietly peering across the open fields before them as sunrise lit the stubble of recently harvested wheat and hay. There was a battle raging across the open field in the Planchette Woods. Within minutes, Joe and Broussard located one of the few remaining officers — Second Lieutenant Keller, who had suddenly found himself in command of the Jomblets line.

"General de Mondesir sends his compliments on your excellent attack," Broussard said. "He wishes to know how the attack is progressing in order to deploy your support."

"We're holding up here pretty well, but we've taken 153 casualties this morning," Keller said. "Fifty-two killed and 101 wounded. Capt. Campbell attacked the Planchette about 45 minutes ago with most of Company M, but they just ran into some heavy resistance. My orders are to hold this fallback position in case things get too hot in the Planchette."

As Joe and Broussard gathered more intel, the shelling in the Planchette increased. Trees shattered and shouts from Company M could be heard across the field. A few minutes into the shelling, Joe could see a steady wall of smoke and flame advancing from the middle of Planchette Woods southward towards Jomblets. In a few more minutes, a line of doughboys ran for their lives out of the Planchette Woods with officers and sergeants screaming "Fall Back!" Then, more German guns opened up on the field between the two woods cutting down many of the fleeing doughboys.

"They're coming, boys!" Get ready to hold this position," a sweat-soaked captain yelled as he dove into 2nd Lt. Keller's foxhole. "They're counter-attacking in force, Art. Ready the men."

After hasty introductions and a quick update, Joe and Broussard prepared to return to the rear to deliver the news as the last of Company M raced back to the Jomblets Woods.

"We'll see to it that 2nd Battalion moves up on the double," Joe said.

"You better grab some rifles on your way, you might have to fight your way out of here. Look over there... and there! The Huns are already trying to get around our flanks to surround us."

Joe could see from this northern-most elbow of Jomblets Woods that columns of German soldiers were running out of Planchette Woods to the west and east of Capt. Campbell's fallback position. Lines of skirmishers were also starting to advance straight out of Planchette. The Americans opened up with everything they had — rifles, French Chauchat machine guns, captured German Maxim machine guns, the few US Hotchkiss guns that hadn't already overheated, and a handful of mortars. Germans fell by the dozens, but there were so many moving so fast that they were already into the Jomblets by the time Joe and Broussard started running to the rear.

Bullets whizzed by and bark flew as the two captains raced past the spiked German machine gun and its dead crew. They could hear Germans who had managed to get around 1st Battalion's left flank moving through Jomblets to surround the Americans. As Joe saw the sunlight from the open field to the south of Jomblets, he noticed four German scouts walking just within the tree line. They were right in the way of the thick stand of brush where O'Neill and Perkins were hidden with the horses.

Joe and Broussard ducked down behind a large oak tree before the Germans could see them. "Let's wait for them to pass," Broussard said, but it was quickly apparent that the Germans had stopped to look out of the woods towards Sergy. Joe couldn't quite make out what they were saying from so far away, but he could pick up the words "machine gun" and "mortar."

The Germans were planning to cut off 1st and 3rd Battalions and prevent reinforcements from reaching the Jomblets.

Joe and Broussard knew what they had to do. They fixed bayonets and readied their rifles. "I'll take the one on the far left. You take the one of the far right. Then, move in on the two in the middle," Broussard said. Joe nodded.

"En trois," Broussard whispered. "Un… deux… trois!

Both men swung around opposite sides of the thick tree trunk, quickly aimed their rifles, and fired at the Germans who were 25 yards away. Joe's shot hit dead center of the German's neck, just below his helmet. Broussard's slug went right through his target's helmet, and both Germans instantly fell. The other two were facing away from Joe and Brossard, and dove for the ground. One managed to get off an ill-aimed shot, but the two captains were on the Germans instantly. Joe's German managed to get to his feet and braced his bayonetted rifle against his hip as Joe rushed him. Joe swatted the German's weapon out of the way with the bayonet end of his rifle and followed with a swift uppercut to the German's jaw with the rifle butt. The coldcock blow disoriented the German for an instant, but Joe was running so fast that he ended up behind the German who tried to swing around and fire his Gewehr 98 rifle at point-blank range.

Joe plunged his bayonet straight into the German's heart and (instinctively recalling the lessons he had been drilling into his own men) used his boot to push the dead Hun off the end of his rifle. By the time Joe had a chance to look up, Broussard was standing over his victim wiping his bloody bayonet off on the German's uniform.

Joe turned towards the field at the sound of hoof beats to see Perkins and O'Neill pull up with Sarasin and Broussard's roan. The captains leapt to their saddles and the Four Horsemen galloped away from the battlefield as more Germans appeared on the south edge of Jomblets Woods firing at them, but they were already too far out of range.

———————

Joe and Broussard's report made it back to Gen. de Mondesir who immediately ordered supporting units forward. But the German counter-attack quickly spread from the west side of Jomblets Woods to the outlying farms of Sergy. The 1st and 3rd Battalions were briefly surrounded by the Germans in the middle of Jomblets and fought their way through to re-establish contact with Sergy, despite being heavily outnumbered. Sergy itself took a vicious beating from German shelling and machine guns, and the 2nd Battalion was bogged down for two days before they linked back up with the remnants of 1st and 3rd Battalions, which had 83 killed and 378 wounded by the end of Aug. 1.

Col. Westnedge kept Joe and Broussard busy delivering orders to the commanders moving up into the fighting. American artillery and more reinforcements kept moving up, and while there was heavy German resistance at first, by the afternoon of Aug. 2, it was clear that the Germans were falling back to the Vesle River some 10 miles north of Cierges and Sergy.

August 3rd started with mist, but soon turned into a glorious summer day. Catching up to Col. Westnedge, who had moved up among the advanced guard to get a better look at what lay ahead, Joe came out the north edge of a forest called Chenet Woods. This was the highest ground between the Ourcq and Vesle rivers, and would have made any landscape painter's heart soar at the patchwork of fields of growing crops, gentle hills, and deep valleys spread out as far as the eye could see. The morning vista, however, was made even more memorable by the sight of dozens of columns of smoke rising in the still air from large fires set by the fleeing Bosche. The Americans were advancing so fast that the Germans were unable to take their ammunition and supplies with them. All across the country ahead, Germans were blowing up their ammunition dumps and setting fire to anything they didn't want the Americans to get their hands on.

"Good morning, Capt. Becker," Westnedge said noticing Joe at his side. "I have never seen so much beauty and so much destruction in the same view. What's the word from the rear?"

Joe passed on his report and waited for Westnedge's next order.

"I have someone I want you to meet. Captain Becker, here's your replacement, Capt. Walter Goodwin. He has something for you."

Joe shook hands and Capt. Goodwin handed him his transit orders back to the states.

"You've been a huge help to me, Joe, and you've served the 126th with honor" Westnedge said extending his hand. "But I believe that it's time for you to catch the next boat home."

————

EPILOGUE

It has been exactly four years to the day since I discovered that my Aunt Vicky was really my grandmother and that Joe and Anna were really my father's grandparents. The legal disputes surrounding the Becker farm have been put to rest, and I am sitting in Joe's favorite wicker rocker on the front porch of The Shack — if you can still call it that. Dan, a couple of his carpenter buddies, and I did a major renovation on the old place. We covered the outside in new cedar clapboards and trim, put in new windows, installed a fully functional kitchen and bathroom, and preserved as much of the original Odawa craftsmanship as we could. I think Joe, Anna, and Dad would be pleased.

The view from the front porch has also been restored. The meadow, the forested bluff line, and the lake in the distance are in full summer regalia. The afternoon winds are beginning to whip up the first whitecaps of the day out on the water, and a half-dozen sailboats and power yachts are heading in and out of Little Traverse Bay. Homer Robertson's insta-forest has been carefully removed from the side of the small hill in front of the house and replanted at the far edge of the meadow. Those white pines have filled in nicely, and they screen out a couple of huge, new houses that now crowd the southern boundary line with Four Fires Estates. There is one opening in the tree screen where the old two-track leaves the meadow and enters the woods that lead up to the neighboring development. The opening not only allows us to walk over and visit friends of ours who have recently moved into Four Fires Estates, but it gives the estaters access to the meadow, which is now part of the eighty-acre *Anna Johnson Becker Memorial Nature Preserve*.

The preserve encompasses the meadow, a quarter-mile of beachfront, most of the bluff between the lake and The Shack, a stand of old-growth red pines near Cummings Creek, some cedar swamp, and about 40 acres of upland hardwoods. Unlike the nature preserve that the State of Michigan was planning to create by taking all 105 acres of the Becker family estate and booting us out, the existing preserve came into existence in a more harmonious and equitable fashion.

The day after my discovery of Dad's true family tree, I learned that an old summer camp friend of mine had recently graduated from Cooley Law School and joined a small law firm in Traverse City. My bald-headed buddy Steve Frasier got an early start on marriage with Sue (a former girls' camp counselor), and they already have two darling daughters—Ella and Olivia. Steve convinced his firm to represent the three remaining members of the Becker family. Steve said he was still pretty green when it came to probate, but he is a former Golden Gloves champion of Saginaw, Michigan, and he proved to be just the man to have in our corner.

Armed with the knowledge of Dad's real lineage, Steve got the State of Michigan to relinquish any and all claims to the Becker family property. What really surprised the folks down at the state capital, however, was that we Beckers still wanted to negotiate after they were ready to drop the whole thing. Once everyone stopped trying to take the land from us, Mom, Sally, and I found the open space that we needed to decide what would happen to the farm — what we wanted to keep and what we wanted give. We decided that Joe's dreams for the place didn't have to result in an all-or-nothing solution. The Becker farm had been in limbo for so long that it had become a

No Man's Land not unlike the one that Joe defended in Alsace-Lorraine. It was no mere private family estate — there was more to it than that.

After all the legal battles were over, the land felt like my home, but it also felt like it belonged to all the Odawas who had tilled its rocky soil for centuries and built the first wood-frame houses here. The land was still connected to the lives of the rugged loggers and settlers who transformed a tribal homeland into a part of America. This land's soul will live on long after I'm gone. But maybe my family has helped to preserve a small piece of the heart of Northern Michigan.

As I walked across my muddy yard in front of The Shack one spring day after all of the new deeds were in place and all of the legal issues settled, I knew what it must have been like for the farmer who owned that wheat field in Alsace-Lorraine that had been Joe's battlefield in the summer of 1918. After the war, that farmer still owned the land legally, but as he began to fill in the bomb craters and trenches in order to re-plant his wheat, he must have realized that he could never truly own No Man's Land. Veterans of both sides who survived the war (and the families of those who didn't) would keep coming to see this ground for many years and decades after the farmer was dead and buried in its soil. It could never really be possessed by one man, but would always remain No Man's Land to those who knew it.

So I have made a home within my No Man's Land. I kept a ten-acre parcel that includes The Shack, the small hill that it sits on, and an adjoining eight acres of woods along the south side of Stanton Road. My sister Sally and her husband kept another ten-acre parcel on the north side of Stanton Road at the edge of the bluff where they hope to build a summer place some day. And Mom held on to five acres next to mine "just in case" she decides to retire Up North.

Instead of swiping the Becker family land through legal slight of hand, the state agreed to work with us and the local land conservancy to come up with enough money to buy 80 acres from us for the preserve. Some of the same local people who had seemed ready to swoop in and kick us out were actually glad to help raise the money for the state to buy eighty of our acres. Mom, Sally, and I discounted the sale of the land by about $200,000, which the state agreed to accept in lieu of the considerable estate taxes we would have had to pay.

In a true legal stroke of genius, Steve filed a legal malpractice suit against Cushman and Joe's old lawyer (Mr. Farmer) for the mistakes (intended or otherwise) which allowed Vicky to get $75,000 out of the property and to almost get away with posthumously stealing another quarter million from her own son's estate. Cushman and Farmer had insurance policies to cover such things. The insurance companies flew into Traverse City with a half dozen lawyers in expensive suits and threats of counter-suits, but Steve and I stared them down, presented the facts, and sent them packing. Cushman was not keen to have the story out just as he was running for appellate judge, and Farmer was happy to rectify any error that he may have caused. The insurance companies settled out of court. We walked away with enough money to pay Cushman for the work he did up until my father died, to recoup all of the $75,000 that Vicky got from the illegal purchase option with Homer Robertson, and to pay Steve handsomely for his time.

I never resorted to tipping off my colleagues in the media about Cushman's shenanigans, but Cushman was soundly defeated in the election for appellate court judge, anyway. The last thing I heard about him was that he left the law practice and was selling health insurance down in Florida.

Homer Robertson didn't get what he wanted, either. Without Phase II of his expanded Four Fires Estates development, Homer went belly up with the bank and his investors. Even the estaters turned on him when they smelled blood. Some of them pooled together at the bankruptcy auction, and bought him out of his own ancestral home and the remaining lots he had within the development. Now, Homer seems to be the one who is no longer welcome on the land that belonged to his family for generations. I saw him in the IGA parking lot a couple of months ago, though, and he seems to be doing all right. After the bankruptcy, he climbed right back into his old rusty pickup and started building houses again. He got in with a couple new investors from downstate, and he's developing a forty-acre farm just a couple of miles north of the ski hills. He may have lost his family inheritance, but he hasn't lost the heritage of his tough, independent, can-do Northern Michigan ancestors.

Lu Ann Wilson's job as executrix of Aunt/Grandma Vicky's estate became a lot easier to handle. Instead of dealing with hundreds of thousands of dollars, there were only tens of thousands to give away to the local humane society and Vicky's Tucson friends. Lu Ann ended up with some money and Vicky's 1987 Lincoln Town Car. She told me that she had never felt right about taking any more than that anyway, since she believed Vicky should have left it to her grandchildren in the first place. Lu Ann willingly gave a deposition that helped establish the fact that Dad was Vicky's son, but we never had to use it in a court of law.

A probate court down in Oswego, New York, however, turned out to hold the secret to the identity of Grandpa X — my father's real father. I was able to ascertain that there was some kind of hearing over custody of my father. The court affirmed

Joe and Anna's custody over Dad, but the court ordered the file sealed, and New York law won't even give me a peek at the name of my grandfather. The Oswego probate court has proved to be a dead end, but Libby and I are hoping to get down there before the summer is out to start digging around in earnest for the identity of a man we only know as "Tom."

Once the land deal was finalized with Michigan and Dad's estate was settled, Mom, Sally, and I were left with about a half a million dollars. Sally and I got a little more than two hundred grand each and Mom got a little under a hundred grand as per her divorce settlement with Dad.

Sally took the money she got from the land, invested it, and eventually bought the Grand Rapids trucking company where she had worked as a dispatcher. Her husband sold his big rig and now works with Sally. She likes having him around more often, and now he only drives about two miles a day carpooling with Sally — at least, on the rare occasions that she lets him drive.

Mom visits every few months, and even likes the winters here, but she has put her share of the money from the land to other good uses. She is a traveling Christian Science nurse and splits her time between caring for those who can afford it and those who can't. She's in Santa Fe, New Mexico, right now taking care of a retired Basque sheepherder who converted to Christian Science in his late seventies, as well as the wife of a successful young financial advisor who moved to the southwest from Boston.

As for me, I have recently become the proud father of Madison Grace Hampton-Becker. She is almost five months old now. I can hear Libby and Madison cooing to each other upstairs in one of the bedrooms that we have turned into a nursery. After Libby finished up her summer field study at

Sturgeon Bay and graduated from the University of Indiana's masters' program for science and biology teachers, she taught in Virginia for a year. Then in 1991, she landed a job in Blue Harbor teaching biology and ecology. Libby moved up here that July. I proposed to her in August, and we were married in Virginia the following April. Libby has taken to the North Country even better than I had hoped. She has become an excellent cross-country skier and snowshoer. She has already bought Madison's first snowsuit, even though it will be four or five months before she can wear it.

The money I received from Dad's estate allowed me to fix up The Shack and start a cozy nest egg for my growing family, but it didn't exactly put me in the same league as the numerous trust-fund babies who make their homes in Blue Harbor after generations of family summer vacations here. In the fall of 1989, Sean Cooper finally came through with his promise to start a northern bureau of the *Northern Michigan Gazette*. My income has only increased slightly from my freelancer days, but my byline was changed from "Special Correspondent" to "Staff Writer." For the past three years, I have run around the Tip of the Mitt counties chasing after stories of loggers who still use teams of horses to skid logs out of the forest, of small-town school superintendents who get caught with their hands in the cookie jar, and of dozens of fatal car-deer accidents.

My newspaper stories got great play, and Sean Cooper and I made a good team. However, Joe, Anna, and Dad kept calling to me from the past. After years of writing other people's stories, I set out to write the story of my own people. In the evenings after filing my newspaper stories, I dove back into the contents of those cardboard boxes from Vicky and began outlining and researching my first novel, which I am calling *The Inheritance*. My book is fiction, but it closely follows the lives of Joe, Anna, and Vicky, as well as a year in the life of a contemporary narrator character who is fighting to hold on to his family's old Northern Michigan farm. I changed all of the names except the historical figures in my novel to protect the innocent and even the not-so-innocent. In the book, Joe became Kurt Radtke, Anna became Sarah Jackson Radtke, Dianna Johnson became Susan Jackson, and Vicky became Veronica Radtke Hemmings. The narrator character was christened Scott Radtke.

The few people who have read my book so far have been curious about which parts are real and which parts are made up. The journalist in me knows that once a writer starts turning a Tuesday into a Thursday he or she sets off a chain reaction of fabrication that really does render the whole work into fiction. The novelist in me, however, has discovered that I can get closer to the truth through fiction than I ever could as a just-the-facts-ma'am journalist. By weaving fact and fiction together, I believe I have told my family's story as well as it can be told.

About two years ago after completing the bulk of my research, I sat down at my old Macintosh 512k computer one night and began writing. Surprisingly, I started close to the end of my story with a World War I scene that had captured my imagination. The scene takes place just after General Pershing has promoted Kurt Radtke to Captain. Kurt catches sight of a grass-camouflaged German raiding party on an adjacent company's petty post at the first light of day. Kurt leads a small squad of his own men into No Man's Land to flank and repel the attackers, but the ground that is thrown up into the air from an exploding German shell in front of him buries Kurt alive. I stayed up until 3:00 AM that night writing that scene, but it took me a couple of years to get back to it because I had to write the rest of the novel from the start.

I felt bad about leaving Kurt buried on the edge of the shell crater for so long, but I needed to flex my imagination further before I felt confident about how to get Kurt out of there. I knew all about the raid from the point of view of the men in the adjacent company that was attacked, but I had only bits and pieces of information about what Joe (a.k.a. Kurt) actually did that day. About a year ago, I was finally able to return to that scene and have Sgt. Miller find Kurt's leather boot sticking out of the shell crater, dig him up in one piece, and get the squad up and going again. Kurt's company killed two Germans and helped to drive the rest of the raiders back to their own lines, but it was the three men of the adjoining Company M who deservedly made it into the history books.

Sergeant Dewey F. Slocum, Private Newton Bell, and Corporal John C. Phillips relentlessly fought back against the Germans who attacked their position. They managed to take down four Germans and hold off the rest until the raiders were driven off. Their platoon commander, First Lieutenant Carl A. Johnson, was killed and became the first officer in the 32nd Division to fall in combat.

I was often tempted to make Kurt — the fictional version of Joe — come off as more dramatically heroic than the real man, but the more I turned to the actual record of Joe's life, the more I admired his quiet, competent career and character. After the June 23, 1918, German raid on Company M that took Lt. Johnson's life, Joe and his company got in and out of the trenches two more times in Alsace-Lorraine with only a few casualties. About a month later, Joe and his men left the trenches yet again and marched through a violent German bombardment near Hecken. The Germans used sneezing gas, which made it impossible for the men to wear their gas masks, but no poison gas shells followed the initial barrage and the company reached Angeot safely. It was there that Joe learned of the Army's sharp twist of irony—his reassignment back to the States as a bayonet instructor.

At first, the official record looked like Joe was sidelined just as E Company and the rest of the 126th Infantry were sent into the Second Battle of the Marne. But after further digging into Sgt. Pomeroy's "Doughboy Journal" and a couple more letters between these two old comrades, I discovered Joe's week of scout-courier duty along the front lines of the Aisne-Marne attack while all hell was breaking loose for the men of E Company. I'm glad that Joe—like a young Lt. George Patton before him—got to have his "big day as a lion" before he reached his next assignment at Camp Pendleton in California where he would spend the rest of the war.

On Nov. 11, 1918, Sgt. Bill Pomeroy and the remainder of E Company were between the Meuse River and the German border when the armistice took effect and an eerie quiet settled across the frontier. The next day, while marching through a landscape littered with hundreds of dead German soldiers, Sgt. Pomeroy tallied up his company's own losses. Of the 437 men who saw service in France with E Company, 222 had been killed and wounded in battle.

———

The real stories of my Becker ancestors, Sgt. Pomeroy, the U.S.S. *Michigan*, Little Ernie Hemingway, Harvey Higginbotham, Mary Jane Keegonee, a young Lt. Patton, and an old Gen. Pershing wash over me as I sit in the old wicker rocking chair on the porch of the home that Libby and I have made out of the past. On a wicker coffee table that I have been using for an outside desk, sits an IBM Thinkpad 700 that I bought last year to help me finish writing my novel. On this brilliant July day, I have reached the last page of the first draft of this book, and the cursor is blinking me on to the finish line.

My family's letters pulled me into their lives in the first place, and it seems only fitting to end my book with a fictional version of one of Anna's letters. After the war and several assignments that sent Joe traveling across America, Joe was given orders to report to Fort Sam Houston in San Antonio, Texas. Anna (a.k.a. Sarah) dashed off a quick note to Dianna (or Susan) back in Michigan to let her know how they are doing.

Oct. 23, 1921

Dear Mother,

We have arrived safely, and all in one piece. Veronica is delighted by the warm weather and has already met some girls in the neighborhood who will be in the same fifth-grade class that she will be entering next week. Kurt is off to report to the Post Commander, and I am left alone with the crates and boxes to unpack.

Our quarters are small but quite handsome, and look to be only a few years old. There are lovely screened-in porches that wrap around the entire house and let in the afternoon and evening breezes. I am perspiring like a farmhand, though. It will take me a while to get used to this hot Texas weather.

The wives on the base have showered us with welcome, but as I sit here with the house finally still, I realize that I feel so at home here because it is the first time in eleven years that Kurt, Veronica, and I have been able to live together under one roof for more than a few months. Our little family has been reunited, and I am so grateful.

Thanks again for all your help getting us packed up and shipped out. Give my love to Dad and Vance.

Love always,
Your Sarah

ACKNOWLEDGEMENTS

Firstly, thank you, Carol Johnston, my delightful wife, for putting up with the endless hours of absence as I researched and wrote *Into No Man's Land* and other works that haven't seen the light of day yet. And thank you Laney – even before you could read or talk you spurred me on to the finish line. Special thanks also go to the rest of the Johnston family – Susie, Joy, Robin, Jennifer, and Norm – for your support. To my sister, Elly Hurd, good job helping track down Grandpa X, and thanks for giving me such a solid sounding board to bounce ideas off. Thank you Janet C. Bachus (mom) for filling in some gaps in the family history. I'm glad you got to read the first draft, but I wish you were still here to see this one.

I'm also grateful for the wonderful works of history that aided me in conjuring up the fictional accounts of life before and during World War I. Some are long out of print, but still make for compelling reading – *The Diary of a Doughboy* by William Pommerening, a sergeant in my grandfather's company from Ann Arbor, Michigan (published by The Washtenaw County Veteran's Council, Ann Arbor, Mich.: 1931); *History of the 126th Infantry in the War with Germany* by Emil B. Gansser (published by The 126th Infantry Association, A.E.F., Grand Rapids, Mich.: 1920); *The 32nd Division in the World War* issued by The Joint War History Commissions of Michigan and Wisconsin, Madison, Wis., for the 32nd Division Veteran Association: 1920). Other books that lit my way through writing this novel are: *Chasing Villa: The Last Campaign of the U.S. Cavalry* by Colonel Frank Tompkins (originally published by the Military Service Publishing Company, Harrisburg, Penn.,: 1934 and republished by High-Lonesome Books, Silver City, New Mexico: 1996); *General Patton: A Soldier's Life* by Stanley Hirshson (published by Harper, New York: 2002), *Hemingway in Michigan* by Dr. Constance Cappel (published by the Little Traverse Historical Society, Petoskey, Mich.: 1999); and *Harbor Springs: A Collection of Historical Essays* edited by Jan Morley (published by the Harbor Springs Historical Commission, Harbor Springs, Mich.: 1981).

Thanks, too, to the talented team of proofreaders who volunteered to help out under a tight deadline—Kevin Brown, Don Hill, Cheryl Howell, Susie Johnston, Vicki McNamara, John MacEnulty, Hedley Pelletier, and Jack Schaberg.

I also owe a debt of gratitude to the dozens of librarians and historians from places such as the National Archives, the Gen. John J. Pershing Boyhood Home State Historic Site, the Harbor Springs and Petoskey libraries, and the Naval History & Heritage Command. And last, but not least, thanks to my editor, Harley Patrick, for giving this novel a shot.

ABOUT THE AUTHOR

RICHARD C. BACHUS has been a professional journalist, English teacher, and advertising copywriter for nearly three decades. He's had thousands of articles, essays, and marketing campaigns published around the world by media such as *The Christian Science Monitor, Newsweek, Ski, The Detroit Free Press, Traverse, Pacific Builder & Engineer, Triathlete,* and *The Traverse City Record-Eagle.*

As the descendant of four generations of U.S. soldiers, Mr. Bachus lives a peaceful life in the woods of Northern Michigan with his small family — living in a house not unlike "The Shack" depicted in the pages of this novel. Joe and Anna Becker are fictional versions of Mr. Bachus's real grandparents, whose Great War experiences are chronicled on the US WW I Centennial Commission's blog:

www.ww1cc.org/index.php/trench-commander-home.html